# change of life

## ANNE STORMONT

Rowan Russell Books

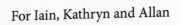

For Iain, Kathryn and Allan

## Acknowledgements

Thank you to all family and friends who have offered encouragement and support to me and my writing – you know who you are.

Special thanks to Ali Smith for telling me I had a novel on my hands, to Maria McIntosh my first critic, to Margaret Bainbridge and Val McIntyre my first readers, to the Romantic Novelists' Association New Writers Scheme for a constructive critique, to the Edinburgh Writers' Club for their recognition, to all my youwriteon.com reviewers for their generous help – especially to Chris Pitt and Andrew Wrigley for going the extra mile.

I'd also like to thank my wonderful editor, John Hudspith, who would accept nothing but the best, and book designer, Jane Dixon-Smith, who has ensured that the book looks good both inside and out.

And most of all thank you to Iain Stormont for giving me the space…

# Chapter One

*Rosie*

I didn't see the boy until the moment of impact. He slammed into the side of the car as I reversed out of the driveway. I got a fright, thought I'd hurt someone, but I couldn't have guessed that this was merely a foreshock to a much greater upheaval. Ten past one, lunch time, Tuesday 17th May. It was the moment when the past caught up and collided with the present.

I got out to check he wasn't hurt. He glanced at me and turned to run. He was about Adam's age, seventeen or so. There was something familiar about him. But I didn't think I knew him. Ours was a small community and with four children of my own, I thought I knew most of the local young people, at least by sight.

"Wait, are you all right?" I caught his arm. "I'm sorry. I didn't see you."

He didn't appear to be injured. He was taller than me, with untidy, dark hair and very deep brown eyes. In one ear he wore a little silver skull. I recognised his tee shirt. Adam had one just like it. It had the words 'Subliminal Messages' written across it – the name of a Slipknot album. As the boy pulled his arm back he seemed to hesitate.

"Do I know you?" I said. "Are you a friend of Adam's?"

He looked me in the eyes for a moment. I stared back. Something passed between us; was it recognition? Then he bolted – obviously uninjured.

I didn't have time to speculate about the boy. I'd only nipped home for lunch and a catch up with Ruby. I needed to get back.

I got the last space in the school car park. I was hurrying towards the main entrance when my mobile rang. I answered it as I went inside. It was the hospital. My stomach tightened.

"Hello, Mrs McAllister. This is Mr Campbell's secretary. He's asked me to set up an appointment for you to come and discuss your test results." The voice was warm, friendly even. But I still had an awful feeling of dread.

"He could see you on Thursday at three."

"Oh, yes, right, Thursday..." My mind whirred through Thursday's schedule. I'd need to get off early. Kirsty, my head teacher and one of my closest friends, would have to cover my class. What would I tell her? I wondered if the doctor needed to see you if it was good news. He could tell you over the phone, surely. It must mean bad news...

"So is that all right then, Thursday at three, with Mr Campbell?"

"Sorry, yes. Is it bad news do you know? I mean, why else would he be bothering?"

"You mustn't jump to conclusions, Mrs McAllister. He'd want to see you either way. Try not to worry and we'll see you in a couple of days."

As the call ended, the bell rang for the start of afternoon lessons. My life went on, even as its bedrock heaved and shifted beneath me.

### Tom

It's Sunday morning. Rosie only met him on Tuesday. Is it really only a few days ago? In less than a week my life has fallen apart – no that's wrong – it fell apart in a moment – in the time it took a boy to speak a sentence. And now my wife is leaving and my heart is broken.

It's the 22<sup>nd</sup> of May, but it feels more like November. I'm standing at the living-room window. It's raining and the sea and sky are slate grey, the horizon obliterated. I feel leaden, unable to move or speak; it's the paralysis of a nightmare. I want to beg her to stay, to admit she's being silly and overreacting.

Rosie and our nineteen year old daughter, Sam, load bags and boxes into Rosie's car. Toby is watching them, barking occasionally. I know I should go out to her and fight to make her change her mind but I'm exhausted, I'm drowning. I'm engulfed in the aftermath of more anger than I've ever felt towards her.

I hear the dull thud of the boot closing. It's done. She's ready to go. Our younger daughter, Jenny, sprints down the driveway, jacket held above her head, and says something to Rosie. Then Max dashes from the house and hands his mother a piece of paper. She looks at it and smiles and they hug each other. She puts the paper down on the driver's seat and closes the door. They all come back in and head for the kitchen.

Jenny calls out, "Dad, Adam, coffee."

A few moments later I hear Adam coming downstairs and going along to the kitchen. I know he's not happy about his mother leaving, but at least he's able to join the others for a coffee before she goes.

I make it to the sofa. I find that I want to cry. This terrifies me. I struggle not to lose my grip, not to howl and kick and scream. I'm Tom McAllister, consultant heart surgeon, professional, practical, in control. Or so I thought. I didn't intend any of this to happen. I'm helpless, lost. I haven't felt this vulnerable or alone since I was a child. I find I'm rocking, curled up, my head wrapped in my arms. I force myself to sit up, to keep breathing.

When I fail to appear in the kitchen, Jenny comes to get me.

"Come on Dad, come and have a coffee. I've made a carrot cake and it looks scrummy, even if I say so myself. Come and say cheerio to Mum."

"I can't. How can you be so cheerful?"

Jenny puts her hand on my arm, "Och, Dad, she just needs a bit of a break." She hesitates and gives my arm a squeeze. "And she needs to get over how cross she is with you."

"So she says, Jenny. So she says. But I can't come and say goodbye as if she was simply going away for a few days holiday. I don't understand how she can go."

"If *we* all understand, why can't you? Even Adam's there to say goodbye. Come and wish her well, Dad, and tell her you'll be here waiting for her. She needs you to say that."

I stand up and hug Jenny. Seventeen and so grown up. The children are behaving better than me. I feel even more ashamed and desperate. "I can't do it. I can't give any of this my blessing."

Jenny walks away. With her long blonde hair and slight frame, she looks and moves like her mother. At the door she turns and says, "It's not your blessing she wants."


### *Rosie*


It's one of the hardest things I've ever done. Yet it feels like the right thing. This is about my survival and I know I can't stay. It's a wet Sunday morning in May. The weather gives the day a heavy, washed-out feeling and it mirrors my mood perfectly. I'm sitting at the kitchen table. My children are with me.

"So, I can come and see you in two weeks?" Max asks.

"Yes, like I said, I'll have had a good rest by then and Grandma will bring you to Edinburgh for a visit."

"I'll miss you, Mum." Max puts down his glass of milk and comes to hug me. I cling to him, glad that, at twelve years old, he doesn't yet feel too old for such displays.

"I'll miss you too. But two weeks will pass quickly and then, in the summer holidays, you can come and stay as much as you want."

"That's a great picture you did for Mum, Maxy." Jenny rubs her wee brother's back. "You could do more for her while she's away – like a sort of picture diary of what you're up to – use the sketch book Uncle Dan gave you for your birthday."

"Mm yeah, I suppose."

"You could start now – draw us all here at the table."

Max considers then nods. "I'll go and get my stuff."

I smile my gratitude at Jenny.

Sam gets up from the table. "I need to go. My shift starts at twelve."

I get up too. "Sam," I say, holding my arms out towards her.

She shakes her head. "I still don't get it, Mum. I'm trying to, but I don't. I think if you just talked to Dad, you could sort it."

I drop my arms. I can't look at her. Then she's over and holding me in a tight embrace. "Go if you have to, but come back soon," she whispers. Then she's gone.

I know I should go too. There's no point prolonging this. I glance at Adam. He's staring into his coffee mug. Max comes back with his sketch book and pencils.

"How can I do my picture if Sam's gone?"

"I better get on my way." I smile apologetically at him.

"You can still put Mum and Sam in the picture, Max," says Jenny. "Even if they're not here – you're a good enough artist."

Max nods and lays his things on the table.

I hug Jenny. "Thanks for the making the cake, it was a lovely thought."

She smiles. "Come on, Adam, let's see Mum off." Jenny places a hand on her twin brother's shoulder. He shrugs it off.

Max takes my hand. At first Adam doesn't move. Then he gets up and stands, hands deep in the pockets of his jeans, shoulders hunched. He's facing me, eyes downcast.

"Bye then, Adam. I meant what I said. I'm really sorry." I will him to look at me. He shrugs and walks past me, head down. I hear him stomping up the stairs.

As I walk down the hall with Jenny and Max, I glance at the closed living room door. I wonder if Tom will say goodbye. I wonder if I should go in. I can't face it. The shock and anger that I've felt for the last few days have hardly abated. Tom has betrayed me. His secret's out.

As I get into the car I glance back at the house. The Victorian villa's sandstone walls are darkened by the rain. It's been my home for nearly twenty years. I love everything about it, its seaside situation in Gullane, one of East Lothian's prettiest villages, its large, light rooms, its period quirks and the memories we've made there. I shall miss it almost as much as the people inside it. I see Tom at the living room window, watching. I think he's about to wave or beckon me back. He turns away.

The appearance of Robbie in our lives has changed everything. And on top of that I now have a dreadful secret of my own.

# Chapter Two

## *Rosie*

I didn't see any of it coming. Tuesday the 17th of May began as an ordinary Tuesday. By eight o'clock, our seventeen-year-old twins, Jenny and Adam, were on their way to school in Edinburgh. It was the day of their higher maths exam. Neither of them said goodbye before they set off. Adam left without a word and all Jenny said was that she felt sick. The rest of the family was having breakfast in the kitchen. I was upstairs dashing around, tidying up before I had to leave for work. Ruby would be in later and I needed to make space for her to vacuum.

As I made our bed, a sea breeze drifted in through the open window and I paused to look out. It was a bright day and the view across the Forth estuary, from East Lothian to Fife, was sharp and clear. Even after twenty years I still loved the view from every window in our big, old house. Several dinghies and yachts were already taking advantage of the wind and fair weather.

"Oh there you are! I've been calling you. Didn't you hear me?" Tom stood in the doorway. At six-foot-two he almost filled the space as he leant against the frame. "Busy, I see." He smiled and came to stand beside me. He kissed the top of my head. He smelt nice and I wanted to push him back onto the bed and undo his tie and shirt. At fifty-one, Tom was still good looking. He kept himself lean and fit. His dark hair was lightly streaked with grey and remained thick, even as it receded slightly at the temples. I looked up at his face. I wanted to stroke his cheek, to touch the laughter lines at the corners of his eyes, to caress the back of his neck. It was too long since we'd made love. It was too long since we'd even just sat and talked. We were always so busy.

"Well," he said, "I can't stand here all morning with you gazing gormlessly at me. I need to get on, even if you don't."

"I've got things to do too. I only stopped for a minute. I never tire of watching the sea."

"I'm teasing, but joking apart- are you okay? Actually you look quite pale. Are you sure you're not overdoing it?"

"I'm fine. Anyway, why were you calling for me?"

"Just to say I'm off to the hospital – it's a full list in theatre today so I better get going. Oh and I need razors – if you're going to the shops. I'm down to my last one and I think Sam's been shaving her legs with it."

He pointed to a couple of little scratches on his chin. "And could you possibly collect my dry cleaning? Please?"

"Right – so I look overworked, but not so overworked that I can't fit in a few extra errands!"

"Well what else do you have to do?" Tom was already ducking as I flung a pillow at him.

"Bye, Tom."

I heard him laughing and then the front door slamming as he left. This attitude of Tom's, that I was the one with the time to do all the domestic stuff, was nothing new, but lately it irked me more than it used to. Whenever I complained of having too much to do, his answer was always that I should give up my teaching job, that he earned enough for both of us. He could never see that what I was actually asking for was for him to pull his weight at home.

I finished making the bed. The clean white linen smelled of the sea air. I smoothed the bedcover. Not for the first time I was struck by how much the bed resembled a boat. It wasn't only the sheets billowing as I spread and smooth and tucked. It was a place of safety with its sturdy old oak frame, like a ship on a sometimes stormy sea. Tom and I had nestled down in it for the last twenty-five years – rolling together, twisting apart. The children had also sought refuge here, first, as babies for the night feeds and, later, climbing aboard in the small hours to escape the terrors of the night. Their warm little bodies snuggled into Tom and me, one back each. I thought of all the birthday breakfasts eaten there, as well as cold, burnt, Mothers' Day ones. Six of us all squeezed up together, laughing and carrying on.

I felt a pang that these days were gone. Our eldest, Sam, was nineteen and about to go to university and our youngest would soon transfer to high school. I wondered what the future held for Tom and me. I'd been thinking 'is this all there is' a lot lately. I both longed for and dreaded a change.

I glanced in the mirror before I left the bedroom. My late mother seemed to be staring back at me. I'd always looked like her and, until recently, that wasn't a bad thing. I'd inherited her slim build, her thick, fair hair and blue eyes. But now there were crow's-feet at the corners of my eyes and grey hairs amongst the blonde. I made a mental note to get my highlights redone. I lifted my chin in an attempt to smooth out the wrinkles in my neck. Next stop would be the menopause. I was sure I'd already had a couple of hot flushes. I wasn't relishing the prospect of turning fifty the next year. Looking worried, it put years on me. Tom was right, I did look pale and tired. I turned and tilted my head, seeking a more flattering position.

I thought of my twin sister too. Would Heather have aged in a similar way to me? My memories of my identical twin were usually well suppressed. But as I stood looking in the mirror both Heather and my mother felt very close.

My mother would've had some comforting words to say about how I was feeling. I smiled at the thought. She'd been the queen of clichés. My sister, brother and I all used to tease her about it, but she often hit the nail on the head, so to speak. She'd probably tell me to count my blessings. In my mother's universe every cloud had a silver lining. She died when I was twenty-six weeks pregnant with Sam. I still missed her.

"Mum, it's after half past eight." Max called from downstairs, bringing me back to the present. I taught at the village primary school, where twelve-year-old Max was a pupil. It was time for us to leave.

As I often did on a Tuesday, I nipped home at lunch time to see Ruby. It was a chance for a chat and a catch up. I sat at the kitchen table while Ruby put the finishing touches to some sandwiches. As she handed me my plate she looked at me closely.

"Are you okay? You're looking pale today. You do too much - wear yourself out - teaching and running around after everyone."

"Oh, I'm all right really," I said. "Yes, a bit tired, but nothing to worry about. And you're a fine one to talk. I don't do half of what you do – with all your children and grandchildren and your two jobs."

"Oh, my lot know the score. I do what I can to help, but they know I have my own life too. I enjoy my work and I don't give up my bingo for anyone. He has to muck in too mind."

She never referred to her husband by name. "And I expect the bairns to sort out their own messes. I do what I do for them because I want to, not because I have to. You on the other hand–"

"I'm fine! I have a life too. I like looking after everyone, as you do with your family - and I enjoy my job as well." I didn't sound convincing, even to myself.

"Well, you look exhausted," she said, putting her hand on mine. "When was the last time you had a night out? Or just some time to yourself? You know you need to look after yourself better. You'll make yourself ill."

"Oh, Ruby, for heaven's sake, you're not my mother!"

It was unreasonable to be annoyed at Ruby. She'd saved my life. When she first came to work for us it was to help with the children, as much as to help look after the house. I was suffering from a completely disabling bout of postnatal depression, brought on by exhaustion, both from a difficult pregnancy with the twins, and from having three children under three-years-old. I could hardly look after myself, never mind the children. Then Heather died and at times during that awful year I wanted to join her. But, Ruby, with her unfailing common sense and good humour, helped me through.

"Sorry, hen, it's just that I worry. You drive yourself far too hard you know."

"No, I'm sorry, Ruby. I'm glad you worry about me – it's nice – but there's no need."

"If you say so – anyway - tuck in". As she poured us both a mug of tea she nodded in the direction of the dresser. "Is that the box of photos you promised to show me?"

"Oh, yes." I got up and brought the box over to the table. It was four years since my father died but I'd only recently got around to sorting through all the small, personal stuff that had belonged to my parents. I passed the box to Ruby. As we ate she looked through the photos and I did my best to fill in the who, when and where of the ones that caught her interest. She came to a packet containing a bundle of black and white snaps.

"Oh – it's you and that has to be your sister – look – bouncing on your mum and dad's bed. You look like a right lively pair! Who's who?" She handed me the photo.

There we were laughing, jumping, holding onto each other, two identical, blonde haired girls. Heather was looking directly at the camera and I was looking at Heather. I was wearing a summer dress. I loved that dress. I could remember it clearly, pink and white stripes with a bow at the back. "That's Heather in the shorts. It's not our parents' bed. It was ours. It was a three-quarter, bigger than a single, but not quite a double. It belonged to my grandmother. We inherited it."

As I handed the photo back to Ruby, I recalled how much we had loved that bed. It had a dark wooden frame, and it came complete with Granny's Irish linen and fat, feather pillows. There was even a bolster. It was grand. The top cover was glorious, a counterpane, Granny called it, with its pattern of white stars on a dark blue background.

"Heather looks a right cheeky wee madam," Ruby said, smiling. "How old were you? Were you allowed to jump on the bed?"

"Oh, she was cheeky all right, much braver than me. We'd be about ten. We weren't really allowed to bounce on the bed, but Dad just laughed and got the camera. We'd been out after tea, playing hide and seek with our friends in the street, and then Dad called us in. It was still light outside and we didn't want to go, especially since Michael got to stay out a bit longer. We were supposed to be getting ready for bed, but Heather still had too much energy and she said 'let's bounce!' So we did."

As Ruby looked through the rest of the photos, my mind went back to my childhood home. "I remember we always used to get washed as quickly as possible – the bathroom was icy, even in summer, and then, in the bedroom, we'd dash over the cold lino and jump onto the bed."

"Ah yes," said Ruby, smiling. "I remember that too - the days before central heating and fitted carpets."

"Yes, indeed. We'd get under the covers as quickly as possible and lie there – facing each other – giggling. In winter, Mum put two hot water bottles in the bed and we'd snuggle together for warmth."

"It must have been nice – together and all cosy in the dark," said Ruby.

"There was a nightlight – it was for Heather. She was afraid of the dark so I used to tell her stories before we fell asleep. But yes, it was nice. The bed was our place. In it we were close and safe. But then we grew up, grew apart…" I gave a little shudder.

"Oh, Rosie, I'm sorry." Ruby put her hand on mine. "I didn't think. These must be upsetting. I shouldn't be so nosey. I'll put them away."

"No – honestly – it's all right. It's nice you're interested, and the photos are a reminder of the happy times. I was thinking about Heather earlier on today, about the less happy stuff. So it's been nice to see these. You take your time looking through them all. I better get back."

I was still thinking about my sister when the boy ran into my car a couple of minutes later.

# Chapter Three

That afternoon, at work, I was distracted, to say the least. I just wanted to get home. The call from the hospital, the encounter with the boy. I needed time to think. As soon as I got home I went to sit in the garden.

I loved my garden. I liked that it thrived on partial neglect – unlike my husband and children, who seemed to need constant attention. It regularly surprised me with some self-seeded beauty or unanticipated flowering.

I wanted to enjoy the late afternoon sunshine, to breathe in the sea air mingled with the smell of next door's freshly cut grass, to catch the perfume of my beautiful shrub roses. I wanted to relish the sound of our resident blackbird, proclaiming his good mood, as he sat amidst the vibrant pink blossom of the cherry tree. But the scents were muted; the birdsong distant, and the scene seemed, somehow, out of focus. Mother Nature had taken on a malignant face. All I could think of was cancer. I tried to keep it in perspective. It could be nothing, something benign. But I was petrified, scared of pain, of dying, of not seeing my children grow up.

No-one knew I'd found a lump. No one knew I'd already been to the doctor or the hospital. I wasn't sure why I was so reluctant to tell. I suspected it was partly because talking about something makes it real. I also suspected that if I told Tom, he would jump in and take control. He wouldn't listen to what I wanted.

Of course, I'd needed some sort of explanation when I went to see Kirsty about getting away early on Thursday. I called in at her office on my way out of school, as I did on most days.

"I'm sorry it's short notice," I said. "I only heard today."

"Oh, that's okay, I'm sure I'll be able to cover for the last hour. Nothing serious I hope?"

"No, no it's menopause stuff. I've to have some tests." It was only a partial lie but I still felt guilty.

I knew that if I wanted to keep my hospital appointment secret and get through the next couple of days without blurting it all out, then I would have to suppress my fears, or at least not give in to them - and try to be optimistic.

Having just about got my health worries under control, my mind switched the focus of its unease to the boy. Why did he seem so familiar? Maybe he simply reminded me of Adam. I tried not to be anxious about him. I was certain he wasn't hurt by our collision – but something about our meeting niggled.

Yes, I was curious. Why had he concealed himself? He must have been hiding, pressed against, or crouching below the hedge. After all, I'd have seen him if he'd been walking down the street. But it was more than curiosity. For some reason I felt protective of him.

I was reluctant to mention it to Tom. He'd assume the lad was up to no good. He'd pay no attention to pleas from me on the boy's behalf.

"I have to be out of here by quarter-past-seven." Sam was just in from work. I was back indoors preparing the evening meal. "When's dinner ready? What are we having?" She rummaged in the fridge as she spoke.

"Around six-thirty and it's bolognaise."

"Mm, any chance of a lift into town. That would mean I could leave later?"

"I could run you, but I do have preparation to do for school tomorrow."

"Great, cool." Sam apparently only heard the first part of my reply.

"How was work?" I asked.

"Tedious," she said, nibbling on a piece of cheese. "I wish I was still in Australia."

"Yes, well welcome to the real world. You need to earn some money for university in the autumn."

"I know. I worked in Australia too, but that was cool. Tesco is so boring!" Sam laid her pickings from the fridge on the worktop. She pushed her hair back with one hand and wound it into a knot on top of her head. With her other hand she unclipped a large hair slide from the neck of her tee-shirt and rammed it into the coil of her thick, wavy hair. Her hands were so like Tom's with their long slim fingers. She was the only one of our children to have inherited Tom's dark hair and brown eyes. She was tall like him too, at about five-foot-nine, a good couple of inches taller than Jenny and me. She even moved with the same long-limbed grace as he did. She was her father's daughter.

"It's not for long," I said. "You'll be in St Andrews before you know it. I do envy you. I loved my time there."

"Yes, Mother, I think you may have mentioned that a couple of times. I'm off for a bath." With that, she scooped up her snack items and left the kitchen.

"Bring all the dishes down from your room please!" I shook my head as I thought of the clutter and disarray that was her bedroom.

A moment later, Jenny appeared in the kitchen, carrying various garments belonging to her older sister. "Madam wants these washed. She needs them tomorrow apparently."

"Ah, okay, I'll do my best."

Jenny shook her head and rolled her eyes. "It's very wasteful to run the machine for just a few things."

"Yes, I know - but you know your sister. Anyway never mind that, how was the exam?"

"Oh – okay really, I suppose. There were a couple of very difficult questions. I don't know if I've passed or not. But it's not essential. I'm more worried about getting an A in my music."

"I'm sure you'll do that," I said. "You sounded superb when

you were practising."

"Mmm, I'm not up to your standard, but fingers crossed I've done enough. Anyway, Mother – getting back to Sam, it's pathetic how you let her walk all over you. She needs to learn to plan ahead and do things for herself."

This sounded so like Tom that I burst out laughing.

"Yeah, yeah, I sound like dad! But she can be such a lazy cow. Anyway, what are we having for dinner?"

"Spag-bol – and don't call your sister a cow."

Max came into the kitchen. "Tut, tut, Jenny."

Jenny put her tongue out at her wee brother. Max returned the gesture and then turned to me. "When's dinner? What are we having? I'm starving." Before I could reply, the phone rang.

"Spag-bol, six-thirty. Could you set the table, please? Everyone's in for dinner."

I grabbed the phone and closed the kitchen door behind me to muffle Max's protestations about the fairness of my request. I went through to the living room to take the call.

It was Tom. "Hi, I'm in the car – nearly home. What's for dinner? I'm famished."

"Oh, for heaven's sake, is that all you lot think about?"

"What?"

"What's for dinner? Adam's the only one not to have asked me that in the last ten minutes and that's only because I haven't seen him. It's spag-bol – nothing exciting."

"Are the kids giving you a hard time?" Tom asked.

"No, not really. I'm merely wondering what you'd all do if I didn't produce a meal one night. What if I wasn't here or wasn't able? It's taken for granted isn't it? Good old Mum keeping it all going!"

"So, get them to help more. I don't know about you, but I'm shattered. I've been in theatre all day. It'll be good to get home and relax. I'll see you shortly."

Dismissive, self-absorbed, complacent, these were some of the words that came to mind as I listened to my husband. I knew I shouldn't ignore how I was feeling. I should talk to Tom about the state of our relationship. But he was unaware there was anything wrong and would make me feel I was being over-dramatic. It also felt like such an effort to confront him and I was so bloody tired.

Before going back to the kitchen, I paused to look out of the living room window. Our house sat high up at the top of a steeply sloping front garden so, even on the ground floor, it was possible to look straight out across the promenade and the top of the dunes over the Firth of Forth to Fife. A ferry was ploughing along the estuary, on its journey to Bruges. I always thought there was something very romantic about the ferry. I spent a minute speculating about the people on board, who they might be and why they were making the crossing to the continent on this particular May evening. I envied them, setting off on their adventure, free from routine. And then I heard my mother's voice saying be careful what you wish for.

# Chapter Four

Max sat at the table, knife and fork in hand, as I put the finishing touches to the bolognaise. He looked angelic with his thick, blond curls and blue eyes. I asked him to tell the others that dinner was ready.

"I do everything round here!" he said, but he was smiling as he left the kitchen. "Hi, Dad!" he shouted, on his way up the hall. Toby barked as the front door clattered shut and Tom appeared in the kitchen.

He held out a bottle of red wine. "It was on special offer at the off-licence – that South African red you like - a treat to cheer you up."

"I don't need cheering up." I said, thinking of Tom's, not insubstantial, wine collection in the cupboard under the stairs. This was clearly not an occasion worthy of wine from his cellar. I also thought that what I needed was for Tom to notice me, not patronise me.

"I'll open it now," he said, rummaging in the drawer for the corkscrew. "We can have a glass with dinner and the rest while we watch one of these DVDs we haven't got around to yet. I can leave the paperwork for one night."

"I can't have a drink now. I promised to run Sam into town. Then I've got preparation to do for school tomorrow."

"Why does Sam need a lift? There's a bus and she has a driving licence come to that."

"She hasn't got time to get the bus apparently," I replied. Jenny started to say something and I threw her a warning glance to be quiet. I knew she wanted to get her tuppence worth in on the selfishness of her sister. "And there's nowhere to park in town," I added. "You know what it's like in the centre of Edinburgh. I know there's the multi-storey, but it's not safe for her to be walking back to it alone."

"She's unlikely to be alone," Tom said. "The usual gang will be there presumably. You're not her chauffeur. I'll talk to her."

"It's fine. I don't mind. It'll only take an hour or so."

He shook his head. I willed him to offer to run Sam, so I could get on with my school work, but it clearly didn't cross his mind.

At that, Sam, Jenny and Adam arrived in the kitchen. Max pushed past them and ran to the table. I started serving up as they sat down. Adam was having a tug of war with Toby over one of Toby's toys. The Labrador's determination not to give in brought a rare smile to Adam's face.

"Adam, not at the table please," I said, as I laid down two plates. "Put him out in the hall. You know the rules for goodness sake."

"Yeah, yeah, I was just going to." He got up and sent Toby to his bed.

Soon we were all settled and eating. I tried to relax, stay in the present, enjoy this shared, family time.

I was chatting to Max about his school project on Bonnie Prince Charlie when I became aware of Sam and Jenny bickering. A new, and as yet unworn, top of Jenny's had found its way into Sam's room apparently. I glanced over at my daughters.

Jenny was quite wound up. She sat back, frowning and folded her arms. "Anyway," she said, addressing Sam, "Dad wants a word with you."

I looked at Jenny and rolled my eyes.

"What?" said Jenny, all innocence.

"Ah, yes," said Tom, turning to Sam. "Is it really necessary to get your mother to give you a lift this evening? She has other things to do. You could get the bus or take Mum's car. Where is it you're going anyway?"

"We're going to the cinema – the one at Haymarket. I haven't got time to get the bus, I'm afraid. Actually, I'll just text the others and let them know Mum's taking us." Sam got up, kissed her father on the top of his head and went to get her phone. Tom looked at me, exasperated.

I smiled weakly and changed the subject. "Adam, how was your day? How was the exam? Jenny said a couple of the questions were tough." I realised, as I asked, that relying on Adam to steer the dinner table chat away from Sam's arrangements was futile. But I did want to know how he'd got on.

"My day was okay. The exam was okay."

Tom looked over at the twins. "So, is that four down and one to go?"

"Yes, it's biology tomorrow. Then we're free!" Jenny answered for both of them.

Adam didn't look up. His dejected demeanour concerned me. He'd been a tense and anxious child and these tendencies had intensified with the onset of adolescence.

Sam returned to the table. "It's kind of you to offer me mum's car, Pops." She patted her father's arm. "But we're going for a couple of drinks after the film. No – don't worry!" She raised her hands to ward off any possible parental protest. "Sarah's mum said she'll pick us up. We've to phone when we're ready. She insisted."

Tom laughed. "I'm not going to win this one. You've got it all figured out. So, how's the world of retailing?"

"Boring as always," Sam sighed. "I might pack it in actually. I don't think I want to spend the summer in that place."

Tom and I exchanged a glance at this. But neither of us got the chance to ask what she planned to do instead, as she continued talking.

"Oh, he was on today, Jenny – on the back shift. He was late actually - got a bollocking from the boss. He gives me the creeps, that boyfriend of yours!"

"He's not my boyfriend! He's not a creep. He's just shy. He's actually quite friendly when you get to know him."

"Jenny's got a boyfriend!" Max cut in. "What's his name? Why's he a creep?" Max asked the questions for the rest of us.

Jenny tried to speak, but Sam leant forward to answer, waving a dismissive hand at her sister. "He's called Robbie. He's always staring and he follows me – I'm sure he does. In fact I think he followed me home last night."

"Jenny's boyfriend's a stalker! A weird, creepy pervert!" Max's eyes were wide as he relished this revelation.

"Don't talk like that!" I said. "What rubbish. Sam, what do you mean he followed you home? Why didn't you say? Who is he? Jenny, is this person your boyfriend?" I knew I was babbling and I suspected I'd met the boy already.

Once again, Jenny's attempts to speak were overridden by her sister. "He's called Robbie - as I said. He's a right weirdo. He's not from here. He comes in on the bus from Edinburgh. He just appeared one day, got a part time job in the shop. He says he's on exam leave, but that he can't spend all his time studying, and he says he needs the money. But it's not like they don't have supermarkets in Edinburgh – why would he want to work here? He must spend loads on bus fares. Like I say – weird. He and Jenny spend a lot of time talking to each other when they're on the weekend shift together. Jen likes him – don't you, Jen?"

All our eyes were on Jenny. "Yes – as a friend – not in the way you're all thinking!" She blushed. "He's not weird. Why would he follow you, Sam? You shouldn't say things like that about him."

"Oh, I know he's not really your boyfriend," Sam replied. "I think he fancies me actually – probably using you to get close to me. But it's all right you can have him. He gives me the creeps with the staring and stuff. And that `earring is so not cool! And he likes Slipknot. I rest my case. Weird!" Sam glanced at her brother, but he didn't rise to the bait. "Anyway, I'm sure he followed me."

Now I knew. "I think I–"

"No, no wait a minute." Tom waved his hand to silence me. "I don't like the sound of any of this. Jenny, you're not to encourage this boy. I could have a word with Andy. Get him to investigate the guy."

"No, Dad, no!" Jenny looked horrified. "Don't go talking to the police about him. He's fine. He doesn't mean any harm."

"I'll speak to Andy unofficially –as a friend. Come on, you know Andy. He'll be low key. You can trust him."

Jenny grabbed Tom's arm. "Please, Dad, don't. He's okay!"

"Well, no coming home alone for the moment, either of you," Tom said, pouring himself another glass of red. "I'll have a word with this Robbie myself."

"No!"

The girls glared at Tom as if he was a lunatic. I used their horrified silence to get a word in. "I think I may have met Robbie already," I said quickly. "I think it was probably him that I hit earlier – with the car." Now the glares swung to me. "He was a young lad with straggly, dark hair..." I had Tom's attention now. No-one was eating anymore, not even Adam, who normally rams his food down his throat as fast as he can, and then leaves the table as soon as possible.

"You hit someone? When? What happened? Was he okay?"

"Yes, yes, he was okay. I didn't actually hit him. He ran into me. It was at lunchtime, when I was going back to school. I didn't see him coming. He must have been pressed against the hedge or bending down or something. He clattered into the side of the car as I was pulling away outside the house. I got out to make sure he was all right, but he ran off."

"What makes you think it was the same boy?" Tom asked.

I looked at the girls. "He was about Adam's height, thin, dark. He had a skull-shaped ear stud and a Slipknot tee-shirt."

Sam raised her eyebrows and nodded. "It sounds like him. When was it exactly?"

"About one-fifteen."

"What was he doing here at that time?" Sam said. "He'd know

I'd be at the shop then. No wonder he was late for his shift. This gets creepier. You don't think he was going to break in do you?" She looked scared now.

Jenny shook her head. "Of course not. He'd be stupid to show himself if he was planning to break in. There'll be a reasonable explanation. Maybe he was just exploring the village and stopped to tie his shoelace or something."

"Yeah, right!" said Sam.

Tom's mind was apparently made up. "I'm going to have a word with Andy. No arguments." He raised both hands once more, to fend off any protests from his daughters. "Come on, everyone, eat up." He turned to me. "Did you remember to pick up my dry cleaning?"

# Chapter Five

When I got home from dropping Sam in town, I made myself a peppermint tea and began to think through my teaching plans for the rest of the week. I took my notebook and sat down at the kitchen table. I sipped my tea as I made my notes. It was dark outside and the lamp on the old dresser threw its soft light around me. The wall clock ticked quietly in the background and the boiler sang to itself in the cupboard in the corner. I heard footsteps upstairs and a door closing. Max would be going to bed. I drank the last of my tea and was just finishing off my preparation when Adam came into the kitchen.

"Hello, how's the studying going?" I asked.

"It's not. I'm trying to study biology, but nothing's going in and it's so boring!"

"Do the diagrams not help – the ones the learning assistant made up to lessen the amount of reading you've to do?"

"It's not the reading that's making it hard," he said, taking the seat next to me. "It's just plain boring. All the diagrams in the world aren't going to help. I don't understand most of it and I can't be bothered. I'm not going to pass anyway…"

"Oh, Adam," I put my hand on his arm. "Don't get discouraged. Of course you'll pass. You're tired. Have a hot drink and an early night." I rubbed his back as I spoke. He twisted away from me.

"No, Mum! A cup of tea and an early night – what – what's that all about? That's not going to help. I'm not going to pass! I'm not going to pass any of them! Don't you understand? I'm not clever like Sam and Jenny, and you can't make it all right with your bloody stupid suggestions and a cuddle. I can't be what you want me to be. I'm too thick."

"What? You're not thick! You have dyslexia, Adam. It's no reflection on your intelligence. Come on, you know that."

"No I don't. It's all a load of shit. Why can't you see it? I'm not going to university, to be a doctor like dad, or a teacher like you. It's not going to happen."

I reached out to him. "Adam, son, I–"

"Don't! It's not all going to be fine. You can't make it all right. I'm not going to get my exams. You and dad, you need to get used to the idea." With that he pushed past me and headed out of the kitchen. He met Tom in the doorway and kept on walking.

"What's wrong with him?" Tom raised his eyebrows.

"Oh, exam nerves I expect. He thinks he's going to fail his exams. He says we need to get used to the fact that he's thick – not university material."

"What? He simply needs to apply himself, get studying, instead of mooning about in his room, messing about with those fish of his and reading those car magazines. He should have cut back on working at that karting place as well, spent more time on his school work. He needs to get a grip on what's important. I'll speak to him. Sort him out."

"No, Tom, please - don't! He needs to calm down and get a good night's rest. It's too late now anyway.  He's probably just a bit insecure because of the dyslexia. He doesn't moon about –not really. I'll have a quiet word when he's not so wound up." I knew Tom would go over the top and shout, and Adam would shout back, and nobody would get anywhere.

"Hmm, you'll be too soft," Tom said. "I know you. He needs a kick up the backside."

I considered arguing, mentioning how vulnerable Adam was. But I knew from previous conversations that it would be pointless.

"Anyway," Tom said, "I came through to tell you your dear brother phoned, wanted to talk over how it's going with the rental of your dad's flat, wouldn't discuss it with me of course."

"No? Right, no, I don't suppose he would." I was never very sure why Michael and Tom had fallen out. They'd been friends as medical students at Edinburgh University. That's how I'd first met Tom – at a party in Michael's student flat. But around the time that the twins were born they began avoiding each other. Then Michael emigrated. "What time did he call? Have I to call him back?"

"It was first thing in the morning in Sydney. Yes you've to give him a call. I know it was your dad's flat but finance is really my department isn't it?

"Yes, I know!" Tom did handle all the finances, and I got bored very easily by all that money management stuff. But he had a way of making me feel helpless sometimes. "I'm not a complete idiot you know. It won't only be the financial details. He'll want to know if the new tenancy is working out. I'm sure I can deal with it. I do manage a demanding job and looking after the house and family." I wanted to add, 'with precious little help from you', but I stopped myself.

Tom shrugged. "Andy called too. He went to the supermarket to see if your mystery boy is the one the girls know."

"Oh, Tom, the girls asked you not to go to Andy. Could you not just leave it?"

Tom merely shook his head slightly, as if I hadn't spoken. "And the plot thickens," he continued. "It's him - Robbie - and he's admitted to hanging about the house. It seems the lad wants to talk to us, all of us, together. Andy's going to bring him round tomorrow evening around seven. He wants to apologise, apparently. More likely Andy's told him he has to apologise!"

"Is that it? Who is he? What does he want with us all? I thought it was Jenny he was interested in."

"Andy didn't say, but I hope he's warned him to stay away in future, away from the house and away from the girls!"

"He's probably harmless you know, got a crush on Jenny, or maybe Sam – as she seems to think."

"Well, he's not welcome here. It's *not* harmless, stalking a young girl."

"Oh, for goodness sake, he's not a stalker. You sound like Max!"

I left Tom in the kitchen and phoned my brother. It was lovely to hear Michael's voice. He'd been living in Australia for about sixteen years. He'd only been home for two short visits in all that time - the last occasion being for our father's funeral four years before. On neither occasion did we get a chance to talk properly, and I don't really know why. Whenever I suggested a trip to Australia, Tom always came up with some reason why it was not a good time. He wasn't even keen on Sam spending her gap year at Michael's home. But, of course, Sam got round him in a way that I never could. Michael hadn't been as close to me as Heather, but he was my big brother and I loved him.

As always, it was good to hear his voice. "So, Rick's working out as the new tenant? He's looking after the flat?" he asked.

"Yes, yes it's fine, much neater than when the students had it. I did a check a couple of weeks ago. Rick wasn't there, but it all seemed in order. Being Lucy's brother, he'll not want to risk her wrath by abusing the place!"

"I suppose not. Upsetting both you and your best friend is probably something best avoided." I could hear the smile in his voice.

"Yes indeed!" I laughed. "He's away working at the moment. Taking photographs up in Skye I think."

"And it's not too much for you – being a landlord?"

"No, not at all. I wish all my responsibilities were so straightforward."

"You do too much, Rosie. God knows how you coped looking after Dad the way you did, on top of everything else – all that going back and forward to Edinburgh and then having him to live with you. I do appreciate all you did back then. You know I do. That's why I wanted you to have the flat. I don't deserve it. You do. I don't need it. I'm only asking about it to make sure you're not having any hassle."

"Yes, I know you are. And I told you it belongs to both of us. I don't want your half. I don't really need a flat either."

"You never know. I like to think that my little sister has a place to call her own." Michael spoke gently as he added, "Should she ever require it."

"I can't see that happening! Like we said though, it's a good investment to hang on to it. And if any of the kids go to uni in Edinburgh, it'll really come into its own."

Michael talked a bit more about our shared rental income from the flat and about the ever changing tax implications, which I did my best to follow. I also knew that this year, as always, I would end up having to get Tom's help sorting it all out. Then I remembered looking at the old photos of Heather and me earlier, and told Michael about it.

"Do you ever think about her?" I asked.

"No, hardly at all," he replied. "How's Sam doing by the way? Jo and I miss having her help around the place. The girls miss her too."

We chatted on, discussing our children, the weather, our jobs. But there was no real heart-to-heart. He certainly hadn't wanted to talk about Heather. I didn't mention my imminent hospital appointment or the incident with the boy. I know I'd made a conscious decision not to mention the hospital, but I've no idea why I didn't tell the story of the mysterious boy.

# Chapter Six

Before leaving for work the next morning, I tried to ensure that Jenny and Adam had eaten something and were calm and organised for their last exam. Jenny was quiet and rather tense, like an athlete focussing on the big race. She refused breakfast as usual, and would only have some orange juice as she looked over her revision notes. Adam was surly and withdrawn and impervious to my attempts to lighten his mood. And, although Robbie's forthcoming visit crossed my mind first thing, it was no more than a passing thought.

Once at school, all thoughts of anything, other than the class in front of me, left my head. The children in my class were a sparky lot and I was completely taken up with teaching primary three.

After school, Max popped his head round the door of my classroom. "Are you going to be long?" he asked.

"Hello to you too, I've had a good day, thanks for asking. And you?" I smiled as he rolled his eyes and sighed.

"Yeah, yeah, but are you? Neil and Connor are going to play footy on the field and I can go too if you're working on here. Oh, and can I go to Ruby's for tea tomorrow? Neil's going to his gran's and he said I can go too."

"Yes, you can go for tea. I'll be away at a meeting tomorrow afternoon anyway." It was sort of the truth and I was glad I wouldn't have to make arrangements for Max when I'd be at the hospital the next day. "And yes, go and play, I'll be about half an hour." He ran off. "Watch your school clothes," I called after him.

"No diving! I'll see you at the field." There was no reply, only the corridor door slamming.

Max made me smile. He was so carefree, so sure of his world. He didn't seem to mind me working at his school, as long as I remembered my place during school hours. He was such an easy child.

Later, over dinner, I asked as casually as I could how Jenny and Adam got on with their exam.

"Fine, Mother," Jenny said. "Don't worry, I think I did enough to pass. But don't ask me anything about cell division or anything else biological. It's all gone now it's over."

"What about you, Adam?" Tom asked.

"What about me?" Adam didn't look up.

"How was the biology exam?"

"Okay."

"Do you think you've done enough to pass?"

"Can we just leave it!" Adam shook his head at Tom, pushed his chair back and left the table. The kitchen door banged shut behind him.

"What's up with him?" Max asked, in a way that suggested he didn't really want to know, but was amused at his brother's outburst.

"I did ask you to go easy, Tom," I said. "I told you he's feeling the pressure."

"Oh, for heavens sake, it was a perfectly reasonable question. I'm interested – concerned that he does well. Is that so awful?"

"Dad, you know Adam loves a drama," Sam said. "He loves being miserable. He'll be fine. And, Mum, stop mollycoddling him. He's a big boy now. He needs to learn to cope with the stress of life." With that, Sam pushed her empty plate away and stood up.

I didn't know who I was angrier with, Tom or Sam. If we'd been alone I'd have tackled Tom there and then. Apart from stressing our vulnerable son, his insensitive mishandling of Adam was achieving nothing. As for Sam, she was so like Tom, just as insensitive to Adam's needs.

So I was distracted, thinking how I'd tackle Tom and Sam separately. I'd momentarily forgotten that Tom still had to break it to the girls that he'd stuck his oar in about Robbie. They had no idea about Robbie's impending visit. I began to clear the table. Jenny got up to give me a hand. Sam pushed her plate in my direction and stood up at the same time as Tom. Only Max remained at the table. He appeared to be responding to a text on his mobile – the mobile he wasn't supposed to bring to the table.

It was then Tom spoke. "Before you go, Sam, there's something I need to tell you."

I froze, my hands clenched on the back of one of the chairs. The kitchen had gone very quiet. I heard the click of a button on Max's phone, it sounded like a pistol being cocked. It wasn't only Adam who was going to be upset this evening. I had such a bad feeling about this whole thing.

"Oh, what?" Sam did her well-practised, bored teenager pose.

"This Robbie, it *was* him watching the house. I got Andy to look into it. He went to the supermarket, questioned the boy." Tom sounded so pompous I wanted to slap him.

Sam glowered at her father. I felt slightly queasy and sat down. I shook my head at Tom in exasperation. He was oblivious.

"Nice one, Dad," said Sam. "That's just great. Wait till everyone hears about this. Are you going to go to the police about all our friends?"

"Don't be ridiculous," said Tom, dismissively. He didn't even look at her. "You said yourself you were uneasy about him."

"Yes, but…" Sam shook her head. I wondered if Tom really did have no idea how misguided he was.

"Anyway," he continued, unabashed, "Andy's bringing the boy round in about half an hour, so he can explain himself."

Sam gasped. Max laid down his phone, looked from Tom, to Sam, to me. I tried to summon up the wherewithal to intervene. I was too slow.

"What?" shrieked Jenny. She'd been standing, a pile of

crockery in her hands, listening to the exchange between her father and her sister. Now she slammed the plates and bowls onto the table. She stared angrily at her father. "I don't believe you sometimes! Listen to yourself. How arrogant can you get!" She looked at Sam and me, turned her palms up and raised her shoulders, as if checking that we were as outraged as she was.

"Robbie's being bloody dragged round here," she went on, "to 'explain himself.'" She made a mocking, quotation marks, gesture in the air. "Christ, you're embarrassing!"

"Look, Jen–" Tom did not sound remotely conciliatory.

But Jenny wasn't looking for pacification. "No, you look, Dad. I begged you not to do this – but, oh no – you always know best." She gave her father a look of such defiance. "Well I'm off, don't expect me to attend this – this repulsive inquisition!"

With that she stormed out and up the stairs. "Bloody control freak!" she yelled, just before her bedroom door slammed.

Tom stood open-mouthed. He looked at me, not for support, surely? I stared back, shaking my head.

"What? Oh, come on!" he said.

"Like I said, Dad, nice one." With that Sam left the kitchen. "Give me a shout when Robbie gets here. He'll need all the support he can get," she called from the stairs.

"So the boy's coming here to see us?" Max spoke at last. Again he looked from Tom to me. I put my hand on his.

"Yes he is," said Tom, looking at his watch. "I suppose we better get ready. Come on, Max, give your mum a hand clearing this lot away. I'm off to phone the hospital – I've a couple of patients to check on."

And then it was just Max and me left in the kitchen. I sat for a minute, stunned. Tom's level of obliviousness was breathtaking.

I could have said no to Tom. I could have said, you organised this, you clear up. I'll get my marking done, and iron Max's school sweatshirt. But I didn't.

In the end we didn't need to give her a shout. It was Sam who ran to answer the door. She brought Andy and Robbie into the living room, where Tom and I were waiting. Sam went to fetch her sister and brothers. I wasn't sure if they'd come, but if anyone could persuade them, Sam could.

"Come in. Sit down," I said, indicating the smaller of the two sofas. "I'm Rosie. You must be Robbie." He looked even more scared than when we met the day before.

"Yes," was all he said as he sat down. Andy sat beside him.

Tom seemed frozen. He was just standing there, staring at Robbie. He looked as scared as Robbie did. I turned to Andy. I felt as if the three of them knew something I didn't.

"Sit down, Rosie. Tom, you too." Andy spoke gently, as I imagined he would when breaking bad news to some poor soul, bereaved in tragic circumstances. Sam returned with all three of her siblings.

Jenny looked embarrassed and glared at her father. She managed to overcome her discomfort enough to say hi to Robbie. He smiled gratefully at her. All four children sat on the large sofa. Max squeezed between his sisters. Adam sat at one end, slightly apart from the others.

When everyone was seated, Andy said, "Okay, Robbie, over to you."

Robbie looked directly at Tom as he began to speak. "I'm sorry for any trouble or worry I've caused you and Mrs McAllister - and Sam and Jenny too. I didn't mean to scare anyone." He glanced at the girls then looked back again at Tom. "I think you know, now you've met me, that I wouldn't want to hurt your daughters, don't you?" Tom shook his head. He looked like a trapped animal.

"Dad, do you know Robbie already?" asked Jenny

"Oh come on, Robbie, spit it out. Is it me or Jenny you fancy?" asked Sam.

"Shut up, Sam!" Tom was on his feet glaring down at Robbie.

"Dad!" "Tom!" Sam and I spoke together.

Robbie raised his hands in a pacifying gesture. "It's okay, Mrs McAllister, Sam, I understand. Dr McAllister, I can see you know who I am. And Mum assumed you'd know all about me too, by now, Mrs McAllister."

"Know what? Tom?"

"Let the boy talk." Andy spoke gently.

Robbie looked me in the eyes. "I'm Robbie Sutherland. I'm seventeen. I live in Edinburgh and I'm your nephew."

He couldn't have shocked me more if he'd pulled a gun. Even as I asked him what he meant, and babbled about not having any nephews, only nieces who lived in Australia, I knew. I didn't understand, but I knew he was Heather's son. I gazed at him, this boy who'd seemed familiar to me the first time I saw him, this boy who was saying a mad, impossible thing.

"No, no, not like this, please, not like this." Tom was pacing now.

"Tom?" I looked up at him from the sofa.

He looked anguished as he ran his hand through his hair. He turned to the boy. "I can't – I didn't – your name – it wasn't – it was James Robert – not Robbie. Christ, I need to think!"

I was on my feet. I tried to grab his hand, to make him turn and face me. "Don't," he said, as he pushed past me and left the room.

Andy stopped me from following Tom. "No, Rosie, leave him. I'll go after him. You all need to hear what Robbie has come to say."

For a moment, after Andy left us, no-one spoke. Robbie stood, looking uncomfortable. Max sat, still cuddled between his sisters. All three of them looked startled and apprehensive. Adam, on the other hand, sat forward, looking intently from me to Robbie.

It was Max who broke the silence. "Mum, you're very white. Are you okay?"

"I'm fine, I'm fine." I tried to sound reassuring. I sank down into the nearest armchair as my knees gave way. "What's this all about, Robbie? What are you saying?"

He spoke so quietly. A gentle assassin. "I'm your nephew. I'm

Heather's son. I was adopted after she died. My parents told me about it as soon as they thought I could understand. Then last year they told me more of the details and that my birth mother had a sister."

I think I made a sound. I don't know. I know I was crying.

"I really didn't want to upset you," he continued. "It was just – I wanted to get to know you – my birth family. It wasn't meant to be like this."

I wanted to stand up, lash out, tell him to go. I wanted him to stop. But I also wanted him to go on. Completely fascinated, I had to hear him out. So I sat and let this lovely, gentle, familiar stranger begin the dismantling of my life.

"I honestly thought you knew about me. My mum, that is Sue Sutherland, my adopted Mum, she told me she met my birth mother's brother and brother-in-law at the time of the adoption. So I assumed you'd know."

I could only shake my head.

"Mum said to wait till I was eighteen and then she'd help me approach you through the authorities.

"So why didn't you wait?" It was Adam who spoke. He sounded angry and cold.

Robbie ran his hand through his hair, a painfully familiar gesture. "I couldn't." He looked back at me. "I suppose, once I knew you existed, I had a way of finding out more about my mother. It was such a strong feeling. I had to do it. I had to see you now. Mum has a folder of stuff from the time of the adoption. I sneaked a look at it. Dr McAllister's name was in there, on a letter he sent when I was a baby. But there was no address, just an East Lothian postmark on the envelope.

"Dad's a surgeon. He's Mr McAllister, not doctor." There was contempt in Adam's voice.

"Yes, but the letter was written a long time ago. I suppose he was still a doctor then." Robbie turned to me once again. "I decided to make East Lothian the starting point for my search. I used the voters' roll and telephone directories. There were a couple of false starts. But, in the end, it wasn't that hard to track you down. I got this address and started to watch the house. Once I worked out where Sam and Jenny worked, I got the part time job at the supermarket. Then I got to know the girls and a bit about the family. I was fairly sure I'd found the right people. I only came round yesterday to check you out one last time before introducing myself. You weren't meant to see me. I'm sorry." He gave a slight shake of his head and held his palms towards me, before sitting back.

I felt very strange. Can a person feel euphoria and dread at the same time? I gazed at this boy, this awful, beautiful boy; Heather's son, my flesh and blood. I looked into his eyes. It was like that newborn moment between mother and child. I knew I loved him already. And I knew it was going to be a costly love. I put my arms out towards him and stood up. He got up to come to me.

"Get away from her!" Adam was between us. He pushed Robbie. "Leave her alone!"

Robbie put his hands out in front of him. "I'm sorry. I'm sorry!" He backed off. "I meant what I said. I didn't come to cause trouble. I didn't want to upset your mum or anyone. I just wanted to meet you all. You're family – my family."

"Get out! Go away! Leave us alone. You can't just come and claim us. You can't come and invade our family. Why should we believe you anyway?" It was Adam's turn to run his hands through his hair. I was mesmerised watching them. My son and Heather's, squaring up, face to face, so physically alike.

"Oh come on, Adam. Lighten up!" Sam stood as she spoke and opened her arms to Robbie. "I think it's cool you're our cousin. Though it'll be a disappointment to Jenny that you're family. Welcome to our world. Sorry about the parents! They'll come round." Sam hugged her new cousin.

Jenny blushed at her sister's teasing, but recovered enough to stand up and stretch her hand out to Robbie too. "Ignore Sam. She likes her little jokes. It's good to know who you really are.

I'm pleased."

"Thank you." Robbie smiled shyly.

"Hi, Robbie, I'm Max," Max pushed in front of his sisters and looked up at Robbie. "Our other cousins live in Australia and they're girls. It's cool to get a boy cousin."

"Thanks, Max." Robbie smiled again.

Adam grabbed Sam's arm and spun her round to face him. "What do you think you're doing? Why are you welcoming him? He's barged into our family – telling us some rubbish about being related. He's made Mum ill – look at her. Max, go and get Dad."

I was feeling quite sick. A wave of nausea had come and gone and I thought I might pass out. The euphoria was passing and the dread superseding it. I didn't quite know yet what the source of this apprehension and fear was. Max looked ready to protest at being ordered about by his brother, but when Adam shouted, "Go!" Max scuttled off.

"Didn't you see how upset Dad was?" Adam continued. "All because of him."

"Oh for heaven's sake, Adam!" Sam shook her brother's hand away. "Why do you always have to overreact to everything? Mum and Dad have had a shock. They'll be fine. This is good news. Robbie is good news."

"It'll be all right, Adam," Jenny stroked her twin's arm.

"Get off me. It will not be all right. If he's who he says he is, then what's he after? He wants to wreck our family – upset Mum - take her away from us. Dad kept him a secret all this time for a reason. He must have known he'd be trouble. We don't know anything about him. He's probably a junkie like his mother."

I will never know what came over me at that moment. I stood up and I slapped my son hard across the face. "That's enough! He's my nephew. I don't need proof. Look at him. He couldn't be more like you if he was your brother. What do you think he wants? He wants to know us, his family. And don't you ever speak about my sister in that tone again. How dare you!"

I was upset, but I was also strangely detached, beside myself.

I could see the shocked faces of all the children. Adam's hand covered his sore cheek. Tears ran down his face. As he ran from the room, he collided with Tom in the doorway. Tom was followed by Max. Tom saw the slap. Mercifully, Max didn't.

"Rosie!" Tom shouted. What were you thinking? That was unforgivable! Max said you looked like you were going to faint, but you've clearly recovered."

"What was I thinking? What about you? Why keep Robbie a secret all this time? Why did I have to find out like this after all these years? That's unforgivable!

Tom started dishing out orders. "Sam, take Max upstairs. See he gets to bed. Jenny, see Robbie out and then go and help Sam with Max."

"I'm not a baby. I can get myself to bed," Max protested.

Sam looked at her father's face, put an arm round Max's shoulder and steered him towards the door. "Come on, Maxy, I'll take you on at that new computer game of yours."

"Thanks, Sam," Tom said. He put his hand on Robbie's shoulder as he was going out the door, "I hope you're proud of yourself. You've had your say, now get out of our house. Andy's waiting in the car to take you back."

Robbie bowed his head and moved towards the door.

But I wasn't having him leave like this. I didn't care what Tom wanted. I stepped in front of him. I touched Robbie's arm. "It's been a shock, Robbie. Give us – give me time to get used to the idea. I'm sorry."

"I'm sorry too," Robbie said. He followed the others out. Tom closed the door behind the children.

# Chapter Seven

"What were you doing, Rosie, hitting Adam? I know you've had a shock but…"

I felt the fury building inside me as Tom spoke. We stood facing each other as the light faded outside. I wanted to shout, scream, cry. But I kept a grip on myself. I needed to focus, to understand. "I don't think it's me that has explaining to do, Tom. Is what Robbie says right?" My voice sounded calm and cold.

Tom sank into a chair. "Yes, yes it's right. Sit down, Rosie. You look terrible. Please, sit down and I'll try to explain."

I sat. "Well?"

Tom leant forwards, his hands clasped in front of him. "Just before she was due to have Robbie, Heather got in touch with me. She wanted to see me, to tell me about the baby. She didn't want you to know.

"Why not and why did you agree to keep a secret like that from me?" My earlier feeling of dread was still there.

"Well, apart from the fact that you'd been estranged for a couple of years, she was – I don't know – embarrassed – thought you'd disapprove."

"But she clearly didn't have a problem with you knowing. Why didn't you say anything? Why did you respect her wishes over telling me?"

Tom got to his feet. He paced. "I wanted to protect you of course. You'd only recently had the twins. You'd had such a difficult pregnancy and birth. You weren't well. I knew you'd worry, want to get involved."

"Yes, so what?" I looked up at him. "It was up to me to decide if I could cope, not you!" I got to my feet to face him.

"Oh really!" Tom leant in close. "Do you remember what you were like, Rosie? Do you? Some days you couldn't get out of bed. You were a mess. What could you have done? You couldn't even look after yourself or your own–"

"What? My own what? My own babies? Is that what you were going to say? How dare you? They never suffered. Not because of me. I was depressed, but at least I was here. Where were you, Tom? Where were you when your babies needed you? You were at your precious hospital or, as it turns out, spending time with my bloody sister." I was no longer calm. I knew I should keep my voice down but I didn't seem able to.

"Now you're being stupid." Tom's voice was also raised, his fists and jaw clenched. "I had to work. I made sure you and the children were being looked after. You had Ruby and Ma to help, thank goodness, because you certainly weren't up to it." Tom stopped as if to catch his breath. He dropped his shoulders. I could see him trying to get a grip on himself. When he spoke again his voice was quieter. "I just thought I'd wait until you were a bit stronger."

"But when I *was* stronger you still didn't tell me."

Tom raised his arms in a helpless gesture. "I know and I would've told you, if Heather had lived. Mind you, if she'd lived, I think she'd have told you herself. She didn't intend it to be a secret forever. She wanted to have the baby first – get her life sorted out – then tell you. But when she died, telling you seemed pointless."

"Why?"

"You were estranged from her, Rosie. I knew how difficult it was for you ending contact. I knew you felt guilty about her death. You weren't in a position to care for Robbie, and that would have made you feel even worse. Robbie was safe and well with good people. He had a new family. A clean break seemed best–"

"Best for who, Tom? No, there must be more to it." Now it was me who was pacing. I struggled to understand. "Yes, Heather and I were estranged. But, you said yourself, you knew I'd want to see her, to see the baby. It was you – you who didn't want that. It was self-interest, wasn't it? You used to get jealous of how close Heather and I were. Were you scared that Robbie would be a way back to that closeness, that his existence might lead to reconciliation? But then there was no danger of that once she was dead. So why…" And it was then that my earlier, formless dread took shape.

"I wasn't jealous, that's ridiculous!" Again, I could see Tom struggle to keep himself under control. Again, he lowered his voice. "Rosie, I saw how Heather hurt you and your family. God, she probably hastened your mother's death with all the worry she caused. I was scared she'd destroy you too. You were so vulnerable, even before her death. But afterwards, you were in pieces. I couldn't do it. I didn't want you torturing yourself any more than you already were. It wasn't easy not telling you, but it was right at the time." He got up and came over to me. He stretched his arms towards me.

"Come here," he said softly.

"Get away from me. Don't touch me!" I backed away from him. "Okay, you say you weren't jealous of Heather, but it wasn't about protecting me. You were protecting yourself! You were having an affair with her. It all makes sense."

Several emotions seemed to cross Tom's face, shock, hurt, anger.

I continued. "You were often out in the evenings when I was pregnant with the twins. We fought about it. I remember. You said it was work. You were so distracted at times. It made me angry. But that's it! It's you isn't it? It's you. You're Robbie's father."

Tom winced, shook his head. He opened his mouth to speak but I didn't stop.

"That's what you're afraid of. That's why Michael hasn't said anything, why you and he don't get along. That's why he doesn't visit. Robbie said Michael was with you at the time of the adoption. Michael knows, doesn't he? It must have suited you fine that Heather and I weren't speaking. How did it happen, Tom? Did you feel sorry for her? I know she fancied you."

"Stop it Rosie! Stop it!" he shouted. He put his hands on my shoulders.

"I said don't touch me!" I pushed his hands away and stepped back from him. I was shaking with anger. Tears came. "What did you expect? You've kept Robbie a secret for seventeen years. Did you think I'd say, 'oh that's okay, never mind, I know now'?"

"No of course not – but I certainly didn't expect this – this overreaction."

"Overreaction! What's the appropriate level of reaction to finding out your husband had a child with your sister seventeen–"

"Shut up – just shut up!" Tom stepped towards me again and leaned in, inches from my face. "I am not Robbie's father. How can you even think it? It's sick!" He turned his back and walked over to the window.

"No, Tom, that's not what's sick. What you've done, that's what's sick." My voice was quiet again. I wiped my tears with the back of my hand. "Christ, her dying must have suited you perfectly. Nobody need ever know. I feel so betrayed, so let down by you, Tom.

Tom let out a strangled howl. He thumped one of his fists down on the window sill as he swung to face me again. I've never seen him so enraged. "Shut up, Rosie! You don't know what you're saying!

"I will not shut up. I know exactly what I'm saying. You've betrayed me – you –you cheating, cruel bastard."

Tom recoiled momentarily. "Stop being so bloody melodramatic! Yes, I've kept Robbie's existence a secret, but I haven't betrayed you." He came over to me. He took hold of me by the elbows and looked into my face. I turned my head away. He gave me a little shake. "Look at me." I wouldn't meet his gaze. "Look at me!" I glanced at him. His breath was hot on my face.

His expression was ugly and cold. "I did not sleep with your sister."

I tried to speak but only a sob came out. I shook my head and looked down at the floor.

He let go of my arms. "Oh, what's the use?" He went back to the window and looked out at the darkening sky. I felt my legs buckling. I sat down. Tom spoke, still with his back to me. "I've told you why I did what I did. It was for your protection."

I managed to find my voice. "So you say, but you could have told me afterwards when I was well again. That's what's so hard to understand. That's why I think there's got to be more to it."

"I did mean to tell you one day – when the time was right. But I don't know – the longer time went on I–"

"It must have occurred to you that Robbie might come looking for his family one day."

He turned to face me and leant against the window sill. "Yes, it did but I thought we'd – I'd get some warning – a letter or something, so I could prepare you. I've always thought of him as James. She named him James Robert after your father. So I didn't make the connection. It wasn't until I saw him tonight–"

"So you weren't going to tell me unless you were forced to, unless Robbie made contact. You weren't really waiting for the right time, were you?"

"When would have been the right time, Rosie – when? Do you remember how ill you were, how deep the depression was? Even as time went on I could never be sure you were strong enough to handle all the facts about the end of Heather's life."

"Not strong enough? How can you doubt my strength? Have you ever considered what I've have coped with, on my own, with no help from you, bringing up the children, working, running this place, looking after my father–"

"Oh, here we go – Saint Rosie – the martyr! You don't have to work, you know that. You put the pressure on yourself. You don't want my help, not really. You shut me out. Everything's always under control. You enjoy being put upon, you smother the children. No wonder Adam's the way he is."

This made me gasp. "So I'm a control freak and a bad mother, am I? What about you, Tom? Absent father and unfaithful, dishonest husband."

Tom looked at me the same way Adam did after I slapped him. "Right, that's enough. This is getting us nowhere." Tom put his hand up to silence me. "Let's leave it for now. We're both tired. We should go to bed. Robbie exists. You know now. You need time to get used to that fact, to get over what's happened. It won't look so bad in the morning. Come on, let's go up to bed."

Now I felt patronised. "No Tom, no. You don't get this do you? Don't tell me what to do and how to feel. Don't talk to me in that 'doctor knows best' way. I'm not one of your patients!" I was shouting again and the tears had restarted. I stood up and headed for the door. Tom was right behind me. I turned to face him, my hand on the door handle. "This is far from over. I haven't even begun to get my head round Robbie and what you've done. I don't know what to believe or what to think. But I do know I'm angrier than I've ever been with you. And I also know I don't want you in our bed."

Tom looked stunned. "Don't do this, Rosie." He tried to turn me towards him as I headed out of the door.

"Get off me. I mean it, Tom. Leave me alone."

I was so angry that my throat hurt as I spoke. At that moment I hated Tom. I hated that he thought he knew best. I hated his need to take charge. I hated that he just expected me to understand.

# Chapter Eight

I went up to Max's attic room to say goodnight but he was already asleep, curled up on top of his duvet. As I crossed the passageway at the bottom of the attic stairs, I glanced at Adam's bedroom door. It was closed. I had to see Adam, to apologise, but not now. I could hear Sam and Jenny. They were in Sam's room, the door was ajar and I glimpsed them sitting on the bed, chatting. They didn't notice me as I slipped into my own room.

I sank down on the bed and, still fully clothed, I crawled under the duvet. I cried for what seemed like hours.

I slept fitfully. Early next morning I heard Tom going out with Toby for their morning jog along the beach. When they returned, Tom didn't come into our bedroom. I didn't get up until I heard him leave for the hospital. I looked and felt grim.

Tom had left a curt note in the kitchen. It said he'd be staying at the hospital that night. Tom staying at the hospital was not unheard of, but it didn't happen often. Occasionally, if there was a patient he was particularly concerned about or an operation ended late in the evening, he would stay over. I suspected neither of these reasons applied to this occasion. I shrugged and dropped the note. I couldn't think about Tom, or any of it, yet. I had to get through this day first. It was easier to keep up a pretence of normality, go to school and then to my appointment. I'd think about the other stuff later.

Sam and the twins slept on while Max and I had breakfast. Sam had the day off and the twins' study leave lasted till the end of the week.

Max was his usual sunny self. He sat opposite me at the kitchen table. "Robbie's nice, isn't he, Mum?"

"Yes, he did seem nice," I replied and I meant it. Whatever else I was unsure of, I knew I'd already made up my mind about one thing. I wanted to spend time with my nephew and get to know him.

"It's so cool to have a boy cousin at last. When's he coming here again?"

"I don't know. We'll have to see." I realised I didn't know where Robbie lived or even have a phone number for him. I also realised I hadn't exactly gone over the top in making Robbie welcome. Neither Tom nor I had behaved well, and it wouldn't have been surprising if he didn't want to see us again. I couldn't bear that.

"Mum, you look sad again, like last night. Don't you want Robbie to come back? Is it because of your sister or because he made Dad so cross?"

I got up and gave Max a kiss. He wiped his cheek with the back of his hand.

"Ugh, Mum!" But he was smiling as he said it. "It'll be all right," he continued. "Dad won't stay cross. He's like Adam and doesn't like surprises." He stood up and put his arms round my waist.

I cuddled him tightly, struggling not to cry. "You're a very wise boy sometimes, Maxy. And I love you very much."

"Love you, too, Mum."

As always, Max had lightened my mood. He was such an uncomplicated and cheerful lad. Despite professing to hate being kissed, he still regularly sought and accepted a hug, and still liked to cuddle up close on the sofa when watching the television. I hoped it would be some time before this changed.

Once at school, I reminded Max I wouldn't be there at the end of the day. And then he was off into the playground, shouting to a friend to kick the ball to him.

Like the day before, I found work to be therapeutic as I had no time to think of anything other than what was happening in the classroom. One of my pupils, Maisie, a shy and reserved child normally, was glowing with the arrival of her new baby brother. She stood up and told her news to the whole class and showed us a photo of the baby. This inspired several of the other children to share stories of wee brothers and sisters. There were tales of a two-year-old having to go to hospital to have a raisin removed from his ear and of a wee sister's potty training accidents. Then it was time to get everyone changed for P.E. As we lined up to go to the gym, Jordan was copiously and colourfully sick on the classroom carpet. This caused hysteria among the other children, who were both disgusted and delighted. I despatched a runner to find the janitor. After break there was a maths test to do, followed by an exploration of the wonders of magnetism.

Before I knew it, it was two o'clock and time to drive to Edinburgh. The traffic heading into the city was not too heavy at that time of day, so I didn't take the by-pass all the way in. It was such a horrible road. I much preferred to approach the city through Musselburgh and Portobello, keeping the sea in view. The sun was out and it was a warm afternoon. The sea sparkled. I threaded through Leith with its new flats, warehouse conversions and trendy bars and restaurants. And soon I was heading west along Ferry Road to the Crewe Toll roundabout and the Western General Hospital. It took me almost as long to find somewhere to park as it had done to drive into the city.

I knew the Western quite well. Tom worked there when he was a junior doctor and it was where my mother had her cancer treatment. I'd accompanied her to some of her appointments. It was still a sprawling, incoherent set of buildings, supplemented nowadays by various portacabins. The breast clinic had moved from where it had been during my mother's time. It had taken me a bit of time to find it on my previous visit, when I came to have the tests done. This time though, I knew where I was going.

The clinic's waiting area was cramped and dilapidated. Two rows of mismatched chairs faced each other; many already occupied when I walked in. The reception desk sat across the top of the small space. In the middle was a low table, its grubby surface littered with ancient magazines and empty plastic cups. I informed one of the receptionists of my arrival and was told to take a seat. I managed to find one that had no one sitting on either side.

Across the corridor from the waiting area were several consulting rooms. The doors to these rooms opened from time to time and a patient would emerge, sometimes alone, sometimes accompanied.

It helped pass the time to wonder about the relationship between patient and escort, and what their story was. Sometimes a patient and partner would come out beaming and embracing. Other times a woman would emerge in obvious distress and supported by a nurse. Then there were those who were impossible to read. Had they had good or bad news? And away they would all go, to face their fate.

Then a nurse would call out the name of the next soul awaiting their verdict and sentencing. Each time this happened my heart lurched. Part of me wanted the consultation to be over, but another part wanted to prolong this time of ignorance. What you don't know can't hurt you – my mother again.

Up until Robbie came into my house and said who he was, everything was normal. Then in the space of a sentence everything changed. My world shattered, certainty fragmented and fell away.

And now, at the hospital, another potentially devastating sentence could be about to be uttered. But at least I was bracing myself in preparation this time. My mind drifted on and on.

"McAllister, Rosemary McAllister?" The nurse's voice sounded impatient as it broke into my thoughts. She was frowning. I wondered how many times she'd said my name. I raised my hand.

"This way, please," she said, without smiling. I followed her across the corridor to the door with Mr Campbell's name on it.

She showed me in and disappeared.

"Good afternoon, Mrs McAllister." Mr Campbell came round from behind the desk and shook hands. As at our first meeting, there was the nice smile and the calm manner. "Do sit down, please." He indicated two chairs side by side at right angles to the desk. The room was very small and stiflingly hot.

"Thank you," I said, as I took a seat. My mouth was dry, my voice weak. I cleared my throat. There was a quiet knock on the door. A nurse entered. She looked friendlier than the one who'd shown me in. She smiled and sat down beside me.

Mr Campbell brought his chair out from behind the desk and sat facing me. He looked down at the file in his hand. "I have the results of the scan and the biopsy." He laid the file down. He leant forward and put his hand on mine. "Mrs McAllister, I'm sorry to have to tell you that the lump in your left breast does appear to be malignant."

So much for bracing myself, it was still a shock. To hear that word –'malignant' – applied to me, to something in me, was devastating.

"Do you have anyone with you today?" He nodded towards the nurse. "Would you like Sister Webster to ask them to come in?" Mr Campbell looked me in the eye, his hand still on mine. He had such a kind face.

"No, there's nobody with me. I came alone. I preferred it that way. My husband would have come if I'd asked him, or any of my friends, of course. But this is how I wanted it. I'll tell people when I'm ready. My husband's a doctor – a surgeon – I didn't want him taking over." I was babbling. I knew I was, but I couldn't help it. For some reason it mattered to me that Mr Campbell understood why I'd come alone.

"That's all right. Everyone copes in different ways. A surgeon you say? McAllister – not Tom McAllister, heart man at the Royal?"

"Yes, Tom's my husband. Do you know him?"

"We've met, but I know him by reputation mainly. He's very

highly thought of. But I take your point about us surgeons wanting to take charge. We make terrible patients and even worse partners of patients!" Mr Campbell laughed at this observation. I managed a weak smile. "Anyway, Mrs McAllister – I know it seems like very bad news, but try not to worry. I believe we've caught your cancer early and it will prove to be treatable. I'd like to get you in as soon as possible and take a good look at what we're dealing with. I need to operate and I'll only take as much of the tissue as is absolutely necessary. Then we'll work out exactly what further treatment is needed. But you will definitely need a course of chemotherapy."

He sat back in his chair and I realised he was waiting for me to respond. I was unable to speak. All I could take in were the words 'your cancer', 'taking tissue' and 'chemotherapy'. They echoed round my head. I felt very strange. I actually thought I was going to laugh. This was all some hideous joke – Robbie, Tom, cancer…

"Mrs McAllister, take a wee sip if you can." Sister Webster was holding a cup of water to my lips. Her arm was along my shoulders.

Mr Campbell was opening the window in the stuffy little room. I took a couple of sips.

"Better now?" Mr Campbell smiled his lovely smile again. "Sister Webster was quick off the mark. She saw you about to hit the deck and caught you. Good catch, Wendy, by the way!"

"I'm so sorry," I said.

"Don't be! These rooms are far too hot and you've had a shock. It's me who should apologise. I was going too fast for you. When you're ready, come over to the examination couch. You're still very pale and I'd like to check you over. But first you need to gather your thoughts. I'll leave Wendy here with you for a few moments. She'll answer any questions you might have and she'll explain the support she'll offer you throughout your treatment." Mr Campbell offered his arm and helped me over to the couch. "Now try and relax and I'll be right back."

Wendy Webster was as calm and reassuring as Mr Campbell. She was about my age, tall and slim with short grey hair and a kind face. She went over everything that Mr Campbell had said and more.

"Don't worry if you don't take everything in now," she said. "That's perfectly normal. Here's my card. You can phone or email me anytime with any questions you might have. If I'm not here when you get in touch, I promise I will get back to you as soon as I can.

In a little while Mr Campbell returned. "You've got your colour back. Feeling better?" He took my wrist. "I'll just check your pulse, Mrs McAllister."

"Rosie, call me Rosie. Mrs McAllister makes me feel like I'm either ancient or at work. I'm a teacher. And, yes, I'm feeling much better thanks."

"Rosie it is then. I'm Angus. I don't like to presume and go straight to first names. Some patients prefer to keep it formal – although it does tend to be the older generation. And that's fine. I want my patients to feel comfortable." He let go of my wrist. "I'll just take your blood pressure, if I may."

I nodded.

"Teacher, eh?" he continued as he removed the pressure cuff. "I couldn't do your job. I wouldn't have the patience. I couldn't put up with the backchat and the cheek."

"Oh, I have the little ones. They're only seven. They can try your patience, I agree, but it's a good job and can be very rewarding." I realised I was smiling and feeling much better. Angus Campbell was a skilled practitioner.

"Seven year olds! Even more scary!" He laughed. " Right, you'll do, pulse and blood pressure are fine," he said. "Now sit up slowly and, when you're ready, come over and sit down.

Once I was back sitting in the chair he asked, "Anything you want to know or has Wendy done her usual efficient job? I take it we can call her Wendy, don't want her to feel left out." He winked at his colleague.

"You said you'd take some tissue during the operation. Did you mean – does that mean that – that you'll – that I'll..?

"Lose your breast?" His voice was very gentle. I nodded. "I could do a lumpectomy, which is only to remove the lump. But I may decide, once I see what's what, to take a bit more than that, and yes, possibly, the whole breast. I will ask you to give consent for the entire visible tumour and as much surrounding tissue as is advisable, to be removed at that operation, because that's how I prefer to do it. However, it's up to you to make an informed decision. Read the leaflets Wendy's given you and do ask any further questions as they arise."

I nodded again. "You said I'd need chemotherapy. Does that mean it's really bad and if it is, is it worth having chemo? It's just my mother had chemo for her breast cancer and it was awful. It made her so ill and she died anyway."

"Rosie, I can't make promises. I don't know the full extent of your disease, but chemo is well worth it. I'm sorry your mother had cancer too, but you're not your mother. Every cancer's different and it's not over till it's over, okay?" He touched my hand again. I nodded. "Talk it over with your husband or someone else close. Let all this sink in. I'll be in touch soon to arrange admission. It could be as soon as next week. And you can be signed off work whenever you want to start your sick leave. I'll be in touch with your GP shortly, so it's just a case of letting him or her know." He stood up. "We'll get this thing sorted. Don't worry."

I stood up too. "I'll try not to. Thank you."

"And you must rest assured that this is all confidential. I know Tom's a doctor, one of the club, but he'll only hear about any of this, if and when you decide to tell him. However, I do urge you to tell someone amongst your nearest and dearest. You will need support. Goodbye for now." He held out his hand. I shook it. I added perceptive to the list of Angus Campbell's good qualities.

# Chapter Nine

I don't really remember the drive home. I know I didn't let myself think about the diagnosis. The car radio hummed its tunes and the roads went by in a blur. All I wanted was a soak in a hot bath and then to sleep and sleep.

The kitchen was strewn with dirty dishes. Sam, Adam and Jenny had obviously had breakfast and lunch. Cereal packets stood open on the worktop and bread and assorted spreads lay abandoned on the table. The washing machine hadn't been emptied. The kitchen bin was overflowing, and Toby had obviously been taken out for a walk recently, judging by the damp, sandy, paw prints on the kitchen floor.

I walked through to the hall to hang up my jacket and saw that the answer machine was blinking. There were two messages. I wandered back to the kitchen as I listened to them. The first made my heart thud. It was from Robbie. He sounded awkward, saying he was leaving a message for Rosemary McAllister and that he hoped I was all right and had got over the shock of meeting him.

The second was from Tom. "I hope you got my note. I thought I'd give you some space. I'll be back tomorrow after work. I hope you've got over it all and seen sense. We'll talk tomorrow evening. Oh, and could you try and get my dry cleaning tomorrow? I need the suit for a conference on Monday. And my car is due a service. Can you book it in? Bye."

I put the phone down on the worktop, turned to the table and swept dishes, food and cutlery onto the floor. I threw my head back and laughed, a horrible, cackling laugh that changed to a howl, and then I sank down onto a chair and cried messily and loudly.

Adam came running to the kitchen accompanied by Toby who was barking loudly at the commotion. "Mum, Mum, what's happened? What's wrong?"

I stared at him. I couldn't form any words.

"Mum, what is it? What should I do? Mum!" He held me by the shoulders and shook me. Then he went to the kitchen door and called out, "Sam, Jenny!" He came back to me. He took my hand and said, "I'll call Dad. It'll be all right."

"No!" This was all I could say. No, no, no!" I shook my head slowly from side to side.

Poor Adam looked distraught. "Sam, Jenny!" he shouted again.

"What?" Sam called from along the hall. "What do you want? We're watching something on TV."

"Come here!" Adam bellowed back over the dog's barking. "Shut up, Toby. Go to bed."

Sam gasped as she stepped into the kitchen. "Jesus! What's happened? Mum, my God, Mum. Adam?"

Jenny followed her sister into the room. She looked scared as she surveyed the scene. "Mum, are you okay? Adam, did you do this?"

"No! I was just coming out of the loo when I heard a crash and Mum laughing like a witch. I came to see what it was and found Mum like this. Didn't you hear it?"

"No, we didn't hear a thing. Did Mum do all this?" Sam pointed at the debris.

"I suppose so. She was sitting there howling and crying when I came in."

"Mum, what's the matter?" Sam came over and sat beside me. I couldn't stop shaking my head and I couldn't stop the tears. She put her arm round my shoulder. "Jenny, Adam, you two start getting this lot cleared up. I'll get her a cup of tea and phone

Dad."

I grabbed her arm. "No!" She put her hand on mine as I gripped her.

"I suggested that already," said Adam. "She said no to me too." He put the broken bits of crockery onto some newspaper and retrieved the cutlery and unbroken dishes.

"Why does she not want Dad?" Jenny asked, as she mopped up the mixture of jams and milk.

"I think they had a bit of an argument after Robbie left last night. Dad's staying at the hospital tonight. There was a note," said Sam.

I could see and hear the children, but it felt like it does in a dream. I tried to speak, but I couldn't. I tried to move, but I seemed to be paralysed.

"I knew this would happen," said Adam. "Him turning up and telling her all that crap. What's he after, for Christ's sake? It's not like Mum's his mother. And did you see Dad? He certainly didn't want him around! And then Mum hit me and now she's like this, and Dad's left home."

"Oh for heaven's sake, Ad, don't go over the top. She shouldn't have hit you. I'm sure she knows that," said Sam. "Robbie didn't mean any harm. He thought Mum knew about him. She just needs to get used to the idea. And Dad's obviously in trouble for keeping Robbie a secret. It'll be fine."

"Oh will it? Well, I don't want anything to do with the creepy little git!"

"This isn't about you, Adam." Jenny spoke gently and put her hand on Adam's arm. He shook her hand away and filled a bin bag with all the broken bits he had gathered.

"Quite," said Sam. She squeezed my hand. "Come on, Mum, I think you should go to bed and I'll bring you up that cup of tea."

I was vaguely shocked that Sam was making me a cup of tea, that was a first. She gently pulled me to my feet.

As she guided me towards the hall she turned to the other two. "Once Mum's settled I'll go and collect Maxy from Ruby's and I'll get us a takeaway for tea on the way back. Can you two finish clearing up in here and that washing needs to go in the drier."

At the foot of the stair my eldest child gave me a motherly hug and said, "On you go. I'll just be a couple of minutes getting your tea. Why not have a nice bath before you go to bed." I clung to her, and wondered at the very concept of a grown up Sam.

I found my voice, "Thank you, sweetheart, I'm so sorry about–"

"Don't be. Go and have a soak."

I did as I was told. I drank my tea in a wonderfully hot and bubbly bath. I lay back in the water. I looked at my diseased breast and I cried for it. Then I thought of Heather and Robbie and cried for them. Later, when I was in bed and propped up on several pillows, trying to eat some of my share of a Chinese takeaway, there was a knock and Lucy came in. Lucy, my dear friend for more than thirty years, was here, exactly when I needed her to be. I pushed my tray away as she approached and sat down on the bed. We hugged.

"How did you..?" I could say no more. I cried again, but this time with relief. It was so good to see her.

"Sam phoned me, asked if I could come over." She took my hand and stroked my hair. "What's been happening to you, Rosie?"

I first saw Lucy Montgomery in the assembly hall on our first morning at the Edinburgh High School for Girls. We were waiting, along with the rest of the new intake, to be called forward into our classes. Heather was instantly at home, talking to lots of girls she'd not met before. But Lucy looked as nervous as I felt.

When our names were called for the same class, she came over and linked her arm through mine. Her fair hair was in two long plaits. She was petite and pretty. She told me she lived with her parents and her brother on their farm in East Lothian and that she'd hardly ever been to Edinburgh before that day. She said, "I think I'll be your friend," and smiled up at me. And that was it, we'd been friends ever since.

And now Lucy held my hand as I told her about the events of the past couple of days. Mostly Lucy listened without comment. Although she did gasp when I told her about Robbie, and about slapping Adam. And, when I voiced my suspicions about Tom being Robbie's father, she couldn't help interrupting. "Oh no, Rosie, no, you've got that wrong. You must have! Tom wouldn't, not Tom."

"I don't know what else to think. I mean why would he keep Robbie a secret all this time? They were attracted to each other, him and Heather, you must remember?"

"Well, yes, I suppose so. But with Tom, it was surely just the fact that you and Heather were identical. He wasn't going to be repulsed by her, was he? And Heather, she was your sister, she wouldn't have done anything. Anyway – she had other – interests."

"She was a junkie. You can say it. She was a no-hope, heroin junkie. Why not sleep with Tom? She had nothing to lose. She and I weren't even speaking at the end of her life."

"I know – but Tom and her – I don't think so. But it's what you think and I'm sorry. I only hope you and Tom can get past it. There's more though, isn't there, more you have to tell me?"

"Yes, there's more." I took a deep breath and told her about the cancer. Then she hugged me and we both cried.

"So now you know. You know it all," I said at last.

"Yes and I don't know what to say, Rosie, except I'm here for you."

"That's all you need to say."

"I'm so glad Sam phoned me. She's a great girl, isn't she?"

"I'm only beginning to realise how much she's grown up. Since she came back from Australia she's seemed like she was before, a messy, self-obsessed teenager, but she surprised me this evening!"

"She just needs a chance to prove herself. With you always

doing everything for her, why would she ever do anything?" Lucy smiled as she said this. She, like Ruby, was always telling me off for running about at the beck and call of the kids. "Sam's got the kitchen gleaming and Jenny's checked Max's homework and got him all organised for school tomorrow."

"What about Adam? Did you see him?"

"He was helping the girls in the kitchen when I arrived, but he disappeared upstairs while I was talking to Sam. Probably needs time on his own to figure it all out. It doesn't take much to unsettle Adam, does it?"

"No, it doesn't. He was already stressed out with the exams. He was very negative about how he'd got on and now all this other stuff has happened."

"I'm sure he'll get over it, especially if the other three are as laid back about Robbie as you say. Anyway, you need to rest. I'll send Max in to say good night. He could probably do with a hug from his Mum. I'll phone Kirsty tonight and tell her you'll not be in tomorrow and that you'll be in touch. I'll also ask Jenny to organise Max in the morning."

"But–."

"Don't even think about arguing. You need looking after and if you really don't want Tom to do it, then you're stuck with me."

"No, I really don't want Tom, and I meant what I said about not wanting him to know about the cancer. And the kids, they're not to know either, not yet anyway."

"Okay – whatever you say. But you'll have to tell Kirsty. And your colleagues will obviously wonder when you go off on sick leave. It'll be difficult to keep it secret. Tom and the children might hear it from somewhere else. You don't want that."

"No, but I need to get used to the idea myself first. I need to be in charge of this."

"I know you do, Rosie. I know you do."

# Chapter Ten

Next morning, Jenny brought me breakfast in bed.

"You can lay the tray down. I'm not going to throw the china around." I smiled sheepishly.

"I'm glad to hear it. How are you feeling?"

"Better, thanks. This looks nice." I indicated the tea and toast she'd brought. "I'm feeling quite hungry."

"Eat up then."

"Yesterday was a really bad day. I'm so sorry I lost it like that."

"Was it the shock of Robbie, and of falling out with Dad?" Jenny sat down on the bed.

"Yes, it all got a bit much. Robbie's announcement was very difficult for me, and for Dad. But you've not to worry. None of you've to worry. We'll sort it all out." I patted Jenny's hand.

"Good. I've seen Max off to school and Sam's away to work. No sign of Adam yet though, so I'll take Toby for a walk and then I'm meeting up with some of the girls to go into town. We're celebrating the end of the exams with some retail therapy and lunch. We might go to the cinema or back to someone's house to crash. Will you be okay?"

"Of course I will. You go and have a good time. You deserve it. You've worked so hard."

"If you're sure. I'll text you later and let you know what we're up to. Oh, that reminds me, I'll put Robbie's mobile number in your phone – you know – in case you want to get in touch with him."

"Thanks, sweetheart. He phoned yesterday and left a message.

I do want to get in touch – to get to know him."

After Jenny left I thought about what I needed do that day. One of the first things was to speak to Kirsty, both as my friend and as my boss. So I phoned and asked if I could see her at lunch time. If she was surprised she didn't let it show. Perhaps Lucy had prepared the ground. Anyway, when I arrived at school she'd put Lesley, the deputy head, on duty over lunch and put the 'Meeting in Progress' sign on her office door. She'd even organised coffee and sandwiches for us.

"I'm sorry to interrupt your lunch hour," I said, as I sat down opposite her at her desk.

"Don't be daft. I wouldn't be getting a lunch hour if it wasn't for you! You know how it is here." She was right of course. A head teacher rarely gets an undisturbed lunch time. But Lesley was obviously on the ball and we were left alone as I told Kirsty what had been happening.

Like Lucy, she listened. And like Lucy, she was shocked. But she was more direct in offering her opinions and advice. "Don't shut Tom out, Rosie. I'm sure he never meant to hurt you over Robbie. How can you even think he was unfaithful? Tom loves you and, yes, he's protective – but I think that's nice. I've always envied you on that score you know."

"You envy me? Right now, I envy you your independence. Actually, I feel quite pathetic compared to you. I'm fed up being protected and treated like some dependent child. Tom had no right to keep Robbie a secret. Why would he do that? What was he protecting me from? No," I shook my head, "he was protecting himself more like – that has to be it."

"I just think you're going to need Tom, with – you know – well now you're – you've got cancer." Even the normally forthright Kirsty had difficulty saying the 'C' word.

"Don't be afraid to say it. It's a fact. I've got cancer." I spoke more sharply than I meant to. The last thing I wanted to do was fall out with Kirsty. Her complete honesty and inability to say one thing and mean another, was one of the things I loved about her. But I didn't like that she saw me as in need of Tom's protection and support, and in need of shielding from the fact of having cancer. I wanted to believe I could be as strong as Kirsty. She reached her hand out to me across her desk.

"I know," she said gently. "I know you're strong, Rosie. I know you can cope. I'm trying to be helpful – and making a mess of it. I can't believe you've got cancer. I don't know what to say, to tell you the truth. I'm more in my comfort zone doling out advice about husbands."

"I'm sorry. I didn't mean to snap." I squeezed her hand. "I don't know what I'd do without you and Lucy."

"We won't ever have to do without each other. You haven't managed to shake me off after thirty years, so it's not going to happen. The three of us will grow old disgracefully together."

Kirsty and I met each other in our first year at St Andrews University. She had the room next door to mine in the hall of residence. She was a striking girl, tall and athletic, with auburn hair. She came from the Isle of Skye and spoke Gaelic. I thought her quite exotic when I first met her. On the face of it we didn't have that much in common. She was studying science and I was doing arts. She was into sports. She played in the hockey and badminton teams and was a keen hill walker. My passions were playing the piano, singing in the university choir and reading, what Kirsty called, soppy novels. However, in spite of how different we were, Kirsty's level-headedness and her ability to be simultaneously kind and direct, were qualities that I found reassuring and stabilising. She also had a wicked sense of humour, something that stood her in good stead over the years. We remained friends throughout our time at university and beyond. I was especially pleased that she and Lucy also became friends when I introduced them to one another.

Thirty years later she was still good looking and she'd kept her lovely accent. "Rosie," she said – I'd always liked how she pronounced Rosie with a soft 's' – like the 'c' in Lucy – "independence is all very well, but it can be very lonely. And

I had no choice, not with my dear ex. Thank your lucky stars, Tom's not like Gary."

I looked at Kirsty and shrugged. I conceded that she probably knew what she was talking about. Kirsty divorced her husband, years before when their only child, Eilidh, was still very young.

"I don't know what to believe, Kirsty. But I know that if Tom finds out about me being ill, he'll leap into action, telling me which doctor to see, which hospital to go to and which treatment to have."

"Would that be so bad?" Kirsty asked gently.

"Yes, it would, actually. Don't you remember what it was like when I had the depression after the twins were born? He had me admitted to that awful place."

"Of course I remember. He didn't do it lightly, Rosie. And of course a psychiatric hospital is no picnic–"

"I hated it there! I hated the way the drugs made me feel, but Tom kept telling me they would make me well."

"And he was right. You did get better." Kirsty still spoke gently, but as always she wasn't letting me get away with any display of self-pity or unfairness.

I couldn't help smiling. She was a brilliant devil's advocate.

"Yes, in the end, the medication did help," I said. "And so did having access to that counsellor. She was good – I admit."

"Well then – perhaps you should trust Tom again…"

"No," I said, shaking my head. "I hadn't realised till now, but I've never really got over the feeling of powerlessness I experienced then."

And I didn't say so to Kirsty, but I'd also just realised how much I blamed Tom. "Oh, I know I sound like a spoilt brat," I continued. "But this is my illness, my body and I want to be in charge for a change."

"Okay, okay!" Kirsty smiled. "I'll support you whatever. I'll help in any way I can. Come here." She came round the desk and we stood and hugged each other. "But I still think you need to talk to Tom," she said as she stood back. "Now, as for school, how do you want to play it?"

"I'd like to start my sick leave right away. I don't think I can do the job justice at the moment. But I'd like to say cheerio to the kids, give them some kind of explanation."

"Of course, do you want to do that today? You could go in after lunch. I'll ask the supply teacher to give you a bit of time alone with them."

"Yes please. I'd like that."

"And the rest of the staff, what do you want me to tell them?"

"For now, could you just say I've got leave of absence for personal reasons and I'll be back some time after the summer holidays. I'll tell you when I'm ready for everyone to know, I promise. I know I can't keep it secret in the long term. But I want to tell the children and – yes – Tom, when I'm ready. I don't want to be rushed and I want them to hear it from me."

"All right, if that's what you want. I'll be discreet." Then the bell rang and Kirsty gave me another hug. "I'll go and see your supply teacher and tell her to wait ten minutes before coming along to the class. You go and say your goodbyes."

So I went along and surprised Primary Three with my presence. I settled them on the carpet and told them that I was starting my summer holidays early. I said I had an awful lot of stuff to sort out at home, and that Miss Mackinnon had kindly said I could have some extra time off. I told them they'd have another teacher for a while, and that I'd see them when they were big Primary Fours. They seemed genuinely sad that I was going and I struggled not to cry in front of them. But I knew that, for now, I couldn't give them the attention they deserved. I needed to go and get my life sorted out.

When I arrived home in the early afternoon there was still no sign of Adam. Toby made it known that he needed to go out, so I set off down to the beach with him. It was a lovely afternoon, the kind we often got in late May, a tantalising glimpse of summer but accompanied by a stiff easterly breeze. The sky was clear and the tide was well out. I threw a stick for Toby and, as we covered the length of the beach and back again, I was able to think. The astringent sea air cleared my head. By the time we were heading back to the house, I'd made some decisions.

While I still had the house to myself, I made a few phone calls. The first was to my mother-in-law, Evelyn, to see if I could go round to see her later. She seemed delighted to hear from me and said she looked forward to seeing me. She didn't betray any curiosity about hearing from me in the middle of a weekday afternoon. Next I called Lucy to discuss her brother and his tenancy of my father's flat.

And after that I called Robbie. Jenny had said he'd be working at the supermarket that day so I wasn't surprised when my call went straight to voicemail.

I wasn't consciously aware of what I was going to say to him. But there was a subconscious compulsion at work. I found myself leaving a message inviting him to join us for dinner the next day, if he wanted to, and if it was all right with his Mum. I tried to sound both welcoming and casual at the same time.

After I hung up, the possible folly of what I'd just done hit me. I hesitated. Should I call back and leave another message, withdrawing or postponing my impulsive invitation? The girls had been furious at Tom's obliviousness to their feelings about confronting Robbie, and now here I was acting without consulting them. And, as for what Tom and Adam might make of what I'd just done… But, I reasoned, Jenny had seemed happy to give me Robbie's mobile number and Sam, well, she liked Robbie, and she'd surely understand my need to get to know my nephew. Wouldn't she? No, it would be all right. I'd explain and hope they'd understand, and if they didn't…

The phone rang, forcing me to abandon my qualms. It was Angus Campbell's secretary. She said they'd had a cancellation on the operating list for the coming Tuesday and that Mr Campbell would like me to come in then for my operation.

And that was the moment when the full significance of what I was facing made its real impact. All my worrying about Robbie, about who to tell about my illness and what to say – none of it mattered, it was just so much displacement activity.

Everything fell away from me. I felt I was on the edge of a void. I shuddered, touched all over by an icy coldness, my hands clammy on the phone. I struggled to breathe. The secretary's voice seemed muffled, far away.

"Mrs McAllister, are you still there? Can you hear me? I need to explain–"

"Yes, yes I'm here. I'm listening." I spoke quickly, just ahead of the nausea that was overwhelming me. I clamped my back teeth together, tried to concentrate on the woman's words. She was saying something about fasting and anaesthetic. I couldn't really make sense of it. I was terrified. I had cancer. A surgeon was going to slice off my breast…

"So we'll see you on Tuesday then?" The voice was as calm as ever.

"Yes," was all I managed to say, before hanging up and fleeing to the toilet to throw up.

It was some time before I could get up off the bathroom floor, but eventually I did. I washed my face, cleaned my teeth, brushed my hair.

Gradually I came back to myself. Slowly the panic subsided. But the underlying fear remained. I realised it would be a long time before that receded. If it ever did. But I also realised I couldn't – mustn't give into it. Doing nothing, hoping it would all go away was simply not an option.

# Chapter Eleven

Before I left for my mother-in-law's, I realised I'd better phone Mr Campbell's secretary back. She didn't seem surprised that I'd taken in very little of what she'd said before, and explained the admission procedure again. I managed to remain calm enough to scribble down the main points of what she told me.

Then, slightly later than planned, I drove to Evelyn's. Tom's mother lived near Haddington, about ten miles inland from Gullane. Haddington was the old county town of East Lothian and is a very pretty, well to do place. Holdfast Cottage was a traditional Scottish, one and a half-storey, white-rendered, stone building. Surrounded by a walled garden, it sat well back off the road. As I was expected, the large, solid, wooden gates stood open. My heart lifted as the car rolled up the gravel driveway. I loved the solid, thick-walled, old house where Tom spent the later part of his childhood, and I loved my mother-in-law.

She was at the front of the house doing some weeding when I arrived and came to meet me as I got out of the car. She was dressed in slim-fitting grey trousers and a blue and white striped cotton shirt, worn with the collar up and the sleeves rolled back. Her silver hair was, as always, in an immaculate French roll. The blue of her shirt matched her eyes perfectly and she had little pearl studs in her ears. She took off her gardening gloves as she approached.

"Rosie, it's so nice to see you. Your call was a lovely surprise." She held her arms open to me. And she smiled her lovely smile, so like Tom's. We hugged each other and I breathed in the scent of Chanel No. 5, a fragrance I always associated with her. It felt good to be embraced by this woman. It felt safe. She was taller than me, and in spite of being well into her seventies, she still stood strong and straight backed. Dr Evelyn McAllister was no little old lady.

She stepped back and looked me up and down. "You've lost weight my girl, and you look tired."

"Yes," was all I could say before those treacherous tears started. I'd promised myself I'd be strong, that I'd calmly relate what had happened and ask for Evelyn's advice.

"Oh my dear girl, come on, come through." She put her arm round my shoulders and guided me inside.

Having installed me in one of the comfy, chintzy, old armchairs in her sitting room, with a box of tissues at my side, she went off through to the kitchen to make us some tea. She left me with the instruction to cry my eyes out as it would make me feel better.

Evelyn's two elderly spaniels were curled up on one of the faded, floral patterned rugs, snoozing in the warmth of the sun coming through the French windows. They'd barely looked up when we came in to the room. The windows stood slightly open, and the fragrance of Evelyn's gorgeous Gertrude Jekyll roses drifted inside. Birdsong came from every corner of the cottage garden, and many little birds flitted from the trees and hedges to the feeders hanging all around. I curled up in the chair and, as the clock on the mantelpiece ticked quietly, I wept once more. I wept with grief for Heather and with sorrow for Robbie and for what Tom had done. I wept with shame for hurting my beloved Adam. But mostly I wept with sheer self-pity and fear. And then I could cry no more.

"I expect you'll be ready for this now." Evelyn reappeared with a tray of tea and cherry cake. She set it down on a large footstool in front of the fireplace. Then she poured the tea into pretty china teacups decorated with little pink roses. As she sat down on the sofa opposite and I settled back with my tea, she said, "Now, tell me what's wrong, Rosie."

So, once more, I related the events of the last couple of days. Lucy and Kirsty had been great listeners and had offered their support. Telling them had made it all seem a bit easier to bear.

But telling it to Evelyn was cathartic. Even though Tom was her son, she didn't jump to his defence, not even when I told her about my suspicions that he might be Robbie's father. But neither did she condemn him. She listened in much the same way Lucy had, but with even greater attention. I realised, as I was speaking, how much I trusted this amazing woman. She was the least judgemental person I knew. Just being with her made me feel better.

Evelyn had not had an easy life. Her marriage to Tom's late father was miserable and she divorced him when Tom and his brother were still children. Maybe her own struggles were what made her so compassionate.

So when I finished telling my story, Evelyn simply stretched out her arms to me. I went over and sat on the sofa beside her. She put an arm round me and I rested my head on her shoulder. I know it sounds daft, but it was as if I could feel some of her great strength seeping into me as we sat there.

After I don't know how long, I had a sudden realisation. "My god, Max, he'll be home from football practice soon. I need to get back!"

"Relax, stay where you are. You're not going anywhere, my girl. It's all sorted out. I texted Sam when I was making the tea and she replied immediately. She's getting away early from work to be home when Max gets in. Although I'm sure he'd be fine letting himself in, Dan and Tom were latchkey children at his age."

"Yes, but–"

"And I've sent Tom a text too, telling him to get home as soon as he can, as you are going to be staying here tonight."

"But, why, how…?"

"I knew as soon as I saw you that you needed time out, even

though I didn't know the reason. So I hope you will forgive me taking charge, but it's a mother's prerogative." All I could do was nod. Evelyn took my hand. "So what are you going to do, Rosie?"

"About what, about Robbie or Tom or the cancer?"

"About all of it, any of it?"

"Well, I need to get started on my treatment and I need to believe I'll get better."

"Yes, you do. Having cancer puts other things into perspective, that's for sure. Tom and Robbie can wait, the cancer can't. And you will get better. But you'll need all your strength to fight that particular battle."

"I'm scared, Evelyn. I'm really scared. I'm scared of losing my breast. I'm scared of dying if the treatment doesn't work. And even if it does, how do you ever get back any peace of mind after this kind of thing? I feel betrayed by my own body. I don't know – I suppose I thought I was immortal. Now I just keep thinking why me, why now? The children still need me, especially Max. And Robbie, what about Robbie? I've missed so much of his life already and now I might be cheated out of – out of…" I could feel new tears starting.

Evelyn put an arm around me once more. "It's all right to be scared. It's a scary thing. Cancer isn't rational. Yes, you can reduce the odds, but nobody's cancer proof. It's not as if anyone deserves it. But it's more beatable now than it's ever been. I know you, Rosie. You'll come to terms with it."

"I don't know if I'm strong enough, Evelyn. What if it's spread?"

"Take it one step at a time. You'll know more after your surgery. You're a survivor, Rosie, like me, made of strong stuff. You've survived so much already. You'll come through this too. And you say Lucy and Kirsty are supporting you, and you've got me. I'll help in any way I can."

"And Tom, what do I do about Tom? We said some terrible things to each other."

"That will become clearer too. You don't want to tell him

about the cancer at the moment, and I understand your reasons. Of course, as Tom's mother, there's a lot I could say in his defence, but I don't think that would be particularly helpful. However, I do know he loves you and I'm certain he's not Robbie's father. But I think you probably need some space and a bit of time to yourself. You could stay here. You know that, don't you?"

"You're so kind. I don't know what I've done to deserve you, Evelyn. And yes, I do need some space. Thanks for the offer, but I don't want to put you in an awkward position with Tom. No, I have an idea about giving myself some time alone. I don't know if it's really feasible. And there's Max. I don't think I can leave him. It's probably daft to even consider it–"

"If you can't be daft now, when can you? What's your idea?"

"Dad's flat, it's empty at the moment. You know how Rick, Lucy's brother, has the tenancy. He's away just now. He's not due back for several weeks. I phoned Lucy earlier and told her what I was thinking. I asked her if she'd contact Rick to see if it would be okay. She said I should go ahead and she'd let him know. She was sure he wouldn't mind."

"Mind what exactly?"

"If I moved in, temporarily, to the flat, while he's away. But I haven't really thought this through. What about the children? Who'll look after them? I shouldn't even think about deserting them should I, especially Max?"

"As I said, I think you need some time out. I think it's a good idea. As for the children, three out of the four of them are well able to look after themselves. And have you forgotten you have an experienced mother's help living with you? Get Sam on board. She was saying, in her text earlier, that's she's sick of working at the supermarket and she's going to hand in her notice. You've got Ruby too, to help with the chores. Yes, Max will need looking after, but I can help with that. There's only a month of school left. He can have sleepovers with you in the holidays. And there's Tom. They're his children too."

"Do you think Sam would do it? I can't see her being willing to take on the role of housekeeper."

"Ask her."

"And what about Tom? He's got his work."

"Yes, and he's fortunate he gets to concentrate only on his work. It won't do him any harm to do a bit of juggling. He has responsibilities at home as well."

"But how do I tell the children I'm abandoning them because I need some space?"

"You're not abandoning them. You're only going to Edinburgh, for goodness sake. They can visit you. You're exhausted and finding out about Robbie has been a shock. You're simply taking some time out. Trust them, Rosie. Trust them to cope without you. And when you're ready, trust them – Tom and the children – to cope with knowing you're ill."

"And what do I say to Tom in the meantime? He'll think I'm leaving him, but I'm not. At least I don't know if that's what I'm doing."

"Then that's what you tell him. Tell him you don't know how you feel. That's the point of you going away, to have time and space to think, away from him."

"And you, you'd be all right with that – me leaving your son?"

"It's not about me or what I think, but I believe it's only by leaving now and doing what you have to do, that there's any chance of putting things right between you. Tom needs to see he can trust you to make your own decisions and that you can cope perfectly well on your own."

"So I should go ahead – move out?"

"It makes sense and you'll be nearer the hospital for your post-operative treatments."

"Well, there is that, but that's a minor reason really, although I remember how grim it was for my mother after some of her chemotherapy sessions. At least I can spare the children from witnessing that sort of stuff."

"Rosie, if you stay at home it will be very difficult for you and Tom to resolve any of this. At best, there'll be a strained atmosphere – tension about Robbie, about your illness. At worst you'll be using precious energy quarrelling with Tom, hurting each other more. No, I'm sure you're doing the right thing."

The phone rang. Evelyn excused herself and went to answer it. I thought over all that we'd said. I felt better, and marvelled again at what a wonder my mother-in-law was.

She came back into the room. "That was Tom. He'd picked up my text and wanted an explanation. He also asked when I'd got the mobile phone."

"Yes, I was wondering that too," I said, smiling at her.

"I got it a couple of weeks ago. Max put all your numbers into it for me when I was last over at yours. And he showed me how to use it. I've been sending practice texts to Max and he's been replying. I think I'm getting the hang of it now. It's cool, apparently, that I have a mobile and it's well-wicked that I can use it, according to Max. At least, I think that's what he said, and I think he meant it as a compliment."

"Oh, there's no higher praise than to be judged both cool and wicked by Max." I smiled at the thought of the conversation between grandparent and child. "And what did you tell Tom?"

"Don't worry. I just said you'd come over for tea and I could see you were exhausted, so I'd invited you to stay the night."

"Did he mention Robbie to you?"

"No, even if he suspects you've already told me, I don't expect he's ready to talk."

"And he accepted what you said?"

"He seemed to. He's going home now anyway."

"I've invited Robbie to come over for dinner tomorrow," I said, realising I wanted Evelyn to approve. "I want to let him know he's welcome – at least as far as Max and the girls and me are concerned.

Evelyn nodded. "Of course you need to get to know Robbie. Adam will come round. He'll make sense of it all in his own way. But I think you should prepare him before Robbie comes to dinner, share your plans with him, make your peace. Don't be too hard on him if he's not ready to accept Robbie yet."

"Yes, I know I need to talk to him. I just hope he understands."

"You shouldn't feel guilty about wanting to get to know Robbie. In fact, don't feel guilty about any of it. It's time to put yourself first."

With that, Evelyn said she was going to prepare some dinner for us. She suggested I go out to the garden. So I went to sit on the bench by the rose bed. My mobile beeped in my pocket. It was a text from Robbie accepting my invitation. I was pleased, but at the same time there was a dull ache of apprehension in my stomach. I was aware I still had to tell Tom and the children that I'd asked Robbie to come. But in spite of that nudging dread and, after talking to Evelyn, I was now even more convinced I was doing the right thing – at least for me –and, I hoped, for Robbie.

I turned my face up to the late afternoon sun and my apprehension lessened. And, as I sat there in Evelyn's glorious garden, I even felt a small surge of wellbeing and confidence. I dared to hope that things would work out.

Dinner was wonderful. There was a delicious homemade quiche and a perfectly dressed green salad accompanied by a glass of crisply dry, white wine. Afterwards I had a long, hot bath. And then, as I settled down to sleep in Evelyn's spare bed, between soft, white, Egyptian cotton sheets and wearing a pair of her beautiful, grey, silk pyjamas, I had a moment of doubt. My earlier resolve and optimism wavered. I wondered again if I should postpone seeing Robbie, or perhaps stay at Evelyn's for a few days and see him at Holdfast. But I didn't – couldn't – give in to my misgivings. I couldn't stumble at the first hurdle. I knew what I was contemplating was going to be painful, but my survival was at stake. I was fighting for my life.

# Chapter Twelve

I left Evelyn's at around ten the next morning and decided to go and see Ruby on my way home. I wanted to tell her face to face what I planned to do. When I arrived she ushered me into her very pink front room. Four of her grandchildren were watching television, still in their pyjamas. There were toys and breakfast plates and glasses all over the floor. Ruby chased the children out.

She ignored their protests and followed them into the hall. "Go upstairs and get dressed. Granddad's going to take you home."

I could hear the children clumping up the stairs.

"Sorry about them," Ruby said as she came back into the room. "I had Gail's kids overnight. He's waiting to take them home." She gestured vaguely towards the back of the house where I assumed her husband must be.

I apologised for disturbing her Saturday. She shook her head and dismissed my apologies as unnecessary. I refused her offer of tea.

"So what is it, Rosie? What brings you here?" she said kindly, as she settled back in her large pink armchair.

I'd intended to keep it brief. I'd intended to tell her calmly that I was ill, that I was going away for treatment and to ask her to do some extra hours. But I found that, as with Evelyn, the whole story came spilling out. While I talked, Ruby came to sit beside me. She put her hand on mine. I gripped it. "I hope you don't think I'm being selfish and I hope you'll be able to help."

"Don't be daft, lassie!" Ruby replied. "You're not selfish enough, that's your trouble. I told you the other day you do too much for them all. I knew you weren't well. I said, didn't I? I said you were looking pale."

"Yes, you did. So will you keep an eye on things for me – at the house – keep an eye on Max especially?"

"Of course I will. And Max can come over here, as usual in the holidays, when Neil's staying."

"You're a saint. I don't know how you do it all, your jobs, the grandchildren..."

"Oh, I'm no saint," Ruby said, "But I do have St Anne and St Monica to help me." She got up and went over to a recessed glass shelf in the corner of the room. On it were two china statues, along with some candles and several rosaries. She picked up the statues. "These are my ladies, my helpers. This is St Anne, patron saint of mothers, and this is St Monica, she looks out for married women. They get me through, never let me down. *He* gave me St Monica actually, after I ran away from home." She turned to replace them on the shelf.

For a minute I thought she meant that God had given St Monica to her, but then I realised she meant her husband. My bemusement must have shown on my face.

"No, not *Him* – him – Ray." It was the first time I'd heard her say her husband's name.

"Oh, right – Ray," I said, "and what did you mean when you said you ran away?"

"It was years ago, before I knew you." Ruby laughed. "I left them, him and the bairns, went to my sister's. I'd had enough, doing everything for everybody, six teenagers and him. So, one morning, I decided that was it. I packed a bag, left a note and went."

"Ruby!" I was aghast. Ruby, who seemed so sorted, so grounded, so family orientated, had walked out, just like that.

"I know, but it was the making of them, and it saved my marriage. They all had to get on and manage without me."

"How long were you away for? What made you come back?"

"Oh, I was away about a month. I always intended to come back. I'm a good Catholic girl and I believe in the vows I made when we got married. But that doesn't mean I'd sit back and be taken advantage of. He came after me, brought St Monica with him, said he couldn't cope without me, came out with all that romantic stuff that made me fall for him in the first place, daft, sweet-talking, Irish bugger. Anyway, it made us stronger as a couple, me going away, and it didn't do the kids any harm either. And, if I'm honest, I missed them all like crazy. I drove my sister mad going on about how great they all were. I was about to give in and come home when he showed up! Of course, I didn't tell him that."

"Oh, Ruby," I laughed. "You're a tonic, you really are."

"It's good to see you laughing, lass," Ruby said smiling. She came back and sat down and took my hand in hers, her smile gone. "I'm so sorry – about the cancer and about Tom and this lad – Robbie, was it?"

"Yes, Robbie." I sighed.

"Come here, hen," Ruby said. As she embraced me I thought for a moment of my mother. "You go and get better," she continued. "I'll do whatever I can to make sure the family are okay,but they'll have to do their bit too. I'll see to that."

"Thanks, Ruby, thank you so much. I don't know what I'd do without you. You saved me seventeen years ago and you're doing it again now." I wiped away some escaped, rogue tears.

"No, hen, I did some cleaning and tidying up. You saved yourself. You're strong, like me, but sometimes, even us strong ones need a break. So stop feeling guilty." Ruby had tears in her eyes too.

"You will come and see me at the flat, won't you?" I said.

"Just try and stop me!"

When I got home, Toby was in his bed in the hall, snoozing. He got up to greet me. His coat was damp and smelled of the sea. "You been swimming Tobes?" I said, as I patted him. I guessed he'd been out with Tom on the beach run. I went through to the kitchen. Tom was sitting at the table, drinking coffee and reading the paper. He was in his running gear. The front of his tee shirt was damp. I could smell his maleness and could see the sheen of sweat on his skin. Part of me wanted to walk over to him and put my arms around him. With hindsight, maybe that's what I should've done. But at the time …

"You're back then," he said. He didn't look at me.

"Yes, I'm back." I picked up the percolator and poured myself a cup. I sat down opposite him. He continued reading his paper. I sipped my drink. I could hear the wall clock ticking, like a bomb about to go off.

Then Tom spoke, without looking up. "I was surprised to hear from Ma yesterday. She said you were too tired to come home and that I couldn't speak to you." He finally looked directly at me. "Are you ill?"

I hesitated for a heartbeat and thought 'He knows'. But, in the same moment, I told myself that was impossible. "I'm okay. As Evelyn said, just a bit tired. Where are the kids?"

"Adam's up in his room. Sam and Jen are both on early shift at the shop. Max is out playing with Neil and Connor. He's having some lunch at Connor's and then Connor's dad's taking them to the cinema this afternoon. He'll be back about five he thinks." Tom's face was expressionless and his voice was flat. "We need to talk," he said.

"Yes, we do."

"I'm sorry, you know, for not telling you sooner – about Robbie."

I nodded in acknowledgement of the apology. I knew he was waiting for me to apologise to him. "Look Tom, I know you just want everything back the way it was."

"Yes, I do. Isn't that what you want too?"

"It's not a case of wanting it or not, Tom. It's happened. Robbie is a fact. Your deception is a fact. Your motives for the deception – I don't know what to think, what to believe."

"I–"

"No, Tom, let me speak. I need to tell you what I've decided to do."

"What do you mean, what you've decided? Is that why you went to Ma's? You went to get her advice, told her all about it. I bet she's on your side too."

"Oh, for heaven's sake, Tom, your mother doesn't take sides. She listened to me. She didn't pass judgement."

Tom shrugged. "If you say so. Anyway, what's this decision you've reached?"

"First of all, I want to make Robbie welcome, to get to know him and to include him as one of the family. I've invited him to come to dinner this evening."

"Oh you have, have you? Well don't expect me to welcome him. Don't expect me to be here for dinner and to play at happy families." Tom pushed his chair back and stood up. He leaned over the table so his face was level with mine. "He's not one of the family. He has his own family. The Sutherlands are his family, not us!"

"Stop shouting, I get the message." I got up from the table and began to clear the coffee things away. "You're not going to have dinner with us this evening, fine. Although it's a shame you won't be here as it'll be the last family dinner for a while."

"What do you mean the last? What do you mean?" Tom looked scared.

"I mean I'm moving out. I'm moving out tomorrow. I'm going to stay at Dad's for a while, at the flat."

"What – why, how can you? What about Rick? Rosie, what are you talking about?"

"Rick is away for a few weeks. Lucy doesn't think he'll have a problem with it. And Evelyn thinks it's a good idea."

"Ma, Lucy – you've discussed this with them? Before you told me?" Tom ran a hand through his hair and shook his head at me.

"Yes, I have. And I know, it's not nice being the last to know something is it?"

Tom looked grim. "Is this some kind of revenge? Is that it?" His voice was quiet.

"No, Tom, no it's not. It's about me and what I need to do. I'm tired, run down and with the shock of finding out about Robbie and – everything – I need some space, some time to myself."

Tom put his head in his hands. Again I was aware of the clock ticking. Then Tom asked how he'd manage without me. He asked how the kids would manage. I told him I thought they'd all manage just fine. He begged me to reconsider. I said I wouldn't, I couldn't. He said I was a selfish bitch. I told him I'd learned selfishness from the master – him. Then he pushed his chair back and walked out. He left the house, clattering the door closed behind him.

I was trembling as the adrenalin, anger and fear subsided. Tom and I didn't really do shouting or raw emotion. I think it was something that scared us both. We'd always been so civilised. I wondered where he would go, dressed only in his running gear and in great need of a shower.

I heard the floorboards creaking above me. The sound reminded me there was another difficult conversation I needed to have. I went upstairs. Adam's door was closed. I heard music playing inside. I took a deep breath and knocked loudly.

"What?" Adam didn't sound pleased to be interrupted.

I went in. "Hi, son."

"Oh, it's you. I didn't know you were home." He was lying on his back on top of the bed. His blind was closed as usual and the only light in his black and white room came from his tropical fish tank. He continued to look at the ceiling.

"Yes, I'm back, obviously." I felt awkward. I perched at the end of the bed. "I'm so sorry, Adam. I'm sorry I hit you. I've never hit any of you. I don't know what came over me. It's no excuse, but Heather was my sister and I couldn't bear to hear you talk like that about her. She was more than a pathetic junkie." I paused, hoping he'd at least look at me. He didn't. "And I'm sorry I lost it in the kitchen and that you had to find me like that. I'd had an awful day and, seeing the mess, I just... I put my hand on his ankle. Please forgive me."

He propped himself up on one elbow and looked at me at last. "No, you shouldn't have hit me. Okay, I shouldn't have said that about your sister. It was just, I hate it when things change."

"I know you do. Robbie appearing was a shock for us all, and it does mean a bit of change and adjustment. But it's a good sort of a change really, isn't it, a new cousin? And Robbie seems nice, don't you think?"

Adam shrugged. "He's not going to be around much, is he? And Dad doesn't seem that happy about him."

"Dad'll get over it. He got a shock too. And I hope Robbie will be around a fair bit. I need – I want to get to know Heather's son. He's part of this family."

"Don't think I'm going to be happy about it, because I'm not. I just want things to go back to normal, and for you and Dad to be friends again, and for Robbie to go away."

This was not going to be easy. "Adam, I've invited Robbie to come for dinner this evening and I hope you'll be there. It'll be easier for you than the other night. Please, give Robbie a chance."

"No, no. I'm working from five anyway, but even if I wasn't, I wouldn't want to be here. I'd be pretending, pretending to like him, pretending I cared. What does Dad think about Robbie coming? Is he going to be there?"

"Well, no, he isn't actually. He can't make it either."

Adam gave a small, disparaging laugh. "Right."

"And there's something else, Adam."

"What?"

"I'm going to stay in Granddad's flat for a wee while."

"Why? What do you mean? How long for? Isn't there somebody staying there already?"

"Yes, Lucy's brother is renting it, but he's away at the moment. I've not been feeling too good recently. I'm a bit tired and run down. It'll only be for a few weeks. I've taken time off work and I need a bit of a rest, a break from everything."

"You can have a break here. We can all help you. Or is it us you want to get away from? Is it me?"

"No, Adam, it's not you. Of course it's not you – not any of you. It's me. I need some space. Grandma and Ruby have said they'll help out here and I'm going to ask Sam to help too, like she did for Uncle Michael when she was in Australia. And there's Dad, of course." I tried to sound positive and upbeat.

But Adam didn't look reassured. "What does Dad think? Does he want you to go?"

"No, he doesn't want me to go. But he understands, I think."

"Yeah, right."

"Look, you can visit me, drop in after school, have something to eat. It's really not a big deal, Adam."

"It is to me." He put his music back on and I could see there was no point in trying to say any more.

I returned to the kitchen, unsure what to do with myself. Then, with her unerring sense of timing, Lucy phoned. She asked if I'd like to come over to hers for lunch. She said she'd asked Kirsty and that she was already on her way.

# Chapter Thirteen

It didn't take long to drive the few miles along the coast to Lucy's place near the village of Aberlady. We had lunch at Lucy's garden table. The spell of warm weather was forecast to end with thunderstorms by the evening, so we wanted to make the most of the sun while it shone. It was good to be in the fresh air, tucking into a delicious pasta salad with my two dear friends for company. I could almost believe that the events of the last few days hadn't happened and, for a little while, the three of us maintained the fragile illusion.

Kirsty chatted about school and Lucy told us how her husband Graham was fretting over the low price their lambs were fetching.

"But you know farming." Lucy stretched out her arm to indicate the spread of fields, beyond the farmhouse garden, that made up their mixed arable and livestock farm. "It's one damn crisis after another. We got through BSE and foot and mouth - and I suppose we'll get through this falling price thing too."

"Of course you will –you two are a strong team," Kirsty replied. "I don't know how you run all this with so little help. I suppose it's a labour of love."

"I suppose." Lucy shrugged. "It's far from idyllic, but I don't know what else I'd do, especially now both the boys are away."

"They'll be home soon for the summer, won't they?" I asked. Both Lucy's sons were at St Andrews University.

"Yes, I can't wait, and not just because they'll be around to help out - although that'll be handy. Graham and I are hoping to leave the boys in charge and get a few days away to celebrate our thirtieth wedding anniversary."

"Good heavens," Kirsty said. "You two going away together! That's a rare event. Where will you go?"

"I don't actually know. Graham's organising it. He says it's a surprise." Lucy smiled and flushed slightly.

"Oh look at you –blushing –after all this time. How romantic of you – and Graham!" Kirsty fluttered her eyelashes and sighed.

"Yeah, yeah," Lucy answered. "You're just jealous!"

Kirsty looked serious for a moment. "Yes, I think I am jealous. I've had enough of being on my own. It would be nice to have someone to share everything with – the good and the bad – like you and Rosie have." Lucy shifted awkwardly and gave Kirsty a look. Kirsty then looked very uncomfortable. "Shit, I'm sorry, Rosie. That was tactless."

"No, no, don't be sorry." I reached over and touched both of them on the arm. "I don't want either of you thinking you've got to watch what you say around me. And you're right, until quite recently I'd have said Tom and I had a good enough partnership."

"But not lately, not now?" Lucy glanced at Kirsty as she spoke. I shook my head and shrugged. Kirsty looked back at Lucy.

"What is it?" I said. "If there's something you want to say – please say it." They looked at each other again.

It was Kirsty who answered. "I, that is we, Lucy and I, - we think you shouldn't delay telling Tom about the cancer – and the kids - you must tell them. We understand how upset you are about the Robbie thing - and there's no question that Tom could have handled that better. But no matter what you think he's guilty of – you're going to need his support – you know – while you're ill."

"And what if you're wrong about Tom – about him being Robbie's father?" Lucy leaned over and took my hand. "Maybe all he's guilty of is being a bit misguided, a bit over-protective – is that so awful? If you don't tell him about the cancer, aren't you just as guilty of deception?"

Before I could answer, Kirsty spoke. "You can't keep it a secret once your treatment starts – that's for sure."

It was now Lucy and I who exchanged glances. "Ah, well, yes you're right about it not being an easy secret to keep – at least, not if I was living at home." I told Kirsty about my decision to go to the flat.

"You really want to do this your way, don't you?" Kirsty said when I'd finished.

"Yes, I do. I'll tell Tom and the children – of course I will – but not till I'm ready. I'll have the surgery on Tuesday-"

Lucy gasped. "That soon!"

"Yes, that soon. I'm glad to be getting on with it, to be honest. Then I'll take things from there. I don't want Tom wading in and taking control – and that would have been the case, even without all the Robbie stuff. And as for the kids – I want to have all the facts ready. I want them to see I'm okay with it all and I'm not yet. And, in the meantime, I'm not alone. I've got Evelyn and Ruby – and you two, I hope."

"Of course," Lucy said. "And what about you and Tom, as a couple?"

"Well, as for my marriage – my relationship with Tom – I don't know. I hope I'm wrong about him being unfaithful – but either way – I don't know if I want to be with him anymore." I was surprised to hear myself saying this. I hadn't realised I actually doubted my long term future with Tom. "It's not only about Robbie and the cancer. Recently, I've realised - oh, I don't know – things haven't been right for a while. Nothing major – not like recent events – just a gradual slide. I think our relationship's been dying of neglect for quite some time." I looked at my friends' bewildered faces. "Oh, look, can we talk about something else – please? Let's leave my sorry life for a while. Can I get us all some coffee?" I made my escape to the kitchen and left the other two to digest what I'd told them.

When I returned, it was Kirsty who moved the conversation into different territory. "So, what's Rick working on up in Skye?"

she asked Lucy, while I poured the coffee.

"It's mainly photos - promotional material for a sound and light show that's on later in the year, on some mountain side," Lucy said.

"Oh yes, it's on the Storr. I heard about it," Kirsty replied.

"But I think he's doing other general stuff for his portfolio of wildlife and wilderness shots," Lucy continued. "And, of course, he'll be fitting in some walking and cycling too."

"He's not changed then. Still the action man he was at uni." Kirsty laughed. "I envy him being up in Skye and all the good walking he'll be able to do. I don't get home nearly enough. I'm planning to go up in the summer holidays – I really need to sort out Mum's house." Kirsty's mother had died at the beginning of the year, within a year of Kirsty's father's death. "I don't know if I'd recognise Rick now. Has he changed much?"

"I don't think he's changed at all – like we haven't either – in the last thirty years. What do you think, Rosie? You saw him when he took on the flat?"

"Oh, not changed at all – still that weird mix of laid back and manically intense – still tall, dark and handsome – yes, okay – a few laughter lines here and there - but still a good looking guy."

"Still fanciable then?" asked Kirsty.

"Oh yeah!" I laughed.

"Oh please – you two! That's my brother you're talking about!" Lucy made a face of mock disgust.

"He was a heartbreaker when we were all at university," said Kirsty. Certainly broke your heart, didn't he, Rosie?"

"That's right – he loved me and left me. We were together for – nearly a year, I think it was – my first love."

"And he's loved them and left them ever since! He's never settled down. Probably never will." Lucy shook her head and smiled.

And so our conversation moved along. Kirsty spoke about her daughter's plans for university the following year and Lucy told us of the latest exploits of her two sons. They were always in scrapes of one sort or another and calling home for rescue or advice or cash. When it was time to leave they both hugged me and didn't need to say anything. I knew I could depend on both of them.

My positive mood didn't last long. There were clouds gathering as I drove home and the atmosphere had become close and stifling. The oppressiveness of the weather matched my state of mind. Dark thoughts now overshadowed the cheering effect of the time spent with my friends. I recalled my earlier dispiriting encounters with Tom and Adam. They'd reacted as I'd feared they would when I told them of my decisions. That was depressing enough, but I was also acutely aware I still had to tell the girls about Robbie coming. In an effort to lessen how demoralised I now felt, I clung to the faint hope that Jenny would understand, would be supportive. But Sam was less predictable. I was also unsure how either of them would be about me moving out. I wasn't at all certain I'd go through with asking for Sam's help with the domestic stuff. And then there was Max – what on earth would he make of any of it?

# Chapter Fourteen

I got home at around four o'clock. I'd shopped on the way for pizza bases and for vegetables and cooked meats to use as toppings. I also got salad ingredients and some garlic bread. I wanted to keep dinner simple.

Adam was already gone and there was no sign of Tom. He was either still very angry or he was in denial. Either way he hadn't seen fit to return home to be there for his children when I told them my plans.

Toby greeted me, tail wagging, as he followed me into the living room. The girls were back from work, watching MTV.

"Hey, Mum, how are you doing?" Sam spoke as if nothing out of the ordinary had happened over the last couple of days and continued watching the television.

Jenny was more demonstrative. She jumped up and came to cuddle me. "Mum, you're home. How are you? Did Grandma get you sorted?"

"Hallo, both of you. Yes, Grandma was a great help, as always. I'm okay, but I do need to talk to you both, and to Max when he gets back."

"Why? What do you want to talk to us about?" Jenny looked anxious.

"I'll speak to the three of you together. Don't look so scared – it's nothing to worry about. And thank you girls, both of you, for looking after me so well - after all the upset. I'm sorry I sort of lost it a bit. You've both been so grown up. Thank you."

"Oh, Mum, give me another hug," said Jenny.

"No worries," said Sam without looking away from the TV. "Give us a shout when the munchkin gets back."

Max arrived home just before five. He was full of his day out at the cinema and was very chatty. He asked me if I'd had a nice sleepover at Grandma's and what we'd be having for dinner.

They were all so happy, so normal, and unaware their mother was about to destroy their equilibrium. Telling Tom about my decision had been easy. I had my anger at him to give me the impetus. But telling the children would require much more effort. I didn't know how I'd gather the momentum to see it through.

Once I had the girls and Max together in the living room, the three of them facing me, in a row on the sofa, I began by telling them Robbie was coming for dinner. I stood with my back to the window, trying not to pace and let my anxiety show. All three seemed happy enough at the prospect of their new cousin coming to eat with us. I'd asked Robbie not to mention my invitation to the girls as I wanted to tell them myself, so I was pleased that it came as a surprise to them. I explained that I wanted to get to know Robbie, even although Tom and Adam weren't very happy about it. I also said that neither their brother nor their father would be in for dinner.

"Are you very cross with Dad for not telling you your sister had a baby? Is that what's made you so sad, and why Dad was so angry with Robbie?" Max asked.

"Yes, I am quite cross about Dad keeping it a secret and, yes, I'm sad about it. I think Dad's maybe angry with himself, more than with Robbie," I answered. Max may have been relaxed and easy going, but he didn't miss a thing.

"Will you and Dad make up?" Max looked at the floor as he spoke. Jenny took his hand.

I went over and knelt down in front of him. "Oh, Maxy, I do hope so. I think we just need a bit of time." I hugged him tightly for a few moments, and then I kissed the top of his head as I stood up.

I sat down on one of the armchairs, my hands tucked under me to stop me wringing them. I took a deep breath, it was now or never. "And that's the other thing I wanted to tell you all. I'm going to stay at Granddad's flat for a few weeks." This got Sam's full attention, although she didn't say anything. Jenny and Max asked similar questions to everyone else about my plans and I tried to offer the same reassurances.

Turning to Sam, I said, "I'm counting on your help."

"What do you mean?" she asked.

"Well, if you're serious about giving up the Tesco job, you could earn a bit of money by helping with things here. I'd need you to be here for Max and to help with housework and cooking and things."

Sam looked doubtful, to say the least.

"Mum, are you mad? She doesn't even know where the washing machine is. And as for cooking…" Jenny looked seriously alarmed.

"According to Uncle Michael," I said, trying to keep my own scepticism hidden, "Sam is quite the professional housekeeper and childminder."

"We'll be able to see you while you're at Granddad's won't we?" Jenny asked.

"Of course you will. It'll be easy for you and Adam. You can drop in after school. And, Sam, you can bring Max at weekends and it'll be the summer holidays in a month's time. I think I'll go away for a wee holiday for the first week or so, but then you can come and see me whenever you like." I didn't really want to go without seeing my children for a whole week, but I was aware I'd be going into hospital soon, and I knew I needed an excuse as to why I wouldn't be in the flat.

"If that's what you want, Mum." Jenny stood up to come to me. I got up to meet her. "But we'll visit lots," she said, clinging to me.

I could see she was about to cry. I held her tight. It was desperately hard to remain convinced I'd made a good decision.

"I'll miss you, Mum." Max joined our hug. His obvious struggle to be brave brought me the closest I came to abandoning the whole idea.

"Oh, Max, I'll miss you too." As I held on to him, I looked up at the ceiling in an effort to contain my tears. "Once it's the holidays you can come and stay with me at the flat as much as you like. And Grandma will be here to keep an eye on you till school stops – and Dad too, of course."

I clung, as if to a life raft, to what Evelyn and Ruby had said about my leaving being the right thing to do.

"And, when you've had a rest, and you're not cross with Dad anymore, you will come home, won't you?" Max stepped away. Once again he couldn't look at me. I wondered if he was subconsciously afraid of what he might see in my face.

I hugged him hard and said, "Of course I will, my darling, of course I will." But I was not at all sure that this was an honest answer. After I let go of him, Jenny guided him back to the sofa. I was glad to sit down again too.

I turned to Sam. I was aware she'd been very quiet since I'd made my announcement. "What do you think, Sam?" I asked.

"About what exactly?" she looked and sounded so like Tom did when I'd spoken to him earlier – hostile and hurt. "About our mother abandoning us?" she went on. "About being asked to work as a skivvy around here? Does it matter what I think? You've got it all worked out. But since you ask, I think it stinks."

"Oh, Sam – please, don't do this," I pleaded.

"Do what?" She was on her feet. "You asked me what I think, but I guess you don't really care about my opinion." She ran her hands through her hair. "You can't be bothered anymore and you're angry at Dad, so you're taking it out on us."

"It's not like that. I'm not like that. Please, Sam, I need your help." I stood up to face her. I tried to get hold of her hand. She pulled away from me. "I need you to understand," I continued desperately. Sam made a face and shrugged.

I sighed, a sound dangerously close to a sob. I rallied, kept my tone level, reasonable. "You said you were going to leave Tesco. So you'll need another job for the summer. I'm offering you another job. It would be like what you did for Uncle Michael."

"No, it wouldn't. It wouldn't be like that at all. That was Australia. It was fun. It was different. Besides I hadn't really thought about another job. I was planning to chill for a while actually, have a break before uni. I certainly don't want to spend my summer cleaning up this lot's mess!"

"Well neither do I, come to that. I do it all the time for you and this – this lot, as you call them. And I don't get paid."

"It's different for you. You're our mother. It's your – your…"

"Job?" I finished for her. "No, it's not actually my job, Sam, but someone's got to do it. Yes, I'm your mother and that is a full time job and one I love. I'm not really taking a break from being a mother. I'm taking a break from housekeeping, a break I desperately need, and I'm asking for your help."

"Look, I'll tidy up after myself a bit more, if that's what you want, but I don't want a cleaning job. Anyway, isn't that why you employ Ruby?"

I hardly knew where to start replying to that one. I took a deep breath. "Ruby is employed to do some cleaning, yes. But she can't do it all. She does what I can't fit in. It's more than just cleaning I need from you. It's shopping, cooking, being here for Max occasionally. Dad, Grandma and Ruby will all be here too, from time to time, to help you. And as I said you'd be getting paid. You can't just – just chill all summer, Sam. You need to earn money somehow."

"I don't. I have some savings, if I want to buy anything."

"That's not the point. You'll need more savings for uni and you need to pay your way a bit here too. You're nineteen, Sam. You need to take a bit of financial responsibility for yourself. You can't simply sit around all summer and be fed and housed for nothing."

"Why not? I'm still your child. You're still responsible for me. But no, you want to do what you want to do, and to offload all your responsibilities onto me. Well, I don't want your life. You chose to do all this. I don't want it! And what about poor Dad? You're taking a break from him. I'll bet he's not happy about it. He kept Robbie a secret, but you know now, get over it, Mother. You always have to be such a bloody martyr!" With that she left the room, slamming the door behind her.

I sank down into a chair and put my face in my hands. Max came and squeezed in beside me. He took my hand. "It's okay, Mum," he said. "Don't let Sam make you sad. She shouldn't have sworn at you. I can tidy up after myself and I don't mind Grandma and Dad looking after me if you need a bit of a holiday. And when school stops, I'll come and look after you in the flat. Don't cry, Mum." Of course this just made me want to cry even more. Jenny came to my rescue.

"Mum will be fine, Maxy – especially if you look after her in the summer and I'll help too. Don't worry, Mum. Sam's a drama queen. She'll get over it and she'll realise her savings won't last long. I could pack in Tesco and be here, if you want."

"No, Jen, you like your job, don't you? And you have school for another month anyway."

"I know I do, and, yeah, I do like working at the store. There's a good crowd of us weekenders and holiday workers. It's hard work but we get a laugh. Sam's a bit older than the rest of us, she's not really one of the gang. That's probably why she doesn't like it as much as she used to."

"Grandma thought Sam would be happy with what I was suggesting, but I must admit I wasn't convinced."

"Look, Mum, don't let this put you off. We can manage. You do look really tired and, if you stay here, you'll end up running around after Dad and Sam, like always, and they'll let you. Take your time out, Mum."

"You're very sweet, love. So are you, Max. But even if Sam comes round, there's still Adam. I spoke to him earlier and apologised. But he's not at all happy about me going, or about Robbie."

"Oh, leave Adam to me. He just needs time to get used to it all. He's not a baby, Mum. He has to learn to cope better with life. He'll get his head round this, you'll see." I wasn't convinced, but it was nice to have Jenny and Max on my side.

I was acutely aware I still had to face telling Tom and the children about the cancer. Telling them I was moving out was the hardest thing I'd ever done, but I suspected it wouldn't be long before it was knocked into second place in that particular hierarchy.

# Chapter Fifteen

I left Max and the girls watching television and went through to the kitchen to begin preparing dinner. I glanced out of the open window as I stood at the sink. The sky was growing dark and everywhere was still, awaiting a clearing of the air.

I looked around the kitchen. I thought how I'd miss this room while I was away. I loved our home, but I especially loved the kitchen. It was a large, square space. My grandmother's dresser stood at one end. In the centre was our big, old table. I ran my hand along its pine top. I knew how it had acquired all of its scars. I thought about all the meals we'd eaten there, noisy birthday teas, leisurely Sunday lunches with extended family and friends, but most of all just the six of us, together, dining, day in, day out.

I decided to make two pizzas and a big, mixed salad for dinner. Jenny came through and offered to help. It was as well she did. My anticipation of seeing Robbie again was intense, and my hands were shaking so much as I chopped the vegetables that I cut myself.

Jenny took the knife from me. "It'll be all right, Mum. You'll like Robbie, and he'll like you."

I could only nod and smile.

We had just finished getting the pizzas assembled and ready for the oven when the door bell rang. I jumped. Toby barked. Jenny shouted at the dog to shut up as she went to let Robbie in.

My heart started to race and my skin turned clammy. I leant on the table. Jenny re-appeared in the kitchen doorway. She beckoned to Robbie who was hanging back.

"Come in," she said, stepping aside to let him into the kitchen. She smiled at me and closed the door behind her as she left.

Robbie was holding a bunch of flowers and a bottle of wine. He looked as tense as I felt.

"Hello, Robbie, how are you? I'm so glad you could come," I said, cringing at how formal I sounded.

"Hi, I'm fine. Thank you for inviting me. These are for you," he replied. "My mum said I should bring something and she thought these would be suitable."

"Thanks, your mum was right, they're most acceptable." I laid the flowers and wine on the table without looking at them. I couldn't take my eyes off him.

I sat down at the table. "Please, sit down," I said, indicating the chair opposite me. "How was your mum – about you coming here I mean – today and the other night?"

"She was furious I'd made contact in the way I did. She says she's really embarrassed. But she was glad you wanted to see me and was fine about today. She'd like to meet you – when you're ready, that is."

I was so relieved Robbie's mother didn't mind me getting to know him. It underlined just how much he meant to me already.

"I'd like to meet her too," I said. "And tell her she mustn't be embarrassed about what you did. I'm glad you made contact, Robbie. It was a shock for all of us. I'm sorry if we didn't behave very well."

"How is Mr McAllister now? And Adam, how is he about all of this? I feel bad about Adam and you..." he paused and looked uncertain, as if searching for the words.

"You mean me slapping Adam? Don't feel bad. It's me who should be ashamed, and I am. I have never hit any of my children, ever. But I couldn't bear to hear him being so disrespectful about Heather, about your mother, your birth mother. I've apologised to him."

"And how is he now about me being here?"

"Adam takes time to get used to things, Robbie. He needs routine and predictability otherwise he gets quite distressed. He hates surprises and some of his social skills – well – he thinks differently from most of us about relating to other people."

"He sounds like Craig, a mate of mine at school, he's got special needs, so they say, but to me he's just Craig."

"And Adam's just Adam." I smiled. "He will get used to you. He's working this evening. He has a weekend job at the karting centre so you'll not see him this time."

"And Mr McAllister?"

"He's out too I'm afraid." I didn't want to say I'd no idea where Tom was. "He's had a lot longer than the rest of us to get used to the idea of you. But he's in shock that we all know about you now, and that we know he kept your existence secret."

"He probably had his reasons, Mrs McAllister."

"Yes, he probably did." But I didn't want to dwell on Tom or his reasons. "Can you please stop calling me Mrs McAllister," I continued. "I'm your auntie – I'm Rosemary – but most folk call me Rosie. How does calling me Rosie sound?"

"It sounds good – Rosie." We smiled at each other. Robbie leaned back and stretched his arms in front of him. His hands rested on the table. I leaned forward and put a hand on one of his. Our fingers interlocked. We remained like that, for I don't know how long, looking into each other's eyes, both of us searching.

In the end it was me who spoke first. "I'm being very rude," I said, patting his hand and pulling away slightly. "Can I get you a coke or a coffee, or anything?"

"No, thanks, I'm fine." He shook his head. He looked awkward again. "Are you still angry with Mr McAllister?"

"Yes, Robbie, I am a bit. Yes, he probably had his reasons for not telling me about you, but I can't help being angry with him for what he's done, keeping us apart." I wanted to be honest with Robbie, but I also wanted to reassure him. "But you and me, we're not apart now."

"No we're not." He smiled. "There's so much I'd like to ask

you. But Mum said I was to take it easy and not rush you."

"Your mum sounds like a wise woman. There's a lot I want to tell you, Robbie – about your birth mother, and about your grandparents and your uncle Michael – but there's plenty time. However, there's one thing I'd like to tell you now, and that's about my immediate plans."

So I told Robbie about my intention to move out. I emphasised that it wasn't his fault I was leaving home for a while. I did my best to explain my reasons.

If he was surprised by this announcement, or unconvinced by my explanation, he didn't show it. I also told him that Tom and the children knew what I was planning, but I didn't mention how Adam or Tom had reacted. I was telling him how much I hoped he'd visit me at the flat, when the kitchen door opened and Max came in.

"Hi, cousin Robbie," Max said, only a little shyly. "Oh cool, pizzas," he added, eyeing them up. "When will they be ready?"

"Hiya, Max." Robbie smiled broadly.

"We'll eat in about half an hour," I said. "Take Robbie through to the living room, Max, and I'll give you a shout when everything's ready.

While the pizzas were cooking, the storm that had been threatening for the last few hours finally got started. The thunder was almost simultaneous with the lightning and rain hurled down. I opened the door to the garden and stood in the doorway for a minute or two, breathing in the refreshed air.

I was putting the finishing touches to the salad when Sam came into the kitchen. She seemed uneasy, not quite able to look at me. "Dinner smells good," she said.

"Yes, it's pizza." I wondered what she'd come to say, but I managed to keep my voice level, neutral.

"Mum, look, I'm sorry, okay? I'm sorry for what I said before. It was a shock, you saying you're leaving us – after everything else that's been happening. I wish you wouldn't go. I don't understand why you have to, but I want us to be friends."

"Come here, you," I said, holding my arms out towards her. She came to me and we held each other tight. "I'm sorry too. Sorry I upset you, sorry you don't understand. I love you very much, but this is something I have to do for me. And don't worry if you feel you can't do what I asked.

"Look, if you're really going through with this – well, I'll give it a try – you know, doing what I did for Uncle Michael. But I'm not promising anything."

"Okay, that's good, Sam." Again I kept my voice level. "I'm pleased, and if you find it doesn't suit you – that's fair enough."

"And what would the pay be?" Sam asked.

I suppressed a smile. "Oh, we can discuss that later," I replied. "But now could you go and call the others through."

We were all relaxed with each other as we ate. Max kept us amused. Robbie and the girls talked about their working life at Tesco. They also talked about the exams and their schools and lots of other stuff. I sat quietly for the most part – taking it all in. My children and Heather's son, all round my table.

But, of course, it wasn't all of them. My heart ached for Adam. I wanted him to be there and hoped it wouldn't be too long before he could accept Robbie.

As for Tom, I couldn't let myself think about him.

We sat at the table for quite a while after we'd finished eating. I told Robbie stories of what the children had been like when they were little. There was a lot of 'oh Mum don't tell him that' from the girls, but they did actually seem to enjoy hearing the stories. Robbie seemed to enjoy it too.

But, too soon, it was time for him to go. I was aware the storm had passed and the rain had stopped. Sam said she would run him home to Edinburgh. Jenny said she and Max would clear up the dinner things, much to Max's disgust.

At the front door, while Sam was backing the car out of the driveway, and with Jenny and Max clattering dishes in the background, Robbie and I said our goodbyes. The night air was cool, newly invigorated after the storm.

"Thanks, Rosie," Robbie said. "I really enjoyed this evening."

"Come here," I said. "I hope you're not too old for a hug from your auntie." I put my arms out and he did too. It was good to hold him close. "Thanks for coming. I'm sure you probably had better things to do on a Saturday night. Actually I'm surprised the girls didn't have other plans this evening."

Robbie laughed, "Oh, they did, but they told me they wouldn't have missed this for anything, and neither would I."

"I'll be in touch soon, after I've settled into the flat. We'll meet up again. Okay?"

"Yes, okay." He smiled. Then he was off down the steps and into the car.

I'd felt good while Robbie was at the house. The anticipation of him coming and then the visit itself had buoyed me up, dissipated some of my apprehension at what the future might hold. But after he left, everything closed in on me once more. I knew I needed to pack in preparation for my departure the next day but I couldn't face it right away. I needed to get out of the house, to try to clear my mind and calm the rising panic I was feeling.

So I took Toby for a walk through the quiet and familiar streets of the village. As we wandered along I wondered when I'd next be able to do it, if ever. Not only was my way of life under threat but my very existence was in peril. A huge wave of homesickness, doubt and fear broke over me. I thought I might pass out and had to stop and sit on a low wall at the edge of a garden. Toby put his head in my lap and whimpered. I realised just how utterly terrified I was.

# Chapter Sixteen

### *Tom*

At first, after Rosie left, it was all a bit chaotic. During the first week, Sam was still working at the supermarket and Jenny and Adam were back at school having finished their exams. There was Max to organise and all the household stuff to attend to. I'm ashamed now to admit it, but I didn't cope at all well.

To begin with, my mother came most days, and sometimes she stayed over. I tried to continue with work as normal, but it quickly became apparent that I couldn't keep that up. Even once Sam was on hand, and with Ruby and my mother both helping, I still couldn't really get my head round all the routines and the million little things that Rosie had previously just got on with.

But more than anything I missed Rosie, and no, not only because of the practical stuff. I was bereft, empty, yearning. In those first few weeks without her, I prowled the house late at night, every night, going from room to room, searching.

I never meant for any of it to happen, all the business with Robbie, the way Rosie found out or how I reacted when she did. I'd always just wanted to protect her and the children, to keep them close and safe and well. I wanted to be a better husband and father than my father had been. And I'd failed miserably.

I didn't even see how Adam was feeling until it was too late. Oh no, I had to keep pushing him, going on at him about school and encouraging his belief that Robbie was some kind of threat.

I let Adam down in a big way.

Instead of reassuring him, I made everything worse for him, until he couldn't take anymore and then he was gone too.

Adam left on a Tuesday, about a month after Rosie moved out. Although Max and the girls had visited her the weekend before, Adam had refused to have any contact with his mother since she'd moved out.

I got home around four-thirty in the afternoon on the day he ran away. I'd left work early, yet again, much to my colleagues' bemusement. I wanted to go straight to the den and be alone for a while. Sam shouted hello, as I passed the kitchen doorway, and asked if I'd remembered to get the shopping. She'd given me a list at breakfast time. I'd forgotten.

"Dad, for heaven's sake, you only had to remember that one thing! I can't do everything. Right, give me your car keys and I'll go to Tesco. Otherwise we won't be having any dinner. I was sorting through a pile of washing. Can you finish that off? Max is out walking Toby, but he needs to get on with his homework when he gets back. He'll need reminding to get on with it."

I half smiled. Sam looked and sounded so like Rosie.

"I don't know what you're smiling at," Sam continued. "Come on, Dad, you need to get a grip. I'm trying to do a good job for Mum. Ruby and I gave the house a really good going over today, but there's more to keeping this all going than hoovering and dusting, you know. I don't know how Mum did it all."

"I know. I'm sorry. I'm not coping very well, am I? I was only smiling because you reminded me of your mum. You're doing a great job, Sam. It's me that's hopeless."

"Och, Dad, you're not hopeless. You just need to think about more than the hospital. Mum's spoiled you, she's spoiled all of us. Maybe if we'd all helped more she wouldn't have needed to leave." Sam looked like she might cry.

"Come here," I said and gave her a hug.

"I miss her, Dad."

"I know, we all do. I'll be calling her in a couple of days. I'll tell her what a good job you're doing and that we all miss her and need her to come home soon." I kissed the top of her head.

After Sam left to get the shopping, I set about tackling the mound of laundry. As I stared at the dials on the front of the washing machine, trying to figure them out, I decided open heart surgery was less daunting.

The phone rang.

It was a teacher from Jenny and Adam's school, a Mrs Wentworth. She asked to speak to Rosie. I told her that wasn't possible and said who I was. I took the phone through to the living room.

"Oh, hello, Mr McAllister, we haven't met, but I know Mrs McAllister of course. She's very supportive of everything we do to help Adam. He's a great lad. I've been his form teacher all through high school, as you probably know, and I was really pleased to become his guidance tutor at the beginning of fifth year."

"Mrs Wentworth – yes – hallo," I said, bluffing that I did indeed know who she was. I'd always left it to Rosie to deal with school matters. "Is there a problem with Adam?"

"Well, I was hoping you could tell me. He hasn't been himself for the last couple of weeks. He's seemed quite depressed actually. I know he was very stressed about the exams, but I'd hoped that once they were over he'd be back to normal. It's probably teenage emotions – and he is such a sensitive boy – but I was wondering if there was more to it and if I could help in anyway. It's not like him to miss school and Mrs McAllister always lets us know immediately if any of your children are ill, so I thought I would phone to–"

"Missed school?" I cut in. "Adam has missed school? When exactly?"

"The last two days. Didn't you know?"

"No, I didn't. What's he playing at? I'll get to the bottom of this, Mrs Wentworth, don't worry." She could probably hear the anger in my voice. As if I didn't have enough to worry about, without him skipping school.

"Don't be too hard on him, Mr McAllister. In my experience when one of our pupils takes time off like this, it's often a cry for help. I suspect Adam's feeling a bit overwhelmed at the moment. Forgive me, but is everything all right at home?"

"Yes, it's fine, everything's fine." I didn't feel able to tell her the truth. "I'll speak to Adam. Thanks for your concern." I hung up.

I stayed where I was, at the window, staring out to sea. What was going on with Adam? He was moody, yes, but depressed enough to miss school?

Adam had always been hard work. Rosie said he wasn't deliberately challenging, it was just he sometimes found it difficult to interact or to understand the way other people did things.

To be honest I didn't really know what to make of him. He had dyslexia and mild autism, according to the experts. But he was at a good school with lots of opportunities. Why could he not just apply himself and make the best of it?

We'd picked the school as much for its reputation for being very good with children with dyslexia, as for its reputation for general excellence.

Since Rosie'd been away, I'd not really seen much of him. We'd had a huge argument the weekend before, when he'd arrived back from his shift at the karting centre. I had a go at him about the amount of time he spent there and suggested he should spend more time studying.

He erupted. He said he wanted to leave school, so what was the point in studying. He said he'd failed all his highers anyway and would probably be kicked out of school after the results came out.

I could have handled it better. Rosie would've calmed him, talked it all through. But not me, I lost it and shouted back. I said that if he'd failed his exams, he'd be redoing them next year and there would be no weekend job at the karting place or anywhere else. I went on about the importance of university and about all the opportunities he'd been given. On and on I went. We were standing in the kitchen and, as we squared up to each other, I remember thinking that he'd soon be as tall as me.

When he couldn't take any more of my ranting he shouted, "Fuck off, Dad. Just fuck off!" He sank down on one of the chairs and put his head in his hands. He was crying. His voice was hoarse, the way that newly broken voices sound when stressed. "I wish Mum was here. I wish bloody Robbie didn't exist and you hadn't upset her with your secret. Robbie's probably really clever and going to university. You can be proud of him instead of me."

"Don't be ridiculous, Adam," I replied. Robbie's no threat to you. I don't want anything to do with him. Especially after what's happened with your Mum. It's you I want to be proud of. You just need to put in a bit more effort."

Adam stood up, pushing back the chair with such force that it fell over. "What's the use?" he said, wiping his face with his sleeve as he walked out of the room.

I hadn't seen much of him after that. He left the house on the Monday morning with Jenny and returned late afternoon. He ate dinner with the rest of us and then disappeared to his room. He didn't speak to me and, I'm ashamed to say, I didn't make any effort to speak to him either.

Now it seemed that for the last two days he'd been somewhere other than school. I made up my mind to tackle him after dinner that night.

But I didn't get the chance. Adam didn't come home. His phone went to voice mail when I tried calling him. As we cleared up after dinner, I mentioned Adam's absence to Jenny. Max was sweeping the floor and chatting to Sam, who was grappling with the laundry that I'd abandoned earlier. I tried to keep my tone casual when I asked if he'd been on the bus to school that morning. Jenny confirmed he had. I asked if she'd seen him during the day or on the bus home. She hadn't, but she said she rarely saw much of him, especially since their timetables had changed after the exams and they were no longer doing the same subjects. I asked if she knew whether he was working that evening.

"Why all the questions, Dad? I know we're twins, but we have separate lives. I don't know if he's working, but he doesn't usually on a school night. Are you saying you don't know where Ad is?"

"No – well that is – yes – I don't know. I'm sorry, I didn't mean to bombard you with questions. The truth is – well – he hasn't been at school for the last two days. Mrs Wentworth phoned. She said he's been depressed lately and was concerned about his absence. And now he hasn't come home."

I was aware Sam and Max had stopped what they were doing and were looking at me.

"Adam's been dogging school?" Max was incredulous.

"Adam! I didn't think he had it in him to break the rules!" Sam sounded admiring.

"Sam," I said, "it's not something to be proud of. And where's he been instead of school? Where is he now?"

"Have you tried his phone?" Jenny asked

"Yes, but it goes straight to voicemail. I've left messages."

"He'll be at a friend's house," said Jenny. He'll turn up. He's probably in the huff about something. I'll text him."

"Have you two been arguing again?" Sam asked. "You have, haven't you? Can you not ease up on him a bit, Dad?

I felt well and truly put in my place.

I tried to justify my actions. "He was going on about failing his exams and wanting to leave school. I just don't want him throwing his future away. If I ease up on him, as you put it, he could end up working at that bloody karting centre for the rest of his life." I put my hand up to stop Max speaking. I knew by his face that he was going to comment on me swearing.

"Would that be so awful?" Jenny spoke to me more gently than her sister had. "He loves cars and engines and all that stuff. He loves tinkering about with the broken down karts. He fixes them too. He got Mum's car started a few weeks ago when it was playing up. He's good at all that mechanical stuff."

"Well, that's a debate for later," I said. "The question for now is, where is he?"

"Right," said Sam, "You call the karting centre, Dad, see if he's there. Jenny and I'll call some of his mates. He'll probably turn up while we're doing it."

But he didn't turn up. None of the people we contacted had seen him. I had a bad feeling. But that night I tried not to show it, both for the sake of Max and the girls, and because I didn't want to admit to myself that I may have driven my son away.

I was pondering what to do next when Jenny's phone beeped.

"Oh," she said. "It's a text from Ad–"

I snatched the phone from her hand feeling a huge surge of relief. The message said,

*IM OK – IN SAFE PLACE –*
*TAKING TIME 2 THINK –*
*DUNNO WEN I B BACK –*
*PLS ASK MAX TO WATCH MY FISH*

I decided it was time to go and see Andy.

# Chapter Seventeen

Andy opened the door to me wearing an apron. He was his usual warm and welcoming self. He told me to follow him through to his kitchen as he was in the middle of baking.

Andy was my closest friend, probably my only friend, if I'm honest. My life didn't have room in it for maintaining friendships. We met through an Edinburgh running club many years before, and we got to know each other in the pub after meets and training. Neither of us was really a club runner and we both found our fellow members to be rather serious and earnest, or as Andy described them, wankers. We left the club but continued running together. Lately the running had become jogging.

It was after his divorce that Andy went into community policing. He got custody of his three daughters, and his career in the CID in Edinburgh wasn't really compatible with being a single parent. I'd never really understood why he took it all on himself and didn't hand it over to his mother and sister. But now, as I watched him assembling ingredients for making bread in some contraption on the kitchen worktop, I looked at him with new respect. Only now did I realise what a difficult road he'd been on for the last decade. I envied him his easy relationship with his children, but I knew that it hadn't just happened.

"You've done a great job with the girls, Andy. I don't know how you do it."

"It's not always been easy, but we're a good team, me and the girls. But you didn't come round on the spur of the moment to tell me what a great Dad I am. What's on your mind? I take it things aren't going too well without Rosie. Do you want a beer by the way?" Andy went to the fridge.

"Yes please. I came on foot, so I can indulge. And yes, things aren't going well at all."

Andy handed me a beer. As he got on with his baking, I told him about Adam and about how hard I was finding it to cope without Rosie. I was aware as I was talking to him that this was the second time in the last few weeks that I'd turned up on his doorstep in need of a shoulder to cry on. The day Rosie told me she was leaving and I stormed off wearing only my running gear, it had been to Andy that I'd come. On that occasion he listened, fed me, let me take a shower, lent me some clothes and put me up for the night. And now, here I was again.

"I don't think Adam will have gone far and I don't think he'll stay away for long," Andy said when I'd finished. "He's probably staying at a mate's." He smiled at me.

"Like his father you mean, running off to a friend's house when the going gets tough?" I managed a wry smile.

"That's what friends are for." He smiled again. "I take it you've contacted his friends?"

"The girls got in touch with everybody they could think of. I'd no idea who his friends are, I'm ashamed to say."

"Don't beat yourself up, Tom. You've always left all that stuff to Rosie, haven't you? And Rosie's let you. It's suited you both. But now the situation is different. It's just a fact."

"Oh, you're being far too understanding! Rosie didn't 'let me.' I didn't give her any choice. I've not been there for the kids like Rosie has. I've been kidding myself that being the provider and protector is my role and that doing that is enough. And I've not been there for Rosie either. I'm surprised she didn't leave before now. What was I thinking of, not telling her about Robbie? And what was I thinking of trying to blame everything on him? And now I've succeeded in driving my son away."

Andy fetched another couple of beers. "Come on, mate, let's

take these through."

So we went to the room that Andy always refers to as his refuge from femininity. It's a small room with a large television, a desk and an old leather sofa. The light was fading outside as we settled at either end of the sofa.

"Sorry, you must think I'm a right prat."

Andy shook his head. "Don't apologise. You can't help being a prat, it's nothing new." He grinned. "But seriously, try not to worry. This is Adam we're talking about. He won't be doing anything reckless. He'll have thought it all through. But you do need to tell Rosie. She won't want to be protected from this."

"I know. It's okay, I've learned my lesson on that. I'll tell her. Maybe she'll come home, you know, to be there if – *when* – Adam comes back."

"Don't get your hopes up, Tom. And don't pressure her. Just let her know about Adam and that you miss her."

"Yes, yes you're right. How did you get so wise?"

"Oh, I've had plenty time to reflect and to regret some of the stupid things I said and did to Jackie. I used to drive her mad, being the policeman at home as well as at work, and being absolutely no practical help as a husband and father. I was hardly here when the girls were little, and when I was, everything had to revolve around me. I didn't see how it was for her until it was too late. No wonder she had to get away." Andy paused for a moment, lost in his own thoughts. "But you've still got Rosie. Give her space, show her you can do things better, show her you can be a real partner, a real soul mate. And accept Robbie for what he is – her nephew. Don't treat him as a threat that you need to protect her from. Rosie's tough. She doesn't need or want your protection. What she does need, is you to be there for the kids while she has some time out."

I could only nod in agreement. I was about to ask Andy if and when I should make a formal report to the police about Adam when my mobile rang.

It was Ruby. Adam was at her house. She explained that he'd

spent the day in her caravan without her knowledge. I knew from Rosie that the caravan was a permanent fixture in Ruby's garden, having been retired from touring many years before. It had since been used as a playhouse by the many children associated with Ruby's household. Adam would've been one of those who'd played in it when he was younger.

"Jenny phoned me earlier this evening," Ruby said. "She told me about Adam not coming home and that he said in his text that he was in a safe place. Jenny remembered that they used to call the caravan their safe place when they were wee. She asked me to check it out and there he was."

"Thank God," I said. "Can I speak to him? Is he okay? I've had a couple of drinks so I can't drive over, but Sam could come and collect him."

"Well – the thing is…" Ruby hesitated. "The thing is, he says he's not coming home and he doesn't want to speak to you at the moment."

"Oh," was all I could say.

"But he's fine. He's having a bath just now and then I'm going to get him something to eat. He can stay here tonight, in the house of course. It'll be like old times."

"That's very kind of you, Ruby. You don't have to do that, but thank you.

"It's not kind. Adam's like one of my own, all your kids are. Look, come over here in the morning. He should be in a better mood after a good night's sleep. You can try talking to him then."

I suppressed the urge to get in a taxi and go over to Ruby's immediately. I told her I'd be over about ten the next morning.

# Chapter Eighteen

Before leaving for Ruby's, I called Sheena, my secretary, to say that I'd not be in to the hospital until the afternoon. There were no elective operations scheduled that day, but I did have inpatients to see and there was a clinic starting at two. I asked Sheena to get Anna, my registrar, to cover the clinic until I got there, and I also said to her to ask if Bruce, the senior consultant, could make himself available if Anna needed him.

Sheena must've been surprised by what I said. Although I'd been leaving early a lot recently, I'd not taken any unscheduled leave in the five years that she'd been my secretary. She was, however, restrained in her curiosity and I didn't feel any need to explain my absence beyond saying 'family matters to attend to'. She said she'd make sure my commitments were covered and she'd see me later.

As I parked the car outside Ruby's, I realised I was feeling quite nervous. I was acutely aware that I had to be careful what I said to Adam. I didn't want to alienate him any further.

I'd no idea what to say to put things right and get him to come home. Part of me wanted to turn the car round and head in to work, to pretend that none of this was happening.

But I forced myself to get out the car and go and ring Ruby's doorbell. As I waited for her to come to the door, I recalled the first time I'd come here seventeen years before. Our GP, at the time of Rosie's depression, had arranged for me to meet Ruby when I told him that I was looking for help in the house. She used to clean at the practice and he thought she'd be perfect.

And she was. She helped to care for Sam and the twins and became a valued friend to Rosie. It was she who coaxed Rosie to make the small steps that led to her getting back to normal life. Yes, the time in hospital and the medication were necessary, but Rosie certainly felt that it was as much Ruby's sheer common sense, sense of humour and compassion that saved her. She said that the family and her friends were actually too close to really help her. They either got upset themselves or were scared of upsetting her. But Ruby said and did all the right things.

And here she was again, coming to the rescue of my family.

Ruby showed me into her living room where there was coffee and biscuits waiting, but no Adam.

"Have a seat, Tom," she said. "Adam's upstairs. He knows you're here and he's going to come and talk you. But he wanted me to talk to you first."

I sat down and took the mug of coffee Ruby handed me. She spoke in a way that was so direct there was no possibility of arguing.

"Right," I replied. "So what did he want you to say to me?"

"He doesn't want to come home, not yet anyway. He says he'll come home when Rosie does and when Robbie's gone away."

"Oh he does, does he? And where is he planning to stay in the meantime?"

"He wants to stay here. He says he's left school and he's working at the karting place. He says he'll pay me rent."

I laughed sarcastically. "I don't think so. He's not left school and he's not making a career at the karting centre. He can't stay here. That's ridiculous."

"He seems pretty certain. He's thought it all through. Okay, he shouldn't have run away and worried you all like that, and I've told him so, but he's finding it all too much to be at home just now. He can't cope with home or school and he's come up with a solution."

Despite Ruby's calm assertiveness, I had to fight to suppress the urge to demand to see my son. I just wanted to force him into the car and take him home.

I took a deep breath. "So what do you suggest, Ruby?"

"Let him stay here. Let him work at the centre for the summer. He can pay me a bit of rent from his earnings. And I wouldn't force the school thing if I were you. Surely, if you explain to the school, they'll excuse him for the rest of the term and hold his place over the summer. I think he needs a break from the pressure of school and home right now."

How could I argue? This woman took common sense to a whole new level. It was infuriating and endearing at the same time.

I shrugged. "Maybe," I said. "And now can I see Adam?"

Ruby smiled inscrutably. "I think you should," she said and left the room.

A minute or so later Adam came in. I stood up. Ruby was nowhere to be seen. He closed the door behind him. We faced each other across the room, but Adam didn't make eye contact.

"Adam," I said.

"Dad," he replied. His hands were shoved deep into the pockets of his jeans. His shoulders were hunched and he looked down at the floor.

It was only now, now that I could see him, that I realised just how scared I'd been for my son.

"Come and sit down," I said. "We need to talk."

And so we talked. Adam told me how he hated school and was afraid I'd make him keep going. He also mentioned how scared he was that having Robbie in our family would change things at home and how he didn't like being in the house without his mum. He said he'd felt he needed to get to a safe place and that's why he'd gone to the caravan, because that had been a safe place when he was a child.

I smiled inwardly when he used the past tense in referring to his status as a child. "But you must've known that you'd be found. Ruby, or one of the family, would be bound to see you sooner or later."

"Yeah, I just needed somewhere to think what to do. I thought I'd move on to Edinburgh or something. I knew I couldn't stay in the caravan for long. I had to sneak into the house to use the toilet today when everyone was out. I remembered where Ruby hides the key. She's always going on about how no one in her family ever has their bloody keys, so she has to leave one under the stone angel beside the back door."

I laughed out loud at this. I think my laughter was prompted by a mixture of relief at seeing him and a sudden rush of affection for my literal-minded boy.

Adam gave me a puzzled look. He'd obviously not intended to be amusing. He was simply telling the facts. He was just being Adam.

"Sorry," I said. "So tell me, what is it you want to do now?"

He told me his plan, just as Ruby had told it to me. I found myself agreeing to do it his way.

Before I left, Ruby assured me she was very happy with the arrangement but I insisted on topping up the financial contribution Adam would be making, to cover his bed and board. To Adam I said I'd phone him regularly and asked if I could come and see him sometimes. He nodded, a little uncertainly, in response to my request. I asked him to go and visit Rosie but he refused, even when I said that his brother and sisters were probably going again at the weekend. I caught Ruby's eye at that point and got the message not to push it.

When she was seeing me out, Ruby told me not to worry and that she wouldn't make Adam too comfortable. She didn't think it would be long until he wanted to come home. I wasn't so sure.

# Chapter Nineteen

It was around eleven when I left Ruby's. On the way to my car I called Rosie. It was Lucy who answered, which threw me a bit. When Rosie came on she sounded as if she'd just wakened up, which also surprised me.

"Tom, what are you doing phoning in the middle of a work morning? Is there something wrong?" She sounded quite weak.

"I need to see you, Rosie. I'm not at work. I'm on my way now. I just wanted to let you know."

"Oh, right, okay then." She sounded bewildered but, mercifully, didn't ask for an explanation there and then. "I'll see you soon."

When I got to the flat it was Lucy who opened the door. For some reason this irritated me.

"Tom, nice to see you," she said, standing aside and gesturing for me to come in. "Come through. Rosie's just out of the shower. She'll be with you in a minute." We went into the small front room. I felt edgy and impatient. "Can I get you a coffee?" Lucy asked.

This irritated me further. I'd come to see my wife. My wife who'd moved out of our home to have time on her own. And yet she wasn't on her own, and I had this bizarre feeling that Lucy was protecting her in some way, protecting her from me. Why was Lucy even here if Rosie was only just getting up?

"No thanks, no coffee. I just came to see Rosie and I'd like to see her alone, if that's okay," I said. I knew I'd sounded rude and I didn't even attempt any small talk. But Lucy either didn't notice, or she pretended not to.

She smiled at me and said, "Yes of course. I've got to go anyway. I'll just say cheerio to Rosie." Lucy left me alone in the room. I heard her and Rosie speaking but not what they were saying. I glanced out of the window as soon as I heard the front door close. It was only a moment before I saw Lucy walking away up the path.

"Hallo, Tom," Rosie was leaning in the doorway.

I was shocked. She looked thin and tired. She was wearing jeans and a loose fitting tee-shirt. Her feet were bare. She had a towel round her head. Her eyes looked enormous, maybe a bit fearful. I wanted to bundle her up in my arms, to wrap her in a blanket as if she was a small child, and carry her to a safe place. But I realised I no longer had any right to look after her or even to hold her. After all, I'd done this to her. I'd worn her out, betrayed her and lost her trust.

And now I had to tell her about Adam. I felt so awkward that I didn't approach her. "Rosie," I said. My mouth was dry and my throat hoarse. I sat down on the one of the armchairs. She came and sat on the sofa. She seemed to be walking rather gingerly, as if she was in pain. She held herself in that protective way that I knew well from my post-surgery patients.

"Are you all right?" I asked.

"Yes, yes I'm fine. Let's not waste each other's time, Tom. I'm sure you need to be getting to the hospital. Why did you need to see me so urgently?"

Part of me was glad she wanted me to get on and say what I'd come to say, but another part of me was dismayed at her coolness. I suppose I'd been hoping she'd greet me with open arms, say she missed me, that our weeks apart had done the trick and she'd forgiven me and was coming home.

"It's Adam," I said. I tried to clear my throat, but there wasn't a drop of moisture left in my mouth.

"Adam?" she leaned forward. "What about Adam?"

"He's gone, left home, he–"

"What? What do you mean he's gone? Gone where, when?" Rosie leaned even further towards me. I could smell the stuff she always used in the shower. I breathed it in. I wanted to close my eyes and lean back, luxuriate in the scent and the memories it triggered. I wanted to hold her.

"Tom, speak to me!" She stared into my eyes, questioning, afraid.

"I don't – that is he…" I was floundering. I needed to get a grip. "He ran away, but he's fine. He's safe. He's at Ruby's."

I told her all about it. I tried to sound reassuring, to stick to the facts and not freak her out, but I think I probably just sounded offhand.

"How can you be so calm? Our son has left home. Adam who can't cope with change, who's so vulnerable…Christ, Tom. How did this happen? Why did you have to drive him away as well?"

Of course, what she was asking was exactly what I'd been afraid she'd ask. And although she was justified in assuming I was responsible, it didn't make it any easier to hear. I would rather she'd hit me than look so wounded and angry. Here I was, letting her down again.

I tried to defend myself, to explain that I hadn't meant to upset Adam. I told her he'd been going on about leaving school and not going to university and that we'd argued about it. I resisted mentioning that Rosie slapping Adam probably hadn't helped him to feel understood, but I did tell her he was still upset about Robbie.

Then the effort of trying to be calm and reasonable got too much for me. I knew as I spoke that I was talking rubbish, but I couldn't help myself. "At least Adam and I agreed on Robbie," I said. "He sees Robbie as a threat to the family and to his place in it." I paused, saw Rosie's look of fury and ignored it. "Bloody Robbie," I went on. "Why did he have to show up? We were doing fine without him, weren't we? I mean, yes, I should've told you about him, but what difference would it have made in the long run? He has a different family now. He's not really one of us, is he? No, I'm with Adam there. Robbie's caused all this, you going away, Adam going away. I wish Robbie'd not–"

Rosie let out a scream and got to her feet. She'd been towelling her hair dry as I spoke. Now she flung the towel down. She winced as she did so. She put her hand up under her left arm. I was about to ask her again if she was in pain, but I was distracted by the shock of seeing that her hair had been cut short. She'd worn it long ever since I'd known her. I loved her hair. It was thick and heavy and a rich, golden colour. I loved the feel and weight of it. I'd always said to her not to cut it.

Rosie didn't seem to notice my shock. She trembled with rage as she shouted at me. "You wish Robbie had not been born. Is that what you were going to say? Then your sordid secret about what you got up to with Heather wouldn't have come out."

I gasped at this, but Rosie didn't even pause, didn't allow me to defend myself.

She went on, "But he was born. He does exist. You should've told me. It would've made a huge difference if you'd been honest. Robbie is my flesh and blood, my family and that's important to me, even if it isn't to you. If Adam had known about him all along, he'd have been able to cope. If I'd known…" She gasped, flinched again. She was definitely in pain. I started to speak, to ask again if she was sore, but she put a hand up to silence me. "How could you deny his existence? Especially if he's yours?" Her voice was quieter now.

I let her last remark go. I realised Rosie wouldn't be receptive to any explanations or justifications. "I wasn't going to say I wished he'd never been born. I was going to say I wished he'd not got in touch in the way he did, then all this could have been avoided."

"But he did get in touch. He's in our lives now. He's been to see me a couple of times. He's a good lad. I like him." She sat down again, the fight gone out of her. "Anyway," she went on, "none of this helps us with Adam. So, he was still upset about Robbie and you encouraged that and you also put pressure on him about school and university. Great, well done Tom." Her voice was full of contempt.

"Look, I'm sorry. I'm sorry, right?" I couldn't bear the way she was looking at me. "I was trying to help him. I was trying to let him see I was upset about Robbie too. I also wanted him to realise how important school is and how important it is to get a degree. I was trying to help him, to protect him."

"Then you didn't do a very good job, did you? University's not the be all and end all. Plenty people are successful without going to university. We can't all be brain surgeons, as they say, or heart surgeons for that matter."

"Are you saying you don't want him to go to university? I just want the best for him."

"What I want, what you want, what about what Adam wants? Maybe he knows his limitations, if that's what they are, better than we do. Anyway, none of it really matters, when he doesn't want to have anything to do with us."

"No, I suppose not. Maybe you should come home. He's insistent he won't come home until you do."

Rosie shook her head. "That won't resolve anything. Oh, he might come home, but he'd still be angry with us. He'd still have Robbie to deal with and you'd still be going on about school. No, I think being at Ruby's is best for him at the moment. And I'm not coming home either, Tom. I don't know when or if that will happen," Rosie's voice was almost a whisper now. She looked exhausted.

Once again I had a strong urge to hold her. Once again it was like a knife in the guts to realise I no longer could, and to realise she wasn't coming home any time soon. She ran her hands through her hair again. It was drying, sticking up in little spikes.

"You've cut your lovely hair, Rosie. Why did you do that? I loved your hair long."

Her hands went to her head. She looked self-conscious.

"Don't you like it?" she said. "Lucy did it for me. We both think it makes me look younger. Robbie liked it too."

"Oh well, that's okay then. But no, I don't like it. You know I loved your hair. Is that why you did it, to get back at me?"

She looked angry again. "No, Tom, that's not why I did it. I did it for me. You see I'm going to lose it all anyway, now I've started chemo. I have breast cancer and I'm having chemotherapy. I just thought it would be easier if it was short. So I asked Lucy to cut it. Not everything is about you."

I just sat and stared at her. I'd heard her words, but I couldn't really process them properly. I knew she'd said something shocking. At first I thought I might laugh. I mean, she had to be joking, didn't she? It was a bad joke, in bad taste, but it was a joke, surely. I even started to smile.

"I'm not joking, Tom. I have cancer. I found out the day after Robbie came round for the first time. I had surgery, a mastectomy, not long after I moved out. I've lost my left breast. It still hurts, but the scar is healing." She had tears in her eyes and was obviously finding it hard to speak. "I began chemo on Monday and it'll be repeated every two weeks until the beginning of October."

"Jesus – Rosie – I..." I couldn't speak. I felt sick, terrified, guilty. Rosie was ill. Rosie had cancer. She'd been going through all this and I hadn't been there. I had to do something. I had to make this right.

"Okay, that's it," I said. "You have to come home now. I'll get you the best doctors. I'll look after you. Adam will come home. And, as for Robbie, he needs to leave you in peace for a while."

"No, no, no." Rosie shook her head. "You really don't get it, do you? It's my illness, my life. I'm doing this my way. I – if you – oh, what's the use? Just go away, Tom. Go away." She got to her feet. "Go away and leave me alone. And don't tell the children about me being ill either. Evelyn and Kirsty are going to bring them here at the weekend and I'm going to tell them then, although I don't suppose I'll be seeing Adam." She sat again, her head down. She appeared to be talking to herself more than to me. "I'll just have to wait until he's ready to listen. Although Ruby knows – maybe she – no that's not fair…" she shook her head. "I'll have to think about what to do about telling Adam."

I didn't say anything, but it hurt that all these other people seemed to know about the cancer before I did.

Then she looked at me and when she spoke it was slightly more calmly than before. "I'd had actually planned to phone you later and ask you to call in, so I could tell you before I tell the children. But you know now."

She looked terrible and I knew I should go, if that's what she wanted. I asked if there was anything I could do for her before I left, but she said no and that she'd probably go back to bed and rest.

Once I was in the car, I just sat there, in shock, gripping the steering wheel as if it was some sort of lifebelt. I'd never felt so powerless. I'd never felt so lost or so fearful. But most of all, I'd never before felt such complete self-loathing.

# Chapter Twenty

I don't know how long I sat there. At some point I'd leaned forward and put my head on top of my fists which were still clenching the wheel. I must've got strange looks from passers by, but I didn't notice. It was bad enough that Rosie might not come back to me because she no longer trusted me, but the thought that she might die was unbearable. I also couldn't bear that, whatever happened, Rosie was going to suffer and I wasn't going to be allowed to help.

As on the day Rosie left, I was horrified to find that I wanted to cry, to give in to all the hurt and rage. Once again, I fought to keep a grip on myself.

I never cried. Rosie had always said I wasn't in touch with my feminine side.

My father had disapproved of crying. He'd made that very clear to me and my brother, Dan, when we were children. He said it was a sign of weakness and that Britain would never have won the war if men had sat around like cissies crying. If he caught either me or my brother shedding tears we were belted. Weeping, he said, was for women.

But I cried when we left him. I was nine and Dan was seven. My mother bundled us in the back of her Mini Clubman. She'd given us each a box to fill with our favourite toys and she'd filled a couple of suitcases with clothes for us all. She said we were going to stay at Grandma's for a while and then we'd be going to a new house. She told us our father would not be coming with us. I cried as we drove away and I looked back at the big grey house where I'd spent my life so far. My father stood at the window watching us go. I waved. He didn't wave back.

Shortly afterwards my father arranged for us to go to his old school, a long-established, private, all-boys school in Edinburgh that he said would make men of us. Neither we nor my mother appeared to have any say in the matter. He paid for our fees, uniforms and books. We rarely saw him after that. I learned to keep a grip on my emotions. I certainly didn't cry when he died.

But that day, in the car, faced with the prospect of losing Rosie permanently, I came close to letting go.

There was no one in when I got home. Toby got out of his basket as I opened the front door. He waited expectantly. When he saw it was me and not, as I'm sure he was hoping for, Adam, his head went down. He'd been pining a bit since Adam left.

I couldn't face going into work in the afternoon, a feeling I'd never experienced before. I called Sheena and said I wouldn't be in after all. I didn't explain or even make much in the way of excuses and Sheena didn't probe.

I decided to go for a run. Toby came too, but without his usual excitement. I went to the beach and ran down between the dunes and onto the sand. The tide was out. I ran eastwards without stopping, until I got to the natural barrier of seaweed-covered rocks at the far end. Toby took his time, stopping to sniff at rock pools and to greet other dogs. I got the impression he didn't want to be seen with me. "Et tu, Toby," I said.

As I jogged back along the shore, I could see Edinburgh along the coast. I wondered what Rosie was doing now. I wondered if she'd ever come back to me, and the wondering set off such a painful longing, that I pulled up and bent over. The pain of missing her took my breath away and I felt sick. I sank to my knees, retching, as the words 'Rosie' and 'cancer' went round and round in my head. I threw up until I had nothing left. It was some moments before I could stand. I was relieved that the other occupants of the beach, the kite-fliers, wind-surfers and dog walkers seemed unaware of my predicament as I did my best to bury the evidence.

When I got back to the house it was still empty. I wandered through the downstairs rooms. I paused beside the piano in the dining room. Debussy's *Claire de Lune* was propped open on the music holder. This was a favourite of mine from Rosie's repertoire but I couldn't remember the last occasion I'd taken the time to listen to her play.

Jenny was as accomplished as her mother on the piano, but Jenny's instrument of choice was the violin. Rosie often played the piano accompaniment when Jenny was perfecting a piece for a recital or an exam. Standing there that day, in the too quiet house, I'd have given anything to hear them play together again.

I also realised, as I stood there, that Max had done little, if any, piano practice since Rosie left. I made a mental note to mention this to him.

Previously, before Rosie left, there would usually be music coming from several quarters of the house by the time I got home. It could be Jenny or Rosie playing, or even Adam on his guitar, or one or more of the children listening to loud music in their bedrooms. Rosie nearly always had music on in the kitchen and often sang along. She had a beautiful, rich, alto voice. I tried to bring it to mind, to hear it. I couldn't. The house remained unbearably silent.

The children weren't expecting me back until dinner time. Max was going to Ruby's with Neil after school. Sam was having a well deserved afternoon off and Jenny never got in from school before five.

I called my mother to ask if she was free and if I could go over to see her. She'd just arrived back from the library and said she'd be delighted to see me.

# Chapter Twenty One

I felt a slight lifting of my spirits as I approached Holdfast Cottage.

My mother remarried after I went away to university in 1972. Maxwell Calder was my housemaster at school. He was a quiet, gentle man who taught classics. He was a childless widower and Dan and I nicknamed him Mr Chips. He and my mother met at some school function and carried on a very discreet relationship while I was in my last year, so discreet that Dan and I knew nothing about it until they announced their engagement. They had a strong and very loving marriage. My stepfather didn't mind that my mother kept the McAllister name so that, as she put it, her name could remain the same as her boys. He was a good man, a good father. Rosie and I named Max after him, something that seemed to touch him very deeply. They had twenty-seven years together until his death in 1999. The cottage had been a very happy home for all of us. My mother had now lived in it for forty years.

She was at the front door as I got out of the car. She came up the path to meet me.

"Hello, son," she said, reaching up to give me a hug.

"Hello, Ma," I replied. I kissed her cheek. She cupped my face in her hands.

"You look done in," she said. "Come through to the back garden. We can sit there and you can tell me what the matter is."

While my mother went to fetch the tea tray, I sat back on one of the garden chairs and closed my eyes for a moment. It was a warm June day. There was a strong scent coming from the roses, and birds fluttered and chirped in the trees. I could feel myself starting to drift off.

"Tom," my mother spoke quietly and gently pressed my arm. I opened my eyes and stretched. "Sorry, darling, were you falling asleep there?" She sat down opposite me.

"Not really, just dozing. That looks good." I nodded at the tray on the garden table between us. There was a plate of sandwiches and some home made cake, as well as a pot of tea. I realised that the emptiness I felt was, at least, partly physical. Not only had I not eaten since breakfast, but I'd thrown up whatever remained of that meal onto the sands of Gullane beach. I was starving.

My mother smiled and poured the tea. "Dig in," she said.

I demolished most of the sandwiches and then set about the sponge cake. I downed two mugs of tea. All the time that I was feeding, my mother watched me intently. She chatted about this and that, about the dogs, who were snoozing at her feet, about the garden and about the choir she was a member of, but I knew she was watching me. When I could consume no more, I sat back and stretched.

"Better?" she asked.

"Oh yes. Thanks, Ma." And I did feel better for having eaten, but the ache in the pit of my stomach was still there.

"Now tell me why you've come. I assume it wasn't just to get fed. It's lovely to see you, but this is the middle of a working day. What's wrong, Tom?"

"I hardly know where to start," I said. "Everything's such a mess."

I began by telling her about Adam and then about having to tell Rosie of his departure. My mother was shocked to hear about Adam, of course, but she was typically stoical and reassuring about it.

"I agree with Ruby," she said. "I'm sure he'll come home when he's ready, Tom."

"But that's not all, Ma," I said. "Rosie, Rosie's got – she's got…"

I couldn't say the words.

"Oh, my darling, she's told you then, she's told you she has breast cancer?"

"Yes, yes she has." My mother was beside me in an instant. She'd pulled a little footstool over and was perched on it at my feet. She reached up and put her arms around me. It was then I gave in. I gave in and I cried. I cried on her shoulder for quite some time. She patted and soothed for as long as it took. The garden became very still around us, even the birds seemed to have stopped singing. Eventually I sat back and Ma slowly got to her feet. The sun had vanished behind a cloud. I shivered.

"Come inside, Tom," she said. "I think we may be in for a shower and I, for one, need a comfy seat."

We moved indoors. My mother sat beside me on the sofa, in the room that looked out over the garden. She took my hand in hers.

"You knew, Ma. You knew about Rosie having cancer and you didn't tell me."

"Yes, I knew. I promised her I wouldn't say anything, but I did urge her to tell you herself."

"When did she tell you?"

"The day she came to see me and stayed overnight. She told me then – about Robbie, about the cancer, and about her moving out for a while."

"But if you'd told me, maybe I could've stopped her moving out. I could've organised the best people to look after her. I could've protected her at home."

My mother shook her head slowly. She put a hand up to my face and stroked my cheek. "Oh, son, don't you see? That's precisely why she didn't want you to know. She didn't want you taking over – organising her treatment. She doesn't want or need your protection. It's her body, her life – she wants to make her own decisions." She spoke even more gently now.

"Yes, yes – she said all that to me herself."

"You need to trust her to take care of herself. Maybe you

should've trusted her when Robbie was born. Maybe you shouldn't have kept all that from her."

"Was it wrong of me? What's wrong with wanting to protect your wife? What could she have done about Robbie? She'd just had the twins. She was totally disabled with post-natal depression. We couldn't have taken him in, could we? So what would have been the point of telling her?"

My mother shook her head and stroked my hand.

"When Heather died I thought Rosie would go too," I continued. She threatened to, you know – at the time – she threatened to kill herself too. I couldn't tell her, Ma. It would've been cruel. I had to think about her and Sam and the twins. I had to protect them. I wanted to be a good husband and a good father. I never wanted to hurt them. I always promised myself I wouldn't be like – like…"

"Like your father? You know, Tom, your father never meant to hurt you or Dan, or me. He was – damaged. He saw unspeakable things during the war. He needed help, but there was no recognition of post-traumatic stress in those days. He did love us in his own way. Even Dan sees that."

In the ten years since my father's death, my mother and I'd regularly had this conversation. She tried to get me to understand him better, to forgive him, to see he was a broken man. But I could never see past his coldness and his bullying. I couldn't understand how Dan could forgive him. My father never spoke to Dan again after my brother came out as homosexual when he was in his thirties. I shook my head.

"I know," she said. "I know you don't agree. And I know he was very mistaken in the way he showed his love. God knows I do. That's why I left him, you know that. But I've always believed he only wanted to protect us – like you want to protect your family. I've said before, you should read his diaries. It helped me and Dan to understand him and to forgive him." I shook my head again. I couldn't talk about my father at that moment. My mother could see that and she let it go.

"But you're not like him, Tom, not in the way you fear. Heather put you in a difficult position. But perhaps you should've told Rosie about Robbie later, when she was strong again."

"Yes, perhaps. But the time never seemed right. And I suppose I didn't want to risk knocking Rosie back. As time went on it was just easier not to say anything."

"Did you not foresee that Robbie might take matters into his own hands?"

"Yes, sort of, I suppose. I forgot all about the letter that I sent his new parents at the time of the adoption, which meant he could get hold of my name. I really thought he'd have to go through the agency to get any information and that I'd get some warning. But I also thought, or hoped, that he might not bother us at all. After all we're not his parents."

My mother took my hand once more and said very gently, "Rosie thinks you might be Robbie's parent."

"She really did tell you everything, didn't she?

"Rosie thinks you were attracted to Heather. She thinks there's more to your motives for secrecy than being protective."

"Of course I found Heather attractive. She was Rosie's twin, and yes, she was an edgier, more dangerous version of Rosie and that had its attractions – at least it did before the heroin took its toll. Even Dan had a thing for her for a while, or thought he did, before he came out, remember?"

"Yes, yes I do. Poor Dan, he was so confused. He went through agonies. But there's more to the story about Robbie, isn't there?

"Oh yes, there's more," I said. "And, if I'm honest, the other part is the major reason why I didn't tell Rosie. It scared Heather enough that she killed herself."

"So, tell me, tell me the rest."

I shook my head. "I don't know if I can Ma, or even if I should."

"Do you mean because of Rosie, because she should hear it first?"

"Yes, I suppose so. Oh, I don't know. It's all such a mess.

Robbie, me, Heather's death…"

"Tell me what you can, tell me whatever you can share. It might help you to begin to sort out the mess. You were obviously in touch with Heather at the time of Robbie's birth. How did that come about? Weren't she and Rosie estranged by then?"

"Yes, they were. I wasn't in touch with her much, just called occasionally. I sort of wanted to keep an eye on her, for Rosie and her dad as much as anything. They'd had to cut off contact, to protect themselves. They couldn't take any more. They told her to stop calling or visiting, said they wanted no more to do with her. But it was hard for them. Then, even Michael stopped seeing her. His wife made him promise he'd stay away from Heather. In the end he broke his promise to Adele. It was one of the things that led to their marriage breaking up."

"Oh really?"

"It wasn't the only reason, but it didn't help when things were already strained. Adele was scared of Heather. You must remember how Heather was. By the mid-eighties, she was funding her addiction any way she could. It wasn't pretty. She'd turn up on Michael's doorstep, when he lived in Edinburgh, demanding money, making threats."

"No wonder Adele was scared."

"Quite. Heather used to turn up at our house too. On one occasion she arrived in a very bad way. She stole Rosie's purse along with her engagement ring and some other bits of jewellery. It was when Rosie was expecting Sam, just a few days before her mum died. Rosie was devastated by the theft. Remember Rosie had the threatened miscarriage when Nancy died? I'm sure what Heather did was at least part of the reason too.

My mother nodded. "No wonder her family got to breaking point."

"Rosie and her dad and Michael were amazingly loyal to Heather. But there was really no doubt that all the worry contributed to Nancy's death. She didn't get help for her own health in time because she was too busy trying to get help for

Heather. Then, when Rosie's mum was in the hospice and asking for Heather, she failed to turn up, even after she promised Rosie she'd come and say goodbye to their mother." I paused and sighed as I remembered that very bleak time. "Anyway, when Rosie confronted Heather about the theft, she begged Rosie not to report it. She said she'd been desperate and it was steal or go with some guy for money. Addicts are very manipulative. You know that. You must have dealt with some in your time at the surgery."

"Yes, indeed."

"Rosie had to tell her it was the end of the road. She said to Heather that she was to stop contacting the family or she'd report her to the police. Having to do that and deal with her mother's death, it tore Rosie apart."

"I didn't know about the theft, but I do remember that Heather broke everyone's hearts – Rosie's, Michael's, her poor parents. What a waste. And she was a talented girl. She could've been a successful artist, couldn't she?

"She could have. And I think that when the family cut her off, it shocked her, really got to her."

"And you kept an eye on her. Even after all she'd done. That was an incredibly good thing to do."

"Not really. Heather was Rosie's other half, more than a sister, a soul mate. Rosie was grieving for Heather even before she died. And I could remember Heather before the drugs took hold, when we were all students. She was as lovely as Rosie. I wanted to help her, but I really didn't know how. I actually asked Dan for some advice at the time."

"Professional advice, you mean?"

"Yes, well, having a psychiatrist for a brother, it made sense to at least ask. He went with me to see Heather a couple of times."

"Did Dan know about Robbie?"

"No, the visits were before she was pregnant. The first Dan knew about Robbie was last month, like the rest of you."

"But Dan couldn't help?"

"No,not immediately, anyway, maybe some of what he said got through to her, made some sense. I don't know."

"I suppose Heather had to want to help Heather."

"Yes, and in the end that's what she decided to do – to help herself. It was at the beginning of 1987. She had a new GP. She was living in the Muirhouse area by then, where most of the city's intravenous heroin users were living, but there was also a lot of good work going on in the area to help addicts get clean. So she got herself onto a rehab programme that was funded by a local charity. And, amazingly, she did it, kicked the drugs, got herself sorted out. She'd never be how she was before the heroin, but she looked well and said she felt great. By the time she found out she was pregnant, near the end of that year, she'd been clean for months."

"And how did she feel about the pregnancy?"

"At first she was thrilled. She had plans for herself and the baby. She had a little flat by then. Her social worker said she would be supervised at first, but that if she stayed clean and showed herself to be a competent mother, she would be able to keep the baby. She asked me to be with her at the birth and I was."

My mother raised her eyebrows at this, but didn't say anything.

"She called the baby James, after her father. The Sutherlands must have changed his name. Anyway she seemed fine, seemed happy to be a mother and to be coping."

"So, what changed?"

I shook my head. I couldn't speak. I put my face in my hands and took a deep breath. "Let's just say there was a complication, something she – *we* – knew was a possibility, and the fear of it destroyed her. She called me after she took the overdose. She said she'd decided that the baby would be better off without her. Of course I rushed to the flat. I got Michael to come with me, told him everything on the way, forced the poor guy to break his promise to Adele, but it felt like the right thing to do. Anyway, we were too late. She was dead when we got there."

"Poor girl…"

"I would never have guessed, before that day, that she'd kill herself. But I knew when she phoned that she meant it. She made sure Robbie was okay and that he'd be found quickly, but not too soon. She didn't want to be rescued. She loved Robbie. I thought she'd rise above her fears, stick around for his sake. I should've made sure we didn't leave her alone. I should've involved Michael sooner. We could've done more."

"You couldn't be there all the time. And Rosie was ill. You had to cope with that *and* your baby twins *and* a toddler. You're not to blame, Tom."

"Maybe not. But Michael thought he and I were to blame. And he blamed me for not telling him about the pregnancy and the rest of it. He blamed himself for not staying in touch with her. We fell out over it all. Then he went to Australia and Rosie lost her brother too."

"You were in an impossible situation. You didn't have to get involved at all, but you did. Besides, you can't change any of it now. Robbie's been brought up by good people who love him. He seems to be a good lad from what I've heard. And now he's found Rosie. Is it not time to sort it all out, to tell Rosie how it was for Heather at the end, how it was for you?"

"Yes, but how? How do I do that, Ma? I haven't exactly been welcoming to Robbie. Rosie is so angry with me, and on top of everything else she thinks I've driven Adam away. And then –then there's the cancer. Where exactly would I start trying to sort it all out? Where would I start?"

My mother put her arms around me. She stroked my back, like when I was a child. "Give it time, son. Give it time," she said. She sat back but kept her hands on my arms. "Rosie has the cancer to fight and she wants to do it her way. You need to concentrate on the children – all of them – Robbie and Adam included. They're all going to need you. Ease up on Adam. Make sure he knows he can come back any time. That's the best way to support Rosie now. Keep the rest of the family together, Tom, and wait for Rosie to come to you when she's ready."

I nodded. "I'm scared, Ma. I'm scared Rosie won't survive. I'm scared she'll never forgive me. I'm scared I can't put things right with Adam, that it'll be like it was with Dad and me. I just want it all to go away, to go back to normal."

"I know son. I know."

My mother took my hand in hers. As she did so she glanced away, just for a moment, seeming to consider something.

"What,? What are you thinking?"

She gazed into my eyes, as if trying to figure something out. Then she said it.

"I'm sorry, Tom. I accept you can't tell me the whole story of what happened, but I have to ask. If I'm going to help you, I need to know…"

I realised what was coming before she spoke the words. I was already shaking my head as she continued.

"Are you – that is – is there a possibility that you are – you could be Robbie's father?

"No!" I pulled my hand away from hers and stood up. "No, no no!"

Even though my mother's tone was far from the accusing one Rosie had used, it hurt just as much that she doubted me.

I put my hands behind my head, looked up at the ceiling, closed my eyes, breathed deeply. There was a sound, something between a groan and a whimper. I realised it came from me.

"Tom, are you all right?" My mother looked worried.

I went back to sit beside her. Now it was my turn to take her hand.

"Sorry, I didn't mean to alarm you. It's just – it hurts – that you – that Rosie…" The pain and frustration of not being able to prove my innocence was almost intolerable. But the question had to be answered. "There's no chance. I didn't sleep with Heather. I'm not Robbie's father. I've never cheated on Rosie. I wouldn't, I couldn't. You must know that."

Change of Life

She shook her head, stroked my face. "I'm sorry. I didn't know what to think. I shouldn't have doubted you, but you seemed to be avoiding the subject of Robbie's paternity – so I did wonder." She looked stricken and, suddenly, old and tired. I could see what the effort of asking had cost her.

I embraced her, angry at myself for causing this wonderful, caring woman a moment's pain. What a guy. First my wife, now my mother.

"I wasn't avoiding the question of who fathered Robbie. It's just that I don't know the answer. I don't think Heather knew. You know what she was, what she did to get money..."

"Yes, but you said she was clean by the time she was pregnant, so why–"

"Why still sell herself? I don't know why, or if. I only know she wouldn't say who Robbie's father was and he certainly wasn't around by the time she told me of the pregnancy."

"And wanting you to be there – at the birth – why you, Tom?

"I'm not sure. I was a link to Rosie, to her family. I was someone she trusted, the only person she could ask..." I shrugged.

My mother nodded. She looked pensive, taking it all in.

I stood up. "I need to get back. Thanks for listening. You look tired out. I'm sorry."

She stood up too. "I'm fine, darling. No need to be sorry." She had tears in her eyes. "I'm your mother and I'm here for you. I'll do whatever I can to help. You know that, don't you?"

I swallowed hard. "Yes, Ma, I know."

A little while later I drove home. I thought about everything my mother had said. Talking it all through with her had helped.

I could see I needed to back off from Rosie, no matter how much I craved to be with her. No matter how much I wanted to gather her up, bring her home and make her better.

I could see the children needed me, and would need me even more once they knew how ill their mother was. No matter that I didn't know how to be there for them.

I could also see I had to rebuild my relationship with Adam.

No matter that I didn't know where to start.

And I could see I had to accept Robbie. No matter that accepting Robbie meant facing up to my guilt.

But the hardest realisation of all was that while the identity of Robbie's real father remained unknown, I would continue to be the prime suspect as far as Rosie was concerned. My mother believed my denial, but she was my mother. Rosie was a different matter. The way she felt about me, she was going to need proof. I'd need to be much closer to Robbie before I could ask him to take a DNA test, even then I couldn't imagine how I'd broach the subject. No, unless, by some miracle, his real father came forward, I would probably remain in the frame for some considerable time to come.

# Chapter Twenty Two

When I got home from my mother's, Sam and Jenny were in the kitchen. Sam was once again sorting through laundry. Jenny was chopping vegetables. She looked so like Rosie that, for a heart-stopping, breath-robbing moment, I thought it *was* Rosie.

"Hi, Dad." Sam and Jenny spoke together, as I walked in.

"Hello, you two, how's things? Is Max back?"

"Things are okay," Sam said. Max is watching telly in the front room."

"Did you see Adam? Is he coming back?" Jenny asked.

"I saw him, but he's not ready to come home. He's going to stay at Ruby's for a while. He says he's not coming back until Mum comes home and Robbie's gone away.

"Oh, Dad." Jenny gave a sob. "I want him home. I miss him so much. I miss Mum. I wish she was here. I wish Adam was here."

I went to her and put my arms round her. She cried into my chest. I kissed her hair and found I was stroking her, just as my mother had done for me earlier.

"Oh, Jen," Sam said. She came over and hugged Jenny's back. Then Sam looked at me. "How did you get on telling Mum about Adam?"

Jenny stepped back and looked at me too. "Yes, what did she say?" Sam put an arm round Jenny's shoulder.

At this point Max appeared in the kitchen. "Hi, Dad," he said. He looked at his sisters and then back at me. "What's wrong with them?"

"Come and sit down, all of you," I said. Once we were seated round the table, I told Max what I'd told the girls about Adam, and then I told them that, yes, I'd seen Rosie and told her what was happening.

"Did Mum say she'd come home to wait for Adam?" Max asked. "Adam would like it if Mum was here when he comes back."

Seeing Max being so brave, not saying outright that he wanted Rosie at home for his own sake, it really choked me up. "Mum will speak to you on Saturday, when you go to see her. She'll explain her plans to you all then," I replied. "And I'm sure it won't be long before Adam comes home."

"Is Adam coming with us to see Mum?" Jenny asked.

I took a deep breath before I answered. "No, he isn't. He doesn't feel able to see Mum at the moment." My heart sank as I looked at the children's faces. It sank even more as I thought that Adam would still have to be told about Rosie's cancer, especially once the others knew. But that was a bridge I'd think about crossing later.

I stood up. "Come here, you three," I said. They came into my outstretched arms and we all hugged for a long moment. As we hugged, I promised myself that I was going to do whatever it took to get Adam and Rosie back home, even if that simply meant waiting. In the meantime, my role as a father was going to have to change.

As we stepped back from each other I said, "Right come on, Maxy, I'll take you on at Monster Rumble while the girls get the dinner ready."

"Cool," Max said. He'd been asking me for ages to play this new game he had for his PlayStation. I'd always been too busy. Sam and Jenny didn't actually say anything, but I did hear a gasp from one of them and I know a look was exchanged.

"We'll clear up after dinner," I said over my shoulder, as Max and I left the kitchen. "Come on, Max, run for it!"

Although I wanted to appear light-hearted to the children, especially for Max's sake, I'd reached some important decisions.

My family was falling apart and doing nothing was not an option.

Later, while we were eating, Jenny told me she'd invited Robbie round for dinner the next night. She looked at me tentatively, probably unsure how I'd react, probably expecting me to make an excuse not to be there. I was surprised to find I was glad he was coming. Yes, I knew if I was to have any hope of getting Rosie back, I had to accept and get to know Robbie. But it wasn't just that. In spite of everything that had happened since he'd come into our lives, I wanted to know him better for me and for him. I wanted a relationship with him for its own sake. I further surprised myself by saying I would cook dinner the following evening.

"Do you know how to cook, Dad?" Max asked, when I blurted out my intention.

"Yes, of course I do!" I spoke with more conviction than I actually felt. All three children looked sceptical. "I'm not completely useless, you know. I'm going to do more round here from now on. I'll show you. I'm perfectly capable."

"I can manage," Sam said. "Ruby and I are keeping on top of things."

"I know you are, love. You're doing a great job but you shouldn't have to do quite so much. No, Jenny did the dinner this evening. Great stir fry by the way, Jen. And Max is helping with Toby's walks and looking after Adam's fish, which is good too. The school holidays start at the end of next week so I think we should get a rota going. All pitch in even more, take some of the load off you, Sam."

Max looked even more sceptical, but Jenny nodded in agreement.

"It's okay," Sam said. "I know I wasn't keen at first, but I haven't actually minded, and you are paying me."

"I know," I said, "but I want to do more and you're going off to uni in the autumn."

"But surely Mum will back before then, won't she?" Jenny said anxiously.

I was acutely aware, of course, that the children didn't know yet about Rosie being ill and that even if she was home, which I really didn't dare believe would be the case, she wouldn't be up to doing all she used to. I tried to sound upbeat.

"I hope so, of course, but even if she is I want to show her that we, that *I*, am serious about changing my ways and not letting her get so exhausted in future. So I'll start by doing dinner tomorrow night. And now Max and I are going to get this lot cleared away. You two can go and relax."

"So, has Mum gone away," said Max, as we stacked the dishwasher, "not just because she's cross with you about Robbie, but because we've all made her too tired? Is she angry with us, with me? And if you have Robbie round for dinner and are nice to him and I do more to help in the house, she'll come home?"

I can hardly describe what it was like to hear Max say those things. I felt sad that he thought any of this mess was down to him and exasperated with myself for not reassuring him sooner. I hugged him to me.

"Mum didn't go away because of anything you, or your brother or sisters, did or didn't do. She loves you and she misses you. She just needs a break, like she said, and yes, she needs me to be nice to be Robbie because she wants him to feel welcome in our family. It's me, Max. It's me that needs to be more of a help to Mum, and I'm going to be. With you and the girls to help me, I'm going to be. You'll see her on Saturday and she'll explain a bit more about why she needs some time away. But I promise you, none of it's your fault, Maxy." He hugged me even harder.

He looked up at me while still holding me tightly. "Are you and Mum going to get a divorce? Ben, at school, his dad left his mum because she was very angry with his dad and told him to get out the house. His mum told Ben none of it was Ben's fault and they both loved him, but they still got divorced."

I was really struggling now. "No, Max, me and Mum are not planning to get a divorce. I love your mum very much. You're not to worry." I was trying so hard not to lie to him, but I also wanted to comfort him and to offer him hope. However, I wasn't at all sure that Rosie was going to come back. I was afraid Max would see this in my face. I pressed him to me. At last I managed to speak. "Now come on, you've got to finish beating me at Monster Rumble."

Later, after Max and the girls had gone off to bed, I went through to the den. Toby followed me. I poured myself a large malt and paused by my i-pod, which was sitting on its dock on my desk. I selected the Dylan collection. I always found Bob to be the perfect background when I wanted to think. I settled on the sofa with Toby at my feet and, as the music played, I reflected on the day's events.

I tried to go with the positives. I was beginning to get my priorities sorted, I was going to get to know Robbie, I was going to be there for my children.

But it wasn't long before Rosie filled my thoughts. Rosie had cancer. I was probably going to lose her whether or not she came home. Confronting this was agony, so I suppressed all thoughts of my poor, darling wife.

Instead I recalled being with Ma that afternoon. Her wisdom and compassion were amazing and it was painful to admit that, yes, I hadn't appreciated her up till now either.

I also wondered what Adam was doing that night and prayed that he'd be okay and come home soon. I did have a bit of a smile again, when I remembered him explaining how he'd headed for a safe place and about him quoting Ruby's remark about her family and keys verbatim. I felt such love for my lad, and such admiration when I thought how difficult he found life at times. I'd let him down. I wanted him home. I wanted to see him attending to his fish, poring over his car magazines, playing with Toby, playing his brother at Monster Rumble, watching the Moto GP and Formula One on Sunday lunchtime television, chatting, as animatedly as Adam ever did, with my brother Dan about motor bikes over Sunday lunch. I wanted to see him struggling to concentrate, and running his hand through his hair, as Rosie tried to help him with his homework at the kitchen table. Toby put his head on my knee, as if he knew what I was thinking about.

And then my thoughts turned to the other three children. As I anticipated how it would be for them when Rosie told them she was ill, I downed what was left in my glass. Rosie… I poured myself another generous dram, struggling not to go there, not to think about her. Christ, it was hard, but I just about managed it.

Then Dylan had to go and start singing 'Lay, Lady, Lay'. I couldn't fight anymore. Regret, shame, fear and an excruciating longing swamped me and my vision blurred with tears. I swiped at them with the back of my hand.  And then, as Bob sang to his woman, I was transported back to the time when I first met Rosie Finch.

I was in my fourth year at medical school in Edinburgh. Rosie's brother, Michael, was a fellow student and a good mate of mine. He was having a party in his student flat. He'd invited his twin sisters, Rosie and Heather, to the party. Heather was at the art college in Edinburgh and Rosie was in her second year at St Andrews University.

I'd just been introduced to Heather and was talking to her when Rosie arrived. I glanced over as she came in. She was arm in arm with two other people. One was a big, dark, hairy bloke and the other was a striking looking girl with auburn hair. Michael called to me to come and meet his other sister and her boyfriend, his old mate Rick. Rosie was wearing a long, pale blue dress and her blonde hair fell almost to her waist. It was weird, looking from Heather to Rosie, they were so alike. But there was something extra about Rosie, about her eyes. There was a connection when I looked at her that I hadn't felt with Heather. I think I fell in love with her there and then. She smiled as we were introduced. She said it was good to meet me at last and that she'd heard what a great guy I was from Michael. Even her voice made an impression on me, rich and sweet and very sexy. She introduced me to the red-haired girl. Kirsty, and we all chatted for a bit.

Then she spotted another friend on the other side of the room. "Lucy!" she shouted. And with that, she took Rick's hand and disappeared through the throng.

I didn't see her again for two years. Michael told me she was serious about Rick. I didn't think I would have any chance, so I tried to put her out of my mind. And I thought I'd succeeded. I went out with Heather for a short time, but I was much too tame for her and she soon got bored. Then after a couple more short-term girlfriends, I got together with Yvette, a fellow medical student, and we went out for about a year until she dumped me for some Arts post-grad. This was more of a blow to my pride than my heart, but I decided I was through with romance and concentrated on passing my finals.

By the summer of 1978, I was almost finished my first year as a junior doctor at Edinburgh's Western General Hospital. I hadn't seen much of Michael since we left university. Being junior doctors didn't leave us much time for socialising. But we met by chance at some lecture at the Royal College of Surgeons one June evening. When the lecture was over, Michael suggested I join him for a pint before going home. He wanted me to meet his new girlfriend, Adele, who was waiting for him in the pub. I didn't really fancy playing gooseberry and made an excuse to get off home. But when he added that his sister, Rosie, would also be there, I reconsidered. He grinned and said something along the lines of, 'I knew you'd change your mind when you heard my wee sister would be there.'

It was a warm, sunny evening and I recall being ridiculously nervous as Michael and I walked across the Meadows to the Mortar bar, on the corner of Bristo Place. Being opposite the medical school, it was an old haunt from our student days.

Adele and Rosie were seated at a table in the corner. They were deep in conversation and didn't see us approaching, so I was able to look at Rosie without her knowing she was being stared at.

She was as pretty as I remembered. She was wearing blue jeans and a thin, white, blouse. Her hair was in a long, golden plait. On one wrist she had several coloured bangles that tinkled as she gestured. Adele often teased me, over the following years, that I hardly looked at her while Michael introduced us and explained how he and Adele had met. Apparently I stared at Rosie, with only an occasional glance in Adele's direction.

When Rosie said it was nice to see me again and congratulated me on becoming a doctor, I lost the power of speech and only seemed to be capable of incoherent mumblings. I desperately wanted to impress this girl, but I'd turned into some sort of moron. I couldn't think of anything interesting or witty to say. I also became completely uncoordinated and knocked Michael's pint over, soaking his jeans. By now I was praying for someone to shoot me. Michael and the girls laughed as he tried his best to mop up.

I went off to the bar to get Michael a replacement pint. When I returned, Rosie was alone. She said that Adele and Michael had decided to go back to his place since he was so damp, and that he'd said I was to have his pint. I sat down beside her and apologised for ruining the evening.

But Rosie grinned and shook her head. "I think the lovebirds were glad of an excuse to go home," she said. "Maybe Michael and you set it up so he didn't have to sit and chat to his boring sister when he had better things to do." She grinned again.

"No, no it was an accident, honestly! There was no plan. You're not boring!"

Rosie revealed her delicious neck as she threw her head back and laughed, a deep sonorous sound that I instantly adored.

She put her hand on my leg and looked up at me. She leant towards me and I could smell her patchouli perfume, a heady smell that I will always associate with that night. I thought I might pass out.

"I'm teasing you, Tom," she said gently. Then Bob Dylan came on the juke box. He was singing 'Lay Lady Lay'.

"Oh, I love Dylan. He's got a great voice. I've got a couple of his LPs," Rosie said. "He's great looking too. Actually, you look very like him, Tom."

"Do you think so?" My voice was a squeak. I felt very light-headed. "I'm a big fan of him myself,great lyrics." Then, as Dylan sang on about wanting his woman to lie on his bed and about what he'd like to spend the night doing and how he'd like her still to be there in the morning, I wanted to cut my own tongue out. "I didn't mean these lyrics in particular. I was thinking more of his anti-war stuff." Jesus, who was controlling my mouth?

"Yes, of course. I thought that's what you meant." There was that laugh again. Then Rosie slapped my leg. "Come on, let's leave the beer and go for a walk. You look like you could do with some fresh air." She stood up and held her hand out to me. I took it and let her lead me outside.

We walked across the Meadows and sat down on a bench at the edge of this oasis in the city. I regained the power of coherent speech as we walked. Rosie asked me about myself, about my ambitions as a doctor. I went off on one about how much I'd love to be a heart surgeon. I apologised for going on and on and for boring her.

She put her hand on my arm. "Listen, if you won't accept that I might be a bore to my brother, then I won't have it that you're a bore either! I enjoy listening to you. You sound so passionate. I hope you achieve your dream, Tom, I really do."

"And you, Rosie, what do you dream of?"

"I want to be a teacher. I start my year's training in October. I also want to get married some day and have lots of children."

I cleared my throat. "And do you have anyone in mind? For the marrying and children bit."

"I'm free and unattached at the moment, no one in mind to father my children. Why do you ask?" She smiled broadly. I knew she was teasing and flirting with me.

"Oh, no reason, just polite interest." I relaxed and smiled back.

After that the conversation flowed. Then Rosie shivered as it got dark and a lot cooler. I saw my chance and ventured to put my arm around her to keep her warm. She said it felt nice and snuggled into me. I offered to walk her home but she shook her head. I was so disappointed.

"I don't want to go home. I still live with my parents, so that won't do." She smiled again. "Have you got a place of your own, a place we could, you know, go back to together, and be alone?"

I could hardly believe what I was hearing. I opened and closed my mouth, trying to form a sentence.

"No, well that is, yes, I have a room in the doctor's residence at the hospital. No girls allowed of course…"

"Of course not." Rosie giggled. "But I fancy you, Dr McAllister, and I want to go to bed with you. So what do you say?"

Of course every taxi in the city disappeared at the very moment I said yes, and we had to walk right across town to get to the residence. On the way we stopped at a phone box so that Rosie could call her parents with some cover story about staying at a friend's. But, at last, we arrived and I smuggled Rosie into my room.

I pulled her towards me as I kicked the door closed and I kissed her lovely mouth. As Rosie returned my kisses, she undid my shirt buttons and ran her hands over my chest and stomach. Then, for both of us, it was a frenzy of undoing zips and fasteners. I did try to apologise for the state of my room. But Rosie just told me to shut up and pulled me down onto the bed.

I wanted to touch and kiss every part of her. I loved her long, slender limbs, the curve from waist to hip, her sweet breasts, the downy softness of her skin and the scent and heaviness of her hair. I loved her laugh, her enthusiasm, her openness, even the way she teased me. I could hardly believe that, at long last, this beautiful, sexy girl was here with me in my bed, whispering my name and obviously enjoying being there. I loved everything about Rosie Finch.

Toby dragged me back to the present. He nudged my hand

and gave a little whine.

"Come on then, old chap," I said, standing up and draining the last of my whisky. "You'll be needing your walk."

As I paced the quiet streets with Toby, I thought some more about Rosie and the children and the life we'd had together. By the time we got back to the house I'd made some decisions.

Tomorrow I was going to start making some changes. Tomorrow I was going to start getting my family back together.

# Chapter Twenty Three

I slept well that night and awoke early. It was a lovely morning. The sun was shining and the sky was clear. I felt more positive and energised than I'd been for the previous month. I went for a run along the beach. Toby came too, of course. He actually seemed to have overcome his huff, and managed to wag his tail now and again. When I got back home, Jenny was in the kitchen having breakfast. Sam was also there, sitting at the table, wearing her dressing gown and drinking tea. Radio One was blaring.

"Hi, Dad," Jenny said. "You look sweaty."

"Thank you, Jennifer," I said, as I filled Toby's bowl with fresh water.

"Morning, Dad," Sam said. "There's tea in the pot."

"Morning, I'll not bother with tea just now, thanks. As your sister pointed out, I need to get a shower."

Max came clattering down the stairs and into the kitchen. He was dressed but would've made a scarecrow look smart. His hair was a mess, his shirt collar was standing up at one side, the shirt itself wasn't tucked in and his school shoes were filthy. "Hi, Dad," he said. His usual cheerful mood seemed to have returned after the previous night's anxieties. "You smell all sweaty."

"Yes, thank you, I've been running, so I've got a good excuse. What's your excuse for the state you're in?"

"What? What's wrong with me?"

"Sort your collar and tuck your shirt in. When did you last clean your shoes and have you brushed your hair in the last few days?"

"Nobody tucks their shirt in. It's not cool." But he did turn his collar down. "I don't know how to clean my shoes. Mum does that. And my hair needs cut. It's too tuggy to brush.

"It's high time you could clean your own shoes. We'll do them later." I realised I'd no idea where, or how often, Max got his hair cut. He had thick, curly hair and, even at its best it was unruly, but I'd never seen it this messy before. This was something else I'd always left to Rosie. "And we'll get your hair cut at the beginning of next week," I added. Meanwhile Max was foraging in the cupboard for his cereal and seemed to have stopped listening.

"What are you going to cook for dinner tonight, Dad?" Sam asked. "I'm going food shopping, so I could get any stuff you need."

I'd forgotten all about my rash offer. "Oh, it's a surprise," I replied. "I'll shop for what I need myself, but thanks for the offer."

"I've got a rehearsal for *Grease* after school and then Robbie's going to meet me in town. We'll get the bus back here together for about six," said Jenny.

"Okay, we'll eat around seven then. Now, I must go and get a shower. Have a good day at school, you two. Are you all organised, Maxy? Got everything you need?"

"Yep, not counting clean shoes and a haircut, of course," Max replied, smiling.

I smiled back. "Yes, not counting those things. See you later."

By the time I got back to the kitchen, showered and ready for work, Sam was also dressed and clearing away the breakfast things.

"Can I get you anything, Dad?" she asked, straightening up from loading the dishwasher and tucking her hair behind her ear. This simple request and the way she moved gave me a catch in my throat. I looked at my daughter. A few weeks ago she'd been a typical, selfish teenager and now here she was behaving all grown up and so much like her mother. There wasn't a strong physical resemblance between Rosie and Sam. Sam looked more like me. But, just then, her manner and behaviour were so like her mother.

"Dad?" she said, when I didn't answer. "Are you okay?"

"Sorry, yes, I'm fine. I'll get myself some tea and toast. I'm very proud of you, Sam. The way you've coped with all this and how you've looked after Max and kept us all going as a family. I can see now why Uncle Michael was so sorry to lose you when you came back from Australia."

"Oh, Dad," Sam said, putting her hands up to her face and shaking her head. "Don't go all soppy. You'll make me cry."

"Come here," I said. "Give your old Dad a hug." She came over to me. I held her. "I meant what I said. I'm proud of you, and Mum will be too, when she sees how well you've done. And I meant what I said about me doing more to help."

"So, is Mum really not coming home soon? I thought she'd be feeling better by now. And you're okay about Robbie now, aren't you? Can't she forgive you for keeping him a secret? Or is there more to this?"

I stroked her hair, then stepped away to fill up the kettle and put some bread in the toaster. She sat down at the table. The nerves in my stomach constricted as I thought of Rosie's other reason for going and for staying away. I'd promised to let Rosie tell the children about her cancer, and I was going to keep that promise. But I could see that the original explanation about Rosie's leaving was not convincing Sam any more.

"You'll see Mum tomorrow. She'll explain more to you then about why she's not coming back just yet."

"Well, it better be good, because I think she should come home now. She said she was only going for a few weeks."

"I know she did. But even though I'm okay about Robbie now, Mum feels very hurt by what I did and doesn't really understand my reasons."

"Have you told her all your reasons? Have you tried to explain? I don't really understand what you did either, but you must have felt you were doing the right thing."

This was almost too much to bear. She was right of course, I still hadn't been completely honest with Rosie. But I couldn't speak to Sam about it either. "I did believe I was doing the right thing. I hope Mum sees that eventually. And, of course now she's also angry about me upsetting Adam and driving him away."

"Adam didn't leave because of you. He left because he's Adam. He's like Mum really, gone away to make sense of things. He'll be okay and he'll be back when he's ready. And so will Mum. They can't be mad at you forever. They know you love them."

"It's nice of you to say so, love, and I hope you're right. And now, I really must get away. See you later." I kissed my daughter goodbye and set off for work.

When I got to the Royal Infirmary it was already bustling.

I made my way up to cardiology and headed along the corridor to my office. It felt good to be back. I'd only been away a day, but it seemed a lot longer. I loved my job. I loved being a heart surgeon. Sometimes when I was driving home after a day in theatre, I would feel so exhilarated, exultant even. To give someone back their life, to pull them back from the edge, take away pain, cut out the problem and make good, there's nothing better. I suppose I was hooked on it, that rush. But like all addictions there'd been a price to pay. And it was a price I'd never questioned before.

When I arrived at my office, Sheena was in the little outer room that was her workspace. Sheena was the medical secretary who worked for me and for Bruce, my boss and head of cardio-thoracics. She worked calmly and efficiently and kept Bruce and I organised. She'd come to work for us about five years before, following the death of her husband. She looked up from her PC as I walked in.

"Good morning, Tom." She smiled her open smile. "It's good to see you back." She betrayed no curiosity about the previous day's absence.

"Good morning, Sheena. It's good to see you too. Sorry about yesterday. What did I miss and what's on today's agenda?"

Sheena took me through it all in her usual efficient manner. She said that Bruce had been very impressed with Anna's handling of the clinic, and with her follow up of our post-operative inpatients. Anna was my registrar. She was very competent and ambitious and was about to complete her cardio-thoracic specialist training.

"So are you saying I wasn't missed then?" I asked.

Sheena looked horrified. "No, no, not at all. It's just you've trained Anna well and she did a good job. I didn't mean…"

I laughed. "I'm joking, Sheena. Don't look so worried!"

"Oh, right, well don't joke. We're not here to have fun!" She relaxed and smiled.

"Sheena brought you up to speed, has she?" Bruce was in the doorway.

"She's just broken it to me that I'm not indispensable after all," I answered.

"Yes, can't say we missed you yesterday," Bruce grinned. "What's today's schedule like for you? I'd like to see you about a couple of your ward patients and one of the clinic cases from yesterday."

"I need to speak with Anna, of course, and then I should do a ward round. What about right after lunch, two o'clock. There's a couple of things I need to discuss with you too?"

"See you at two then." With that he disappeared into his office, next door to mine.

The morning passed quickly and it was true, everything seemed under control despite my unscheduled absence. Anna actually seemed very glad to have had the chance to get on with things without me. She was a very able doctor. Her surgical skills were developing well and she had a good way with the patients. She certainly put in the hours, but it wasn't until recently that I'd begun to appreciate how hard it must be for her.

"How's Evie?" I asked, after she'd finished updating me on the previous day's patients.

She looked mildly surprised at the question. I wasn't exactly in the habit of asking about Anna's family life.

"She's fine, thank you," she replied. "She had her fourth birthday last week. I think I mentioned it."

"Oh yes, how did that go? There was a party?"

"I got home in time for the end of it. Kenny had done a great job in the afternoon with all her friends from nursery, and I was there in the morning when she opened her presents."

"How do you and Kenny do it? Manage, I mean, with both of you working, and looking after Evie."

Anna now looked a bit suspicious. "It's not easy. You must know that. Kenny works part time, for now, so he can be there for Evie some of the week, and my mother helps out the rest of the time."

"And Kenny doesn't mind being part time at work?"

"No, he enjoys being a dad. I envy him actually, being at home with Evie so much, but I'll not get to be a consultant by working part time. Once Evie starts school, Kenny can build up his hours again. And maybe, once I'm a consultant, I can job share or something. There are a couple of female consultants in ENT who do that already."

"But it bothers you, does it, not being around for Evie as much as you'd like?"

"A bit. I've had to compromise to keep my career on track. I knew it would be difficult combining motherhood and being a surgeon. But I try to make up for it at the weekends, and I make sure I take my full holiday entitlement. Look, what's this about Tom? Are you questioning my commitment to the job?"

"No, no far from it. I just wondered how you did it. Working and being a parent, with the hours you have to put in. I never had to think about it. Rosie stopped work for a few years, when the kids were small, and went back when Max started school. But I didn't really do much at all at home. I still come in here most weekends, at least once, and I've hardly ever taken a full fortnight off."

"I did wonder. I know you've come back early from holiday while I've been here. To be honest I thought it was so you could keep an eye on me. But you've never, even for a family holiday, – you haven't ever taken your whole entitlement?"

"Very rarely. I usually end up coming back early, leaving Rosie and the children wherever and coming back to work. It's not to keep an eye on you. I can assure you. You're one of the best registrars I've worked with."

"Right, well, thanks for the compliment. But why are you asking all this now?"

"Oh, ignore me. It's no reflection on you, I promise. No, it's just things – well– things have been happening at home. I've realised I haven't been there enough. I've left Rosie with far too much to do."

Anna looked bemused.

"Sorry," I said. "You must think I've gone a bit mad. I know we never really normally talk about our home lives."

"It's okay. But yes, it's a bit weird. You're always so focussed on work, which is good of course, but…" she was floundering.

I smiled at her. "Relax, normal service is resumed. Let's go and see some patients."

In what seemed like no time, it was two o'clock and I was knocking on Bruce's door.

"Come in, Tom. Take the weight off." Bruce looked over the top of his glasses and pointed to a chair piled high with files. I moved the files to the floor and sat down. "Sorry," Bruce said. "I had the clinic yesterday, and then I was in meetings most of the morning, so I haven't got that lot processed yet. You know how it is."

"I do indeed," I replied. "Which patients was it that you wanted to have a word about?"

"None of them really. That was just an excuse for Sheena's benefit, though I don't think I fooled her for a minute. I wanted to talk to you about you."

"Oh, right, look, I'm sorry about yesterday, not coming in

and at such short notice. It was family stuff. I needed to be there."

"Oh that. That's fine. Don't give it another thought. Anna coped magnificently. You've done a good job training her up, Tom. You've always been good at that side of things."

"It's all part of the job, passing on the skills. You taught me."

"Yes, I did and, even if I say so myself, I did a good job. But I'm a bit concerned about you, Tom. You don't seem to have been your usual self for a few weeks. Don't get me wrong, your work has been exemplary as always, but you have seemed a little distracted. It's not like you, and this is not a criticism, but it's not like you to be out of here by five in the evening, or to miss a day. I'm speaking as a friend, not as a boss. Is everything all right? Is the family stuff, as you called it, all sorted out now?"

I hadn't expected Bruce to be taking the lead in this conversation, but I was glad it hadn't been left up to me to broach the subject of my domestic turmoil. "Not exactly, no." I told Bruce about the events of the last five weeks.

"I'm so sorry, Tom. Poor Rosie. What a shock for her, and you of course. And, as for Adam, I'm sure he'll be back. You should've told me all this sooner. I could've covered for you, arranged some time off."

"Yes, I know. It was just, I guess, it was hard to admit it was happening, and that I only had myself to blame, driving my wife and son away."

"Don't be too hard on yourself. I'm sure whatever you've done, you've done in good faith. You wanted what was best for the family."

"Thanks for saying so. But I think I need to change the way I do things as regards my family, if I'm to have any hope of getting them back."

"So, what things are you thinking about changing?"

"The way I work has to be the first thing, at least in the short term. I need to spend some time at home, being a proper father and, – if I get the chance, a proper husband. I need to cut my hours."

Bruce looked momentarily surprised, but he recovered well. "I see. That's brave in our game. I'm retiring next year, as you know, and I had thought you'd be after my job. Chief of cardio, it's what you've been working towards, isn't it?"

"It surely wouldn't put me out of the running?"

"You know what it's like, Tom. Part-timers don't get the top jobs. Competition at this level is fierce. You have to be seen to put in the hours, publish the papers etc, etc."

"If losing the top job is the price for getting my wife and son back, then it's a price I'm willing to pay." I hadn't realised I thought that until I voiced it.

"Let's hope it doesn't come to that. And I must say, I admire you. Maybe if I hadn't been so ambitious, I'd still be married."

"I wasn't getting at you," I said.

"I know you weren't. And anyway we were as bad as each other, Karen and I. We were far more married to our jobs than to each other. She didn't want children and I did. I wanted her to give up work and be a mother, and there was no way she was doing that. I never even considered giving up my job in order to be a father. So it all ended in tears, mine mostly."

Bruce had never told me anything this personal in the twenty years I had worked with him. I knew he was divorced of course and that Karen now had the Chair of forensic medicine at Edinburgh University. I knew they were still friends and that Bruce was very proud of her achievements, but I didn't know why their marriage had broken up. I didn't know what to say.

But Bruce didn't seem to expect me to say anything. He went on, "I'm surprised, Tom, but I think you're doing the right thing. So how do you see this working? How will you go about reducing your hours?"

"Anna's done her final exams for membership of the Royal College, and I think we can assume she's passed them. So, she'll be eligible for a consultancy post. I wondered if you could make a case for Anna and I to job share, at least until a full time post comes up for Anna. And I hoped you'd supervise her to begin with."

"You have thought this through, haven't you? It's a good idea and I'll support it with the powers that be. Have you spoken to Anna?"

"Not exactly. But earlier on today she was talking about her future as a consultant, and she did mention the idea of a job share as being something she'd be up for. I didn't mention my plans. I wanted to run it by you first."

"Okay, talk to her. You could also consider a sabbatical. God knows you deserve one. And you'd also be eligible for some compassionate leave right now, you know."

"Yes, I know. Thanks, Bruce. I'll speak to Anna. I did wonder about a sabbatical. I'll give it more thought now I have your approval."

"I hope you didn't doubt my approval. The hospital will go on without us you know. It's Rosie and the children that are most important thing. You have something precious there. Don't make the mistakes that I have. This place is no substitute for family life." Bruce sounded quite emotional now. "Do what you have to do to get Rosie and Adam back."

Once more I was thrown by Bruce talking in such personal terms, and once again I didn't know what to say.

"Right that's enough of all that," Bruce said. "Pull yourself together, man. I take it you're at least going to do some work while you *are* here. Go on. You've patients to see." Bruce laughed, back to his normal self, as I stood up to go.

"Yes, sir," I said.

As I returned to my own office I felt relieved, lighter. It was good to be doing something positive at last.

The afternoon passed as quickly as the morning. I saw two patients who were hoping to be discharged, and was able to give them both the good news that they could indeed go home. I also checked on a couple of others in the High Dependency Unit, both of whom, I was pleased to see, were making good progress. And then, as always, there was paper work to attend to.

Later, as I prepared to leave for home, I remembered I still had dinner to sort out. What on earth was I going to cook? "Damn," I said to myself. "What was I thinking of?"

"Sorry, what was that?" Sheena said, from the doorway.

"Oh, did I say that out loud?" I said, embarrassed. "I was talking to myself, sorry."

Tom, tell me to mind my own business, if you want to, but are you all right?"

"Yes – well that is no – not really."

"Do you want to talk about it?"

I wasn't sure I could face telling the whole sorry story yet again, but it also crossed my mind that I probably owed her an explanation, as much as I'd owed one to Bruce. She was always discreet and didn't generally indulge in the gossip that travelled faster than any virus round the hospital.

She saw my hesitation. "I'll put the kettle on," she said.

And, over a cup of tea I told Sheena it all. I also asked her to tell my theatre team the edited highlights. She listened, without interrupting, except to make sympathetic noises here and there.

"I really hope you sort out things with Adam and that Rosie gets better. Try not to blame yourself. Adam and Rosie are their own people. They've made decisions about what they need to do and where they need to be at the moment. But if there's anything I can do to help you, I hope you know you only have to ask."

I realised for the first time, as Sheena spoke, how fond I was of her and how much I relied on her steady, calm manner. Here was someone else in my life that I'd been taking for granted.

"Thanks, Sheena, for everything I mean, all that you do. Heart surgery I can do, but all the paperwork and all the organisation, I'd never keep on top of it all without you. I know I don't say it often enough, but I do appreciate it."

"Don't be daft. It's what I'm paid for," she said. The normally unflappable Sheena was blushing.

"It's not daft. You do more than you're paid for and you know it."

"Don't start being nice to me now. I know where I stand with the distracted grunts that Bruce and you usually use by way of communication. I won't be able to cope if you start treating me as a person!"

I smiled at her. "That just proves how badly we treat you! Actually, I need to ask you to help me out in a way that, I don't think, either Bruce or I have asked before."

"Oh," she said cautiously, "what's that?"

"I volunteered to cook dinner for the kids tonight and I haven't a clue what to make. I can boil an egg, but that's about it as far as my culinary skills go. They think I'm not up to the task and I don't want to prove them right. Have you got any suggestions?"

Sheena laughed, rather too gleefully I thought, then got a grip of herself. "Right, I admire your bravery. Is a take-away out of the question?"

"Oh yes, I have to be seen to actually cook, that's what I promised."

A little while later I was on my way to the supermarket, to get the ingredients for dinner that Sheena had written down for me. She'd also written out, what she described as idiot proof instructions, for the assembly of said ingredients. I was going to make coq au vin.

# Chapter Twenty Four

I arrived home around five thirty. It was a beautiful June evening. Sam was watching Neighbours in the living room. She said that Max was taking Toby out for a walk and had actually done some piano practice when he got home from school. We had a brief chat about how our days had been. Sam reminded me that Max's end of year school concert was on during the following week and that he'd brought home a note about tickets. She reminded me too, that Jenny's school production of *Grease* was also on during the following week, as was the prize-giving. I assured her I'd organise my attendance at all three events.

Before going to the kitchen, I phoned my mother to confirm the arrangements for the next day, when she and Kirsty would be taking the children to see Rosie. She said that Dan was with her and that he sent his love. I also told her a bit about my plans as far as my work was concerned. I know she was quite shocked at this, but she did her best to cover it up. Mind you, I think she was equally shocked when I told her that I had to go and cook the dinner. She laughed, a bit too enthusiastically for my liking, and wished me the best of luck, and said she'd pray for her grandchildren. I thanked her for her vote of confidence and she laughed some more.

Then I decided to phone Adam. I wanted to ask him if he would reconsider going to see Rosie the next day. But his phone went to voicemail. I wondered if he was working or if his caller ID showed it was me phoning. On a mad impulse I left him a message asking him to join us for dinner, though I didn't really expect he would.

Then I couldn't put it off any longer. I went to the kitchen and got down to cooking dinner. I washed and chopped mushrooms, shallots and peppers. The garlic baffled me. How on earth were you supposed to tackle that, and did you peel it or not? Sheena's recipe said 3 cloves of garlic. How much was a clove? If it was only one section, then that didn't seem very much. In the end I chopped the whole thing up and put it all in. I opened a bottle of red wine for the sauce and poured myself a glass as well. As I did so, I heard the front door open and close. Max and Toby came into the kitchen followed by Jenny and Robbie.

"Hi, Dad," Max said, as he went to fill Toby's water bowl.

"Hi, son, hi, Jen and Robbie," I said. Robbie hung back behind Jenny. He looked as awkward as I felt.

"Come in, Robbie, come in," I said.

"Hello, Mr McAllister," he said, as he came over from the doorway. "Something smells nice, but I think it might need a bit of a stir." He nodded in the direction of the cooker.

"Oh, God, yes, thanks." I grabbed the lid off the pan and stirred hard. The chicken breasts were just beginning to stick and I prayed I'd caught them in time.

"It does smell nice, actually," said Jenny. "What are you making?" she asked, as she peered into the pan.

"No need to sound quite so amazed," I said. "It's coq au vin."

"It's what?" said Max.

"Chicken in a red wine sauce. It has a French name. Coq means chicken and au vin means in wine," Jenny said. "Stop giggling, Max, it's not grown up."

Max looked at me and we both sniggered. "Coq!" said Max, hugely enjoying the double entendre.

"Oh, for heaven's sake!" said Jenny. "It's not big and it's not clever. Grow up, both of you! I'm sorry, Robbie. My father and my brother are very immature."

"I'm only eleven. I'm allowed to be immature!" said Max, still giggling hysterically.

I was now laughing at him laughing. "And I'm only fifty-one," I managed to gasp, before collapsing into more laughter. I noticed Robbie was grinning.

"I give up," said Jenny, rolling her eyes. "I'm going to get changed." She left, shaking her head.

"Can I do anything to help?" asked Robbie.

"No, it's okay, I think I can just about get control of myself on my own, but thanks for offering," I said. This set Max off again. I was pathetically pleased that I was so amusing to an eleven-year-old.

"I think he means with the dinner, Dad," giggled Max.

"Oh, right," I said feigning surprise. "Sorry, Robbie. I don't know what got into me. It's Max laughing like that. It set me off too."

"Don't blame me!" Max said, as he went away, with great glee, to tell Sam what we were having for dinner.

"Now, would you like a beer or anything?" I asked Robbie once we were alone.

"A beer would be great," Robbie smiled.

"Help yourself," I said, indicating the fridge. "Bottle opener should be in the top drawer."

"Thanks, Mr McAllister."

"Tom – it's Tom. We're family after all," I said. "And please, have a seat."

Now as the laughter wore off, I felt uncomfortable, remembering how I'd been towards Robbie before. I turned away to the sink and filled the basin with water so I could start peeling the potatoes. I raked around in the cutlery drawer trying to locate the peeler that I'd seen Rosie and, more recently, Sam using. I found it, eventually, in a jar on the worktop where various implements were kept. I sensed Robbie watching me.

I began, as casually as I could, to peel the potatoes, not something I'd ever really done before. I cleared my throat. "And, Robbie, I'm sorry. I'm sorry, I was out of order, you know when–"

"There's no need to apologise. It was my own fault, shocking you like that. I honestly thought that Mrs, that Rosie would know I existed. I didn't mean to cause all this trouble."

"None of what's happened is your fault. Rosie leaving, your arrival, let's just say, it's not the only reason she's moved out. And Adam, well, Adam got scared with all the changes and I didn't help him. So he left too."

As I spoke I was gouging great chunks out of the potatoes. It was only partly because of the stress of what I was saying, of what I was admitting to Robbie. I actually couldn't get the damn peeler to glide like it's supposed too.

"I went to see Rosie after school yesterday," said Robbie. "She said you'd been round earlier and she told me about – about her illness." He spoke gently and very quietly. "She told me Jenny and the others don't know yet and that she's telling them tomorrow. She wanted me to know now so I could help the girls and Max a bit, you know, afterwards."

"I see," was all I could say. I gripped the edge of the sink. "Does she not think I'll be able to help them?" I stabbed at a potato.

"I don't think it's that. Let me help." He was standing beside me now.

"I can look after my children, Robbie, no matter what Rosie thinks!"

"I meant with these poor things," he said, holding his hand out to take the peeler from me and peering into the basin.

"Oh, yes, yes, okay. I'm making rather a mess of them. Give me open heart surgery any day. It's not as hard as this. Sorry." I handed him the peeler. "Be my guest."

I decided to return temporarily to my comfort zone and fed Toby. This I could do. Once Robbie had finished peeling the potatoes, I suggested he might like to go and watch television with the others.

As I continued making the dinner, I found I was thinking about Rosie. I thought how she would've enjoyed Max's

amusement earlier and I yearned to have her back. I couldn't
conceive how a true bereavement must be. This was bad enough.

Then my mobile rang at the same time as the doorbell. I
grabbed my phone from my pocket. The display on the phone
said it was Rosie calling. My heart turned over. I shouted along
the hall for somebody to get the door, and then went back into
the kitchen and pushed the button to accept the call. My hands
were shaking.

"Hello, Rosie," I said, trying to keep my voice even.

"Hello, Tom," Rosie's voice sounded faint, far away. "I
just wanted to check that the children were still coming here
tomorrow – so I can – so I can tell them."

"Yes, they are. Although not Adam, as you know. I tried
calling him to ask him to reconsider, but he isn't answering his
phone.

"Oh, that was good of you. Actually I was hoping you would
have a word with him, tell him about the cancer, try and persuade
him to see me." This surprised me. Was it a small breakthrough
between us, that Rosie was asking me to do something for her?

"If you're sure you want it to be me who tells him, I'll certainly
try to talk to him."

"Thanks," she said, even quieter now.

"They're looking forward to seeing you. But of course they've
no idea what you're going to be telling them."

"I know that. I know it's going to be hard for them. It's going
to be hard for me too."

"Yes…" I didn't know what to say that would be of any
comfort. The whole situation was just too awful. I changed the
subject. "Robbie's here. I'm cooking dinner for us all."

"Oh, are you? That's nice." Her voice sounded really weak.

"How are you, Rosie? How are you coping with the chemo?"

"Not very well. I've been throwing up today, not pleasant,
but I'm told that will subside and I should get one good week
before the next dose. Anyway, I better let you go if you've a meal
to cook. And, Tom…"

"Yes?"

"That's good that you've got Robbie round. He's a lovely lad, isn't he?"

"Yes he is. Listen, I don't like to think of you alone, especially when you're not feeling so good. I could come up to Edinburgh after dinner, be with you for the evening."

"No, no,- that's not necessary. I'm not actually alone. But thanks for the offer. Bye, Tom." She hung up

I was a bit thrown by her hanging up so abruptly. I did wonder who was at the flat with Rosie. Most probably it was Lucy or Kirsty, but I didn't get a chance to speculate for very long, as the kitchen door opened and my brother, Dan, came in. I'd almost forgotten about the doorbell ringing when I was answering the phone. Dan had long been in the habit of dropping in on the spur of the moment, and his impromptu visits often coincided with mealtimes, at least they did when Rosie had been at home.

"Hi, Tom, I hope you don't mind, but when Ma told me you were cooking I thought I had to see it for myself." He produced a bottle of wine from behind his back. "Have you got enough for an unexpected guest?"

"I could do without the pressure of your presence actually, you devious, smug bastard."

"And good evening to you! I'm well. How are you? That's the customary greeting in polite society."

I raised my eyebrows at my smirking brother and shook my head. "You can stay, if you insist. But there's to be no mocking of my culinary abilities, or the lack of them." Dan was a great cook, so I felt justified in feeling defensive.

"No, I promise, no mocking. It smells good anyway." Dan settled himself at the table and I set another place. "You look tired, Tom," he said. "Ma's filled me in on the latest developments. I know you already had a lot on your plate with Rosie's reaction to Robbie turning up. But Rosie's diagnosis and Adam leaving, I'm so sorry."

"Yeah, well, just when you think things can't get any worse…"

I shrugged.

"And Ma also told me what you'd said about you not being Robbie's father." Dan paused, looked up at me.

"Yes, what of it?"

"I never thought you were. I couldn't see you being unfaithful to Rosie. No way, and with Heather, no, it's just unthinkable. I don't think Rosie believes it either. She's angry, yes, in shock. But she'll come round. I'm sure she will."

I smiled at my brother. "Thanks for your faith in me. I just wish Rosie shared it."

"Like I say, give it time. Anyway, how are you coping?"

"Oh, you know, not very well really," I said, stirring the sauce. "And remember, the kids don't know Rosie's ill yet. She's telling them tomorrow."

"I know, don't worry. I won't mention it in front of them." As I put the finishing touches to the meal, I told Dan about my plans to cut back on my work hours

"That's a big step to take isn't it, cutting back your time at the hospital? It's a brave thing to do career wise. Have you really thought it through?"

"Of course I have. We, or at least I, always took it for granted that I would pursue my career and Rosie would do the hands-on parenting thing. With the result I don't know my kids, or the first thing about running a house, and Rosie's worn out and ill."

"Surely you're not blaming yourself for Rosie having cancer?"

"No, not directly, but she has had a stressful time, teaching, looking after all of us. Meanwhile all I've had to do is go to work and do a job I love. Then I completely mishandled the Robbie situation. I've not exactly been a support to her, have I?"

"I suppose not, not when you put it like that. But, for what it's worth, I think you were right not to tell Rosie at the time about Robbie being born. There's no way she could have handled it."

"No, she certainly couldn't," I replied, glancing at my watch. "Anyway, time to dish up dinner. Could you give the kids a shout?"

The meal went well. There were some comments about ambulances on standby, and Max said a grace that went along the lines of 'for what we are about to receive give us strong stomachs to stand it'. However, there were lots of noises of approval and mostly clean plates. Max picked out the mushrooms and the peppers and left them on the side, but said that, apart from those, it was 'well tasty'. There were some remarks on the strong garlicky flavour, and Dan laughed heartily when I admitted that I'd put in a whole garlic bulb. But, all in all, my cooking was well received. I couldn't believe how pleased I felt with myself. I decided I owed Sheena a big thank you.

There was lots of good chat round the table while we ate. Dan kept it all going and kept it light-hearted, for which I was very grateful. He and Robbie seemed to really hit it off. But that was Dan, people took to him. He was warm and easy-going and had a great sense of humour. However, even by his standards, he did connect very quickly with Robbie. I knew he was a psychiatrist and therefore it was to be expected he'd know what made people tick, but with Dan it wasn't simply a professional skill, it was him, it was how he was as a person. I watched him charming Sam and Jenny, and making Max laugh, and putting Robbie at ease. And, as I watched him, I had moment of – what exactly? I don't know. A moment of revelation, I suppose, of realisation of how much my brother meant to me. He caught my eye and winked at me, and I could see in his look that he understood exactly the turmoil I was going through. I knew too that he was very aware of the terrible news that the children would get the next day from their mother.

We finished the meal by polishing off two tubs of Luca's vanilla ice-cream, locally produced, and not only a McAllister family favourite, but the best ice-cream in the universe.

It was after nine o'clock when we got up from the table. Dan detailed the children to clear up the meal so that he and I could go and relax in the living-room. He also announced that he'd drunk too much wine to drive home so would be staying over.

I found myself suggesting to Robbie that he stay over too, if it was all right with his parents, and if he didn't mind the sofa bed in the den. "Dan better have the proper bed in the spare room as he needs a firm mattress at his age," I said, while dodging a smack to the back of my head from my brother.

Robbie seemed pleased to be asked, and said it would be cool not having to leave and get the bus back to Edinburgh, as he was enjoying the evening so much. I was very touched at that. He said he'd phone home and check it was okay, but that his Mum and Dad would be fine about it.

"That went well," Dan said, once we were settled on the sofas with a brandy each. "You did a good meal. Well done."

"Thank you. I think I did a not bad job," I said. "And thanks for keeping the children's spirits up. They're finding it hard at times, missing Rosie and Adam, and they're going to have a rough day tomorrow."

"You don't have to thank me for that bro. They're great kids. I love them all to bits, you know that."

"I know you do and they love you."

Dan had always been very involved in the children's lives. He was very generous at birthdays and Christmas, but it was more than that. He spent time with them. He and his late partner, David, had taken the children ice-skating, swimming, out on picnics and on lots of other jaunts. Dan and Max had a particular bond. They shared a love of football, and of the Heart of Midlothian football club in particular. Dan gave Max his first Hearts season ticket for his ninth birthday, and the two of them had attended all the Hearts home matches together ever since. Dan was also the only person who could regularly beat Max at Monster Rumble on the Playstation.

"You'd have been a great Dad, you know," I said to him.

Dan smiled. "I like to think so. Who knows, maybe if David had lived we might have had a child or two. Things are moving on in that regard now, but when David was alive, gay couples couldn't adopt. We did talk about it. But then David died."

Dan and David had twelve years together before David's death in a road accident. Dan was silent for a moment before he continued. "I do envy you. You have four such lovely young people that are part of you and Rosie. I can't really imagine what that must be like. And now you have Robbie too, a late addition to the family. You're a lucky man, Tom."

"I know I am. I just hope I haven't realised it too late. It's such a cliché, but it's true, we don't appreciate what we've got till it's gone."

"Oh, I know that, living without David has taught me that."

"Sorry, I didn't mean you. I meant in general, and myself in particular."

Dan shook his head. "Don't apologise," he said. "It applied to me too. I always thought David and I'd be together until a ripe old age. I didn't savour all the good bits enough. I still miss him five years on. It's rubbish, you know, what they say about bereavement, that with time you move on and you get over it. Life does move on, relentlessly and you're forced to move on too, but you don't get over it." Dan ran a hand through his hair and took a gulp of brandy. "In some ways," he added, "It actually gets worse rather than better. Anyway, I don't want to get over it."

"I've never really appreciated what it must have been like for you, losing David, not until now. Not until I've been faced with the prospect of losing Rosie." I should have been there for you more, at the time and since. Christ, I've been such a selfish git."

"No, you haven't. You were there as much as I wanted you to be. There was nothing anybody could do. If I'd needed you, I'd have asked and you'd have come. I know that."

"I'd like to think I would've been there if you'd asked. But–"

"Look, Tom, don't take this the wrong way, but Ma says you've been torturing yourself about being like Dad. You're not. You're a good bloke. Mind you, he wasn't the monster you think he was, really he wasn't."

"I don't know how you can defend him. The way he treated you, cutting you off because of your sexuality, how can you overlook that, quite apart from the fact that he was a cold, sadistic–"

"Tom, I know now's not the time, but later when this stuff is all over, you must read his diaries." I shook my head. "No, no," Dan continued, "I know you can't contemplate it at the moment. But since all this business with Rosie and the past, I think it'd help you. He manages to say it all in writing, all the stuff he couldn't speak of. His motives, the way he treated us, it wasn't out of wickedness."

"I don't believe there's anything he could've written that would justify the way he was."

"I could tell you what he wrote. I could tell you, try to make you see, but I know that wouldn't work. Reading his diaries, it's like he's communicating directly with us. I think that's what he intended."

I got to my feet. "Please, Dan, not now." I picked up the brandy bottle. "Top up?"

Dan nodded held out his glass. "Okay, I'll back off," he raised a hand in submission. "But you, Tom, you've been a good husband and father. Rosie never had any complaints before all this, did she? I know you think you've let her down. It's not selfish to want to protect your wife or to establish a career that lets you provide well for your family."

"It's nice of you to say so. Andy and Bruce have said much the same things and I'd like to believe them."

We sipped our brandy in silence for a moment. Then Dan spoke.

"From what Ma's told me, there's more to this Robbie business than Heather having a baby and then dying of a drug overdose isn't there?"

"Oh, yes, there's more, stuff I've still not told Rosie, things only Michael and I know."

"So are you going to tell her the whole story now?"

"I think I have to, yes, as soon as she'll let me. I have to."

# Chapter Twenty Five

Next morning, Max and the girls were up early. They were excited at the thought of going to see Rosie. All of them had bits of news to tell her.

Max had recently been to visit the high school in Edinburgh that his siblings attended, and where he would be starting as a pupil in August. He was keen to tell his mother all about it. He also had his school concert and Primary Seven leavers' ceremony on the coming Wednesday evening. He had a ticket order form for Rosie, for these events. I doubted Rosie would be up to going. But I couldn't say anything, of course.

Jenny was also hoping that Rosie would be at the prizegiving at her school on the following Monday. Jenny was receiving the fifth-year music prize and still had to give her mother the good news. And she wanted her mother to see her playing one of the Pink Ladies in the school's production of *Grease*.

Sam was quiet over breakfast, while the other two chatted about the forthcoming final week of their school year. But she did say she'd be telling Rosie about the good dinner I'd cooked the previous evening, and that Robbie and I had got on well. She said that was the sort of news that would make her mum want to come home. She also suggested that, in view of all the end of term stuff happening the next week, it would make even more sense for Rosie to come home very soon.

The other two were very taken with Sam's assumptions. It was gut-wrenching to see the children so excited and happy at the prospect of visiting their mother and of her, as they saw it, imminent homecoming. I didn't have the heart to even try to dampen down their expectations.

Kirsty and my mother arrived at about half past ten to collect the children. It didn't seem to have occurred to any of them that it was strange to be taken to see their mother. After all they normally got to Edinburgh under their own steam, or I could have dropped them off. Rosie had said to them that Grandma wanted to come too but Grandma's car wasn't big enough for them all. She explained Kirsty had offered to drive them in, as she was shopping in the city anyway. They seemed to have accepted the arrangement without question. As the children got themselves organised to depart, I had a brief chance to talk to my mother and Kirsty.

"They're all excited about seeing Rosie," I said. "It's going to be so hard for them when she breaks the news about the cancer. They were actually saying that they think she'll be ready to come home."

My mother gave me a hug and said she'd do her best to help them. Then Max shouted that he couldn't find his trainers and she went off to help him.

"It's good of you to be taking the time out to drive them to Edinburgh," I said to Kirsty. "You must have lots of weekend stuff of your own to do. I don't understand why Rosie didn't ask me to drive them."

"I don't think it's any reflection on you, Tom. It's going to be difficult enough to tell the children her news without..."

"Without my presence making it even more difficult for her." I finished for her.

"Sorry, I didn't mean..."

"It's all right. I'm glad you're going along, really I am, if it can't be me. You are a good friend to her, so is Lucy. Was it you who was with her when she phoned me yesterday evening, or was it Lucy?"

"It wasn't me. And Lucy's away for the weekend with Graham, the boys are home, minding the farm. Why do you ask?"

"Oh, just curious," I said, trying to sound casual. "Rosie phoned to check that everything was sorted for today. She said she wasn't feeling very well and I offered to go over so she wasn't on her own. But she said there was no need for me to go as she wasn't on her own."

"Right, well it's good she wasn't alone," Kirsty replied. I may have imagined it, but she looked a bit uncomfortable. She certainly seemed keen to change the subject. "Adam's not changed his mind about coming?" she asked.

"No, he's still angry with us. Rosie's asked me to tell him about the cancer and to try again to persuade him to come home."

Kirsty raised her eyebrows. "That's not going to be easy. When will you do it?"

"I thought I'd go later on today, in the afternoon, before the others come back. I think Adam should know about Rosie when his brother and sisters do. But you're right, it's not going to be easy. I just wish he'd come back. I know it's only been a few days, and Ruby'll look after him, but I want him here with the others. He's the most vulnerable of all of them."

"Of course you want him home. But don't underestimate Adam either. He'll get his head round it all in his own good time. He'll be back."

"I hope so. I've made such a mess of things, haven't I?"

Kirsty shook her head and smiled at me. "What matters is what you're doing now, Tom. You're doing well, holding it all together, keeping things as normal as possible for the other children. Your mother was saying how she didn't need to stay here much at all. She said you and Sam are doing a great job of looking after Max and everything else. She also told me about your intention to cut your working hours. That can't have been an easy decision. It's something I often considered when Eilidh was younger, but financial considerations always made it difficult. At least, I used that as an excuse not to go part time."

"At least you thought about it. I never did. But I can see Max needs me to be here, and after today even more so. And I'm still not doing as much as Rosie did for us all. I mean it's nice of you to say I'm doing a good job, but Rosie did it for years and I don't think anyone ever told her they admired her."

"Well, no, I never told her, but I did admire her. I used to think she was as much a single parent as I am, with you working so much."

"In the end it was quite an easy decision, about work, I mean, something I should've done years ago. Maybe, if I had, I wouldn't have lost Rosie."

"That's the benefit of hindsight, Tom. And Rosie's never been one to admit she can't cope. She likes being in control. I don't know that she could've handed over the mothering stuff to you before now. Her leaving, it's not only about you. It's very hard for her being away from the children, especially Max, but she really believes it's best for them. She's so scared of them seeing what she witnessed, when her own mother had cancer. This way she can see them when she's having good days and spare them the bad ones."

"Maybe…"

"Come here. You need a hug," Kirsty held out her arms and I stepped into them. It felt good, to hold and to be held. It felt very different to holding Rosie, but it was soothing and a momentary salve to my loneliness.

Kirsty looked up at me "It's just bad timing. Robbie arriving when Rosie was already at low ebb and then the cancer diagnosis on top of that. You'll come through this. Hang in there."

I couldn't help thinking that a strong relationship would have survived these events, without resulting in a separation, but I didn't say so. I just hugged her close once more.

"Thanks, Kirsty," I whispered.

"Any time," she replied, softly.

"Sorry to interrupt." My mother was back. "We need to get going, Kirsty. The children are ready and Rosie will be waiting." She spoke sharply.

Kirsty quickly stepped away from me. "Of course, yes, sorry.

I'll go and open the car. Bye, Tom."

"Bye, Kirsty, and thanks again." As Kirsty left the room, my mother gave me a disapproving look.

"What? Why are you looking like that?" She shook her head at me. "Oh no, no!" I said. Now it was me shaking my head. "No, Ma, you can't, you don't think that Kirsty and me–"

"No, Tom, I don't, but I do think you need to be careful. You're vulnerable. And you and Kirsty, you're both lonely. It would be easy to… Well, you know. And it wouldn't be right, Tom, not for you or Kirsty, and–"

"Stop it, Ma! Kirsty was simply offering a shoulder to cry on, being reassuring. She said I was doing a good job of keeping my family, what's left of it,  together. It was just a hug between friends. How can you think it would be anything more?"

"I'm sorry. I'm just worried for you, and for Rosie. I suppose I'm trying to keep my family together too. But I do know what it is to be lonely. Just be careful." She reached up and stroked my cheek and then she turned and walked towards the front door. I followed her along the hall and said goodbye to the children. I couldn't watch as the car drove off.

I was finishing clearing away the breakfast debris when Robbie appeared in the kitchen. I'd almost forgotten that he and Dan were both still in the house.

"Good morning," he said shyly.

"Good morning," I replied. "Did you sleep well? I don't know how comfy that sofa bed is."

"Yes, it was fine. I woke up a while ago, but I thought I'd wait till the others left before coming through. I thought you'd want to be with all of them, without me in the way."

"You wouldn't have been in the way, Robbie, but thanks." Not for the first time, I thought what a good job his adoptive parents had done raising him. And I marvelled at how generous they were being about the time he was spending with us. "And your mum didn't mind you staying?"

"No, she was just worried that I was outstaying my welcome,

but I told her that it was you that asked me to stay, not the other way round." He yawned and stretched and scratched at his hair. He looked so like Adam when he did it. For a moment I couldn't speak. I could only stare at him.

"Are you okay?" Robbie asked.

"Yes, yes, sorry. I'm fine. Do you want some breakfast?"

"Yeah, toast and tea. I can get it myself if you tell me where the stuff is."

Having shown him where to find things, I said I was going for a run and that I'd take Toby with me. I told him Dan might appear at any time and to say to him to help himself to breakfast too.

It was a lovely morning, already very warm. The tide was well out. There were other joggers strung out along the length of the beach, as well as dog walkers and couples strolling hand in hand. Even although it was only mid-morning, there were already family groups appearing on the beach with rugs and windbreaks, forming their separate camps on the sand.

There was a young father coaxing two toddlers, twins I reckoned, to leave the security of their blanket and to step out onto the sand with him. The mother laughed from where she was sitting on the blanket. I found myself wondering what troubles might await this happy little family group in the future. The young mum caught my eye and smiled. I thought of a younger Rosie with our twins. I smiled back and then I ran.

I ran hard along the length of the beach. I wouldn't let myself think about Rosie or the children. It was more than I could bear to let myself imagine how it was going to be for all of them today. Toby, who was still being a bit off with me at times, came along, but rather grudgingly I felt. He gave up trying to keep up and went off down to the sea for a swim. He loves the water, but he is not often allowed to partake because of the mess he makes back at the house as he shakes the sand and salt water from his coat. But, that day, I appreciated his need to do something he enjoyed and, for a short time at least, to be free from worrying about other things. I knew Toby probably didn't actually have the capacity to worry, but he was definitely missing Adam and was not his usual self. So I left Toby to his swim, and I ran and ran until I could run no more. I doubled over trying to catch my breath. My chest hurt and my leg muscles were protesting. I thought how embarrassing it would be for me, a cardiologist, to keel over here, on the beach, with a cardiac arrest. My legs buckled and I fell down on my knees. I was gasping for air. Toby appeared. He barked and then let out a little whimper. He licked my face and whimpered again. He sat down beside me. A shadow fell across me. I felt a hand on my shoulder. Toby barked.

A voice said, "Shut up, Toby." He went back to whimpering.

"Crikey, Tom! Breathe mate, breathe. You were going at a hell of a speed. Remember your age, old man." I looked up. It was Dan. I fell back on the sand. He knelt down beside me. "Tom, can you hear me?"

I nodded.

He put his ear to my mouth. "That's it, keep breathing," he said. He took my pulse. "Crikey," he said again and dropped my wrist. "Are you all right?" I nodded again. "Do you need a doctor, an ambulance, or something?"

I shook my head and made a face at him. Wasn't he a doctor? Eventually I could speak. "Where did you spring from?"

"I've been trying to catch up with you all the way along the beach. Robbie told me you'd gone for a run and I fancied joining you. I had my running stuff in the car, and he said you'd just left and I'd easily catch you. Didn't you hear me calling after you?"

"No, sorry, I wanted to push myself, to clear my head of it all for a while, you know?"

"You nearly cleared it permanently. I thought I was going to have dredge up what I could remember of CPR."

"Yeah, trust me to collapse when the only doctor around is a bloody psychiatrist."

"Lucky I was here, you cheeky bugger! I'm no expert but you shouldn't be pushing yourself as hard as that. You were a bit blue around the gills there. You were holding your chest in an alarming way too. When was your last health check, blood pressure, cholesterol, all that?"

"Never you mind," I said.

"What do you... You've never had them checked have you? You haven't, have you? Christ, Tom, you of all people–"

"Yes, yes I just haven't got around to it. I'm fine. I'm not overweight and I jog regularly."

"Oh yeah, you're clearly as fit as a fiddle. Look. promise me, bro' – promise me that you'll go and get a check up."

"Yeah, yeah," I said. Dan shook his head.

We walked back to the house at a sedate pace. Even Toby walked slowly and kept very close to me. Once we were back, Dan said he wouldn't come in and that he'd get off home for a shower and something to eat, if I was sure I was okay. I assured him I was. He said he'd come back later to see how we were all doing.

# Chapter Twenty Six

Robbie was getting ready to leave when I walked in. I couldn't face being in the house on my own, so I said that if he didn't mind waiting while I got a shower, I'd drive him up to Edinburgh. He said a lift would be great and he'd call his mum to let her know. Then he offered to hose Toby down while I was getting ready. And, even though Toby knew what was coming as Robbie opened the back door and called him, and despite the fact he hates the hose, Toby went willingly, in a way he would normally only ever do for Adam.

When I came back down to the kitchen, Toby was getting a blow dry. He looked blissful, as if, at any minute, a grin would break over his doggy face.

"I hope Jenny doesn't mind. I've borrowed her hair drier," Robbie said.

"Toby's certainly not minding," I said, laughing. "He usually has to make do with his stinky old towel."

Robbie switched the drier off. "That'll do you," he said, patting Toby's back. Toby looked hopefully at the drier. "No more," said Robbie. "Go and lie down." The dog retreated to his basket and curled up.

"You're a hit with Toby. He's missing Adam. He's mostly Adam's dog really, he just tolerates the rest of us. And he's been in a real huff with me since Adam left. It's like he knows it's my fault."

"But it's not your fault. It's down to me. I really messed things up and you're all being so nice to me. Maybe I should stop coming round." He looked really stricken.

"Robbie, I told you yesterday, none of this is your fault. Now, no more talk of stopping seeing us. You promised Rosie you'd be around for Max and the girls, didn't you? And apart from that, I want you around."

He seemed to relax a little and he grinned shyly. "Thanks, Tom. I guess I'll be coming back then,"

"And besides, who'll peel the potatoes for me if you're not around?" I said, smiling back at him.

Before we headed off to Edinburgh, I called Adam and prayed he'd answer. He did. I asked if I could come to see him later that afternoon. He sounded a bit wary, but he said he wasn't working till the evening and yes, he would see me. Part of me rejoiced that he'd agreed and part of me was filled with dread because of what I was going to tell him.

Once through Leith, we headed out along Ferry Road towards the Muirhouse area where Robbie lived. "You'll need to give me directions from here," I said, turning down Pennywell Road. Within a few minutes we were drawing up outside Robbie's place.

The house was a neat and modern white-walled semi, situated next door to a primary school. Robbie told me, with obvious pride, that his mum was the school janitor. I'm ashamed to admit I was amazed because I never thought that a woman could, or would want, to be a janitor. The area looked a lot different to the last time I'd been there, when Robbie was a baby. There had been a massive amount of demolition and regeneration.

"Mum said I was to invite you to come in, if you'd like to," Robbie said.

"Oh, right, yes I'd like that very much,"

"Cool."

There was a small, neatly paved garden in front of the house with pots of bright red geraniums placed against the house wall. This was a far cry from the low-rise flats with their long walkways, graffiti covered walls, and general rundown air that I remembered from seventeen years before. The Sutherland's flat had been in one of these grim blocks, though the flat itself had been cosy and welcoming.

Robbie let us in and shouted, "Hi, I'm back," from the hallway.

Sue Sutherland appeared from a room at the end of the hall. She looked older, of course, than when I last saw her. She'd be about fifty now, but she hadn't changed very much. She was still a person of presence, tall and strong looking.

"Dr McAllister," she said, stepping forward with her hand outstretched. "How lovely to see you. How are you?" The smile was the same as I remembered, very wide and warm. Everything about her bearing was reassuring and calm.

"I'm very well, thank you, and it's nice to see you too," I shook her hand. "Please call me Tom."

Robbie said, "Mum, I told you he's not doctor anymore. He's a consultant surgeon, so he's a mister."

"That's me told," his mother replied. "I'm still Mrs Sutherland but you can call me Sue," she said to me, laughing. "Come on through, Tom. Come and have a seat."

Robbie went off upstairs to 'do stuff', as he put it. Sue went through to the kitchen to get us some tea. While I waited I had a look around the room. The walls and shelves were covered in lots of family photographs. Many of them were of Robbie at various ages. One, which looked like a first day at school photo, could easily have been a photo of Adam apart from the hair colour. I was fascinated by the pictures of Robbie and I thought how Rosie would love to see them. I felt a sharp stab of guilt as, once again, I realised what I'd deprived Rosie of by keeping Robbie a secret. To distract myself from this painful line of thinking I looked out of the window. Outside was one of the most colourful gardens I've ever seen.

"Here we are," Sue said, arriving with two mugs.

"Thank you." I said, taking one from her. "I was admiring your lovely garden. You must spend a lot of time getting it to look so good."

"Oh it's not me that's responsible, that's Bob's department. He spends all his spare time either working in the garden or tinkering with engines."

Sue told me how her husband had kept their various second-hand cars on the road over the years, as well as tending to his beloved motor bikes. She said that with the family to look after, and her job as janitor at the local primary school, she had quite enough on her plate.

"Mind you," she said, "I'd not be able to do it without Bob. He's always got stuck in at home. We couldn't have done all the fostering or the adoption if we hadn't both been pulling our weight. I couldn't be doing with a man who didn't roll his sleeves up and do his share at home." I'm not sure I didn't blush when I heard her last statement.

I ended up staying for lunch. Robbie was there and I met Julie, also seventeen years old, and also adopted. She was very quiet and was dressed all in black. Bob arrived when we were half way through lunch, having finished his shift driving the number twenty-three bus. He appeared in the kitchen, where we were all squeezed round the table, and he seemed to completely fill the space that was left, standing there in his motor bike leathers, with his crash helmet in his hand. He greeted me warmly, as if it was the most natural thing in the world for me to be there.

After lunch both Robbie and Julie said they were going out for the afternoon. Sue, Bob and I went through to the living room, where I was talked through the family photo gallery. I saw pictures of Robbie from babyhood to the present and heard many stories of his childhood. They seemed to be a very close couple with tremendously big hearts.

Bob was keen to show me Robbie's paintings. He guided me through the contents of a large folder. There were sketches and paintings of family members and pets, as well as some still-life and landscape work. He also pointed out two framed pictures on the living room wall that he said had been done by Robbie. One was a small still-life of motor bike parts. The other was a watercolour, showing part of the garden. Robbie had clearly inherited his mother's artistic talents.

Bob said Robbie's art teacher spoke very highly of his talent, and that Robbie wanted to study art when he left school. Sue commented that this was great, but she felt that he should do something more practical and keep art as a hobby.

However, Bob said that if Robbie really wanted to work as an artist then he should go for it. "Robbie has choices, opportunities I never had and I think he should go for it. Imagine us being the parents of a famous artist one day!" Bob beamed at the thought.

"Robbie's biological mother was an artist wasn't she?" asked Sue.

"Yes, yes she was," I replied. I felt a bit awkward talking about Heather. It must have shown.

"I'm sorry," Sue said. "I know it didn't work out for her and it must be painful for you to talk about. At the time of the fostering, and then the adoption, we were told a bit about Robbie's mother and her circumstances of course, as you know. And you and the other man, your brother was it, who came to see us at the time? You told us bits and pieces too."

"My brother-in-law," I said. "It was Heather's brother, Dr Finch, who came with me. How much does Robbie know about his birth mother?"

"He knows most of what we know. We've told him it bit by bit as he's got older. He knows that she had a difficult time as a young woman because she was on drugs, and that it took many years for her to get clean. But he knows too that she was sorting her life out by the time she was pregnant with him and that he was a very wanted baby. He knows she loved him. We just told him this year that she killed herself, although he's always known that she died." Sue paused, cleared her throat. "We haven't told him about the reasons yet, but we will, once the knowledge of her suicide sinks in."

I felt even more awkward now. "How did he take it – the suicide?" I asked.

"He was shocked, of course. It led to lots of other questions. It was then he started talking about finding your wife and you, and your family. He started to ask about his father too, of course – his biological father. But we said we couldn't answer that. He wanted to know everything he could possibly could. We tried to persuade him to wait. We thought we'd convinced him. We did intend to go through the proper channels."

"Yes, he explained that. Don't worry. He said he'd acted without your approval."

"It must've been such a shock for you all, him turning up. We know you wanted a clean break at the time."

"It was certainly a shock. We knew a young lad was coming to see us at the house, but the name Robbie didn't mean anything to me. I still thought of him as James, the name Heather gave him. It was her father's name." Then it clicked, her father was James Robert. "You changed to using his middle name," I said.

"Yes, with Robert being Bob's name, we decided it was a nice father son link, and Robbie suited him," Sue said.

I nodded. "When I did realise who he was, I didn't handle it well. I'm sure Robbie's told you. And I had my reasons for not telling my wife about him."

"Robbie's told us about your – your situation with your wife," said Sue. "And he also told us about your son, Adam. He feels bad about him and that he's to blame."

"I know he does and I've tried my best to reassure him that it's not his fault. It's down to me, I'm afraid. I've mishandled the whole matter."

"Well, from what Robbie says, you're fine with him now. The past can't be undone and we never doubted you wanted what was best for him. We've always told him that."

I was touched by that and I said it was clear Robbie couldn't have had better parents.

"It's very nice of you to say so," Sue said. "We couldn't have children of our own, but it's been a privilege to have Robbie, and we're grateful to have had the chance to be his mum and dad."

Hearing Sue say this, I wished Rosie could hear it too. I said it would be good if they could meet Rosie and the rest of the family some time, and they agreed that it was something they'd very much like to do. By the time I left their house, I felt my burden of guilt to be slightly lighter.

# Chapter Twenty Seven

As I drove along Ferry Road, heading for home, I thought about the Sutherlands and Robbie and the closeness of their family. It gave me a strong urge to go and see Rosie and the children. Rosie would've told the children about the cancer by now, and I wanted to be there for all of them.

Next thing I knew, I'd turned the car and was heading over to the south side of the city. I made the unlikely find of a parking space in the Morningside street where the flat was. As I walked up the path to the stair door, I glanced in the bay window of the front room. What I saw stopped my progress and flooded me with a clammy nausea.

Max and the girls were together on the sofa. Sam had her arm round Max's shoulders and her head was inclined towards him obscuring his face. She seemed to be talking to him. Jenny was leaning forward and looking up, as if about to stand. I followed her gaze and saw that she was looking at Rosie. Rosie, standing in the arms of a man, in the arms of Rick Montgomery to be precise. Rick, Lucy's brother, supposed absentee tenant of the flat, and one time boyfriend of my wife. As I watched he stroked Rosie's back and then held out an arm to Jenny. She walked over to him and her mother and he embraced her too.

I turned and ran. It took all my self control not to throw up there in the street. I got into the car, my mind buzzing with questions. What was going on? How long had Rick been back? Was he staying at the flat? What was he doing with his arms round my wife and my daughter? Where were Kirsty and my mother?

I don't remember much about the drive back to East Lothian. But I do remember deciding I wasn't going to mention the fact I'd gone to the flat to anyone. Not yet anyway, I needed to think. And before I could do that I had to visit Adam. I fought to suppress the ghastly image of that man's arms round my Rosie.

Ruby was aware I was coming and knew what I had to tell Adam. When she let me into the house she didn't say very much. She must've sensed that I just wanted to get it over with, and I was grateful to her for that. She did say that no-one else was in and to stay as long as I liked. Then she called upstairs to Adam and left me to wait for him in the front room. I felt dreadful, very apprehensive and took several deep breaths to calm myself down.

As I waited for my son, the scene I'd witnessed at the flat broke through my fragile defences. The nausea and panic returned. My hands trembled and sweat trickled down my back. Even though I was sitting down I felt unsteady. So I grasped at whatever I could, at whichever of the myriad thoughts racing round my head offered any kind of hope. If I could just persuade Adam to come home then Rosie would come back too. She wouldn't be able to resist being with her beloved Adam, would she? And she'd be so impressed with me, grateful even. Then I could work on her, show her I'd changed, wrestle her out of Rick's clutches. Maybe when I told Adam that Rosie was ill and he was still in shock he'd be susceptible to the suggestion. Looking back, I'd like to think that there was, somewhere in my mind, a seed of self-disgust that I would even consider manipulating my wife and son in this way, but at the time…

"What do you want, Dad?" said Adam, coming into the room. He sat opposite me.

"I wanted, that is, your mother wanted, your mother asked me to come and see you." My mouth felt parched. "And I wanted to see you too," I added hastily.

"I'm not coming home, if that's what she wanted you to say."

I didn't miss a beat. "Of course, that's what Mum and I both want, but no, that's not why I'm here, not the main reason anyway."

"So, what is the main reason?"

"I need to tell you something, something important and serious about your mother. Max and the girls have been told. They went to see Mum today as you know."

He looked wary now. "What do you mean serious?"

"Adam, your mum's ill. She has cancer – breast cancer – and she's undergoing treatment for it at the moment. She's had an operation and now she's receiving drug therapy." I tried to swallow, tried to keep breathing.

Adam looked horrified. "I don't believe you! Mum can't have cancer. She can't. You're lying, trying to make me come home." He was on his feet, pacing, running his hands through his hair.

I stood up too. All thoughts of using his distress to my advantage were gone. Christ, we could lose Rosie to the cancer. I couldn't manipulate us out of that.

I went to him. I put my arms round him. He fought me off, but I persisted in trying to hold him. "It's true, son. It's true. I wish it wasn't, but it's true." I had tears in my eyes. He looked into my face. I nodded at him. He crumpled and stopped fighting against me.

He was crying now. "No, no, not Mum," he sobbed into my shoulder.

"She's getting good treatment. She'll get better." I stroked his back.

He broke away from me. "You don't know that! You can't know that! People die of cancer. Gran died of it, didn't she? Mum might die too." I reached out to him, but he pushed me away. He sat down and put his head in his hands.

"Yes, it's serious, Adam," I said. "Yes, people die from cancer, but lots of people survive it."

"And you think Mum'll survive?" he looked up at me.

"I can't – I don't – we can't know for sure, son," I sat down again too. "But she's taking all the treatment she's offered and she's got lots of things in her favour. The cancer was picked up quite early and she's being well looked after." I didn't sound convincing, even to myself.

"So, is Mum coming home – so you can look after her?"

And there it was. The question was back, hanging there. I could take it down, use it. "Not at the moment," I answered. "She prefers to do this her way. She thinks she can cope better if she stays at the flat for the time being."

"Why – why does she? She's still angry with you. isn't she – about Robbie?"

"It's partly that, but it's – it's complicated. I know she'd like it – and so would I, of course, if you'd come home."

I could have left it at that. But no. The Rosie and Rick scene was back. Adrenalin spurred me on. I jumped to my feet, began to pace. "If you'd come home, if you'd just come back, then Mum–"

"No!" Adam stood up to face me. "No, way! I'm not coming back. A look of fear crossed his face. "I can't come back."

He sank into the nearest chair and looked up at the ceiling, pressing the heels of his hands into his eyes. But tears still ran down his face. "Mum," he groaned. "Oh fuck, oh fuck."

I went to him and put my hand on his shoulder.

He pushed me away. "Get off me! Leave me alone! Mum's going to die and I'm never coming home."

"Don't, Adam, please. I don't care about the exams, uni, it doesn't matter, please just come back." I meant what I said. It wasn't a sly move. Yes it was born out of desperation, but Adam's future was just that, something for later. Right now it was the present that mattered.

But Adam wasn't having it, wasn't convinced. I couldn't blame him.

"Yeah, right," was all he said.

I held up my arms in a gesture of despair. I looked at Adam, at his face. I wasn't sure exactly what his expression was. I'd expected anger, contempt even, at my manoeuvrings, but no, it was neither of those. I think what I saw was pity. He slowly shook his head. I had to look away.

I stood looking out the window for a moment, hating myself. Christ, had I learned nothing lately? This wasn't about me or what *I* was prepared to do. I turned back to face my son.

"Will you at least think about going to see Mum?" I pleaded. "I know she'd like that, Adam. I know you're angry with us both, but Mum needs you to forgive her and she needs to see you."

He looked wary again. "I don't know."

"Think about it. Will you, please?" He nodded slowly. I knew I should probably go. I'd got as far as I could for that visit. I told Adam to call me anytime and that I'd see him again very soon.

He shrugged and said, "Whatever."

I couldn't help feeling I was getting the blame for Rosie being ill, on top of everything else he held against me. On my way out, I spoke to Ruby and asked her to keep an eye on him. She said she would and patted my arm comfortingly as she said goodbye. I didn't deserve her comfort. I did not feel good about myself.

Not long after I got home, Kirsty and my mother arrived with Max and the girls. The children were very quiet as they came into the house with their grandmother. Kirsty stayed in the car. All three had obviously been crying. Sam was very pale. I held out my arms to them.

"Oh, Dad," Sam said, as she came to me. I put one arm round her. Max ran and put his arms round my waist and Jenny came into my other arm. My mother looked stricken too. She said she'd phone me later. I could only nod at her as she left.

All thoughts of Rick, and what was going on with him and Rosie, had to be put to one side as, for the next couple of hours, I comforted my children and tried to allay their fears about their mother. I had to focus only on them, for the time being. I didn't mention Rick, and they didn't speak about him to me.

Dan arrived around seven. He'd brought three large pizzas with him and he did his usual thing of lightening everyone's mood.

When my mother phoned later, I asked her if she'd stayed with the children while Rosie broke the news. She said she hadn't, that she and Kirsty had dropped the children off and then gone for a walk in the Hermitage Park nearby, and from there to a coffee shop. She said that Rosie had wanted to be alone with the children. I didn't say that Rosie hadn't been alone. My mother didn't mention Rick, and I felt sure she was unaware he'd been there.

I phoned Kirsty after speaking to my mother. I thanked her for what she'd done that day. She said that was what friends were for and it was a small thing to do. She didn't mention Rick either and, for some reason, I couldn't bring myself to ask her if she knew anything.

When I called Rosie the following morning, I told myself that I was just phoning to check how she was, and to tell her about my visit to the Sutherlands, and to Adam. But I knew that what I really wanted to do was to suggest going to see her. I wanted to see her face to face and tell her about my visits the day before. But I also wanted to tell her all the stuff that had happened with Heather seventeen years before. And I wanted to see if she'd tell me about Rick.

The conversation began pleasantly enough. Rosie wanted to know how the children were. I told her they were coping and that I realised the previous day must have been very difficult for her. I asked how she was doing. She said she was very tired.

I told her how I'd got on with Adam, leaving out my pathetic pleadings. She was concerned about how he'd taken the news of her illness. I tried to put as positive a spin as I could on what he'd said. She was grateful I'd told him. She seemed to accept I'd done my best.

She asked me to explain, again, to Jenny and Max that she wouldn't be at their end of term plays and prize-givings. Apart from not feeling up to it, she'd been advised to avoid large gatherings of people because of her lowered immunity due to the chemo. She said she'd tried to explain it to the children already, but she wasn't sure they'd taken it in.

She was keen to hear how the meal with Robbie had gone, and was surprised and interested when I told her about meeting his parents.

It was when I asked if I could see her later that things deteriorated. "I'd like to come to the flat, Rosie. I'd like to see you. I can tell you about the Sutherlands and all the stuff that happened around the time Robbie was born. I need to tell you more about that."

She hesitated before she answered. "I don't know. It's–"

"Please, Rosie." I'd like to see you. I came to see you yesterday, actually. I needed to be with you and the kids."

"You came yesterday? When?"

"In the afternoon, on my way back from the Sutherlands. I got as far as the stair door. I looked in the window. I saw him, Rosie. I saw Rick with you and the children. So–"

"So, what?"

"So I couldn't come in."

"Why not? Why couldn't you?"

"Because he was there. Rick was there. He had his arm round you. I thought–"

"You thought what, Tom? What did you think?" She sounded angry now.

"I don't – I didn't–"

"You think me and Rick, you think we're together, in a relationship – a sexual relationship, don't you?"

I was thrown by her directness. "Yes – no – I mean I–"

"Fuck off, Tom! Fuck off! How dare you? How dare you spy on me and then make assumptions and judgements? After what you've done!"

"I didn't. I wasn't. I thought he was away.

"Rick is home just now, home here at the flat. Remember it's his home? He pays us rent." She sounded sarcastic now. "He arrived back last week. And it's been good to have him around.

193

He's been very understanding about my situation."

"Well, that's nice for you." Now who was being sarcastic?

"Yes, it is. It's very nice actually. We're going out for a short walk and then he's going to cook, see if he can tempt me to eat. So don't come to the flat, Tom. It's not convenient and I really don't want you to."

"Please, Rosie. I need to see you. I could go for a walk with you, cook you something. You don't need Rick Montgomery to do that. I love you, Rosie. Please."

"No, Tom. I can't see you just now. If you really do love me, then please leave me be."

"I don't want to. I want you to be with you. We need to talk at least."

"I know we do, but not yet. I'm not ready. I need to be by myself for now."

"But you're not by yourself are you? You're with him, with Rick."

"You're being ridiculous. I'm not with Rick, not in the way you mean."

"What am I supposed to think, Rosie?"

"I don't know. That's up to you and whether you trust me. It's not a nice feeling is it, not knowing whether your partner can be trusted?" She spoke more quietly now. "Look, I have to go. Thanks for letting me know about the children and for telling Adam. I'm glad about you and Robbie and the Sutherlands. It's great, really."

"Yes, but–"

"And I do need you to let me know how the children are. I mean how they *really* are. I know they'll put on a brave face for me. So do keep calling me. And keep in touch with Adam, keep trying with him. You'll do that, won't you?

"Of course I will."

"Good. But please, don't come round. Please, promise me you'll let me do things my way for now."

"I don't understand this need you have to be away from us,

from me. I just want to take care of you."

"I know you do. That's how we got into this mess, Tom. You taking care of things and me letting you. So can you promise to let me take care of myself for now?"

Reluctantly, I promised.

# Chapter Twenty Eight

For the first few days after their visit to Rosie, Max and the girls were in shock.

Max asked lots of questions and got very cross if I couldn't give definitive and positive answers. Like Adam, he wanted me to answer the question of whether his mother would die from her cancer with an unequivocal no. He wanted to know exactly how long his mother would be ill. He wanted to know why I wasn't treating her and making her better. He wanted to know why she wasn't coming home and having me as her doctor. These and other questions were asked several times over and on different occasions. They'd be reworded and reframed, as if, by reshaping them, he would get a different and more acceptable answer. I didn't want to mislead him or give him false hope, but I also wanted to give him something to hold onto. I don't think I made a good job of it.

One evening, about two weeks after Rosie told the children she was ill, and just after he'd returned from staying with Rosie for several days, Max came through to the den. I was busy doing some paperwork. He was in his pyjamas, standing just inside the door and his expression was fearful, almost haunted.

"Does the doctor that's treating Mum really know what he's doing?" he asked, yet again.

"Yes, Maxy, as I've said before, he's one of the best there is."

"And have the other people that he's treated – who had the same as Mum – have they got better?"

I so wanted to lie, but I knew I mustn't. "Well, yes, he has made some of them better."

"But not all?"

No, not all. But I'm sure he'll do his best to make Mum feel better."

His face flushed and he started to cry. I went to get up, to console him, but he flew into a rage, pummelling the sofa with his fists and feet. I let him go, let him get it all out.

Eventually he said, "But will he be able to cure Mum? Will he? What if he can't? What if he can't?" He was all anger and fear. His eyes were huge and there was such pain on his face.

I got up and went to him. I put my arms round him. He hammered at my chest with his fists. He tried to push me away but I held on tight as he sobbed and shouted, "No, no," and "Mum, Mum."

When he was exhausted and offering no resistance, I guided him over to the battered old sofa under the window and sat with him. He leant against me and I stroked his hair. He wept quietly and for a long time. In the end he fell asleep there on the sofa. I picked him up and carried him upstairs to his room.

As I bent to put him into his bed he opened his eyes and whispered, "Your bed." So I took him through and placed him on Rosie's side of our bed. "Love you, Dad," he said as he settled in under the duvet.

From then on it became a regular thing for Max to sleep beside me. He would appear during the night and climb in the bed. He seemed, at those times, to be in a semi-sleepwalking state. It didn't bother me to have him with me. In fact it was a comfort to me too. I'd been finding it increasingly difficult to sleep alone in the big, empty bed.

The girls on the other hand were quiet and didn't share their worries very readily with me. They talked to each other about Rosie's cancer and I know they looked up breast cancer on the internet. They were very sweet with me, very sensitive to how I might be feeling.

One time, during the first couple of weeks after hearing of

their mother's illness, I walked in on them in the den and they were at the computer. They quickly closed down what they were looking at, but not before I noticed that it was a cancer website they'd been on.

They talked to my mother about the disease and about Rosie's chances of survival. It was she who confirmed that they were doing their own research because they didn't want to upset me.

Sam swung between wanting to be with her mother and feeling very angry and resentful at Rosie's absence. One day I came home earlier than expected and found Sam sitting in the living-room crying. She tried hard to cover up the fact she was upset, but I couldn't play along. My heart went out to her and I couldn't pretend not to have noticed her distress.

"What's wrong, sweetheart?" I sat down and slipped my arm round her shoulders. It turned out she'd been to see Rosie that day. Rosie had been feeling unwell and her hair had started to fall out. She'd had her second dose of chemo earlier that week.

"I hate seeing her like that, Dad. She seems so weak, not like Mum at all."

I hugged her. "I know. It's the treatment, the chemo. Try not to worry. Once she's finished the course she'll get stronger."

"But you didn't see her. She kept being sick and she's really thin. You should go and see her. You'd know what to do, wouldn't you, if you saw her?"

I shrugged. "I don't think–"

"You could persuade her to come home, if you really tried. She's being stupid, being angry about you and Robbie. She should've got over that by now."

"It's not only about me not telling her about Robbie. There's more to it than that." I wanted Sam to understand, but I couldn't tell her what Rosie suspected about me and Heather, or about how much she resented my over-protective attitude. "I'm not what your Mum needs right now. I promised her I'd let her do this her way, on her own."

"You shouldn't have bloody promised!" With that, Sam left,

slamming the door behind her.

I agreed with Sam. I wished I hadn't promised to stay away and I desperately wanted to see Rosie and to help her. I hadn't seen her for about three weeks at that point, not since the day I'd told her about Adam and she'd told me she was ill.

Fortunately, Sam did not remain angry with me for long. Later, the same day, she came and put her head round the door of the den. "Sorry, Dad," she said.

I stood up and held out my arms to her. "Come here. I'm sorry too," I said, as we hugged.

"You don't need to be sorry. I'm just worried about Mum and I wish she was here with us."

"I know you do, love. We all want her well and home. But we have to be patient and give her the time and space she needs."

"It's just, it's hard, you know?" Sam was crying again. All I could do was hold her.

Jenny was probably the strongest of all of us. Although she could be very intense and serious about all sorts of things and had a very sensitive nature, she was also very resilient and determined. She was just as worried about her mother as the rest of us and she missed her twin terribly, but she was able to channel her worry and concern into practical action.

For Rosie, Jenny researched breast cancer treatments and sources of support. Jenny'd been learning to drive since her birthday, the previous April, and she got me and her Uncle Dan to take her out for practice sessions. In the middle of July she passed her test first time. I told her about the Maggie's Centre, a place of respite for cancer patients at the hospital, and suggested she might like to drive Rosie there, which she did. She also drove Rosie to her chemotherapy appointments on a few occasions.

But, it was in her efforts to get Adam back home and communicating with Rosie, that Jenny was at her most indefatigable. Jenny'd always been protective of her twin brother. Adam didn't speak until he was nearly four and, up till then, Jenny did all his talking for him. Even once he started talking, she continued to speak up for him, if she thought his needs weren't being met. She'd interpret his mood for the uncomprehending adults at home and nursery school, telling us when he was hungry, or tired or scared. She also stood up for him if another child looked as if they might be about to bully or hurt her brother, even if she got into trouble for being over zealous in her protection. And Jenny continued to feel she had to look out for her brother, even into their teenage years. She said to me that she felt guilty she hadn't realised how Adam was feeling before he ran away. She was annoyed at herself for being so wrapped up in her show rehearsals that she didn't notice he wasn't at school. No amount of reassurance from me would ease her sense of having failed her brother.

So she made it her mission to get Adam talking to Rosie and to get him to come home. She went to see him regularly at Ruby's. At first she went alone. Then later she got Robbie and Eilidh to go with her on some of the visits. Kirsty's daughter, Eilidh, was one of Jenny's closest friends. Jenny explained that Eilidh being there made the visits less intense. She also said that Eilidh was someone who Adam liked and trusted. She was sure that if Adam got to know Robbie, he'd be much more relaxed about coming home. Sometimes they all hung out at Ruby's, but at other times the three of them would visit Adam at the karting centre. They'd even been to Robbie's house on a couple of occasions.

Apart from our worries about Adam and Rosie, the four of us, Sam, Jenny, Max and I, got along quite well.

Ruby propped us up with her sheer common sense and practical support. Her unyielding positivity was refreshing and energizing. She watched over Adam and, although, at the time, we missed having him with us at home, he was in the best place. It was good Jenny was seeing him, but if he'd been at home the strain would have been unbearable for both of us. I think we'd have continued to argue and resolved nothing. I'd have been impatient with him and he'd have dug his heels in. It would also have been difficult to have Robbie round and get to know him.

There really was no thank you big enough to express my gratitude to Ruby for what she did that summer. But when I tried to tell her so, she'd just shake her head and walk away, embarrassed.

In the last week before school broke up, I went along to Max's school concert and Primary Seven presentation. I felt very proud of him as he was awarded his graduation certificate and his book token. He also took part in a leavers' rap he'd written it with his friends, Connor and Neil. He brought the house down with his impressions of various members of staff.

I also visited Rosie's class one afternoon, to deliver a letter from her to them. I'd been a bit apprehensive about doing this, but Rosie was very keen that I go in person with the letter, and it felt good to be able to do something for her. It was scary speaking to the class, but they were thrilled to hear from her and had made her a card. I hadn't realised how loved she was as a teacher, another humbling experience in what was becoming a long list for me.

During the same week I went to see Jenny in *Grease*, at her school. I thought she was the best actress and singer in it, of course. It was nice to be at the school for a happy reason. My previous couple of visits had been to discuss Adam's situation, and to get the school to agree to hold his place until the new session.

I videoed both Max's and Jenny's performances for Rosie to watch, and I heard from the children that all three of them enjoyed an evening at the flat spent watching the footage.

As the summer progressed, I settled into my job-share with Anna. She'd been taken aback when I asked her about job-sharing the consultant's post. But she'd been very happy about it once she got over the shock.

Sam continued to do a lot of the domestic work at home, but she and Ruby also took me in hand and trained me up in the many tasks that had hitherto been a mystery to me. I was soon able to do the weekly shop at the supermarket and to both load and set off the washing machine.

Sam, Ruby, my mother and I also made sure that one of us was always around for Max, when he wasn't staying with Rosie. Andy was enlisted to teach me the rudiments of cooking and Sheena supplied several more recipes. I took Sheena out for a meal as a thank you for her life-saving coq au vin recipe. We spent a very pleasant evening. Sheena was good company, and I saw a much more relaxed side to her than I did at work.

My mother supported me in my efforts to get the garden into some sort of order and I conscripted Max to help me. I felt connected to Rosie while I worked amongst her beloved plants. It was like it gave me something tangible to offer her. And it was also good fun to be working with Ma and Max.

About half way through the school holidays Max, his friend Neil and I went away for a few days camping up north. Dan and Andy came along too. I actually enjoyed our time away and I think Max did too. The five of us had a lot of laughs and it was good to see Max enjoying himself. For me it was good to get a break from the house.

I loved our home, but without Rosie and Adam it could be unbearable at times. I missed the thumping base that used to emanate from Adam's room and the sound of him clattering down the stairs. And I continued to miss Rosie's music.

One summer afternoon, when I came home from work, I heard the piano being played. It was a Chopin piece, one of Rosie's. I flung open the dining-room door. But, of course, it was Jenny playing. She could tell by my face what I'd been hoping, that for a few insane seconds, I'd hoped it was Rosie playing. She apologised, saying that she found it comforting to play things her mother loved. I told her not to be sorry and asked her to play again for me. It was both painful and pleasurable to listen.

During the school holidays I also managed to get Max to the barber's and to an overdue dental check up. I grew to admire Rosie even more as I discovered first hand how tricky, and how tiring, it could be doing all the domestic stuff and working.

However, much as I enjoyed being with the children and, much as I regretted all the time I'd missed being an active father to them, I still loved my job. I still found myself driving home on a high after a day in theatre. I found my work to be great therapy when the missing of Rosie and Adam got to be too much.

At times the craving to see Rosie was agonising, but I stuck to my promise and let her be. I got into a pattern of phoning her twice a week, once at the weekend and once during the week on a day when I wasn't working. I looked forward to these calls so much that they became the highlights of my week. I longed to hear her voice, and even managed to make her laugh at times, with some of the daft stories I told about how we were all getting along. To hear her laugh made me feel so good, for a few, all too brief, moments. I would find myself saving up little bits of chat about the kids or my mother or Ruby or even about work, just so I could keep her on the line a bit longer. I think we both tried to keep the calls as light-hearted as possible.

Because the children went on regular visits, I knew from them that Rick was still staying at the flat. Jenny explained he was between assignments and that his job up north had finished earlier than expected. She said he was going away again soon and that he usually went out when any of the children were visiting. Jenny seemed completely relaxed about Rick being at the flat.

Sam, on the other hand, was not. She asked me about Rick one day, when we were putting away the grocery shopping.

"Dad, if I ask you something will you please not get upset?"

My heart missed a beat, in a way that will be familiar to any parents of teenagers when asked this type of question. I'd no idea what might be coming. Was it a request for permission for a tattoo? Was she going to ask me how I'd feel about her moving in with a boyfriend whose existence I knew nothing about? Or did she want to know how I'd feel about becoming a grandfather sooner than expected? My mind whirled through the potential questions.

"I'll do my best," I answered weakly.

"Are Mum and Rick, that is, do you think they're having an affair?"

I hadn't seen that one coming. It was a question I couldn't bear to think about, even although it popped into my head several times a day. But Sam was looking at me with expectation. She clearly needed me to think about it and to tell her my thoughts.

"I – I don't think so. That is, I hope not. They went out together at uni, before Mum and I met, and they've sort of kept in touch, but that's mainly because Mum and Lucy are friends. It just so happens that they're sharing Granddad's flat now. It wasn't planned or anything. I think Mum's got enough on her plate getting better. She's not going to be…" I couldn't complete that sentence. "They're mates Sam. That's all, just mates. I love Mum and she loves me." I ran out of things to say.

"Are you sure, really sure, Dad?"

"Yes, Sam," I tried my best to speak with conviction. And then I couldn't help myself. "Why do you ask?"

"Oh, it's just he's usually there when I arrive, and comes back before I leave. Mum's always so pleased to see him, and he puts his arm round her and stuff. I don't like it. I can't explain."

It wasn't easy but I tried to keep my voice neutral, reasonable. "It must be nice for Mum to have company, especially if she's feeling poorly. No wonder she's pleased to see him. According to Jenny he gets her shopping and helps her around the flat. And anyway he'll be away again soon."

"I suppose so. I don't know how Jenny can be so cool with it, though. I think he's a creep."

Somehow I restrained myself from openly agreeing with her sentiments. "Try not to worry about it, sweetheart. There's nothing going on, I'm sure."

Max was simply happy to spend time with Rosie and, mercifully, he wasn't distracted by Rick. He never really mentioned him in relation to Rosie. He said Rick had a cool car and was impressed by all his camera equipment, but that was about it. My mother or Sam took Max to see Rosie regularly. If Rosie was up to it they went for a walk. If not they watched DVDs together or he played his football manager game, a gift from Dan, that Dan had installed on Rosie's laptop for just such occasions. At those times, Max said, Rosie would lie on the couch while he played and they'd chat about stuff or Rosie would sleep for a little while.

It was through the children that I got to know how Rosie really was. She never said much to me about the illness or her treatment when I phoned. I knew she was often sick at first, but that the anti-sickness drugs helped a bit. I knew she'd lost all her hair. Jenny thought she looked cool bald. Sam said it was awful to see her without hair. Max wouldn't let her go out without her wig, which the girls said she hated, and he was terrified that anyone he knew would see his mother without her hair. Apparently she didn't eat much, as she said everything tasted of metal, but she'd developed a liking for Starburst sweets and Jaffa cakes.

Then, at the beginning of August, just after I'd returned from the camping trip, there was a breakthrough. Adam asked to see Rosie.

# Chapter Twenty Nine

He just came out with it. Jenny was visiting Adam one Friday, after she'd finished work and, while they were in the middle of talking about something else, he said he wanted to see his mother.

When Jenny got home she hurtled through the front door, shouting, asking where I was. She almost collided with me in the doorway of the kitchen. She was so excited.

"Dad, oh, Dad, you're not going to believe this!" She grasped both my arms. "It's Adam, he wants to see Mum. Isn't that just the best news?"

It was encouraging, of course, the kind of progress I'd been desperate for, but I was wary of getting too carried away. However, Jenny's enthusiasm was infectious.

I laughed as I hugged her. "It's great, Jenny. How did you do it?

"Well, I'd like to take some of the credit, of course, but I think it was Robbie who swung it in the end. The two of them have been spending quite a bit of time together, at Ruby's and at Robbie's. Adam just said that something Robbie mentioned to him yesterday made him think he needed to see Mum and he wants to see you too."

I took a minute to digest this. "Did he mention coming home? Did you ask him?"

"Of course I asked. He said no, he isn't coming home, not yet anyway, but that after talking to Robbie he wanted to see you and Mum and talk to you both together."

Again I paused to absorb what she'd said. Jenny shook my arm. "What are you waiting for, Dad? Phone Mum, let her know. We need to get this set up."

"Right," I laughed. "Yes, Ma'am. I'll call her right now." Jenny went off to tell Sam and Max, and I did as I was ordered.

"Hello, Rosie," I said, as I took the phone through to the relative quiet of the den. I told her Jenny's news.

"Oh, Tom, that's fantastic. Clever Jenny!" I could hear the smile in her voice as she spoke. "I'm, I can't believe, I..." her voice broke up. "Oh, Tom," she said again, really softly this time.

"I know, Rosie. I know. It's great, isn't it?" My own voice had gone quite weak and there was an ache at the back of my throat. I paused as, despite my efforts to maintain a sense of perspective, relief and joy flooded through me, threatening to reduce me to a whimpering idiot.

"So what do we do now?" Rosie regained the power of speech before I did.

"I don't know. He says he's not coming home, not yet anyway. He wants to see us both and talk before he'll consider it."

"We could both meet him here, at the flat. At least that way it won't matter how I'm feeling. Would he do that do you think? Would he come here? Would you bring him here?"

I hesitated before I answered. I was amazed Rosie wanted us to meet Adam together, amazed and heartened. But I knew I mustn't over-react or read too much into it.

Rosie must have sensed what I was thinking. "I think Adam needs to see us united, as his parents, that's what he's asking for. So we should meet him together and explain what's going on. He needs reassurance from us both, Tom. We didn't make a very good job of reassuring him before and now we've got a second chance. And I'd like you to be here when he sees me for the first time since – since my – since the cancer."

I did my best to keep my voice level. "Okay then, let's ask him to come to the flat. I'll get it set up and let you know."

It was actually Jenny who set it up. She phoned him the

same evening and asked him to come to the flat the next day, a Saturday, in the afternoon. She had the day off work and offered to come too, something we all thought was a good idea. For me, that evening, there was the very pleasant task of phoning my mother, and of course, Ruby to give them the good news. At least, I hoped it was good news. As I came out of the euphoria of the mere fact that Adam wanted to see Rosie and me, some niggling doubts appeared. What if Adam wanted to tell us exactly what he thought of us, and not in a good way, and that he was leaving, going travelling, off to London, Africa, Australia, and to hell with us?

The next day I was up very early. I'd been too wound up to sleep properly. It was the first night in a long time that Max hadn't come through to sleep beside me, which was just as well, for his sake, as I was so restless.

It was a dull, damp morning but I was hopeful the sun would break through by lunchtime.

I couldn't wait for the afternoon but I also felt apprehensive. I'd be seeing Adam and Rosie, which was good, but I was also scared. I was scared that if Adam was prepared to come home, I'd say the wrong thing and mess up in some way, or that Adam would declare his contempt for us and announce his imminent departure from Scotland, and Rosie would have even more to blame me for. As usual, when the pressure was on, I decided to go for a run along the beach. Toby came too.

The running helped. I managed to focus on the possibility of a positive outcome to the meeting with Adam. After all, Jenny had been so enthused, hadn't she? She would have picked up on anything negative in Adam's manner or intention. I was still nervous, but optimistically so.

The dog seemed to pick up on my nervousness and would periodically stop running along beside me and jump up and bark. I found myself saying to him in a barely suppressed shout, "They're coming home Toby, they're coming home! Adam and Rosie are coming home!" This made him bark all the more.

Of course, I knew they wouldn't come home right away, that day, but surely they'd come soon. I was now convinced Adam wanted to see us for all the right reasons. I was getting on okay with Robbie. And, once I told Rosie the whole story of what happened seventeen years ago, she'd understand and come home. Adam would see everything was back to normal and then he'd come back. It didn't matter if Adam had messed up his exams, the results were due the following week, he could re-sit next year, if he wanted to, and I'd be around more to help him. Oh, I had it all worked out. I simply had to be careful not to say the wrong thing. I just needed to show them I'd changed and everything would be fine.

My mother came to the house later that morning. I was surprised to see her.

"Sorry to interrupt your morning, Tom," she said, as I showed her into the living room.

She refused my offer of coffee. "I'll just say what I've come to say. I think that's probably best." She wouldn't even sit down.

"Okay," I said warily. I knew this tone of Ma's voice only too well.

"This afternoon, when you see Adam, I want you to remember, Tom – it's not all about you. If you want Adam back, it has to be on his own terms."

"Yes, Ma, I know." I felt hurt by her lack of faith in me. It was one thing to doubt myself, but to hear my mother voice the same doubts, it was hard to take.

"I mean it," she said, putting her hands on my shoulders and looking me in the eye. "Don't blow this, Tom. Adam – and Rosie too – let them make their own choices."

I couldn't hold her gaze. I looked upwards. "Yes, I know. I do know what's at stake." I sighed, closed my eyes.

"Yes, I'm sure you do." Her hands touched my face.

I looked down at her as she stroked my cheek. Her expression had softened.

"Oh, Ma," I said. "I'm so afraid I'll mess this up."

She hugged me and said, "Just don't expect too much, my darling. Go easy on Adam. Let him see you love him no matter what and that the door is open for him when he's ready to come back."

"Of course I will. I don't want to do anything to scare him away again. But I want him home. I want both of them home so much, you know?"

"I know you do, son, I know you do." As she released me from her embrace she said, smiling, "I could do with that coffee now."

We went through to the kitchen. Sam and Max were there and were delighted to see my mother. She offered to stay at the house with Sam that afternoon. Sam seemed glad of the offer of her grandmother's company. Ma also said Dan would be over later to take Max out for the afternoon. This cheered Max up considerably.

He had begged to be allowed to come to the flat that afternoon. He had spent the morning cleaning out the fish tank so that Adam would be pleased with the level of care the fish had received from him. Although he didn't say so, I knew he was hoping Adam would come home that day. I almost gave in and let Max come. But I sensed that just meeting with me and Rosie, with Jenny there in support, would be quite enough for Adam at this point.

Sam and my mother made lunch for us all, but I could hardly eat anything. Then I couldn't wait any longer. It was ridiculously early but I had to get on the road. So Jenny and I set off for Edinburgh. In the end it had been decided that Jenny would meet Adam in town and they'd come to the flat together. It was the arrangement Adam was most comfortable with. I would go straight to the flat after I dropped Jenny in the city centre.

As I'd hoped, the sun had come through and it was a warm afternoon. I opened the windows and sun roof as soon as I started the car. As Jenny got in, the sun shone in her eyes, and she swept her long, fair hair back from her face as she searched in her bag for her sunglasses. She looked so like Rosie that it knocked the breath out of me.

"What?" she said, as she caught me staring at her.

"Oh nothing. It's just, you're a beautiful young woman, Jennifer McAllister and I love you." I leant over and kissed the top of her head.

"Och, Dad, you're a soppy git," she said, smiling. "Give me a big Daddy hug." This was something she used to say a lot when she was little, but it was quite a while since she'd last said it. I was happy to oblige.

"It's going to be okay, Dad," she said.

I tried to relax as we approached Edinburgh. It wasn't easy. I dropped Jenny off and, before I knew it I was walking up the path to the flat.

It was Rick who opened the door. "Tom, good to see you," he said, extending a hand.

How could I have forgotten him? But I had. In my daydreams about reconciliation with Rosie I'd not factored Rick in. How stupid could you get?

"Eh, yes, hi," I said, shaking his hand quickly, as much to displace the urge to punch him as any attempt to be polite. I didn't really stop to look at him. I just wanted to see Rosie.

I went through to the front room. And there she was. Rosie, sitting in an armchair with her feet tucked up under her. She was looking down at a book in her lap. She wore a dress, long and loose, made of some sort of light, floaty material and on her head she had a little blue hat with an upturned brim. She looked up as I came in and got to her feet.

"Hello." She smiled at me. She looked so lovely. My need to hold her was even more intense than the last time I'd been there. I wanted to pick her up and carry her off. But all I could do was gaze at her. She was so familiar and yet so strange. It reminded me of the first time I saw her, this mixture of familiarity and strangeness. I was scared to speak.

Rosie took a step towards me. "Tom?" she said, looking

puzzled. "Tom, are you okay?"

She was standing very close now. I inhaled her scent. Christ, how I wanted her. She put a hand on my arm. She looked up into my face.

Tentatively, I put my hand to her cheek. It was cool and soft.

"Rosie," I said. It came out as a whisper. I cleared my throat. It felt as if she leant her face, just ever so slightly, against my hand. She closed her eyes briefly. She opened them again and looked right into mine. With my heart pounding, I contemplated kissing her.

Then Rick was there in the doorway. "I'll get away, Rosie. I'll be back to make us some dinner. See you later." He looked at me. "Tom, take care. Great news about Adam by the way."

I didn't really want to answer him. But I made the effort. After all, I wanted to impress Rosie with how reasonable I could be. "Yeah, thanks." Despite my endeavours it still came out grudgingly and I was aware of my free hand tightening into a fist.

If Rick noticed my barely suppressed aggression, he didn't seem in the least fazed by it. He turned back to Rosie. "Hope it goes okay," he said.

"Thanks, Rick. See you later," Rosie replied, smiling at him, as she stepped back from me.

I wanted so much to hit him. "He's still here then?" I said, as the front door closed behind him. I couldn't help myself. So much for trying to impress Rosie.

"Clearly," Rosie replied. "Look, please, Tom, don't start. Sit down, please."

I bit back what I wanted to say and sat down opposite her. She was right of course. Today was not about Rick Montgomery and his relationship with my wife.

"Oh, by the way," I said, reaching into my pocket. "These are for you." I held out a couple of packets of Starburst sweets. "The kids told me you've developed a liking for them."

She laughed as she took them from me. "Thank you. Yeah,

they're one of the few things I can eat with any pleasure. Most stuff tastes like its been dipped in metal or has no taste at all."

"So, how are you?" I asked, as we both sat down.

"I'm okay. You know, as well as can be expected, as they say. I just had my fourth dose of chemo a few days ago. So this is a tough week. It's a two week cycle, get chemo, feel grim for a week, recover during week two, feel almost human and then it's the next dose. Still, I'm saving a fortune in shampoo and conditioner."

"It must be hard going. Have you lost it all?" I asked, pointing to her head.

"Oh yes," she nodded and removed her hat. "Look."

I couldn't help myself. I gasped. She was completely bald.

"I know," she said. "Scary, isn't it?" She rubbed her head with her hand. She smiled and added, "Max said I looked like an alien at first, then he said I looked like the robot in that film 'I, Robot'. His latest comparison is to the person in the Munch painting. You know, The Scream. None are very flattering!"

I smiled back at her. "Typical Max."

"Yes, he thinks I should wear the wig at all times."

"But you don't like it?"

"There's nothing really wrong with it. It's realistic enough and everything, but it makes my head hot and itchy. I prefer hats and scarves if I want to cover up. Jenny and Sam have been lovely about it. They've bought me a couple of hats and a pretty scarf as well. They tell me I look cool. They're probably just being nice, but I choose to believe them."

"You look fine," I said. "It's a shock at first, that's all."

"I was so scared of losing my hair. It scared me as much as the cancer at first, if I'm honest, but now I'm used to it. And do you know the really annoying thing about it?"

"What?" I asked.

"I still have to shave my legs. Those hairs are unaffected!" She laughed. It was a lovely sound. I laughed with her.

"And what are the doctors saying about how you're doing?"

"Oh, Angus Campbell is usually upbeat and reassuring. He's pleased with how the surgery went. The scar is healing well. I lost the whole breast which is, well, it's been difficult, you know?" She swallowed.

I so wanted to reach out and touch her, but ...

"But it could have been worse," she continued. "At least it doesn't seem to have spread, and I have my prosthesis to balance things up. I might have a reconstruction later."

I could only nod.

"Anyway, the main thing is the tumour's gone," she went on. "So, I suppose, so far so good. Karen Knox, the oncologist, she never gives much away. She just keeps saying it's early days. Once the chemo's over they want me to have radiotherapy."

"I'm glad to hear it," I said. "They should throw everything they've got at it. What sort of tumour was it, if I'm allowed to ask?"

"Of course you can ask!"

"I don't want you to think I'm asking so I can go and question your doctors. You know, take over, like you were afraid I'd do."

She looked away for a moment before she answered. "I'm sorry, Tom. I'm sorry. The way I told you, it was cruel. I should have told you about the cancer right at the start. It seems a bit daft now, but I felt it was my battle, my body and I wanted to do it my way."

"And now, Rosie, how do you feel now? Can you share any of it with me now?" Of course I wanted to ask her so much more. Like was she coming home and how did she feel about me? Could she forgive me? Would she listen to my story? But I somehow managed to hold back.

She bit her lip and took a steadying breath. "I've got a fairly aggressive version, but it was caught at stage two and there is no sign of any spread to the lymph nodes or anywhere else at the moment. So, if the chemo does its job and if I have the radiotherapy and drug treatment afterwards, it seems I have a fairly good chance of survival. Of course, they can't promise anything but, as Angus Campbell says, none of us has any guarantee of a ripe old age."

"Thanks for telling me." My voice was a croak. I fought to hold myself together. I cleared my throat. "I've been wondering about the medical nitty-gritty, the occupational hazard you were afraid of, I know. But it sounds like your medical team are on top of it."

She smiled again. "I'll tell them you said so. They'll be relieved to hear it." I knew she was teasing me. I smiled back weakly.

I was restless. I was enjoying being with Rosie but my nerves were shredded. The combination of trying to say the right things, of listening to Rosie talk about her illness and anticipating Adam's arrival, made me shaky in a way I never was with a scalpel in my hand. I suggested a cup of tea. Rosie said she'd love one. She looked tired already.

Once I was back with the tea, which I noticed she didn't touch, we talked about Adam and about Jenny, Robbie and Eilidh all rallying round in support. Rosie told me that, according to Kirsty, Robbie and Eilidh had been on a couple of dates. I told her a bit more about Robbie and how we were getting along well and she seemed pleased. She also seemed as excited and apprehensive as I was about seeing Adam. She got up periodically to look out of the window for him.

Watching her looking out, scanning the street for our son, I was uncomfortably aware of my part in Adam's leaving. "I'm sorry, Rosie," I said. "Sorry I caused Adam all this anxiety and then didn't exactly reassure him when he needed it. I've let you both down but I am sorry. I want to put it right. There's other stuff I need to tell you about Robbie and Heather and – everything."

"It's not all your fault. I didn't exactly handle Adam's distress well either. And, yes, we do need to talk, and we will, I promise, but not today. Today is about Adam." As she finished speaking she put her hand up to her mouth. She looked very pale.

"Sorry," she said through clenched teeth. "Sick!"

I jumped up and went towards her. She got to her feet. I put out my arm to help her and she threw up down the front of my shirt.

"Sorry," she said again. And then she fled from the room. As I peeled off my shirt, I heard the bathroom door clatter against the wall. I went after her. She was crouched over the toilet. I knelt down beside her and rubbed her back as she vomited. She retched violently and not always productively. Then, at last, I could feel her body relax. She leant back against me. I got hold of a face flannel from the side of the bath. I managed to dampen it under the wash-hand basin tap without having to completely leave my position beside her on the floor.

"Here," I said and she turned her face towards me. She was still very pale. I gently wiped her face with the flannel while supporting her in the crook of my arm. She rested there for a few minutes, her head against my chest. We didn't speak.

It was me who broke the silence. "Better?"

"Yes, sorry about that," she said, turning her head to look directly at me. She put her hand flat on my chest. "Sorry about your shirt too." She smiled, even managed a little laugh. "But you did step into the firing line." She continued to look at me. I held her gaze. I felt like I had lost the power to breath. Rosie this close, even in these circumstances, I was lost.

Then she rallied, smacked me on the shoulder. "Come on, we better get you a shirt before the kids get here." She stood up and held out her hand.

I took it and stood up. She led me through to the back bedroom. It was full of camera equipment and bags and other clutter. The bed was unmade. She opened the wardrobe.

"Good job you and Rick are roughly the same size," she said. "What about this one?" she asked, taking out a checked cotton shirt.

"Yes, anything," I said.

She handed it to me, and then made a face as she said, "God, my mouth feels disgusting, like a dry, furry, tin can." She glanced at herself in the dressing table mirror. "I'll leave you to get dressed. I need to freshen up."

I put on Rick's shirt, not with good grace I have to say. It was Rick's shirt, enough said. I wondered if her easy presumption that it was okay to give me one of his shirts was an indicator of an intimate relationship between them. I refused to pursue that thought.

I went to the kitchen and searched in the small freezer. I found what I was looking for. I put the ice cubes in a small bowl and took them through to the living room. My shirt had gone from where I'd dropped it on the floor.

Rosie came back wearing a different dress. She wasn't quite so pale now. She smiled and sat down. "That's better," she said. "I've rinsed off your shirt. I'll wash it and get it back to you."

"Oh don't bother. Chuck it out. It's ancient." It was an old, faded, blue denim thing.

"I couldn't do that. I know it's old. I bought it for you, and I like you in it. It suits you. Mind you, you suit that shirt too," she added, nodding at Rick's one, teasing me again.

"Do I?" I mumbled vaguely. "Here, I thought this might help your mouth, you know, with the nasty taste and the dryness." I held out the bowl of ice cubes.

She took the bowl from me and immediately popped a cube in her mouth. She seemed to savour it. "Mmm, that is soothing, thank you. It's numbing the mouth ulcers too, another side effect of the chemo, I'm afraid."

Glad it helps. It's something I've seen the nurses on the ward do for patients from time to time. Surgery often leaves them with very dry mouths."

She popped another cube in her mouth and sat back in her chair. She closed her eyes momentarily. She was clearly very tired. I hoped meeting up with Adam wasn't going to be too much for her. I let her doze. I sat and looked at her while she did. My Rosie, my darling, sick Rosie.

# Chapter Thirty

When the door bell rang, Rosie opened her eyes. We stared at each other for a moment. There was no need for words. I got up and went to open the door. Jenny stood there on the doorstep. I moved back to let her pass into the hall.

Then Adam stepped into view. "Hello, Dad." He looked right at me, into my eyes.

I met his gaze. "Hello, son, come in."

Jenny beamed at us both. She led the way through to the living room. "Look who's here, Mum," she said, standing aside to let Adam go in before her.

Rosie stood in the middle of the room. She was facing the door with her hands up at her face. Adam went to her.

"Adam," she whispered. There were tears on her cheeks.

"Mum." He rubbed at his face roughly with the back of his hand before gathering her in an embrace. Jenny came to me, and I put my arm round her as we watched Rosie take Adam by the hand and sit him down beside her on the sofa.

Rosie stroked Adam's face and rubbed away his tears. "My darling, darling boy," she said. "I am so sorry, so sorry that I hit you and that I didn't realise how worried you were. I'm sorry I left you, without making sure you understood why I was going. I love you, Adam and I've missed you so much."

"I've missed you too, Mum. I'm sorry too. I'm sorry I upset you saying that stuff about your sister and that I've made you worry. It just all got muddled up in my head, Robbie and you and Dad and school. I had a horrible feeling in my stomach all the time. I didn't feel safe anymore. Everything had changed. I just had to get away."

"Yes, yes I can understand that," Rosie said. "And, now, how do you feel now?"

"I don't have the horrible feeling in my stomach any more. And, like I said, I miss you."

"Come here," Rosie said, reaching forward to embrace him again.

As I watched and listened to him talking, I was aware Adam had changed. It wasn't a dramatic change. Yes he was taller and a bit thinner, but that wasn't it. It was something about the way he held himself, his general demeanour. He was less diffident, more confident than before. He was grown up.

As they moved apart, Adam spoke. "Mum, are you going to be all right? Dad told me about you being – about you having cancer. Jenny said all your hair's fallen out and that you're sick a lot."

"I'm going to be fine, son, I'm going to be fine. The drugs they give me to fight the cancer, they make me sick and, yes, I've lost my hair because of them. But I'm going to get better."

"But you don't know that, not for certain. You can't know that." His voice was louder now. There were shades of the more familiar Adam. He stood up. "People die of cancer. You might die."

Rosie looked distressed. I was unsure if I should say anything. I was trying hard to keep out of the conversation, to let Rosie and Adam speak to each other. I was still so aware that I might ruin the reconciliation by saying the wrong thing. There was a momentary silence. Rosie looked over at Jenny and me.

"Stop it, Adam." Jenny was on her feet now. "Stop it." She put her arms around him. "Calm down. Mum's going to be all right. They got it early. They can treat it. She'll get better." She stroked his back as she held on to him. He seemed to relax.

"Sorry, sorry, Mum," Adam said, as he sat back down beside her. "It's just it's not fair. Why do you have to have it?"

Rosie took his hand again. "Don't be. Don't be sorry. You've a right to be angry. God knows, I was angry when I found out. I know it doesn't seem fair. I asked why me, at first. But then when you think about it, why not? Why not me?"

"Because you're my mum. That's why not," he said. He turned back to me. "And what are you doing for Mum? Are you helping her get better? You must know stuff to do.

"It's not my field Adam. I fix hearts. You know that."

"Yes, but have you checked that they're not missing anything, that Mum's got the best doctors and the right treatment?"

"I – well – I–"

"I'm getting the best treatment, Adam," Rosie rescued me. "There's really nothing your father can do. He offered to check things out for me, but I told him not to. I'm doing this my way, love. I need to do it my way."

"But why won't you let Dad help you? You could go home and he could look after you. Jen told me that Dad's not at work so much now. Why don't you go home? Are you still angry with him for not telling you about Robbie?"

"I'm not ready to go home, Adam. It's complicated. I can't think about it all just now. I need all my strength to get better. The important thing now is that *you* go back home and then I don't have to worry about you."

"No! I'm not ready to go home yet either."

Rosie and I exchanged a look.

Jenny spoke. "Why, why not, Ad? Why won't you come home? I thought you were cool about Robbie now you know more about him, and after you and him spoke about Mum."

"I am cool about Robbie. He seems an okay guy. But he wasn't the only reason I left. I hated it at home without you, Mum. I'm not going back without you. And Dad," he paused and looked at me. "Dad was always on my back about school and university and I couldn't deal with it. It was too much pressure."

"Look, Adam," I said. "I'm sorry I caused you such upset over Robbie and I'm sorry you blame me for Mum leaving. But please come home. We all miss you. And don't worry about the school stuff. The exam results will be out next week and I don't care how you've done." I tried to sound sincere and it was partly true. I didn't care at that moment. But somewhere within me, I still held onto the hope that he'd re-sit if necessary.

Anyway, Adam wasn't convinced. He stood up. He looked right at me and shook his head. He raised his arms in a despairing gesture. "No, no, no," he said. "I don't believe you. You say you don't care if I pass or not. Since when? Since you've been trying to trick me into coming back. That's when!"

I shook my head at him and glanced at Rosie. She was looking at Adam and frowning slightly.

I tried again. "Adam, all I'm saying–"

"Oh, I know what you're saying! And you don't get it! I'm not going back to school, no matter what happens. I've had it with school. I'm not going to university. I'm not coming home."

"Adam, please." Rosie got to her feet and put a hand on his arm. "Please go home. We can talk about the school thing, work something out. But please go home." He shook her off.

"No, Mum, stop, please stop. You're a fine one to talk. You're not going home. Why should I? You don't want to live with him either, do you?" He pointed at me. He was obviously still very angry with me and I know I wasn't exactly saying all the right things. I felt quite hopeless. He was right. Nothing had really changed. Neither he nor Rosie wanted to come home. Neither could stand to be with me.

"That's different," Rosie said. "You don't understand. You can't understand. Please, Adam, go home."

But he wasn't having it. "I'm glad we've made up. But Dad's just the same, still on my back. I'm not going home. I could come here and live with you. What about that? I could take care of you since you don't want Dad to." He looked pleased with himself at this suggestion.

"I'm sorry. That's not possible. There's no room. Rick's living here at the moment. You know Lucy's brother? He's renting this place while he's working in Scotland. He's between projects at the moment and he's staying here for now."

"Could he not rent somewhere else? Or you and me could."

Rosie shook her head. "No, Rick has a tenancy here. I can't throw him out, even if I wanted to. And I'm not up to moving house. Please, just go home."

"So you'd rather live with this Rick than me. Are you in love with him or something?"

Jenny gasped. I held my breath.

Rosie shook her head and put her hands up to her face. "Please, Adam, don't."

I could see she'd had enough. I tried to gather my thoughts. I needed to bring this to some kind of satisfactory conclusion, for all our sakes. "Adam, I think we need to let Mum rest now. It's been good to see you, and it's great you're talking to Mum. But it's still difficult for everybody. Maybe we should leave it for today. I could run you back to Ruby's if you like, and we can arrange to meet up again soon. I wish you could believe me when I say the exams don't matter." By this point I was actually starting to believe I truly thought so.

But the look on Adam's face showed he was nowhere near accepting what I said. I persevered, determined to end our meeting on a positive note. "It's clear none of us is ready to resolve anything more yet. So let's stop and just be glad that we've met up."

At that, Adam seemed to relax a little. "Yes, okay. Sorry, Mum. I didn't want to upset you. Sorry."

"It's okay, darling," Rosie said, and she stood up and hugged him. "I love you, son. We'll work all this out, I promise. Come back and see me soon and keep in touch."

Adam hugged his mother back. Then he said to me, "Thanks for the offer of a lift. But I'd rather make my own way back."

"I'll come with you, Adam. If that's OK with you?" Jenny said.

"Yes, whatever," he replied.

Rosie and I said our goodbyes to both of them. It was hard

letting Adam go, but there really was nothing else for it. And he promised Rosie he would be in touch. That would have to be good enough for now.

After the children left, the feeling of anticlimax was awful and I felt it was down to me that things hadn't gone all that well. I was about to apologise to Rosie for messing up again. But she spoke first.

"Thanks, Tom. I couldn't take any more. You did the right thing, calling a halt. We're going to have to take it slow with him."

"You're not angry with me then?" I said.

"Angry? No, I'm not angry. You want the best for him. I know that. He just doesn't see it that way." She sighed.

"Come on, Rosie, you're shattered. You need to rest. Go and lie down. You've gone very pale again."

"Yes, Doctor," she said, managing to smile. She stood up, but then she staggered a bit and held the arm of the chair. She seemed even paler, if that was possible. "I feel a bit faint," she said. She swayed forwards.

I was on my feet in an instant. I scooped her up and carried her through to the front bedroom. I was shocked at how light she was. She'd lost a hell of a lot of weight. I laid her gently on the bed and put the pillows under her feet. I sat on the edge of the bed beside her and took her pulse. It was weak and her breathing was shallow. I opened the window and returned to sit on the bed beside her. I stroked her hand and bent and kissed her forehead. "Take deep breaths," I said.

She gripped my hand. Her pupils were dilated and she looked frightened. "Don't go, Tom," she whispered.

"I'm not going anywhere. Try and relax. Don't be scared. Your blood pressure has dropped to your boots. It's okay, love, it's okay." I continued to stroke her forehead. "Are you in any pain?"

She shook her head. "No pain," she said. She closed her eyes. Her skin was clammy. I removed her sandals. I stroked her hand. Gradually her colour returned. She shivered. I pulled the duvet over her and knelt by the bed. She reached for my hand again.

"Thank you, Tom," she said, without opening her eyes. Then she fell asleep. I checked her pulse again. It was stronger now. I raised her hand to my mouth and brushed it with my lips. Then I stood up and drew the curtains. I left her to sleep.

I went back through to the living room and sank down on the sofa. Then I too dozed off. The next thing I knew the front door was banging shut and Rick was shouting hallo. I jumped up as Rick came into the room.

"Hi honey, I'm home," he said. Then he saw it was me. "Oh, Tom, it's you. Sorry I expected Rosie."

"You don't say," I said.

"You're still here then," said Rick.

"Evidently."

"Sorry, sorry mate. I'll try and stop stating the obvious. I just got a surprise seeing you and not – God, I'm doing it again, sorry." I almost felt sorry for him. He was clearly as uncomfortable as I was.

"Rosie felt a bit faint so I put her to bed. I didn't want to go away and leave her on her own."

"Oh, right. Is she okay now?"

"She should be. She's still sleeping."

"No, she's not," Rosie was standing in the doorway.

"Rosie, are you okay?" Rick asked.

"Come and sit down," I said.

"I'm fine, thank you," Rosie said. "Don't fuss both of you." She smiled at the two of us.

Rick was looking at me. "Is that my shirt?"

"Ah," Rosie said. "That's a long story. I'll tell you over dinner. I'm quite hungry actually."

"Right," Rick said. "I'll get started on the food right away. Will you join us, Tom?"

I swallowed hard. For the second time that day I wanted to punch him. "No, no thanks," I managed to say. "I better get home. My mother and the others will be waiting to hear how this afternoon went." I turned to Rosie. "Rosie, you seem better now and in good hands, so I'll get away." I tried not to sound sarcastic.

"Okay then. Give Evelyn and Max and Sam my love. She came over to where I was standing and reached up and touched my face. "Thank you for everything this afternoon."

I put my hand on hers. "Don't mention it," I said.

# Chapter Thirty One

### *Rosie*

When I was first told I had breast cancer, I couldn't really grasp it. I was in denial. Yes, at some level, I knew it was a fact. I was shocked and scared, but only up to a point. There was a barrier, a distance between me and my cancer. Robbie's arrival, and my anger at Tom, meant that I focussed on my need to get away, rather than on the full significance of my illness.

But once I'd had the mastectomy, I had to face up to it. After days of refusing to look when the dressings were changed, I found myself saying to Wendy, my wonderful cancer-care nurse, that I was ready. I was ready to see.

"Are you sure, Rosie?" Wendy paused from preparing the dressings tray on the bedside trolley.

"Yes, if you'll stay with me." It was less than a fortnight since I'd first met Wendy but I already depended on her. She'd been there to meet me when I arrived for admission to the hospital. She accompanied me to the operating theatre, and she was there when I came round afterwards. She'd looked in on me most days since.

"Of course I'll stay. If that's what you want."

I nodded.

Wendy gently slipped my hospital gown off my left shoulder and down my arm. Despite her gentleness, I winced at the movement.

"Sorry! I'll just fetch us a mirror. Okay?"

I nodded again.

As I prepared myself, I felt grateful for the privacy of the side room I'd had to myself since admission. Angus Campbell denied he'd pulled any strings for the wife of a fellow consultant, but I wasn't sure I believed him.

"Here we are." Wendy returned and handed me a small hand mirror. "Right, let's get the dressing off."

I looked away as she peeled back the gauze. She leant in close to examine the site of the operation. "It's healing nicely." She straightened up. "Ready?"

I took a deep breath and held the mirror level with my chest. I made myself look. I gasped. My left breast was completely gone, its absence marked by an angry, red wound.

Like viewing the corpse of a loved one, seeing was a sure way to believing. As the realisation of what I was seeing sank in, the shock gave way to rage. Rage at this betrayal by my own body. I flung the mirror down. Wendy moved towards me.

"No! Please, leave me, leave me alone!" I pulled the gown up and turned my back on her. I heard the door close behind her as I gave way to the fury and fear. I've never felt so alone.

Over my remaining two days in hospital, I talked a lot with Wendy about how I was feeling. I ended up telling her the whole story of Tom, Heather and Robbie. "I'm sorry," I said when I'd finished. "I didn't mean to offload all that onto you. But you must have wondered where my family is, why they haven't visited."

"No need to apologise. I'm here to listen. I did wonder about your family, and it helps me to help you if I have the full picture. I can't offer any advice on your predicament with your husband. But I do know that your emotions would be all over the place even if you only had the cancer to concern you."

"So you're used to emotional wrecks?"

"Yes, indeed!" She smiled and put her hand on mine. "As for the cancer, your feelings about it are all absolutely normal. You're grieving, Rosie. You're grieving for your breast, your past certainty, the pre-cancer Rosie. The denial, the anger, they're absolutely normal. It will pass. You'll find the strength to accept what's happened. Things aren't going to be the same as before and you've got a fight on your hands."

It was Evelyn who brought me home from hospital after the mastectomy. When we arrived back at the flat she insisted I go to bed.

"You look tired out," she said. "Come on, I'll help you get undressed." She was right of course. I was exhausted and still very sore. I flinched as she gently removed my blouse. "Sorry, I know you must be feeling very tender. How's the wound healing?"

"Oh, they say it's doing well. The painkillers help but moving my arm is agony at the moment."

"My poor dear. Come on, in you get." Evelyn held back the duvet and, once I was in bed, she made sure I was well propped up by the pillows. She perched on the edge of the bed and stroked my hair. "Did you consider having a reconstruction?"

"Mr Campbell did suggest it. But I couldn't face thinking about it. I can have it done later, if I decide to go ahead."

Evelyn nodded. "And you've seen the oncologist?"

"Yes, Karen Knox, and I liked her. She seems very capable, down to earth, a bit cagier than Angus Campbell about my prospects. She was honest with me, didn't make any promises, but she did say my prognosis is fairly good, at least for remission, if not cure."

"Oh, Rosie, my darling girl," Evelyn held my hand in both of hers. "You've got a rough road ahead, but you've got to believe you'll get through this."

I nodded. "I'll be starting my chemotherapy in about a month. It'll be high dose and once a fortnight."

"That'll be tough. Will they admit you for some of the time?"

"Dr Knox suggested that. She said my immunity will be compromised. I'll need to avoid people with colds and other bugs, and I'll need lots of rest. But I told her I'd be living on my own, that I'd abdicated my responsibilities, abandoned the children. What must she have thought, what must everybody think?" I felt tears starting.

"Now stop it, how many times do you have to be told? You've not abdicated, or abandoned anyone. God, if you were a man you wouldn't be thinking like that. Nobody thinks badly of you. You need to be away and you've got lots of support in place for the family. And if you being here, rather than at home, means you don't have to be hospitalised for most of your treatment, then all the more reason."

"I know, but–"

"Rosie, you've got a lot to cope with. I told you at the outset, I think you're doing the right thing."

"Yes I know you did. It means a lot that you don't think I'm being selfish. I know I'm fortunate to be able to step out of normal life for a time."

"And it's my fervent hope that by doing so, you'll be able to return to it, that you'll get well, forgive Tom…" Now it looked like Evelyn was going to cry.

I squeezed her hand. "Oh, Evelyn, I hope so too. It's all such a mess at the moment. But your support, your approval, they're very important to me."

And indeed, Evelyn was a tremendous prop over the following few months. She visited regularly, often bringing her delicious, home-made soups and other light meals, designed to tempt my feeble appetite.

But Evelyn did not approve of Rick, or at least of his presence in the flat. Although she never put pressure on me regarding Tom, it was obvious by her coolness whenever she saw Rick, or if I even just referred to him, that she saw Rick as a threat.

# Chapter Thirty Two

I lost my virginity to Rick Montgomery. I was nineteen, he was twenty one and I was in love for the first time. The event took place on the single bed, in my room in the university hall of residence. It was a sweaty, awkward and uncomfortable experience. But Rick assured me it would get better. In fact, I think what he actually said was that *I* would get better at it and he would be my teacher.

And it wasn't only in matters of sex that Rick initiated me. He opened my mind to many new things. He was into whole foods and ecology, at least twenty years before most people gave them any thought. His politics were Scottish socialist. He loved Scotland, its landscape and its history. He took me hill-walking all over the country. He told me about the flow of the ice-age glaciers, of how the ancient ice gouged out the glens and shaped the peaks, leaving mounds of moraine in its wake. He took me to Glencoe and brought the story of the massacre there to life, in a way it never was at school. And always, he was taking photographs.

It felt strange seeing him again, after a gap of nearly thirty years. It was early April, several weeks before I met Robbie or knew I was ill. We'd arranged to meet at the flat, in the afternoon. I got there ridiculously early. I busied myself making a coffee, mainly so I'd stop going to the window every few minutes to see if he was coming.

I knew him before university, of course, but only as Lucy's big brother. He was way out of reach as boyfriend material when I was a schoolgirl. During my first year at St Andrews I only saw him in passing. It wasn't until Lucy's engagement party that we met up properly. I fell for him in a big way and I think he was flattered.

We went out together for eight months. I dumped him after I walked in on him in bed with another girl. He broke my teenage heart. I got over it.

When I opened the door to him that spring morning all those years later, he was leaning on the door frame, head to one side. I'd forgotten how tall he was, and how loud.

"Hey, Rose-Marie!" he boomed, using the name he called me by when I was nineteen. No-one else ever called me that. He looked me up and down, and the next thing I knew I was engulfed in an enormous bear hug. "You're still a fine looking woman – if you don't mind me saying so." He released me and took a step back, his hands still on my shoulders. "Tom McAllister's a lucky man. Is he here?" He stepped into the hallway of the flat, looking round as he did so.

He looked older, of course. His, once, thick, dark hair was thinner and greying, and his beard was flecked with silver. He was less slender than he'd been at university. But all these changes suited him. He was still attractive and his smile was the same.

"Rick," I said, feeling slightly flustered. "It's good to see you. Come in. No, Tom's not here. He's at work." It didn't take long to show him round the flat. We finished up in the living-room. "So, that's it," I said. "Would you like to look round again, on your own, or is there anything you want to ask?"

"No, I've seen enough. This will suit me fine. Lucy told me how much the rent is and that it's a standard six month lease. It's available now, is that right?"

"Yes, you could move in any time. I didn't renew the previous tenants' lease at the end of the spring term. They were students, three girls. They had little respect for the neighbours or the flat, or for that matter, paying the rent on time." I knew I was rambling on, disconcerted by Rick's presence. God, how ridiculous, how embarrassing!

And Rick wasn't about to make it easier for me. "So, you'd be happy with an older man then?" He grinned and raised his eyebrows.

Was he was flirting with me? If so, I was out of practice. "Oh, yes, that is, yes I'd be happy for you, a man, to have it, the flat. I mean, our first tenants were two lads, students. They were here three years and were no trouble at all."

"I'll do my best not to let the male side down and will show the place due respect. You can come and inspect me any time." Again there was that grin, that dangerous twinkle in his eye.

I tried to keep playing it straight. "So you're coming home to Scotland, to stay?"

"Yes, ready to settle down, at last. It's time to re-establish my roots. I've got a project on Skye for the next few months, as well as some other commissions around the country. There's also a retrospective exhibition of my stuff, during the festival, here in Edinburgh, in the autumn. So I can use this place as a base while I prepare for that, and do a bit of house hunting as well."

"Do you really think you'll be able to settle in one place, after all this time?"

"Got to, Rose-Marie, I've had enough of the globetrotting, the dashing around. It's been a blast. I wouldn't change it, but it's a young man's game."

"But won't you miss it, all that mountain climbing, camping in the deserts, trekking in the Arctic and whatever?"

"In some ways. There's nothing like the buzz of spending hours, days, months and then, finally, getting the perfect shot, but it's a case, now, of been there, done that. Now I look around and think is that it? International acclaim and recognition is very gratifying, but it's come at a price."

"What price?"

"No wife, no kids, no home, no meaning, I suppose."

"You'd have hated the wife and two kids thing. Anyway,

there's more to life than being married with kids. How can you say your life's had no meaning? You've done all those daredevil expeditions, been on TV, published books, had exhibitions. You're a hero to my daughter, Jenny, with all the stuff you have to have say on saving the planet."

"Am I, a hero, really?" He looked genuinely pleased at this. "I've tried to do my bit, use my photos to get people to realise how beautiful and fragile our wee planet is. And yes, you're right, I couldn't have settled when I was younger. I did have a couple of longer-term relationships. But in the end the long separations killed them off. When I had to choose, I chose work."

"So there's no-one, no significant other, at the moment?"

"No, no-one. I'm not really looking, not desperate or anything. But, I don't know, getting to fifty, you realise you've not got forever, less ahead of you than behind you. If there's stuff you still want to do, you better get on and do it. And I want a home, time to stand and stare, and yeah, if the right person were to come along to share it with…" Rick paused and laughed. "Blimey, I don't know where all that came from. I've never put it into words before. It's you, you always were a good listener, that was one of the things I loved about you."

I felt flustered again. "Shall we look at the tenancy agreement?"

A week later Rick moved in. Tom wasn't all that happy about it. I found it amusing that, all these years later, Tom still didn't like Rick. In early May, Rick let me know he was off up to Skye. He wasn't sure how long he'd be away.

Then, at the end of June, he was back. I'd been living in the flat for about a month. I'd just returned from my first chemo session. Kirsty was with me. She'd insisted on being my driver and moral support for my first time at oncology. She was about to leave me and get back to school.

"Thanks, Kirsty." I said. "For being with me, taking time off work, it was good of you".

"No problem. Being the boss has its perks. I can take time off to help a friend if I want to. Are you sure you're going to be all right on your own?

"Yes, you get away. I think I'll just rest for a while." I lay back on the sofa. Then we heard the front door clatter shut.

Rick stumbled into the living room, laden with bags and cameras. "Oh, Rose-Marie! And, and good lord, it's Kirsty isn't it?" I hurriedly sat up. He grabbed hold of Kirsty by both hands and stepped back to look her up and down. "You're looking good! How are you?"

Kirsty was only momentarily thrown by Rick's enthusiastic greeting. She recovered quickly. "Yes, it's me, and I'm well, thank you. Rick, isn't it?" She smiled, teasing. "How are you?"

"Glad you remember me! I'm good." He turned to me. "You're not looking so great though. What's up?"

While I tried to work out how to answer this, Kirsty said she'd have to go. Rick insisted on seeing her out. I heard them speaking in the hall for a couple of minutes, but couldn't make out what was being said.

When Rick returned to the living-room he sat down beside me. "So, Rosie, I knew you were going to use the flat for a little while, but I didn't expect you still to be here. Not that it's a problem, but what's going on? What's been happening to you?"

I told him.

"Christ, what a tough break! The big 'C', that's a bummer. And Tom, you really think him and Heather, that this boy, Robbie, is …" He looked at me, at the tears running down my face, and then he took me in his huge embrace. He stroked my hair and rocked me gently.

Later, when I'd composed myself and we were drinking tea, he said, "I'm sorry I didn't make the funeral. I heard she'd died, that Heather had died. Lucy let me know, but I was out of the country."

I shook my head. "Don't be sorry. I didn't make it to the funeral myself."

"Really?

"Really. I'd just had the twins. I wasn't – I wasn't very well."

"I met her again, you know. It was years after we'd all graduated, late eighties it must have been. We met at a fund-raising exhibition in Edinburgh. I'd been asked to put in some pictures, and Heather was there as a beneficiary of the charity. We went for a drink. She said she was off the drugs, was on this supported programme, had a wee flat."

"I wouldn't know." I couldn't keep the bitterness out of my voice.

"She said you two were estranged."

"It's a long and nasty story. She did some terrible things, Rick. I find it hard to believe she was clean when you met her."

"So did I, I'm afraid. She seemed pretty sorted, happy even, but I didn't trust what I could see. Lucy had told me, over the years, how deep Heather was into drugs and all the rest. Anyway, I walked away. Maybe I should've stayed, supported her on the programme, been a friend."

"It wasn't your responsibility. I didn't see her at all in the last year of her life. We all gave up on her."

We were both quiet for a moment, remembering our own versions of my sister.

It was me who spoke first. "So, what's next for you, work wise?

"I've finished the first phase of the Skye project, done my research and preliminary photography. Now I need to do some processing, editing and writing up. I also need to do a bit of prep for the retrospective."

"Sounds like you'll be busy."

"I've rented workspace at a mate's studio, over at Inverleith. So don't worry, I'll be out a lot."

The side effects of the chemo kicked in a few days after Rick's arrival. I couldn't bear the thought of him seeing me throwing up, but he seemed to know to keep out of the way when I fled to the bathroom. He was a good cook and saw it as a challenge to find food that I could tolerate, coaxing me to try morsels of this and that.

He was particularly supportive when my hair succumbed to

the toxic consequences of the cancer drugs. Even though Lucy cut it short, before my treatment started, it was still a shock when it started to go. I first noticed it coming away in the shower. I'd just begun to rub in some shampoo and it felt like my hair, not my scalp, was sore. Then I saw clumps of it in the shower tray. I felt more of it between my fingers. I wept as I watched it clog the drain.

Later, when I went back through to the living room, Rick was waiting. "Can I help?" He brandished his hair clippers. I nodded. He led me to the kitchen and sat me on one of the stools. Then he gently shaved off what remained of my hair. When he was finished he fetched the little mirror from the hall. "There was no point in prolonging it, was there?" He handed me the mirror.

I gazed at my newly bald head. It was shocking, but it was also a relief. "Losing my hair, I was dreading it more than the chemo. But now it's done, it's happened, it's over. Thank you."

"No problem, Rose-Marie."

I appreciated that he didn't make a big deal out of it. I suspected that having one of the family, or even Lucy or Kirsty, shave my head, would have been unbearable. There would have been way too much sympathy.

Rick made sure he was out the day I told the children I had cancer, but he returned at precisely the right moment. It was just as I was beginning to struggle in my attempts to reassure them. He took one look at me standing there, trying not to cry, failing to reassure Jenny. I must have looked shaky. "Whoa, careful," he said, as he put his arm around me. "Hello everyone, I'm Rick, Lucy's brother, and you must be Jenny. Come and give your mother a cuddle. She looks like she could do with one. I'll go and get you all some tea and biscuits." He handed me over to Jenny's embrace. "And you're Max, right?" Max nodded. "Can you come and give me a hand, tell me how the girls like their tea, if they like tea?" Max nodded again. "And, Sam, it's good to meet you too." He smiled at her before turning to me. "I'll get the tea made, and then I need to go out again for a while. I only popped back to fetch something I forgot earlier."

I didn't believe a word of it, but I appreciated what he'd done, coming back to check on us.

It was the same sort of thing that he did the day Tom and I met with Adam at the flat. Once again he gauged exactly how much support to offer and, once again, he could offer it in his slightly detached way. Rick didn't add to my stress.

And yes, there was some chemistry still between us. We flirted a bit and I must admit it lifted my spirits.

# Chapter Thirty Three

However, Rick did have work commitments and sometimes had to be away from home, so for a lot of the time, I lived alone and, for the most part, I didn't mind the solitude.

It gave me time and space to reflect. I could begin to come to terms with the mastectomy. I allowed myself to grieve for my breast, to measure what I'd lost. I'd nursed my babies there. It was part of my sexuality, a source of such tender pleasure. It was part of my feminine identity. But I came to accept that its loss was a tolerable one, part of the price of my survival. The anger I'd experienced when I first saw the results of the surgery subsided and, gradually, I acknowledged that my breast was gone.

And for some reason that I can't really identify, the acceptance of this loss enabled me to grieve, at last, for my sister. I thought about her a lot, allowed the memories, good and bad, to come to the surface. For the first time since her death, I could think about her without anger. I conceded that there was probably more to her death than I'd chosen to believe.

I mentioned my thoughts about Heather to Michael, during one of our regular phone calls. I told him that I felt better about her, asked him again how he coped with her loss.

But, as always, there was his customary reluctance to talk about her. He changed the subject by asking how my treatment was going and offering, as he did during every phone call since I'd told him about the cancer, to fly home to see me. And as I always did, I told him to wait until my treatment was finished and then we could really enjoy each other's company.

As the summer passed, the rhythm of my life was dominated by the chemotherapy schedule. I was glad that the children didn't have to witness just how sick and wretched the toxic medication made me feel. I was an adult when my mother went through it and it had still been harrowing to watch. I didn't want my children to remember me like that.

Ruby kept me in touch with how Adam was, as well as how things were at home. And if Adam had to be away from home, I couldn't think of anyone I'd rather he was living with. I tried to voice my gratitude to her one day when she was visiting. It wasn't long after Adam had visited Tom and me at the flat. She was doing some cleaning, despite my protestations that she was visiting as a dear friend, and not in her working capacity as a cleaner.

"Ruby, will you stop and sit down," I begged. "Please, it's embarrassing."

"Och, it's nothing," she replied. "I just want to look after you. I can't help myself."

"You're doing more than enough for me as it is, especially with Adam."

"I want to do it, all of it. Adam is one of the family. He's like one of my own. I don't run around after him, not like…" she hesitated.

"Not like me?" I laughed.

"Yes, not like you," Ruby smiled. "He has to get himself up and out, do his own washing and ironing, muck in with the meals and the cleaning. Mind you he's a very tidy lad, could teach my lot a thing or two."

"Yes, well, he's always liked things tidy, hasn't he? I did think when he visited that he'd grown up a bit since being with you."

"I think that would have happened anyway, Rosie. Maybe I've just hurried it along a bit. He's been able to see he can cope without his Mum, but he's missing you all, I know that. His time out has been good for him, but I don't think it'll be long before he's back at home where he belongs."

"I hope you're right."

"And you, Rosie, have you any idea when you'll be back? I'm sorry, hen, I know it's none of my business but…"

"It's okay. The truth is I don't really know when, or if. I've another month or so of chemo then maybe I can think about what I'm going to do."

"Tom really misses you, you know. He made a mistake with the Robbie business, but I'm sure that's all it was, a mistake. I remember how worried he was about you when the twins were born and when your sister died. You were really ill. And sometimes, the right thing to do isn't the best thing to do. For what it's worth, I think Tom did the right thing at the time."

Ruby paused and looked at me. This was blunt, even by her standards. A small part of me conceded that she had a point. But there was also the question of Robbie's paternity. Ruby seemed to know what I was thinking. "Oh, I know there's more to it than Tom not telling you about Robbie, and I'm not saying anything about that. That's between the two of you."

"Yes it is, but thanks for caring. Now what gossip have you got for me from Gullane?"

"Ah, now, funny you should say that. I do have a couple of titbits. I'll get a cup of tea and fill you in. I've also got the latest copy of 'Hallo' in my bag, so we can get stuck in to that too."

Another of my regular visitors was Robbie. I wished the circumstances could have been better, but I was delighted to see him and to be getting to know him.

He had a summer job in town. He'd quit Tesco once he made contact with us. He was working as a kitchen porter at the Bruntsfield hotel, quite near the flat. When he was on his week of split shifts, he would often turn up on my doorstep, rather than going all the way across town to get home between the early and late stints.

I loved when he visited. I became consciously aware of his shift patterns and would anticipate his probable arrival. We were, by then, completely at ease with one another. He had lots of questions about Heather and the rest of the family and I enjoyed answering them. I was fascinated by my sister's boy. He was likeable, intelligent and mature and I loved him utterly.

He was very keen for me to meet his mum, and I was curious to meet her. So, one afternoon in early August, Robbie brought her to the flat. I was quite nervous waiting for them to arrive. It was important to me that Sue Sutherland would like me. For some reason her approval mattered.

She smiled nervously as Robbie introduced us. Her hands shook as she handed me the large bunch of flowers she'd brought. "From our garden. I hope you like them."

"I love flowers, thank you," I said, inhaling their scent. There were yellow and cream roses along with similarly coloured freesias and sweet peas. "They smell gorgeous. Freesias are my absolute favourite, but I've never been very successful growing them."

She smiled again and gave a little shrug. "Glad you like them." She didn't seem comfortable doing small talk. There was wariness in her manner.

But, once she was in the living room, she went straight to the family photos I'd recently put out on the mantelpiece. She seemed fascinated by them. She exclaimed over the resemblance of Adam to Robbie. She lingered over Heather's photo, after I pointed it out to her. She picked it up and held it out to Robbie, "Have you seen this son?" she asked. "She was a pretty girl, your mother."

"Yes, Mum, I've seen it." He took it from her and looked at it for a moment. Then he replaced it on the mantelpiece. "Rosie's shown me a lot of photos of her and of the rest of the family. I told you that." He spoke gently and squeezed her hand.

She nodded. "I know you did, son. I know you did."

"I hope you didn't mind me showing him the photos," I said.

Sue shook her head. "No, of course not, but can I ask you something?"

"Yes, of course, and please, both of you, sit down."

Sue looked anxious and paused before continuing. "Do you think it would have been better for Robbie to have been with you, to have grown up with his biological family? Do you think you would have done a better job than us?"

Robbie touched his mother's hand. "Mum, don't do this to yourself."

She put her hand on his arm and gave a slight shake of her head. She was sitting forward, intent, looking at me.

"No! That is, I don't know," I said. "You've done a great job. Robbie's a lovely boy. He was lucky to get you and your husband as parents."

"But it would have been better to be with his blood relations? I know you must think you could have done better by him. You're a teacher, Tom's a doctor. You've got money and your children are at private school." Her voice had got quieter. She looked down at her hands, twisting her wedding ring as she spoke. "Bob and I, a bus driver and a janitor, it's not in the same league, is it?"

"No, honestly, that never occurred to me. Good parents are good parents. Jobs and money, they're incidental. You work in a school. You must see that all the time. It's love and security that's important."

"And the biological connection? Is adoption second best?"

"No, not necessarily. Like I say, just because someone gives birth to a child doesn't guarantee they'll be a good parent. I suppose it's just that I didn't get the choice with Robbie." My voice cracked as I spoke. I could feel tears starting.

I looked at Sue and saw she had tears in her eyes too.

I managed to continue. "God, Sue, this is hard. But I feel nothing but gratitude to you. What I feel about the adoption is very selfish, I'm afraid. Robbie is a connection with my dead sister, and being with him is very comforting to me. I'm sad for me, for what I've missed. But I couldn't have loved him any more than you obviously do."

I desperately wanted to reassure her. She looked slightly less wary, but not exactly relaxed. "And part of me can see Tom was right," I went on. "I couldn't have coped with another baby at the time. I just wish he'd told me."

"Well, what's done is done and neither of us can change that. And thank you for being so honest. I've been desperate to know what you think." She hesitated and then said, "So you're not going to take Robbie away from us then, ask him to live with you?"

"What? No, no, of course not! Why? Is that what you thought? Robbie's your son. I'm just delighted that you're generous enough to be willing to share him with me and my family."

"Thank God," Sue was smiling and crying. "Thank God. Yes, I've been worrying about that. Actually, I'd like to think we're all part of the same family now."

I smiled back at her. "I'd like to think that too."

Robbie added to the easing of the tension by saying, "Right, can you two, please, stop talking about me as if I'm not here!"

# Chapter Thirty Four

To say I missed the children doesn't fully describe the sometimes physical pain of my longing to be with them. But at least when I did see them, it was on my better days.

I knew that Evelyn and Ruby and, yes, Tom, kept a close eye on Max. And, as I'd promised, he often came to stay for a night or two, once the school holidays began.

At the start of one such visit he let himself into the flat, calling "Hi, Mum," as he slammed the front door shut. He bounded through to the living room, where I was stretched out on the couch watching daytime television. "Kirsty dropped me off. She says hi, but she's not coming in because she's still got a bit of a cold."

I sat up to greet him. "Hi, son, come and give your mum a hug."

He backed away. "No hugs or kisses. I was in the car with Kirsty and she could have transferred some germs to me. Better to be safe than sorry. Remember your white cells are rubbish." He sat down on the armchair furthest from the sofa and began unpacking his backpack.

"And what do you know about white cells?"

"They're what protect you from infection. Dad explained it to me. They're in your blood."

"Okay, Dr McAllister." I shrank back on the sofa with my hands over my mouth and nose.

He rolled his eyes at my feeble attempt at humour. "I'm serious. You need to be careful." He held up his sketch pad. "Do you want to see my drawings?"

"Yes, please. Have you done more since your last visit?"

"Uh huh." He turned the pages. "This is one of Dad and Toby." He passed me the book.

"Oh my goodness, Max, this is really good." I stared at the picture. He'd drawn Tom and Toby together on the sofa, sleeping. Some of the proportions were slightly off and the shading wasn't perfect, but Max had captured such an accurate likeness of his father.

"You okay, Mum? You're not crying, are you?"

"No, I'm not crying. I'm just very proud of you, Maxy. You're a talented artist. It's a great picture."

"Dad and me had been working in the garden all day. He's been getting me to help him tidy it up. He says we've to keep it nice for you coming home. Grandma's been telling him what to do. Anyway, he was knackered when we finished, said he just wanted to sit for a few minutes before he made the dinner. Next thing he was snoring away on the sofa. It was Jenny's idea for me to draw him."

I nodded. I told myself to focus on the excellence of the drawings. Determined not to cry in front of Max, I said, "Go and get yourself a drink. There's some Coke in the fridge." He didn't need persuading to indulge in this rare treat. While he was in the kitchen, I blew my nose hard and tried not to think about Tom and the garden.

"Whose car is this?" I asked, pointing to another of his sketches, when he came back into the room.

"Uncle Dan's. It's his new one. It's wicked, black, and the top folds down. He took me and Grandma for a run in it. We went over the Forth Road Bridge and got fish suppers in Anstruther. He says it's the best chippy in the country. He told Dad to take you there, when you're better, and won't throw up. He even said he'd lend Dad the car to take you in."

"Mm, it looks like a really cool car." Once again I'd to concentrate really hard on the drawings. At the end there were a few sketches of some of the Harry Potter characters. "Oh, have you got the next one yet?"

"Yep, 'The Half-Blood Prince', here it is." He produced it from his bag. "Dad got it from Amazon for me. I'm racing Grandma to read it. We keep texting each other to say how far we've got."

"Who's winning?"

"Grandma's a chapter ahead at the moment."

"Are you enjoying it as much as the others?"

"Yeah, but it's a bit soppy with Ron and his girlfriend, and with Harry fancying Ginny. I sort of skip those bits. Why are they wasting time with all that love stuff?"

"They're growing up, Maxy. You'll be the same."

"Never!"

"Oh look, come and sit beside me. Kirsty's germs must have worn off by now." I held out my arm to him. "And since when are you calling her Kirsty?"

He came over and curled in at my side. "It's been for a while now. Since I left primary school at the end of term. She said she wasn't my head teacher anymore, so I didn't have to call her Miss Mackinnon."

I smiled and gave him a squeeze. "See, you are growing up! Now, do you think it would be cheating, in your contest with Grandma, if I read some chapters of Harry P. to you?"

"Nah, anyway, we won't tell her."

"You're on. Are you sitting comfortably?" Max remained nestled by my side as I read. At some point his hand slipped into mine. After a while he took over the reading and I just relaxed and enjoyed his soothing, easy company.


Jenny's visits were livelier than those of her little brother. She was lively, bright and opinionated on many issues; climate change, poverty, and politics were just a few of the topics on which she regularly held forth.

During her visits she often talked about her hopes for the future of the planet. Her enthusiasm and optimism were infectious, and listening to her knowledgeable and passionate take on the world lifted my spirits. After one such discourse I couldn't help smiling at her bright-eyed zeal.

"What?" she said. "What are you laughing at?"

"I'm not laughing. It's just you make me feel good. Listening to you makes me feel good."

One day, in the middle of July, she arrived at the flat looking very excited.

"Guess what!" she said as soon as she was in the door. "I've passed my driving test!"

"Oh, Jen, congratulations!" I hugged her. "You kept that quiet. I didn't even know you had a test date. When was it?"

"Yesterday. I wanted to surprise you and tell you in person. Isn't it great?"

"It's fantastic. Well done." I hugged her again.

"Now, you need to put me on the insurance to drive your car, because there's somewhere I want to take you."

"Right, okay. I don't suppose you're going to tell me where we're going."

"No, just get the insurance sorted out and then all will be revealed."

It turned out Jenny had found out about the Maggie's Centre, at the Western General and that was where she wanted to take me. Wendy had mentioned the facility to me and I'd passed the building many times. It was in the hospital grounds, but I'd never ventured in. I had a distinct feeling of role reversal the day Jenny drove me there for my first visit.

"Isn't this a lovely place, Mum?" Jenny said, as we were shown round by one of the volunteers who worked there. "You can get support, therapies, counselling and all sorts of stuff to help you."

The volunteer smiled at me. "Your daughter's done her homework."

"Yes, indeed she has. This is a lovely place. I'll definitely be back."

The centre had an atmosphere that was both tranquil and

energising. And I did become a regular visitor. Jenny even organised Lucy to drive me to the centre when she couldn't do so herself.

"It was Dad who told me about this place," Jenny said, as we walked back to the car after our first visit. "He talks about you a lot, Mum, thinks about you and what you need. He said I wasn't to tell you it was him who suggested the Maggie's, because it would put you off the place, but I just think you should know." She took my arm. "I'm not telling you to upset you. It was nice of him wasn't it? To suggest it. And it was just a suggestion. He wasn't saying you must go or anything."

I couldn't answer her immediately.

"You're not angry are you, with Dad or me?" She looked at me, serious and uncertain.

"Oh, Jen, don't look so worried. No, I'm not angry. It was thoughtful of both of you."

As we approached the car, she stopped walking and turned to me. "You are coming back to live with us, with Dad, aren't you, once you feel better about everything?"

Again I couldn't answer right away. I shook my head.

"I mean, I understand. At least I think I do. I think I get why you felt you had to go. And I'm not taking sides or anything. But you've not left forever, have you?"

"I don't know. I didn't intend it to be forever. I still don't intend it to be. But I'm not ready to come back yet. I do know that." I took her hands in mine. "And I know it's hard for you, and it means a lot to me that you've been so understanding and supportive."

She held me close for a moment before getting into the car. "I love you, Mum. I love you and I miss you."

For Sam it was even harder than it was for Jenny. She felt for her dad, and she struggled to understand my reasons for leaving. Like Evelyn, she was also suspicious of Rick.

During one visit to me, in the middle of July, not long after

Rick had returned to Skye, she seemed especially tense. "The creep not here then?" she said, looking around when she arrived.

"If you mean Rick, then no, he's not here. He's gone back up north, to do the next phase of his project."

"Good. I hope he doesn't come back." She flung herself down on one of the armchairs, and crossed her arms in a way that reminded me of a much younger and sulking Sam.

I sat opposite her and tried to change the subject, lighten the atmosphere. I asked her about her social life, her friends. Her answers were monosyllabic. I battled on. "Grandma and Ruby have been telling me what a great job you're doing keeping things in order at home. I'm so grateful, Sam, for what you're doing. It means I don't have to worry about all that."

"I'm not doing it for you. The money will come in handy and, unlike you, I actually like doing it."

Although I was aware of her mood, I was taken aback at the vehemence with which she spoke.

She got to her feet, began pacing, ran a hand through her hair. "You could come home and I'd still do it," she continued. "I know what you said, about having to be careful to avoid infection while you're having the chemotherapy, but are you not just using that as an excuse not to come back?"

"What, no! No I'm not! What nonsense!" Of course, I recognised a grain of truth in this and I probably protested too much. "Come on, Sam. I've been over all this. Surely you wouldn't rather I was in hospital a lot of the time."

"Yes, I would actually, if it meant you were at home in between. And you can't still be angry with Dad."

I stood up, tried to catch hold of her arm, to stop her pacing and make her face me. She shook me off, went to the window, looked out.

"Look, Sam," I said, "how I feel about Dad, about him and Robbie, and me being ill, it's complicated. I–"

She turned, leant against the sill, arms folded again. "No, it's not. It's simple. You're punishing Dad. He doesn't deserve it. He was trying to protect you. Why's that so bad?"

"It's not bad. It's not just about that. I think–"

"Oh, I know what you think. You think Dad's Robbie's father. You think that's why he didn't tell you. How can you believe that? There's no way Dad would've done that. You're just being stupid."

I wasn't surprised that she'd worked out my suspicions, or that she sided with her father, but it was hard to hear her say it.

And she wasn't finished. "All this, this wanting time on your own, your – your stupid cancer – it's just selfish. It's just a way of making Dad suffer."

"Sam, don't do this," I begged. "I know this is hard for you. But sometimes we can't explain our feelings or our actions, not fully, even to ourselves. Please believe me. I'm not trying to hurt your father. Yes, I was angry and, yes, I don't understand what he did. I can't help how I feel. I can't help having cancer. Of course I want to come home, but the time's not right at the moment."

"When will it be? When will it be right?"

"I don't know. Look it's difficult for you. You're young–"

"Oh, don't do that speech! I'm young. I can't understand adult stuff blah, blah, blah. Heard it! You're just bloody stupid and – and fucking selfish! It would be easier on all of us if you were dead!"

I gasped as if she'd slapped me. I'd have preferred it if she'd struck me. I put my hands to my face, trying unsuccessfully to prevent a sob escaping.

A momentary flicker of alarm crossed Sam's face. Then she picked up her bag and fled from the flat.

I didn't see or hear from her for a couple of weeks. At first she wouldn't answer her phone when I called. Then I got a couple of terse texts in response to my messages.

It was the last day of July when she came back to the flat. Jenny was with her. It was early afternoon when they arrived, and I was resting on top of the bed. I sat up and shouted hallo when I heard the key in the front door. They came straight through to the bedroom.

"Hi, Mum," Jenny said, as she gave me a hug and a kiss. "I've brought camomile tea for you to try. You said you'd gone off the ordinary stuff. I'll go and get the kettle on."

Sam, who'd been hanging back in the doorway, looked at her sister, pleadingly, but Jenny just smiled and patted her arm as she passed.

"Come in, Sam," I said.

She took a step into the room. "Mum," she spoke quietly. "You look tired. Are you feeling bad?"

"I feel better after my rest. And I feel better seeing you. Come here." I held out my arms. She came into them so quickly, she nearly knocked me over. We sat on the bed, holding each other tight.

When Sam released her grip, she sat back, looking into my eyes. She was so like Tom that my breath caught in my throat.

"I'm sorry, Mum. I'm so sorry. What I said, it was horrible. Jenny was so cross when I told her. She's the only person I've told. I've been too embarrassed to talk to you. But you know Jenny. She wouldn't let it go. She persuaded me to come. She said you'd forgive me."

"Oh, my darling, there's nothing to forgive." I kissed her and stroked her hair. "I'm sorry too. Sorry you've been so hurt by all this. I love you so much, Sam."

"I love you too, Mum."

"Right, I'm glad that's all sorted!" Jenny was back in the bedroom. "Now dry your tears you two and come through for some camomile infusion."

"Sounds revolting," Sam said. "I think I'll have a Coke." Jenny rolled her eyes as Sam went off to the kitchen, but she gave me a huge grin.

"Have you given Mum her present?" Jenny said, when Sam joined us in the living room.

"Oh, yes!" Sam scrabbled in her bag and produced a prettily wrapped package. "For you, from me" she said.

It was a hat, a pretty little blue hat with an upturned brim. "Oh, Sam, it's lovely. Thank you." I took off the hat I was wearing, an earlier present from Jenny, and tried on my new one. Sam looked at me and smiled, a wonderful sight.

"It suits you, Mum. Good choice, Sam." Jenny nodded in approval. She reached into her bag. "Here." She handed me a mirror. I looked at my reflection. I'd been avoiding looking at myself for weeks. In fact I'd turned the bedroom mirror to the wall. I let out a little gasp. I looked pale and my face was much thinner, but the hat was flattering. Jenny rested her head on my shoulder and looked at us both in the mirror. "It matches your eyes perfectly, but that face could do with some colour."

"It certainly could!" Sam said. "So get that tea finished, and then sit back for your makeover."

"What?" I asked, as my daughters laughed. They'd come prepared. I was treated to a facial by Jenny. Then Sam applied some makeup to my face. And I had to admit, when I surveyed the result, I looked much better for their ministrations.

"And this is from both of us," Jenny said, handing me another package.

"This is too much, girls!" I unwrapped a beautiful, turquoise and lilac, tie-dyed, cotton scarf.

"No, no, it isn't," Sam said. "You deserve a treat, Mum. Here, I'll show you how to tie it round your head. We thought you could wear it as a change from your hats."

After that day, my daughters and I had regular girlie afternoons of makeup and manicures and I treasured every moment.

# Chapter Thirty Five

I meant it when I said to Jenny that I'd never intended my leaving to be permanent. I missed home and I loved it when the children visited me. They really did lift my spirits. So, what was stopping me going back? Yes, there was the risk of infection, but seeing family and friends at the flat was only marginally less risky. I didn't tell my medical team just how many visitors I had, because I didn't want to be hospitalised. But if I was honest, as the summer progressed, my low immunity was a convenient excuse to stay on my own.

And, as I'd also said to Jenny, that day at the Maggie's centre, I wasn't ready to go home.

For one thing, I was putting on a brave face about the cancer whenever I was with my family or friends. But it was just that. An act, an utterly exhausting act. It was something I noticed. People seemed to expect bravery from cancer patients. It was seen as admirable. It seemed if the patient was stoical and serene throughout, it made the unafflicted feel less threatened by the whole filthy, painful business of cancer. Oh yes, I felt that bitter. I resented the healthy. I'm not proud of it, but sometimes, when my mood was the very darkest black, I hated the relentlessly cheerful, look-on-the-bright-side brigade.

Because the truth was, I wasn't the least bit brave. I was absolutely petrified. I was an emotional wreck. The physical pain, the vomiting, my ulcerated mouth and bleeding gums were nothing compared to the internal terror.

It could happen any time, day or night. I'd think I was coping but then *she* was always there, just biding her time, waiting for the slightest sliver of self-pity or fear. She was an ever-present, dark shadow waiting in the wings. As soon as there was a chink in my defences, she was out of the wings and at centre stage. And yes, I'm sorry to say, it was a she. My cancer was a malicious, marauding, merciless witch-bitch from hell, a most wicked Queen, offended by healthy femininity. She was a hideous and heartless entity, a violating and invasive, alien presence. She plotted my death.

Sometimes she made me cower. At those times I could only curl up on the bed and cry, and try to keep the sickening pictures out of my head; images of my mutilated chest, or of my morphine-clouded deathbed, and my bereaved and motherless children. But the bitch would be there screaming and cackling, "Look! Go on, look!

And sometimes, she'd win and I would look. I'd look at the fiery, jagged scar that served as a sickening marker of what I'd lost. And I'd cradle my remaining breast, stroke, press and prod it. I'd convince myself there was a lump. I'd check again and there'd be nothing there. And how the evil, festering crone would laugh. These were my darkest times and, on these occasions, I felt my sanity hanging by a thread.

I had to come up with a way of fighting this truly awful entity.

It was speaking with Dawn, a young patient I met at the Maggie's, that helped me come up with my battle plan. Dawn was very young, just Sam's age, and was being treated for secondaries in her bones. It was humbling enough just conversing with this amazing girl. It certainly helped me regain some perspective. For one thing, I was utterly grateful it was me and not one of my children who was the cancer patient. But it was Dawn's visualisation technique that really resonated with me. She pictured herself as Lara Croft swinging through tombs blasting her nasties, her tumours.

"It works for me, Rosie. You feel strong, like you're the boss and you're in charge and kicking the cancer's ass. Try it!"

And so I did. The choice came easily. The Alien movies were some of Tom's favourite films. We saw the first one at the cinema when we were just married and we got it on video as soon as we had our first VCR. It remained our favourite of the series. We watched it many times, with a takeaway and a bottle of wine, in the years before we had the kids. I bought it on DVD after my conversation with Dawn. I watched it over and over.

I was going to be the gutsy Ripley, the armed-to-the-teeth Sigourney Weaver character, the heroine of the movie. My body was the spaceship Nostromo and I was going to rid my craft of the stinking, malevolent witch-bitch alien.

As Ripley I'd scream my threats at the ghastly hag that was stalking me. I'd stand my ground and I'd yell at her to do her worst, shout that she wasn't going to get me. She'd got my mother but she wasn't going to get me. And she needn't even think about getting her scrawny, wraith-like hands on my daughters, because I was going to obliterate her from my life and she wasn't ever coming back.

I'd patrol my spaceship and, always, that stalking bitch was waiting, tucked round a corner, ready to lunge out in front of me, forcing me to stay and fight or, to turn and flee. Being Ripley brought me strength, helped me look past the shadow in the wings, helped me get to know my enemy better.

I researched symptoms and treatments obsessively on the internet. I quizzed my doctors. What were the chances of a recurrence, of a carcinoma in the other breast, of a genetic link that meant my daughters were vulnerable? Mostly they answered patiently and kindly, but never with the unqualified assurances that I sought.

But it was from Dawn and my other fellow patients at the Maggie's Centre that I got the most practical support. We exchanged information about therapies and treatments. And we shared a black humour, tumour humour, we called it. And when my sense of humour failed me and I needed to weep, to grieve for the loss of my breast and the loss of my self, no-one at the Centre minded. No-one made bloody stupid, bland remarks about how it would all be fine.

So, by August, the bitch and I reached an understanding. I wasn't going to waste any more precious energy being angry. I would still get scared, but if I remained strong in the face of my fear, then I believed I would win. This was not bravery, but a strong desire to survive. I no longer trusted my treacherous body, so I had to rely on my strength of will. I'd negotiate the road on my terms. To do it, I needed space to manoeuvre and to react as I saw fit. And agony though it was, at times, to be separated from them, I honestly believed my children were better off not witnessing the full horror of my journey.

My resolve, my determination to be in control, also meant that I couldn't be with Tom. Not only had my own body betrayed me, but Tom had too. And I still feared the force of his belief that he knew best.

However, my feelings of anger towards him did subside.

I realised that I'd never given him the slightest inkling that I was ready to talk about Heather's suicide. I'd blocked the whole malignant business and let it eat away at me. The irony of the parallel with my present physical condition was not lost on me. I knew there was more to the story regarding Tom's part in the end of my sister's life and the beginning of Robbie's. And although it might hurt like hell, I also knew that I needed to hear it.

And I was grateful to Tom, that he did as I asked and gave me my time alone. But though it was what I wanted and needed, I did yearn for him. I missed him in every way, physically, mentally, emotionally. I longed for his touch, his smell, his maleness and, perversely, I know, at times I longed for his strength.

I found that I looked forward to his twice-weekly phone calls. And I had to admit to myself that, on the day Adam came to meet us both at the flat, I was as excited about seeing Tom as I was about seeing Adam. He was so kind and gentle that afternoon, even after I threw up on him.

A week after that visit, the exam results came out. Jenny's

results were very good, four As and a B. Being Jenny, she was, of course, more annoyed about the B in History than thrilled about the four As. She phoned me to let me know how she'd done. She'd got the grades she needed for university and we chatted about the pros and cons of the courses offered by Edinburgh, St Andrews and Aberdeen.

Adam arranged for his results to be forwarded to Ruby's. He said he'd call me to let me know how he'd got on and that I was to tell Tom. He clearly didn't want to discuss the outcome with his father. I rehearsed how I would react when he phoned. I was determined not to say the wrong thing, no matter what he had to tell me, but the trouble was I didn't know what the right thing would be. If the results were better than expected, I told myself not to gush, but to sound pleased in a controlled way. If the results were bad, then I mustn't sound pitying. I would be positive, but not overwhelmingly so. By the time his call came I was a nervous wreck.

"Hi, Mum, how are you feeling today?"

"Hi, son," I replied keeping my voice calm. "I'm well, thanks. No chemo this week."

"That's good. I've got my results here."

"Yes?"

"I got my maths. I got a C in my maths! How cool's that?"

I could hear the smile, the delight in his voice. I smiled too as I spoke. "It's very cool, son, very cool. Well done. You're obviously pleased about it, and so am I. Higher maths is a great achievement. Really it is!" I stopped at that. Don't gush, I reminded myself.

"I've never done anything this nerdy before. Me, higher maths! Still, a C's not too nerdy, is it."

I laughed.

"What you laughing at?" He didn't sound defensive. I could still hear his smile.

"You, Adam, you, but in a nice way."

He laughed back. "Okay, if you say so. I failed the others by the way."

I took a deep breath. "And how do you feel about that?"

"Okay. I got a D in English which is better than I expected, and an E in biology.

"Right, well, you sound positive. I'm glad. I'm really proud of you. Well done, Ad."

"I guess. Anyway, I better go. You'll tell Dad about my results, yeah?"

"Yes, I will. Bye, son."

I called Tom at the hospital right away. I guessed he'd be feeling as nervous as I'd been. Sheena answered. She told me Tom was just out of theatre and she'd page him.

When he came on the line he sounded out of breath. "Rosie, hi, are you okay? Everything all right?"

"Yes, Tom, everything's fine. Thanks."

"He called then?"

"Yes, he called. He passed his maths, got a C." I heard a little gasp from Tom. I wasn't sure if this was because of joy or disappointment. Did Tom see it as *only* a C?

I continued. "He thinks it's cool and not too nerdy. Don't you think he did well to pass?"

"Yes, yes I do," Tom said. "It's good. What about the rest?"

"He failed the rest. But as he said, not as miserably as he'd feared."

There was momentary pause before Tom spoke. "I don't suppose the subject of him going back to school came up?"

"No, it didn't. I think he's made it clear what he thinks on that score. I really don't think we should push it. The main thing is he's feeling positive."

"Yes, you're right of course. I need to let the school thing go, don't I?"

"Yes you do. Adam's made it clear. He's going to be making his own decisions from now on."

"God, I really screwed up with Adam, didn't I?"

"No, no you didn't. You want the best for him. That's a good thing. You care. I got it wrong too. I stifled him. I was far too protective. I thought he couldn't cope on his own and he quite clearly can. We both need to give him space."

"Yes, and thanks, Rosie. It means a lot that you don't blame me." He spoke very quietly.

I wished we were together in the same room. I wanted to touch him. But I was aware he was at work, and I wasn't sure if he was alone. So I didn't say anything.

Then he added, even more quietly, "Over Adam at least."

# Chapter Thirty Six

As September began, Edinburgh quietened down and settled herself. The crowds of summer tourists had gone home and the bustle of the festival was over. It had been the hottest summer for years, but the weather broke with several dramatic thunderstorms at the end of August. Autumn's muted tones were reflected in the city's more sedate pace, and I experienced a similar calming down after my own fraught summer.

The cooler air, misty mornings and wash of glorious autumnal colour over the city's parks, gardens and tree-lined streets were all soul soothing. And as the season changed, I sensed I too had reached a turning point.

It was during the first week of September that Adam came to have dinner with me. It was his suggestion. I hadn't seen him since he visited Tom and me at the flat a month before. I was apprehensive, like when awaiting his exam results phone call. As then, I knew I must be calm and not rush anything.

He brought me flowers, freesias, which surprised and delighted me. He'd never done anything like that before.

"They're my favourites," I said. "Thank you." I wanted to kiss him, but settled for patting his arm. He looked at the floor, embarrassed. He seemed to have grown again and had become even ganglier.

But the thing that struck me most, was how like Tom he looked. He was becoming a fair-haired version of his father. As he ran his hands through his hair, a flustered gesture straight from Tom's repertoire, I had such a strong desire to be with Tom that it knocked the breath out of me for a moment.

"God, Mum, are you okay?" he asked. "I know it's a shock, me giving you flowers. It was Robbie's idea. He said they were your favourites."

"Yes, I'm okay. Sorry, never mind me. I was just thinking how like your Dad you're getting. And it made me think I was missing him. That's all." I hadn't meant to blurt that out to Adam.

"Right. That's good, isn't it. You missing Dad? Maybe you're ready to talk to him, maybe go home?"

"I don't know about that," I said , before changing the subject. "So, it was Robbie's idea, the flowers?"

"Yes, I had dinner at his house yesterday. He invited me and Jenny round. He's a good bloke."

"Yes, he is." I smiled and I relaxed and spent a lovely afternoon in the company of my son.


A couple of weeks later, another significant milestone was reached when I had my last dose of chemo.

Sam took me to the hospital and stayed with me while the noxious mixture dripped into my vein.

Wendy was upbeat. "Last time," she said, smiling at Sam and me as she hooked me up.

I know I should have been pleased it was the final shot. But I wasn't. I was in turmoil. For one thing, I could hear witch-bitch cackling in anticipation. I was frightened by this major disarmament. She'd be there in a flash, spreading her malignancy round my body. How would I fight her then? These toxic chemicals were the bullets for Ripley's guns and Wendy was stealing away my ammo. It felt like I was losing control. I considered begging Wendy to let me have another six months treatment.

Then there was Tom. I suspected he'd see the passing of my last chemo as the end of my need to be away. I was unnerved to realise, I'd probably agree with him. Contemplating going back to Tom, I felt like I had when I was at the top of the Nemesis ride at Alton Towers, both wanting and dreading at the same time.

"So how do you feel, Rosie? About stopping." Wendy's voice broke in on my thoughts.

"Oh, I'm glad, of course," I lied. "But I must admit I'm a bit scared of stopping." Oh, the understatement. "Does that sound daft?"

"No, not at all, it's a very common response actually. Patients often feel it's like they've stopped fighting when they stop getting this stuff. Let's just hope it's done its job."

"Oh, yes, don't get me wrong, I'm not up for getting more." Liar! "It's just, it feels like letting my guard down."

"Well the fight's not over yet, but you get a bit of a break now, before radiotherapy. You'll be seeing Dr Knox soon, to find out if the chemo's been effective. And, just think, your hair will start to grow back now."

Wendy made sure I was comfortable and then left us while the potion made its journey from bag to bloodstream. Sam had brought a couple of gossip magazines with her and, for a while, she distracted me by reading aloud from them. We shared a laugh at some of the crazier stories and I realised how much I was going to miss her.

Soon she'd be going away to university and we were trying to spend as much time together as we could. Tom was going to be running her to St Andrews and, as she drove me home, she broached the subject of me going along too.

"I don't know, Sam. What if I feel sick?"

"It's two weeks away Mum. You'll have stopped being sick. And this is a big occasion. Your number one child going off to uni. You can't miss that."

"You've been thinking about this, haven't you?" I said smiling.

"Yes, I have. Please, Mum. Dad would like it too, if you came."

"Would he, now? You've asked him then?"

"Yes, but he said you wouldn't come. Prove him wrong, Mum. Go on."

I didn't need much persuading, not after my realisation in

the chemo ward earlier. And, like I'd said to Adam, I was missing Tom. I was probably as ready as I'd ever be to listen to what Tom had to tell me. The time had come to try to rebuild my life, our lives.

"Okay, I'll come," I said, and I found I was laughing.

I phoned Tom that evening and told him I'd be going to St Andrews with them.

"You're coming, in the car, with Sam and me?" he asked.

I laughed. "Yes, that's the plan. Sam said she'd asked you."

"Yes, she did, but I didn't think you'd agree. Not if it meant being with me."

"I think I'll cope. Maybe we can have a bit of a talk on the journey back." There was silence at the other end. "Tom, Tom, are you still there?"

"Yes." He cleared his throat. "I'm still here. Right, it's a date then. I'll call you nearer the day and we can fix up a time to collect you on our way north."

Over the following few days I was hardly sick at all, and even the nausea disappeared. By the end of the week I was feeling quite well.

Robbie called in to see me on the Friday. Over lunch he told me that Adam had been to visit him on several more occasions. "My dad and him seem to have bonded over engines, which is fine by me. It takes the pressure of me having to pretend to be fascinated by pistons and carburettors."

I smiled. "Adam certainly won't have to fake an interest."

"Adam also seems to have bonded with my sister, Julie, and I don't think their mutual interest in motors is the only attraction." Robbie raised his eyebrows and grinned.

"Oh, really, bonding as in..."

"Yes, as in..." He laughed and put both hands over his heart and fluttered his eyelashes.

This was the first I knew of Adam being interested in a girl. He certainly was changing. When Robbie was leaving, he said he was going to meet Eilidh in town for a little while before going back to work.

"So you and Eilidh are still bonded then?" I said.

Robbie nodded. "She says she needs a break from her mum, who's in love apparently, and is driving Eilidh up the wall."

"Pardon?" I said. "In love? Kirsty's in love? She hasn't said anything to me. Who with? Who's she in love with?"

"Oh, you better ask her that yourself." And off he went, leaving me amazed and very curious.

That afternoon, Sam and I went shopping in Princes Street for clothes and other bits and pieces that she'd need for starting university. It was several months since I'd been on an outing like this. I felt liberated and we had a good, girlie afternoon together.

I had mixed feelings about Sam leaving home. It felt more final than when she went to Australia. My first child was grown up and it made me feel old and a little sad. But I was happy for her too and quite envious of all she had to look forward to.

She was very excited about going up to St Andrews the following weekend. "I'm so glad you're coming up too, Mum. Oh, it'll be great, the three of us together. Dad's excited too."

I smiled at her. "It's an exciting time. I'm excited for you, just like Dad is. You're going to love being at uni."

"No, Mum, Dad's not just excited for me. He's excited that you're coming. He says you two are going to have a good talk and get things sorted out. He misses you, Mum. He wants you back, I'm sure he does."

"Oh, sweetheart, I'm not sure what either of us wants. We've changed. The Robbie stuff, me being ill. But we're both proud of you and excited. And it'll be nice for us both to see you off."

"But you will talk to him, won't you? He says he has a lot he wants to say to you."

"Yes, Sam I promise we'll talk."

Later the same day, Rick phoned to say he'd be back in Edinburgh the following Friday. He asked how things were going. I told him about the plan to go to St Andrews and he sounded genuinely pleased that Tom and I were going together.

He laughed when I told him what Robbie had said about Kirsty being in love.

That evening I couldn't settle. My thoughts kept going back to Tom. I wanted to see him. I almost got in the car and drove to Gullane, but it was about ten o'clock and I was very tired. Then I thought if I could just hear his voice, then I could settle. So I phoned home. Max answered. We had a bit of a chat and then I asked to speak to Tom.

"Oh, he's not in. He's out for a meal with Sheena. You know, the lady at the hospital? Except, oops, it's a secret. I'm not supposed to tell you that!"

"Oh, right, with Sheena, and it's a secret." I kept my voice as level as I could, trying to keep the shock of what I'd just heard on the very edges of my consciousness.

"Yeah, don't say anything. Dad says he'll tell you when he's ready. Uncle Dan's looking after me. Well, he's supposed to be. He's fallen asleep on the couch. Will I ask Dad to call you when he gets back? He's not usually late when he's with Sheena."

"No, no it's okay. It's not important. I think I'll get off to bed. Goodnight, Max."

It was a sickening blow and I'd been completely unprepared for it. Tom and Sheena, it sounded like they'd been out a few times. And Max didn't sound bothered at all. I felt wounded and ill. I put my hands over my mouth to stem the nausea and rocked with the gut clenching pain. Tom obviously wasn't missing me as much as Sam seemed to think. A low, agonised groan escaped from my lips as I began to sob.

Tom and Sheena, I hadn't seen that coming.

# Chapter Thirty Seven

The next day, Lucy and Kirsty came for lunch. They'd suggested an end of chemo celebration. I tried to put thoughts of Tom out of my mind as we set out the food they'd brought, but the pain remained as a dull ache. There was a gorgeous, creamy quiche and salad from Kirsty, courtesy of M&S's food hall, and Lucy's homemade bread and her wonderful, chocolate cheesecake. They'd also brought pink champagne, my absolutely favourite drink. It all looked lovely and I actually ate some of it. I even managed some champagne.

"How's your course going?" I asked Lucy, as we ate. She was training in aromatherapy, reflexology and therapeutic massage.

"I'm loving it. I can't wait to start putting it all into practice. Graham's got really enthused by it, and he's talking about converting part of the steading into a treatment salon for me."

"That's great," I said. "So, you'd have your own business?"

"Yes, I was planning to try and get work in an established practice, but Graham's made me think. He says it's high time I had something that was just for me. To tell you the truth, I've been struggling a bit since the boys left home. There's always plenty to do on the farm of course, but it's not been the same, having no one to mother."

Typically, Lucy hadn't said anything about how she'd been feeling, how she'd been struggling, missing her sons. I put my arm round her shoulders and gave her a squeeze. "Oh, Lucy, you should have said sooner how you were feeling."

She shrugged. "Yes, maybe, but it seems so trivial compared to what you're going through. I'll get over it. Graham's been great as always. He says the boys still need me and they always will. And I know he's right. It's just so different when they're not around in term time. But Graham's right. I need to change, do things for me, now I've got the chance."

"Here's to you, Lucy," Kirsty said, raising her glass. "I think you'll be great. Go for it girl!"

"Hear, hear," I said, raising my glass too.

"And to you, Rosie. Slainte!" Kirsty toasted my health.

We chatted on about lots of things. Kirsty seemed happy, but not in any over the top way. When I got onto talking about Robbie's visit the previous day, I saw my chance to ask the question that I'd been desperate to ask since the girls arrived.

"Robbie mentioned that Eilidh needed a break from her mother – her lovesick mother. Is there anything you'd like to tell us?"

Kirsty and Lucy exchanged a glance and smiled at each other.

"Okay," I said. "I can see I'm the last to know. What's going on?"

Kirsty blushed. "I'm sorry, Rosie, darling–"

"Don't you 'darling' me!" I laughed. "You've been keeping secrets from me!"

"Not really. It's just that I've been so happy and you – well you've not been. It didn't seem…" she faltered and looked at Lucy.

"Kirsty and Rick," said Lucy, "Kirsty and Rick have got it together They're an item. Isn't that great?"

I stared from one to the other. Then I started to smile and my hands came up to my mouth.

"Oh my God, Kirsty! You and Rick. Wow! He was on the phone last night. He laughed when I said I thought you were in love. It's amazing. I had no idea. When? How?"

Kirsty laughed. "It was just after he came back in June. Remember I was here with you the day he showed up?"

I nodded.

"He went to see Lucy later that day. However, when he got to Lucy's she wasn't there, but I was. Lucy and Graham had some cow-related emergency and I was waiting for her. We were supposed to be going out for something to eat. So Rick and I sat and chatted while we waited. When Lucy and Graham eventually got back, Lucy was, to put it politely, in need of a bath, and I'm afraid she cancelled our date. But, she made up for it by suggesting that Rick and I go out to eat."

"Yeah, so it's all my fault." Lucy said, laughing.

"Yes, it is," said Kirsty. Anyway, we got on really well and it's just gone on from there. The real clincher was when he showed me his photos of Skye and told me how much he loved my island." She smiled widely. "What do you think, Rosie?"

"I think it's wonderful. He's obviously making you happy. I'm pleased for both of you. But you didn't have to keep it from me. It's nice to get good news."

"I'm glad you're glad," said Kirsty. She reached over and squeezed my hand. "We just need to get you and Tom sorted out now. You're still going up to St Andrews together next weekend?"

Tom, oh Tom, I thought. nd the deep, gripping pain in my gut was back, full on. I didn't think I could bear to voice my fears, so I tried to keep bright and positive. "Yes, we are and we're planning to have a bit of a talk. I've been missing him lately. He's surprised me the way he's coped with being a single parent. He's done everything I asked, stayed away, given me space."

"And maybe he needed to be given some space too, to be a Dad and do some of the domestic stuff," Lucy said gently.

"Yes, I never really let him in, in that respect, did I? I had to be in control, doing everything myself, quite a martyr. Anyway, I asked for space and he gave me it, so I suppose it serves me right." I couldn't hold back. I had to share my dreadful suspicions.

"What does?" Kirsty asked.

"That he's now seeing someone, a woman from work. Max told me last night. I phoned to tell Tom I was missing him. I just wanted to hear his voice, but he wasn't there. He was out with this woman. Max didn't even seem bothered. He was more bothered that he wasn't supposed to mention it to me. Tom's going to tell me when he's ready, according to Max. And it wasn't their first time together apparently."

I knew I was going to cry. I tried to stop myself, but it was no use. The tears ran down my face.

Lucy got the tissues. "No, Rosie, no, that can't be right. Tom still loves you."

I blew my nose, but I couldn't stop crying.

"Come on, come over to the sofa." She guided me over and sat down beside me. She put an arm round my shoulders. Kirsty came and sat on my other side.

"Oh, I think he still cares," I said, between sobs. "But I can't really blame him for looking for some affection elsewhere. I've been horrible to him. I've accused him of deceit. I've accused him of fathering my sister's child. I've moved out. I've not let him support me through all the cancer crap."

Kirsty took my hand. "But you had a right to be angry and you had a right to ask to do things your way. Tom knows that. He loves you Rosie, that's why he's let you be. God, Rick says the sexual tension fairly crackles in the room, when you and Tom are together."

"Does it? I don't know about that. The last time I saw Tom, when we met Adam here, I threw up on him. Then, later, I passed out. I think it was probably just plain, ordinary tension that Rick picked up on, tension about what I'd be doing as an encore." I managed a bit of a smile. Kirsty and Lucy were offering a sliver of hope.

They both laughed.

"I even let him think that Rick and I were having some kind of liaison, just teasing him really. I found it funny and nice that he thought anyone could find me attractive in my present state."

"There you go then. He's besotted. He still fancies you, bald and covered in vomit. And he thinks other men do too. No, Max is wrong. There's no way he's seeing this – this floozy," Lucy said.

Kirsty laughed. "Yeah, she'll be some airhead, all young and pretty and shallow, with some kind of doctor fixation.

I managed a laugh at this. I hadn't met Sheena, but I'd spoken to her on the phone. I was fairly certain she was no young floozy. "Describing her as young and pretty is not really making me feel any better," I said, smiling at Kirsty.

"Look, whatever is or isn't going on, I think there's no contest between you and whoever she is. Tom probably just needed some female company. It'll be quite innocent. I can't believe he's given up on you. And you clearly want to be with him. So talk to him, Rosie." Kirsty shouted this last bit.

I raised my arms in surrender. "All right, all right. Everyone's telling me that. I'll talk to him! You know, I don't even care any more if he's Robbie's father. If he is I'll deal with it somehow. For now, I just need to hear exactly what happened seventeen years ago."

After Lucy and Kirsty left, I felt quite tired and went for a lie down. I slept for a couple of hours. It was getting dark when I woke. When I tried to get up, I realised I wasn't feeling at all well. I felt like I was coming down with flu. My bones and my head ached and my throat was sore. I lay back down.

The room seemed to be spinning. And then the nausea started and I had to dash to the bathroom. I was very sick. I knew I shouldn't have had the champagne. I crawled back into bed. I was sick another couple of times and had a restless and disturbed night.

Next morning I couldn't get up. I felt hot and shivery and very weak. Thank goodness Evelyn was due to visit. As usual she let herself in. I remember her calling my name and then her standing at the side of the bed with her hand on my forehead. Then I saw her with the phone in her hand and she was holding my wrist. She washed my face. I can remember the cool flannel on my hot skin, and I think I can remember her helping me into a clean nightdress. But, after that, nothing.

# Chapter Thirty Eight

*Tom*

I'd just come out of theatre. It was Monday morning, the second last week of September. The surgery on an elderly patient had gone well. I was in good spirits. Bruce was due in the theatre for the next couple of hours and I intended to get on with some post-clinic paperwork. I wasn't due back in theatre until after lunch and I was changing into fresh scrubs when my pager went.

It was Sheena. I called her immediately.

"Tom, thank goodness. You're out of theatre at last."

"What is it?" I asked.

"I'm so sorry, Tom. It's Rosie. Your mother's been on the phone. Rosie's very poorly. She's in hospital, here, down in the receiving unit. Your mother came in the ambulance with her."

I didn't wait to hear any more. I flung the phone down and I ran. I didn't bother with the lift. I charged down the stairs and flew along the corridors. I burst in through the receiving unit doors and nearly fell over Karen Knox. She caught hold of me as I crashed into her and I read her ID badge.

"Steady on," she said. "What's the rush?"

"Where is she?" I asked. She took in my scrubs and glanced at my badge.

"Ah, Tom McAllister," she said. "I'm Dr Knox, Karen, your wife's oncologist. It's all right. Rosie's here. Your mother's with her. It was fortunate that I happened to be here this morning

271

when Rosie arrived. Your mother phoned ahead to try to track me down."

I must have looked frantic, like a complete madman probably. I kept looking over Karen's shoulder as she spoke, and only nodded vaguely in her direction.

"Can I see her? What's wrong with her?" I asked.

"Come and sit down Mr McAllister, in here." She indicated a small office behind the nurses' station. I followed her inside and sat down on a plastic chair. She sat opposite and spoke gently.

"Rosie has an infection. It's quite severe. You know, of course, that chemotherapy compromises the immune system, so she's not able to fight it very well. She's very poorly, but we're pushing drugs and fluids into her and keeping a close eye on things. She's been taken along to HDU. I was just heading off there when you arrived. She's stable and sedated and as comfortable as we can make her. I'm sorry. It's such a shame. She's been doing so well and come so far. She's had her last chemo and things should have been starting to get easier. We have to hope that she has enough in reserve to overcome this."

It all felt unreal. Karen's voice seemed to be coming from a long way off.

"No, please, no," I said. "This can't be happening. Not now. We're going away at the weekend. We're going to talk. It was all going to be all right."

I could hardly breathe. I jumped up and knocked the chair over. I wanted to scream and rage, throw the furniture. It was agony. I punched the wall and sank to the floor. I'd witnessed this kind of shock so often, breaking bad news to a patient's relatives, news they were completely unprepared for. Up until that day I'd never really understood the primal, visceral nature of this kind of response. I used to wonder why they couldn't keep a lid on their feelings, maintain some dignity. I mean, I was sympathetic to their shock, but I never really understood it until that day.

"Tom, it's okay. Shh, now, it's okay."

I felt arms around me. It was my mother.

"Ma, oh, Ma," I clung to her, as the room seemed to slip away.

A little while later I was sitting once again, still in the little room, sipping some water. My mother sat beside me with her hand on my arm.

"Better?" Karen asked. She smiled kindly.

"Yes, thanks, sorry, I sort of lost it for a minute there, not very professional, sorry."

"You're not required to be professional, Tom. This is Rosie we're talking about. You're allowed to be emotional."

I turned to my mother. "Thanks, Ma, for being here and for looking after her."

She patted my hand. "Go and see your wife."

So, I went to Rosie's bedside, in a single room in the High Dependency Unit. She wasn't conscious, well not fully anyway. I couldn't tell if she knew I was there or not. She looked fragile and so pale. Drips were hooked up at her right hand side and there were the usual monitors doing their tracing and bleeping. I went to her left side and kissed her forehead. I took her hand. I noticed she wasn't wearing her wedding ring, but I couldn't dwell on what that might mean. I sat down beside her.

"Stay with me, Rosie," I said.

At some point Bruce put his head round the door. I went to speak to him. He told me not to worry about work. I wasn't. He said he'd do my two scheduled operations that afternoon and would contact Anna to see what she could do. He said that everyone upstairs in cardio sent their love and good wishes.

Some time after that, Dan appeared with Jenny and Max. My mother had called him, apparently, and asked him to bring the two of them from school. Then Andy arrived with Sam and Adam. My mother's doing again.

It was good to have everyone there and my colleagues in HDU were wonderful. We were given the relatives' room to ourselves, and the children were able to go in pairs to sit with their mother for a little while. Andy had to get back to work, but he made me promise to let him know if anything changed. I couldn't speak when he said this. I just gave him a clumsy hug.

I stayed at Rosie's side after that and the children, Dan and my mother took it in turns to sit with us. By evening I was concerned that my mother had been running around all day and was looking beat. Dan said he'd take her home to his place and then come back for the kids. I was going to be staying at the hospital and we were standing in the corridor outside Rosie's room trying to figure out where the children should spend the night, when Kirsty arrived.

"Tom," she said, giving me a hug. "How is she?"

"She's hanging in there, but it's difficult to tell, she …" I struggled to speak. "Kirsty, what am I going to do? I can't lose her. I can't." I fell into her arms and came dangerously close to sobbing on her shoulder.

"Oh, Tom." Kirsty held me tight. "Rosie's a fighter. She'll beat this. She will. She'll beat this."

I suddenly felt very weak and absolutely shattered. I hung on tightly to Kirsty as I staggered a little.

"Oh, careful, mate," came a voice.

I was held round the shoulders in a strong grip and led to a seat. The corridor swam around me.

"Deep breaths, Doc." The voice came again.

Kirsty's voice said, "Give him this."

The other voice said, "Here, take a sip."

I took the cup and sipped the cold water as instructed. Gradually the corridor floor stopped moving and things came into focus again. I looked up. Kirsty was further along the corridor talking to Dan.

"Tough day?" It was the voice again. I turned to where it came from.

It was Rick. "Thought you were going to hit the deck. Good job I was here. Don't think Kirsty could have caught you."

"I might have known you'd show up. How did you find out Rosie was in here?" I couldn't be bothered to make the effort to even pretend to be civil.

He ignored my tone. "I was at Kirsty's. We'd arranged to meet at hers after she finished at school. We were going to have a takeaway at her place. Then your Mother phoned about Rosie."

"You were at Kirsty's? You don't waste time do you? You've not changed. One woman still not enough?" I knew as I was saying this that I was being ridiculous, but I couldn't help myself. Again, Rick let it pass.

"I'm with Kirsty. We're together, a couple, have been since I came back in June. I'm flattered that you think I've still got the old, amazing, pulling power, but I'm strictly a one woman fellow nowadays."

I almost managed a smile. "Oh, so you and Rosie, you're not, she's not–"

"No we're not. She's not." He shook his head, smiling. "Rosie's a mate. I care a lot about her. She was special to me a long time ago, but I blew it. She's yours, Tom. Only an idiot wouldn't see that. Present company included."

I cleared my throat.

"Accepted," he replied.

Kirsty came up to us. She said that Dan was heading off with my mother. It was Rick who suggested that he and Kirsty took the kids home to Gullane and stayed with them. I reminded Kirsty that Adam would need to be taken to Ruby's. But she said that he wanted to spend the night with the others and he was quite happy to go to Gullane. In any other circumstances this would have been the best possible news, but that evening it simply underlined how serious things had become.

As they were leaving, Rick gave me his keys to the flat. He told me to make use of it to grab a shower or to sleep.

"We'll bring you some clothes and stuff from home tomorrow," he said. "But feel free to borrow a change of clothes from my wardrobe if you want to, in the meantime. After all it won't be the first time." He smiled. I found that the desire to punch him had gone.

After everyone left I went back to sit with Rosie. At about

half-past-nine there was a knock at the door.

It was Bruce again. He beckoned me to the doorway. He had a tray of food with him. "I hear you've not eaten all day. Get this down you. And I suppose it's pointless to tell you to get some rest."

"Yes, it is. But I am starving, thanks. And I suppose it's pointless asking what you're still doing here at this time?"

Bruce shrugged sheepishly. He sat with Rosie while I went to the relatives' room and ate my food. As I was about to go back in, Bruce came out.

"Doctor's with her just now, checking her over," he said.

"Right," I answered.

Soon the door to Rosie's room opened and a young lad, who looked about twelve, came out. "Mr McAllister?"

"Yes."

"Doctor Williams, Dave Williams." He shook my hand.

I fought the urge to ask him if he was qualified and listened while he made the usual speech about the patient, my Rosie, being comfortable and holding her own, and the next twenty four hours being crucial.

That night I dozed, fitfully and uncomfortably, in the chair at Rosie's bedside. The night nurse came and went, doing her observations and changing the drips. Every time she came in she offered me a cup of tea or the chance to go and stretch my legs. I only took her up on her offers on a couple of occasions.

There was no change in Rosie overnight. When the morning shift of nurses arrived I was told, politely but firmly, to go away for a while. I was assured I would be called if anything changed.

As I was leaving, one of the nurses called me back. She handed me a small plastic bag. "You better take this for safe keeping, Mr McAllister. It's your wife's ring. She was wearing it on a chain round her neck. I guess she must have lost weight and was scared of losing it if she kept it on her finger."

I couldn't say anything. I just took the bag from her and clasped it tightly.

I didn't go far, just up to the cardio theatre area for a quick shower and a shave, and then down to the canteen for some breakfast. While I was there, Bruce and Anna came in. Once they had their coffees they joined me at my table.

"The nurses downstairs said we might find you here," said Bruce, as he sat down.

"How are you bearing up?" Anna asked, touching my arm.

"Oh, I'm fine, you know…"

"They're pleased with Rosie down on the ward. She's no worse, so that's good," said Bruce.

I nodded. "Yes, I suppose so."

"Don't worry about us upstairs either," he went on. "Anna's in for the next two days."

"I can do Thursday and Friday as well," said Anna. "And I was doing the weekend on-call anyway, so that's fine. Then I'm supposed to be on holiday for the next couple of weeks. But I can postpone. It's not important."

I'd forgotten about Anna's holiday plans. I'd arranged my own leave for the two weeks after Anna got back, when Jenny and Max would be on half-term holiday from school. Yes, I'd booked a fortnight off work. That was a first. And not only that, I'd decided that I was going to get my sabbatical set up before the end of the year.

I shook my head at Anna. "Your holiday is important. It's all arranged. You need to spend time with your husband and daughter."

"Yes, indeed," Bruce intervened. "You're going, no arguments. Time with your family is what's important. Don't take as long as Tom and I have to reach that conclusion. We'll manage. I'll sort it out."

I was back in Rosie's room, trying to concentrate on reading the newspaper, when Karen Knox arrived. She spent a few minutes checking Rosie's chart, which I'd already scrutinised, and then she told me she'd spoken to the rest of the team caring for Rosie.

They were all agreed that Rosie was responding well and they were going to decrease her sedation over the day. I thanked Karen and clung to the fact that this was a good sign.

As the day went on Rosie got more restless. All I could do was hold her hand.

In the afternoon I called Dan and asked him to phone round everyone with the latest news. I also said to tell people not to come in to the hospital that day as, if Rosie did come round, she wouldn't be up to visitors. Dan said he'd stay with the children in Gullane until I came home, however long that took.

My mother called me to say she'd contacted Michael and that he was on his way to Scotland. She didn't say, 'just in case,' but we both knew the implication.

Then at around four o'clock in the afternoon, while I was grappling with the Scotsman crossword, Rosie started to speak. She became agitated and struggled to get the oxygen mask off. I lifted it away from her face and took her hand. I put my face close to hers. She opened her eyes.

"I'm here, Rosie. I'm here," I whispered.

"Tom," was all she said.

For the next few days, Rosie remained very weak as she battled to overcome what could have been an overwhelming infection. She slept most of the time and wasn't up to talking very much. I was persuaded to go to the flat to sleep and to take a little time out each day, but for the most part I stayed at Rosie's side.

At some point, Michael arrived. He came straight from the airport to the hospital. Rosie looked astounded when she opened her eyes to find him standing by the bed. They hadn't seen each other for several years, and their joy at their reunion was moving to watch.

I knew that Rosie had been in regular contact with her brother and had told him what had been happening in the last few months. I didn't know exactly what she'd said, or if she'd asked him about the events surrounding Robbie's birth. I felt a bit awkward with them so I decided to leave them alone for a while. Michael followed me out the door as I was leaving.

"Tom, before you go, mate, we need to talk. You know what about."

"Yes," I agreed. "Not here. Not now. But we *will* talk."

"Does Rosie know the whole story? Have you explained everything?"

"No, she doesn't. She only knows that I was in touch with Heather, during their estrangement and knew about Robbie and the adoption. I was going to tell her everything this weekend. We were going away together, taking Sam up to the uni, and then this happened."

"Well, she won't hear it from me. This is your call, your story, and, for what it's worth, I'm sorry that I ran away after it all, after Heather, and everything. I couldn't face Rosie, couldn't face not telling her. But you did the right thing."

"Look, go back in and be with her now. She'll drift off to sleep quite quickly. But just sit with her. We'll talk soon." I left the two of them together.

As I wandered along the corridor, I passed the hospital sanctuary and found that I was drawn inside. I'd never been in before. I had it to myself and I took a seat near the front. I wasn't really religious but, since Rosie's diagnosis and departure from home, I'd often found myself praying to somebody, I wasn't sure who, especially in the desperate hours in the middle of the night. I'd prayed she'd get better and come back to me. In the last few days I'd prayed even more. I begged for Rosie to survive. I told God that even if his price was that I couldn't have Rosie back, then that was fine, he was just to make her well, let her live. I even asked him to take my life instead.

I was sitting in the little chapel, saying this prayer once again, when I became aware that someone else had come in. I looked round.

It was Reverend Jack Martin, one of the hospital chaplains. I knew him from his visits to my ward. Jack was a popular person around the hospital, with staff and patients. He was a big man, taller than me, broad and bearded, a man of presence. His distinctive laugh was well known around the wards, but I'd heard from many of the patients' families and friends that he was also enormously comforting when the worst happened.

He came and sat beside me and shook my hand. "Tom, I'm glad to see you. I was going to come and find you. I heard about your wife. How is she?"

"She's fighting back, but not in the clear yet. I just thought I'd put in a word for her, you know, with…" I looked upwards. "I know I've probably no right to ask."

"We all have the right to ask."

"I've not been – I'm not – you know, religious. I don't know what I believe, if I believe. You don't think it's a bit of a cheek?"

"No, not at all, and even if I did, it's not for me to judge. I think God can probably cope with any presumption on your part."

"Do you think it works? You know, 'ask and you shall receive', all that stuff."

"I believe in the power of prayer, yes. Whether we get what we think we ought to receive is another matter. We don't get what we want, but we do get what we need. God is mysterious, but I believe he hears us when we call to him."

"I don't deserve any attention, but Rosie doesn't deserve to die. I'd rather he took me to fill his quota."

Jack smiled. "I don't think God is some kind of middle-manager with a list of targets to achieve. Neither do I think you have to deserve his attention. We can't do deals with Him. We just have to trust that what happens is for the best, for reasons we can't understand. And if we're suffering we're not alone. He's there beside us, beside you, beside Rosie. Right now he's holding Rosie in the palm of his hand and he'll do right by her."

I don't pretend that I really understood what Jack was saying, but it was comforting nevertheless. He said he'd sit with me for a while and that if I wanted him to visit Rosie I'd only to ask.

I felt better when I left the sanctuary. The optimism that I'd started to feel before Rosie had succumbed to the infection had returned.

And over the next couple of days, it began to look like Rosie was winning. She was awake for longer periods and able to cope with short visits from the children, as well as from Michael and me. She didn't have the strength to say very much, but she liked to be read to. This was something Ma had suggested. Ma even got me a copy of 'Other Stories and Other Stories' an anthology by Ali Smith, an author she knew Rosie liked.

And so I would spend part of each afternoon reading aloud to Rosie. Neither of us could have coped with a heart to heart discussion at that time, but I found I enjoyed the time that I spent just sitting and reading to her. She seemed to find it soothing, so much so that she sometimes dropped off mid story.

Jenny suggested getting her an MP3 player, which I did, and she and the other children spent a lot of time downloading music that they thought their mother would like. Rosie was delighted with it and with the children's thoughtfulness in their choices of music. Listening to her favourite tunes also tended to send her to sleep.

On one such occasion, as I sat at her bedside, watching her as she slept, I wondered if it would ever be all right between us again. I took hold of her hand and held it to my face. I'd been so hopeful that going to St Andrews together would be a turning point for the better. Of course, it was an indescribable relief that Rosie had overcome the infection, but now that she had, the worry and fear were replaced by a leaden disappointment. Any chance of a proper heart to heart seemed as far away as ever.

I kissed the tips of her fingers and whispered, "Forgive me, Rosie, forgive me.

# Chapter Thirty Nine

It was decided that I'd take Sam up to St Andrews, as planned, on the Sunday. Rosie, despite her weakened state, insisted, and I was glad to do something real and practical for her.

Adam surprised me by saying that he'd come along too, so that I wouldn't have to be on my own on the way back. Naturally, I was both pleased and touched by this and determined to make the most of it.

So, on the Sunday morning, the car was packed and the three of us set off.

Adam sat in front with me and immediately plugged himself into his i-pod. So at this stage, at least, I didn't have to worry about saying the wrong thing, conversation clearly wasn't on his agenda. It wasn't my intention to say anything to upset him. I could see that Rosie had been right all along. I'd fully accepted that he would be the judge of what was best for him. I'd come to terms with the fact he wasn't going to university and that it really didn't matter. I'd come to trust that he would sort out his own life on his own terms. But I still felt wary with him. It still seemed we circled round each other, unsure and tentative. However, he was there in the car and by his own choice. I took it as a good sign and tried to relax.

Sam was very quiet in the back, but not because she was listening to music. She'd been subdued since first thing. I glanced in the mirror at her from time to time. She just seemed to be staring out of the window. There was none of her usual chat. I hoped she was going to be all right away from home.

What if she hated university or couldn't make friends or some lad mistreated her.

"Are you okay, in the back there?" I asked.

"Yes, I'm fine," she replied.

"Not worried about going away, are you?"

"No, not really. I want to go to uni, to St Andrews, it's just…"

"What? It's just what?"

"It's Mum. I'm worried about her. And I'm worried about you, both of you, if you'll get back together. I can't really get into uni and all that stuff. I need to know Mum's going to be all right and that you…"

"Oh, Sam, I know it's hard. But really, try not to worry. Mum's over the worst and me and her, we're going to meet up as soon as she's strong enough. We'll sort ourselves out."

I wasn't sure how convincing I sounded. I glanced sideways at Adam, concerned he'd heard my conversation with Sam, but he was oblivious, eyes shut, drumming on his leg and moving to his music.

Next time I looked at Sam she too had her i-pod on. She saw my look in the mirror and gave me a little smile. I smiled back and told myself she'd be all right.

The roads were fairly quiet and we arrived in St Andrews in a little over an hour.

It was a bright autumn day and the east wind was bitingly cold as we unloaded all Sam's stuff at the halls of residence. She seemed to brighten a little as the three of us carried everything indoors. She was in the newest of the university's residences, on the North Haugh and she was pleased with her room.

We went for lunch in the town and I couldn't quite believe that the three of us were doing this very ordinary thing. Six months ago I'd probably have left it to Rosie to take Sam up, and I'd have got on with paperwork or gone to the hospital.

And more recently I would've found it difficult to believe that Adam would volunteer to take a trip with me. I hoped there was no hidden agenda on his part, and that he wasn't planning to tell me a few home truths before announcing his permanent departure. But he seemed fairly chilled and, though he didn't directly engage me in conversation, he laughed and chatted with his sister as he ate his pub meal.

The intensity that was part of what made him Adam was still there, but I got the impression that he could cope with it now, cope with himself. His former tense demeanour was mostly gone. I realised he'd achieved this new way of being through his own efforts, on his own terms. I was definitely going to leave him be.

As for Sam, I was quite overcome with pride; pride in her achievement in getting to this university,yes, but much more than that. I felt pride in how she'd matured over the summer and taken on so much of her mother's role. In May, she'd seemed so self-centred and carefree that it was hard to believe how much she'd changed in a short time. I hoped she wouldn't worry too much about Rosie and me and that she'd get back some of that earlier, blithe, untroubled quality, as she set out on student life.

After lunch we went for a walk round the town. We visited the quad in North Street and located the various buildings where Sam would be having lectures and tutorials. We found the library and the student union and then made our way back to the residence. There, Sam met a girl from school who was going to be living just down the hallway from her. After an enthusiastic greeting, the girls talked excitedly of the hall and freshers' events and the joy of finally getting started on their adventure. This was more like the old Sam and it was great to see. The girls arranged to meet up half an hour later to compare notes. It seemed like a good time to leave her to it. And so we said our goodbyes.

I hugged her close and told her I loved her. "If there's anything, anything at all you need, or if you're unhappy, or anything, you call me and I'll be here. Promise?"

"I'll be fine, Dad. But thanks, for today and for the last few months and everything. You're the best Dad and I love you."

"And you promise you'll tell me the minute you need me to

do anything?"

"Yes, if you promise me something."

"Anything."

"Talk to Mum. Get you and Mum sorted."

"I promise," I said.

Then she hugged Adam. "And you, you be good. And look after Dad for me."

Adam tolerated being hugged and said, "I'll try, sis. You be good too. And if you don't want the old guy to rescue you, then call me."

"I will," she said, laughing.

I laughed too. "Cheeky bugger," I said to Adam. "And less of the old!"

God, just that little bit of banter with my son, it felt so good.

We waved until we were out of sight. I'd always felt a strong bond with Sam, but had feared she'd grown away from me in her later teenage years. However, the last few months did seem to have made the bond stronger than ever. I was so torn between the feelings of rightness and pride in my daughter leaving and the need to keep her close and safe.

"She'll be okay, Dad," Adam said, once we were in the car.

"You think so?" I said, as we pulled away.

"Yeah, I do. And I'll be okay too."

"Yes, I think you will, son." I smiled at him, but my heart was thumping.

"And what about you and Mum? Will you two be okay?"

"I really don't know, if you mean as a couple. Mum's getting over the infection and I'm sure she'll beat the cancer too. But we've still got a lot to talk about. And I think your Mum may have discovered that she's happier not living with me."

"But what about you? Would you be happier away from Mum?"

"Well, I sort of did a deal actually."

"What sort of deal?"

"I told God, that if the price for Mum getting better was that I had to let her go, then I'd pay that price. And if he wants to hold me to the deal, well that's fine."

I glanced at Adam when he didn't reply. He was looking out the window. We drove on in silence for a few minutes, but it was a companionable silence. I felt quite calm as the car purred along.

Then Adam spoke. "That was a stupid deal and God is stupid if he made it. What if he made her better so that you two could get back together? Had you thought of that?"

"No, no I hadn't," I replied, smiling at him. "You could well be right. Thank you for that, son, thank you."

And so, Adam gave me a wee bit of renewed hope. It was true that when Rosie had said she was intending to come on the St Andrews trip, I had dared to hope that there was a thaw and that she was moving closer, ready to listen and to talk. But as she began to recover from the infection, I sensed she'd withdrawn again. I'd been prepared to back off. However, Adam's insight made me resolve not to give up just yet.

A little while later, Adam said, "Where are you staying tonight?"

"At the flat," I replied.

"Can I crash with you then?"

I struggled to keep driving in a straight line. "Yes, yes, of course you can. That would be great."

And, if Adam's plans for that night were a shock, there was more to come. We were a few miles north of the Forth Road Bridge when Adam spoke again.

"I want to come home, Dad."

For a moment, I thought he was still talking about coming back to the flat that night. He guessed as much. I could see him, out of the corner of my eye, looking at me.

"No, not to the flat. That's just tonight. I mean I want to come home to our house. If that's all right?"

Once again I had to struggle to focus on my driving. But it was no use. The tears in my eyes made it difficult to see. I tried wiping at them with the back of my hand but they were instantly replaced. I had to get off the motorway. I pulled over on to the hard shoulder and flicked on the hazards. I took off my seatbelt and turned to face Adam.

I cleared my throat. "Of course it's all right, but are you sure you want to?"

Adam reached into the glove box and produced a handful of paper hankies. "Here," he said, handing them to me. "Yes I'm sure. I've missed you, Dad, and Mum and the girls of course, even the munchkin." He gave a little smile. "But if it's going to upset you this much..."

I shook my head. "Oh, don't read too much into this." I pointed at my face. "Something in my eye, would you believe? I don't do crying." I managed to smile.

Adam laughed. "Yeah right!"

"It would be great to have you back home. We've – I've – missed you too. A hell of a lot, actually. But I thought you were happy at Ruby's."

"I was. I am. Ruby's cool and all that. I've been able to think about stuff at her place." He was quiet for a few moments. Then he spoke again. "Robbie's cool too, Dad – don't you think?"

"Yes, I do."

"We weren't very nice to him at first, were we?"

"No, son, we weren't."

"But it's all right now. It was Robbie, you know, that told me to come and see you and Mum at the flat. He said how worried you'd all been about me and that I had a cool family. He said he had a cool family too and he wasn't going to be spoiling ours."

"Right, so you don't see him as a threat any more then?"

"No, and neither should you. I know you kept him a secret and everything and Mum is really mad at you about that. But once you explain, she'll understand. Like Robbie explained to me. I hate it when people don't explain what's going on. It's scary. And then when you're scared, you get mad."

I could only nod. I swallowed hard and looked at my son.

"Come here, you," I said. And for the first time in a very long time, I embraced my boy. And he let me. In fact he didn't just let me, he hugged me back, hard. When we moved apart we both needed some of those hankies from the glove box.

It was beginning to get dark, and I knew we should get on our way, but I sensed Adam had more to say and I didn't want to break the spell. "There's a café not far from here, just at the Kelty turn off. Do you fancy grabbing a snack?"

"Yeah, sounds good."

It wasn't long before we were settled in the warm cafe with steaming hot mugs of tea and a huge slab of chocolate cake for Adam. He demolished the cake in about ten seconds and I just watched in awe. I'd forgotten how he hoovered up food.

After a couple of mouthfuls of tea he said, "I've been to Robbie's house a few times. His mum and dad are nice and his sister, Julie, she's cool too."

Adam smiled as he mentioned Julie's name. I smiled too.

"Yes, the Sutherlands are good people," I said.

"So, if it's all right with you, I'll move back next weekend. It's my weekend off from the karting centre, and Julie's off too, so she said she'd give me a hand with my stuff."

"Right, and have you told Ruby you're coming home?"

"Yes, I told her. She said she was surprised it had taken me this long to realise what I was missing at home. Ruby and her family have been really good to me, but they weren't you, weren't us. It wasn't the same. Do you know what I mean?"

"Yes, I do."

"Julie said I was lucky to have a family who loves me. Her real parents didn't love her. They hit her and didn't look after her, didn't feed her or give her proper clothes or anything. She doesn't see why I had to run away from a dad like you and I can see what she means." He cleared his throat.

So did I. We both took a gulp of tea.

Then he continued, "Julie, she's, well she's sort of my girlfriend, you see."

"I see." I nodded, smiling at him again.

"Anyway, Julie and me are doing up an old car with Bob, Mr Sutherland, and, when it's safe and ready for the road, Bob says Julie can have it. She's just passed her test and I'm going to apply to do mine soon."

"So, Julie's into cars too?"

"Oh yes. She's so cool. She's not like Jen and Sam into all that girlie rubbish. She's not always talking about clothes and make up. She's really into engines and stuff. She's going to college this year, to get the grades she needs to do mechanical engineering at uni. She's found school hard, like me. She's not dyslexic, but she sort of had a bad start in life and she found it hard to catch up. But now she knows what she wants to do, she says she's going for it."

I'd never heard him talk so much about anything in his life. I didn't want it to stop. I got us more tea.

"Julie says I should go to college too," Adam continued. "She brought home the book thing that explains about courses. There's a mechanics one that sounds really good and Julie says there's tutors at the college that help you if you have dyslexia. I'm going to see about enrolling tomorrow morning. Julie's coming with me."

I nodded, amazed and proud, but not trusting myself to speak. Fortunately, Adam wasn't waiting for a verbal response. He wasn't finished yet.

"Bob says I'm a born mechanic and he says he can see where I get it from."

"Oh, where?"

"From you. He says I'm really patient and good with the fiddly stuff and have great dex, dexi something…"

"Dexterity," I offered.

"Yes, dexterity. Surgeon's hands, he says. He reckons an engine's like a heart, and you need the same sort of skills to rebuild them and keep them going."

I swallowed hard. "It sounds like you've made the right

decision then, to train as a mechanic."

"I never thought I could. I thought I was too thick to do anything much. I've known for a long time that I wouldn't get into uni, and I didn't want to go anyway, but I didn't know what else I could do. Bob says he'll take me into the bus depot to see what goes on there, and he has a pal who's got a garage down at Granton where I could maybe do some work experience."

"You have got yourself sorted out, haven't you?" I said.

"Yeah, I have, and now it's your turn."

I nodded. "Yes, son, I believe it is."

"Right, I'll pay for this," he said. "Then we should get on the road. It'll soon be dinner time and I'm starving."

I thought of the cake he'd just devoured and smiled to myself.

Once we were back at the flat, I phoned Ruby to tell her Adam was staying the night. I also told her about what he'd said in the car. I told her that thank you was totally inadequate for expressing my gratitude to her and her family. To say I was tired and emotional that evening doesn't really cover it.

However, tired as I was, I knew Rosie would want to know how today had gone. I phoned the hospital. Rosie was sleeping. She'd had a lot of visitors during the day and was very tired. The nurse said it would be best not to come in and to let Rosie rest. She assured me if Rosie awoke, she'd give her the message that everything had gone fine. I decided to keep Adam's news for when I saw her face to face.

By the time I was off the phone, Adam had rooted out the takeaway menus that Rick had accumulated in the kitchen drawer. He'd already made his choice, an Indian, and he was on his mobile ordering for the two of us.

"I couldn't wait," he said. "I ordered you the lamb bhuna. That's still your favourite, right?"

"Certainly is," I answered, ridiculously pleased, not just that he remembered this fact, but that he knew it in the first place. "There's a couple of beers in the fridge. Do you fancy one?"

"Yeah, cool," he nodded and switched on the television.

We watched a movie while we ate, Austin Powers in Goldmember. We both laughed at exactly the same bits. It was magic.

The next morning, I was up early. I'd not slept very well, as the events of the day went round and round in my head. But by morning I'd made some decisions.

First off, I wanted to make Adam breakfast before he left to meet Julie at the college. I did us the works, bacon, eggs, fried bread, the lot; not good for my heart specialist credentials, I know, but good for the soul. It was especially good for my soul, watching Adam tucking in and enjoying the food I'd prepared for him.

"That was ace, Dad," he said, wiping up the last of his eggs with his bread. "Didn't know you could cook like that."

"Oh, I've been learning. I'm quite proud of myself, actually. I can produce a few good dishes now."

"Well if they're all like that, I'm glad I'm coming home." He glanced at his watch. "I better get away. Don't want to miss my chance to get signed up."

As he stood up to go, he caught me looking at him.

"What?" he asked.

"Oh, nothing," I replied. "Only, it's just, I'm very proud of you, Adam."

"Daft bugger," he said. But he was grinning broadly.

After Adam left, I cleared away the breakfast things and gave the flat a bit of a clean up. Then I packed up my stuff. But I didn't head straight for the car. I found myself gazing out of the window, then pacing, then back at the window again. I was keen to be on my way, but I was also procrastinating. I knew I should phone Bruce. Now that I'd finally made up my mind, I owed it to him to give him as much warning as possible. I turned from the window, pulled my mobile from my pocket and called his direct line. He was slow to answer and I almost hung up.

"I don't quite know how to tell you this," I said, without preamble. "But I'm not coming in tomorrow. In fact I'm not coming in for the next month."

"Right, that's–"

"I'm taking compassionate leave for the next fortnight, right up until my annual leave starts."

"Okay I'm–"

"I'm sorry, Bruce. I know this will make things really difficult especially with Anna's leave coming up, but the truth is I'm not up to the job at the moment."

"Look, Tom, don't worry–"

"But–"

"Tom, let me speak!" he laughed.

I hadn't exactly expected him to laugh.

"It's okay, really," he went on. "I've been expecting this. I'd already started making contingency plans."

"Oh, right."

"I'm just surprised it's taken you this long," he said.

"Ah." I gave a little laugh.

"What?"

"Adam's decided to come home and the friend he's been staying with, she said the same to him when he announced his decision."

"That's good news! Like father, like son, eh?" Bruce laughed again.

"Yes, I suppose so." I had to swallow hard to get rid of a sudden lump in my throat.

"So, all the more reason to be at home now," said Bruce.

"Yes, but how will you manage, and what about Anna's leave?"

"Not your problem. As I said before, no one is indispensable. And to be honest, if you'd taken much longer to decide for yourself, I might have had to order you to take leave anyway."

"But–"

"Don't misunderstand. You haven't put a foot wrong in theatre throughout all your troubles. But what if, Tom, what if? You'd never have forgiven yourself, and I wouldn't have forgiven myself for not insisting you take time out. You're doing the right thing. Right now, your place is at home. I'd feel better knowing you were getting your personal life sorted out"

"So I'd be doing you a favour?" I laughed.

"Exactly." I heard him smile.

"You're one smooth operator, Bruce, pun intended."

"Yes, I am. Now go and see to your wife and kids."

So, I headed home, home to Gullane. Dan had been great staying at the house, but now I knew that Rosie was out of danger, my place was at home, full time, with the kids. They needed their dad, and I needed them.

# Chapter Forty

*Rosie*

When I woke up on the Monday morning, the day after Tom had taken Sam up to St Andrews, there was a note on the bedside cabinet from one of the night nurses. Tom had called and left me a message. I was relieved to read that everything had gone well. He'd said he'd be in to see me later that day. I knew he'd be back at work, so I wasn't sure when he'd drop in. I was looking forward to seeing him and hoped we'd at last start to sort our lives out. But as the day wore on I became increasingly anxious when Tom didn't arrive.

It was after four o'clock when my bedside phone rang. It was Tom.

"Hi, Rosie, how are you feeling today? When I rang last night the nurse said you'd been very tired yesterday."

"Not bad, still tired."

"Look, make sure you take it easy. Don't let the visitors tire you out."

"I thought you'd be visiting today." I paused, trying to keep the tremor out of my voice. I really needed to see him. "Where are you? Aren't you here in the hospital?"

"No, actually. I'm at home in Gullane."

"At home? You're not staying at the flat anymore? And weren't you due back at work today?"

"Yes, I'm back at home and I'm not going back to work for

at least a month. Things happened yesterday, and not wasn't just yesterday, but I reached a decision. My place is here with the children."

"Right–"

"The most amazing thing happened, Rosie. Adam, he's coming back. He's coming home to stay. He just announced it while we were driving back."

"Oh, Tom, that's fantastic!" I lay back against the pillows, savouring this good news.

"Yes, it is. We got on so well yesterday. You were right. He's grown up, made his own decisions. But he'll want to tell you all about that himself. The main thing is he's coming back."

"And Sam, she was okay? You said in your message you'd left her getting settled in."

"Yes, she was fine. She was a bit quiet on the journey up. She's worried about you, about us."

"Oh." My feelings of joy about Adam were replaced by guilt about Sam. Tom and I had to get things sorted out.

"I did my best to reassure her, and she did brighten up when she saw her room in the residence and met a friend from school. I'm sure she'll call you later."

"So are you coming in to the hospital to see me? I was hoping, expecting…" A tear ran down my cheek as I lay back looking up at the ceiling. I just wanted to see him.

"Ah, now you've not to worry, it's not serious but–"

"What, what's not serious?" I sat up, alert and tense.

"I'll not be in to see you for a while I'm afraid. It's Max, he's got some sort of tummy bug. Started around midnight apparently. He was sick several times. Dan was up most of the night with him."

"Oh, right," I lay back again.

"When I got home this morning, Ma was here. She'd been about to phone me. The thing is, he passed out in the bathroom this morning and bashed his head. Ma was concerned he had concussion. So I bundled him up and took him off to the Sick

Children's to get him checked out.

"And is he okay?"

Yes, we've to keep a close eye on him for the next twenty-four hours and to watch out for dehydration. This bug's a vicious one apparently. A lot of people have fallen victim. He's tucked up in bed now feeling very sorry for himself."

"Poor Max, I wish I could see him."

"I know you do. And that's the other thing, Rosie. I called Karen Knox. She says we should all stay away for at least ten days. It's possible that some of the rest of us will come down with it during that time, or could carry it without actually succumbing. Her advice is no visiting you until we're in the clear."

"I see." My tears flowed freely now. The disappointment was devastating. A sob escaped.

"Are you all right? You mustn't worry. Max will be fine. It's just a tummy bug, and I'll be here to look after him."

"It's not that, Tom. It's just, it's just I, we were going to have a talk about everything." Another sob escaped.

"I know we were." His voice was very soft. He cleared his throat. "I'm disappointed too, but we can't take any chances. If you were to catch this bug, it could be extremely serious."

"I know. You're right, but it doesn't make it any easier to accept."

"I'm going to have to go, Rosie. Max is calling for me. You take care. We'll all phone often and we'll see you as soon as we're allowed."

A little while after the phone call ended, Michael came to see me. He knew about Max and the quarantine situation, and assured me he'd not been in contact with the others. He'd visited every day since arriving from Australia and I was very relieved that he could continue to do so.

It had been lovely spending time with him, despite the circumstances. We certainly had plenty to say to each other.

I caught up with his life in Australia. He told me about his GP practice and about his wife, Jo, and his three girls. One afternoon, after he'd told me about a family holiday to the Whitsunday Islands, I said he sounded very happy.

"I am," he said. "After Adele and I split up I didn't think I'd get a second chance."

"Yes, you were very miserable when you left. So was I. And I was angry with you, at the time, for going off to Australia just when I needed you."

He looked uncomfortable.

"No, Michael, no, it's okay. I got over it. I don't blame you. And now I kind of understand why you went."

"Because of Robbie, you mean? I'm not proud of deceiving you, Rosie. Tom took charge. He was so insistent that you weren't to know. It just seemed easier to go along with it. I got to the point that I couldn't stay. I was grieving for Heather, but I was so bloody angry at her too. It was all such a mess. It finished my marriage. I just fled. I'm sorry." He looked dejected.

I took hold of his hand. "Don't be too hard on yourself. To be honest, I wanted to get away too. Only..." I hesitated. It was hard to admit out loud, but I knew it was high time we were all more honest with each other.

Michael was looking at me, waiting for me to finish.

I took a deep breath. "I wanted to get away too, but I had something more permanent in mind." I had to look away as I spoke.

"Oh, Rosie," Michael said softly, as he stroked my hand. "Tom said he was afraid of that. I thought he was exaggerating. He was so scared for you."

I turned back to look at Michael. "He wouldn't let me talk about her. Every time I mentioned her name he'd change the subject, say not to dwell on it. But I needed to try and make some sense of it all. One of you should have told me the whole story."

"Yes, maybe what Tom and I did was wrong, but we did it with good intentions. Look, sis, when you've got your strength back and when the danger of you getting this bug has passed, talk to Tom, get the whole story from him. Then maybe you can forgive us, Heather and me and Tom.

He loves you, Rosie."

"Everyone keeps saying that. 'Talk to him. He loves you.' And I want us to talk, but I'm scared too. I don't know what to think. Is he Robbie's father? Does it matter? And if he's not, what is it that neither of you felt you could tell me? Does he even still love me?" I shook my head and shrugged.

"And you, Rosie, what do you feel about Tom?"

"I still love him. No matter what he has or hasn't done. I love him."

"So you must talk to him. As soon as he's in the clear and you're up to it, talk to him."

"I will. I have to. But I'm afraid it's too late. I'm afraid too much damage has been done. I'm afraid I've lost him, that he's moved on.

Michael looked sceptical. When I told him my suspicions about Tom and Sheena, he looked even more sceptical. "I don't think so, sis. I think you're way off there. But, if there's even a chance that you're right, then all the more reason to get talking to him."

Michael was right of course, I had to face Tom. The time had come to resolve things.

When I was alone all I could think about was Tom. The situation we were in now was tearing me apart. At best, my longing to see him was a dull ache deep in my stomach. At worst, it was agony, more unbearable than any of the physical pain I'd endured lately. And all I could do at those times was curl up on the bed and wait for the yearning to pass.

But I was also afraid. Much as I wanted to see Tom, part of me dreaded having it all out with him, because then I would have to know, would have to hear him say that he'd moved on. I didn't think I'd ever be strong enough to hear that.

I was further tortured by the thought that I only had myself to blame. I'd left him. I'd shut him out. Yes, I'd been hurt by him, but I'd hurt him too. I'd pushed him into starting a relationship with Sheena.

To preserve my sanity, I tried to focus on getting well, on the good news about Adam and on enjoying my time with Michael. But the turmoil I was experiencing was never far from the surface.

# Chapter Forty One

Just over a week after Tom's phone call about the need for the family's quarantine, I got some much-needed good news. Angus Campbell came to see me and told me that the latest tests showed my infection was completely gone. He said Karen Knox would be in touch about a date for a scan to check that the chemo had done its job. He also said I was to have a month off, no treatment or hospital appointments, before my course of radiotherapy. He said I could go home the next day.

I was glad to be getting out of hospital, but it was a similar feeling to stopping the chemo. The hospital offered a form of security. It was a protective cocoon.

Before succumbing to the infection, I'd reached an understanding with my cancer and the loss and changes it had brought in its wake. Now I realised I had a similar struggle ahead of me to make sense of all the other stuff that had been happening in my life. Leaving hospital would be the first step.

The medics weren't keen on me living on my own when I was first discharged. I was unsure whether just to move back to the flat and hope for the best, or to impose on one of my friends. It was Michael who came up with the solution to my dilemma. He'd been staying in a B&B near the hospital since his arrival, but proximity to the hospital was no longer necessary and, as he'd arranged to remain in Scotland until the end of October, he needed somewhere more comfortable to live. So he suggested moving into the flat with me. With Rick now living at Kirsty's, there was room for us both and I'd have my own private GP to keep an eye on me. It seemed like the perfect solution.

So on Wednesday, the sixth of October, Michael came to fetch me. As soon as we got back to the flat, he told me to put my feet up and went to make a cup of tea. I heard him on his mobile while he was in the kitchen. When he returned with the tea, he said Tom had been on the phone checking we'd got back and that I was okay.

"That's nice," I said, feeling really pleased that Tom was thinking about me. "How did he sound? How are the kids?"

"Max is much better and Jenny and Adam are up and about and starting to eat again. Adam isn't impressed with his welcome home present."

"No, being given a tummy bug probably wasn't what he had in mind. Poor Adam." I shook my head and smiled. "And Tom, is he okay?"

"He said he was, but he sounded tired. You could phone him yourself later." Michael looked at me. It was a meaningful look.

"Yes, I think I will," I said, surprised by my resolve.

"And will you see him soon?"

"Yes, I'll arrange something when I call him later. I think I'm up to seeing him for a proper talk, strong enough now to hear it all, whatever he might have to tell me."

Michael glanced away for a moment, looked awkward.

"What is it?" I asked.

"I sort of asked him, asked Tom, if he was seeing someone."

I gasped.

Michael shook his head. "I didn't tell him your suspicions. I just asked casually. I can't repeat what he replied, but it was along the lines of telling me to mind my own business."

"Oh, Michael, did you have to? I thought you were staying out of it."

"I am. It was just Kirsty, Lucy and I were talking, the other day at the hospital. None of us could believe Tom was seeing anyone and they thought one of us should ask Tom, and I sort of volunteered.

"What, you were all talking about it, about Tom, about us?"

"Yes, we all care about both of you. We can see what you two have, even if you can't. We just want you to–"

"Talk! Yes I know. So you all keep saying. We're going to. We'll talk! Now can we drop it?"

"Okay, okay." He raised his hands. "I'll stop going on about it. I promise."

Later that evening I phoned home. Jenny answered. The news wasn't good. When I asked to speak to Tom, she said he couldn't come to the phone. The inevitable had happened. Tom had caught the bug. It would be some days before we'd be seeing each other. It was a crushing disappointment. I'd got myself psyched up to make the call, thought through what I was going to say, and all for nothing.

Michael held my hand while I ranted at the unfairness of it all, and passed me the hankies to dry my angry tears. He did his best to put a positive spin on this latest setback. He said that at least I'd a few extra days to build up my strength before I met Tom. I wasn't convinced, but I was grateful to him for trying.

Michael and I got along fine as I convalesced. He and I'd not spent so much time under the same roof since we were teenagers. It felt strange but comfortable at the same time.

We went for walks in the mornings. It was lovely to get out in the fresh air. And it was very fresh. Early October was frosty and clear. We walked in the Botanical Gardens, beneath the bare trees, and drank hot chocolate at the terrace cafe.

We walked briskly along the seafront at Cramond, with the wind slapping our faces and snatching our words away.

We reminisced about our childhood and about happy times with Mum and Dad and Heather.

Michael also spoke about Robbie and what a lovely lad he seemed and how he'd like to get to know him better.

And I was able to share my feelings about the cancer. On one of our beach walks, I told him about my fears of a recurrence, and of the disease spreading, and how I dealt with the witch-bitch.

"Good on you," he said, when I described exactly how I viewed my cancer demon. "You're going to beat it. I have a good feeling about your future. That bitch claimed Mum far too soon. She's not getting you too."

"That's just what I told her or rather screamed at her, and I used words that would make even you blush!"

Michael laughed. He picked me up and spun me round. I laughed too. When he put me down, we both looked up at the sky and shouted, "Fuck off, bitch!" Fortunately the seafront was deserted and we only startled a few seagulls.

In the afternoons, I rested. Then later we cooked together. My appetite had certainly returned, and Michael was greatly amused that I ate more than he did.

On the Saturday, my phone rang as we were finishing breakfast. It was Kirsty. She asked if she and Rick could come to see me that morning as they had a couple of things to discuss. I was intrigued.

They were at the flat within an hour. It was weird seeing Kirsty and Rick as a couple. They sat side by side on the sofa. Michael said he'd go out and leave us to it. But Kirsty said no, he should stay, because what Rick had to say concerned Michael too.

Rick leant forward and looked at the floor. He twisted his hands together. "The thing is, Rosie, Michael, I suspect it's me. I suspect I'm Robbie's father." He reached for Kirsty's hand and looked from me to Michael.

It was me who was able to speak first. "You, you're Robbie's father?"

"Possibly, yes. I began to wonder, that day after we talked about her, Rosie. After we talked about Heather and I told you we met at that exhibition in 1987. Well we didn't only have a drink that night. We, you know, we had sex."

"Oh," was all I could manage.

Michael was quiet, but staring intently at Rick.

"I know it was probably a very stupid thing to do, unprotected sex, with our histories, but those were less aware times, and we were rather drunk. Anyway, I was lucky, I got away unscathed. That is, at least as far as any transmittable nasties are concerned. But after you and I spoke, Rosie, I did my sums and worked out it was just possible I was Robbie's father."

"So, what now?" Michael had found his voice.

"At first I didn't know what to do. I'm ashamed to say part of me didn't want to know. It seemed such a massive thing. It is a massive thing. I thought about it for quite a while and then I talked it over with Kirsty." He paused and looked at Kirsty. She smiled at him and squeezed his hand. "Anyway, with Kirsty's help I realised I couldn't just ignore it. So I contacted Sue Sutherland. Her number was stored in the phone here in the flat. Sorry, Rosie, if that seems a bit sneaky."

"No, it's fine." I shook my head as I spoke. "It doesn't matter."

"I didn't want to bother you with it, not if it wasn't going anywhere." Sweat trickled down his forehead. He wiped it with the back of his hand. "Anyway, I told Sue what I suspected. She was great about it, very understanding, very kind."

"She's a remarkable woman," I said.

"Yes she is. She said she'd talk to Robbie and Bob for me. I wanted to know how they would feel about a DNA test, to establish if I'm Robbie's father. She promised to get back to me once they'd discussed it."

Michael was leaning forward in his chair now. "And?"

"And she did, a few days later. She asked me to come to the house, to meet her and Bob, and to see Robbie too, of course. Kirsty came with me. I don't think I'd have managed without her, to tell you the truth." He turned and looked at Kirsty as he finished speaking.

"And they agreed to a test?" Michael asked.

"Yes, they did. Robbie said he'd started the search for his biological family because he wanted to understand why he'd had to be adopted. He knew his mother was dead, but he also knew from Sue and Bob that he had other family. He found all of you, and finding his biological father would be another important part of the jigsaw. He said that Sue and Bob were his parents and nothing would ever change that, but this was something he needed to do. He said it would be fine if I turn out to be his father, but it would be fine if I wasn't. As he said, he has nothing to lose."

"Robbie's extraordinarily mature for his age, isn't he?" I said.

"He certainly is," said Rick. "I've only spent a short time with him, but I was very impressed. He's very grounded. Mind you, with parents like the Sutherlands, I suppose it's not surprising."

"And Bob, how was he about it?" I asked.

"He was great, very supportive of Robbie. He said it was Robbie's decision. It was about Robbie's roots. If it was important to Robbie, then it was important to him. I was kind of blown away by the guy. What a big heart. What a big man." Rick stopped speaking, obviously struggling.

Kirsty stepped in. "Long story short," she said. "Rick saw my solicitor, the chap who handled my divorce. He sets up these tests for clients fairly regularly. He can organise it. It's a simple procedure. It's just a mouth swab. But the thing is, Rosie, they need a DNA sample from Robbie's mother and it would have to be you who provides that. As identical twins, you and Heather shared identical DNA."

"I see," I said. Rick was staring at me. I looked at Michael.

"It's your call," Michael said.

I was momentarily aware of Heather. It was an awareness of her that was stronger than any I'd felt since her death. I was also aware of wanting Tom beside me. But mostly I was aware of Robbie, of his need, and of his right to know.

"Okay, let's do it," I said.

"Oh, Rosie, thank you," Rick was on his feet, arms outstretched. I stood up too and we hugged each other. We both had tears in our eyes. "Thank you," he said again and kissed me on the cheek. "Thank you, thank you." He held me tightly. I felt slightly light-headed.

Kirsty rescued me. "Put her down, Rick. She can hardly breathe."

"So what happens now?" I asked, as I sat back down.

"If you're up to it, an appointment's been made for Monday. It's only provisional, so feel free to say no if it's too soon. I've just to confirm to the clinic place on Monday morning if we're going ahead. Here's a card with the address and stuff. We should be able to go back for the results on Thursday."

"Okay, Monday it is," I said. "I should have taken all this in by then. It's funny, I suspected it was Tom who was the father, and then I decided I didn't care if he was or he wasn't, because I still – well that's another story." I turned my attention back to Rick. "How do you feel? How will you feel if you're Robbie's father?"

"I don't know. Shocked, proud, thrilled, terrified, take your pick. I'm just going one step at a time, and so is Robbie, so is everyone I guess."

Michael suggested coffee for us all, which everyone agreed was much needed. He and Kirsty went through to the kitchen to make it.

Rick looked at me. "I mean it, Rosie, thank you for being willing to do this."

"I need to know too, Rick. Like it is for Robbie, it helps me with my jigsaw of what happened."

Once we all had our coffee, Kirsty said, "And now, can you cope with a second announcement?"

"Probably not, but you're going to make it anyway," I smiled.

"Rick and I are getting married a week today, next Saturday, in St Andrews, and I want you to be my bridesmaid along with Eilidh and Lucy."

I was speechless.

"Congratulations, mate!" Michael said, getting up to shake hands with Rick. "And well done, Kirsty, for doing what no other woman has ever managed." He kissed Kirsty.

"Rosie, what do you say? Will you be my bridesmaid?"

"Yes, of course I will. Sorry, it's just a bit of a shock. Congratulations, both of you. Come here." I hugged Kirsty and then Rick.

"You two haven't wasted any time!" Michael said. "What's it been, three months?"

"Oh I know!" Kirsty laughed. "It's mad and exciting and–"

"And at our age we don't want to hang about," Rick said. "I haven't felt like this about anyone before. As soon as I got together with this lovely girl, I just knew. I felt I'd really come home. At last. I want to grow even older with her." He took Kirsty's hand while he was saying this and looked into her eyes.

"What a lovely thing to say," I said, delighted for both of them. God knows, Kirsty deserved to find a good man and to be happy. I tried not to think about me and Tom and to just enjoy their happiness. "So, is everything organised?"

"Yes," said Rick. We did all the paperwork about three weeks ago. We were just about to make the announcement and then you stole our thunder getting taken into hospital."

"Sorry!" I laughed. "So where's the wedding taking place?"

"We were incredibly lucky. We managed to get the Bay Hotel. The ceremony will be at three in the afternoon," said Kirsty. "Then everyone can have a few hours off and we'll meet up again in the evening for drinks and a meal. We want it all to be chilled and low key. Rick and I have booked a cosy, romantic wee cottage for our wedding night, just outside town, complete with log fire. The plan is for us girls to travel up together on the Friday and have some pampering at the hotel and a good old girlie night in. Ask Sam to join us if she'd like to, Rosie. The men will travel up on Saturday. You lot are all booked to stay at the hotel on Saturday night. And then we're off to the Maldives on honeymoon on the Sunday." Kirsty was glowing.

"Sounds wonderful," I said. "So who exactly is going to the wedding?"

"Well, there's me, you, Lucy and Eilidh on the girls team, and Sam if she wants. And there's Rick, Graham, Robbie and Tom for the boys. I've asked Tom to give me away. That's all right, isn't it?" Kirsty asked.

"Yes, of course it is. It's a lovely thought. How was he, when you asked him?"

"He was really sweet about it, even though I disturbed him on his sickbed. He seemed really chuffed to be asked. He's going to bring Robbie to St Andrews with him. We'll know by then if Rick is Robbie's father. But he's invited as Eilidh's boyfriend, whatever happens, and being the laid back guy he is, that's fine by him."

I suddenly had a thought. "What will I wear? It's only a week away! What on earth will I wear?"

"Ah, well, I've taken a bit of a liberty there. Lucy and Eilidh have got their outfits, their own choices, and I went ahead and chose one for you. I know your taste and I guessed your size, but if it doesn't fit, Evelyn's on standby to alter it." Kirsty reached down behind the sofa and produced a carrier bag. She brought out a beautiful, forget- me-not blue, silk suit. The skirt was narrow and knee length and the jacket was short and fitted with three quarter length sleeves. "I hope you like it," she said.

"It's gorgeous! And I love the colour," I replied.

"Thought you might," Kirsty smiled.

"Go on then, sis, try it on," Michael said.

It fitted perfectly and was a very flattering shade for me. I twisted and turned as I looked in the full length mirror in the bedroom. I'd only recently turned it back round the right way. For the first time in a very long while, I liked what I saw. I'd removed my headscarf and I looked at my new hair. It had just started to grow again before I went into hospital, but I was still a bit self conscious about it. However, looking at it now, I realised that here was no longer any bare scalp to be seen. There was a good centimetre or so of new hair.

As I stood admiring myself, there was a knock on the bedroom door and Kirsty came in. I turned from the mirror to face her. "Will I do?"

"Oh, Rosie, you look beautiful. You look so well. And your hair, it's coming back! I'm so pleased to see you looking like this." She hugged me. "Are you feeling as good as you look?"

"I'm feeling a lot better, stronger each day. And, yes, my hair's coming back! Isn't it great? I love this Kirsty." I smoothed down my new suit. That was pretty clever guessing the right size."

"I did do well, didn't I?" She grinned and took my hands "And you're sure you don't mind me asking Tom to be at the wedding?"

"Of course not, I'm sure we can get along for a day or so. I'll be calling him later to see how he is and to check the kids are still coming here tomorrow, so we can discuss how to keep things civilised on your big day. After all it will be about you and Rick on Saturday, not about us, if there's still an us."

"He wanted to know if you were coming, and when I said I'd be asking you to be my bridesmaid, he seemed very happy about it. And what about Robbie? The paternity test, I mean. It seems you'll soon have proof Tom's not his father."

"Yes, but as I said, I'd got past that. I either trust him or I don't. If he says he's not the father, then I believe him. And if he had been, I think I could handle that too. It was just such a shock, at first, when it came out." I sighed, recalling Robbie's first visit.

"Oh, Rosie," Kirsty rubbed my arm. "I didn't mention about Rick and Robbie to Tom. I wanted to tell you first, but if you want I could tell him now. It seems only fair,"-

"No, no it's all right. I'll tell him. I think it should be me. Like I said, I'll be calling him later. I'll do it then. Now come on, let's see what the boys think of my new outfit."

Rick gave a loud wolf whistle and Michael gasped and said wow, when I gave them a twirl. It was just the boost I needed. I was still smiling as I got changed back into my jeans.

The four of us decided to go out for a pub lunch. We went down to Leith, to one of the waterfront places. I enjoyed being out and doing something so normal after such a long time of confinement. I'd certainly found my appetite and having polished off every bit of my fish and chips, I then tucked into apple pie and ice cream. It was great.

The other three teased me about not being able to get into my outfit the following weekend. I felt relaxed and it was a joy to see how happy Kirsty and Rick were together. It was also good to be with my big brother. We chatted about old times and some of the people we'd known then, speculating about what had become of them. We all agreed that sometimes we didn't feel any older in our heads than we felt at nineteen, in spite of everything that life had thrown at us.

We laughed affectionately at our younger selves, and commiserated with each other about the process of getting older. All the time we chatted and laughed, I was aware of Tom, of his absence. I thought how he'd enjoy the conversation and the banter. I missed him, but I managed to keep the ache at the edge of my consciousness. I was also aware how careful the others were not to mention him.

After lunch we headed into town. Kirsty and I were going shopping for shoes for me to wear at the wedding. Michael wanted to buy Scottish-themed presents for his daughters, so he went off to do that and Rick went to buy his own wedding outfit. We all met up back at the flat later.

I'd not only got shoes. I had the beginnings of a new wardrobe, new makeup, including mascara for the new improved eyelashes and, joy of joys, a bottle of shampoo. It had been true retail therapy.

By the time I said goodbye to Kirsty and Rick at the end of the afternoon, having arranged to meet Rick on Monday morning for the DNA test, I felt renewed, liberated and optimistic. I no longer had to worry about needing to throw up. I had my appetite back. I could make plans to go out and about. I was looking forward to the next weekend. I also found that, like Robbie, I had a fatalistic attitude to the outcome of the DNA paternity test. If Rick was Robbie's father, I'd adjust to that and if he wasn't, nothing would've changed.

That evening, as planned, I phoned Tom. I felt nervous as I rehearsed telling him about Rick and Robbie. However, I knew it had to be done and it would be a start, a start to us finally sorting things out, one way or another. But my over-riding emotion as I called home was longing. I just wanted to hear his voice.

Tom answered quickly. "Rosie, hi, it's good to hear from you. How are you?"

"I'm good, very good. I've had a lovely day with Rick and Kirsty and Michael." I chattered on about what we'd done and how well I was feeling. I knew there were other more pressing matters to discuss, but I at least wanted to start by being fairly light-hearted. Then I became aware that he was very quiet, letting me blether on and on. "Sorry, Tom, I didn't mean to witter on. How are you? Are you feeling better?"

"No need to apologise. I was enjoying listening to you witter." I could hear him smile as he spoke. "And, yes, I'm getting better. I've stopped being sick, just a bit weak from lack of food. I might try eating something later."

"That's good."

"Yeah, if I follow the same pattern as the kids, I should be much better by mid-week, and certainly fine for the wedding."

"It's great news isn't it, about Rick and Kirsty, I mean? They seem very happy."

"Yes indeed, great news. And you're going to be a bridesmaid?"

"I am, yes, though I think Lucy and I are a bit past it to be classed as such. But matron-of-honour just sounds horribly ancient!" I laughed.

"Well I'm acting as father of the bride, so that makes me feel rather ancient too. But I feel honoured to have been asked. Kirsty says I remind her of her late father. I think she meant it as a compliment!" Tom laughed too.

"Oh, I'm sure she did. She adored her Dad," I said. Right, now or never, I thought. My mouth went dry. I took a deep breath. "And speaking of fathers, it seems there's a possibility, or rather

311

a probability, that Rick is Robbie's father."

"What, sorry, what do you mean?"

I told him. As I finished speaking, I became aware that he hadn't said anything while I'd been telling him. "Are you okay? Are you still there?"

"Yes, yes, sorry. It's just, it was a shock. It means... I had no idea. Christ, Rick."

"Sorry, it was a shock to me too at first."

"And now, Rosie, how do you feel about it now?"

"I don't really know what to think. I'm just going to wait to see what the result is and take it from there."

"Doesn't it matter to you that you might get proof that I'm not Robbie's father?" He asked this very gently. There was no implied reproach.

"No, not really. I think I've got past all that. For what it's worth, Tom, it's the future that matters to me now, now that I'm daring to hope I might have one. What did or didn't happen in the past is just that, in the past." I could feel my voice starting to crack. This was getting dangerously emotional. Again Tom didn't speak. I got a grip on myself. "Anyway, I also phoned to check that the kids are still intending to come tomorrow and to find out what the arrangements are for next weekend childcare wise." I tried to get back to sounding light-hearted.

"Yes, right." He cleared his throat. "Yes, they're all much better and are coming to you in the afternoon. They're looking forward to it. Adam's got news. He's starting college on Monday, as you know, and he's got lots to tell you about that. But he's also heard today he's been offered an apprenticeship as a mechanic. That friend of Bob Sutherland, who has the garage in Granton, he's said he can start in six months, as long as he gets on all right with the access course. He's really excited. But he'll tell you himself. And don't worry about next weekend. Max is going to Dan's. They've got the Hearts match to go to on Saturday, local derby against Hibs, and they've got a cinema trip planned on Sunday. Jenny and Adam have got their own plans of course and they'll be fine. Ruby and Ma are available if they need any adult input. And Ma is having Toby."

"It's all under control then," I said, smiling. "How is Toby? I miss him."

"Toby was ecstatic when Adam came home, so excited. It was lovely to see their reunion. He still misses you, though."

"Maybe I'll come and see him soon," I said.

"He'd like that."

Maybe neither of us was still talking about Toby.

I was aware that though we'd made a tentative arrangement to meet and talk the following week, as soon as everyone was free of the bug, neither of us had committed to a time or place.

"And, Tom, I'm looking forward to the wedding and I hope we can try and just enjoy each other's company on the day." The last thing I wanted to know before the wedding was that Tom was leaving me for Sheena.

"Yes, yes, of course. I'd like that too."

"And after the wedding, maybe I could travel back with you and come to the house. We could have our postponed talk and I could see Toby." There was a heartbeat's pause.

"Toby and I'd like that very much."

The next day was as much fun as the previous one had been. I phoned Sam in the morning. She sounded very happy. She'd had her first week of lectures and tutorials and was loving university life so far. I told her about the wedding. She was thrilled at the news, and at the fact that her father and I would be in St Andrews the next weekend. She said she'd meet us at the hotel on Friday and, of course, she'd come to the wedding.

The other children came up to Edinburgh on the bus and were all in good form. Jenny was enjoying sixth year and spoke a lot about a boy called Stewart, from North Berwick, who she'd met at a party. She insisted they were just friends, but there was a definite light in her eye when she spoke about him. She said it was really romantic about Rick and Kirsty getting married, something which caused her brothers to pull faces, and to remark on the grossness of old people having anything to do with romance.

Max said he couldn't wait for the half-term holiday in a week's time, as school was such a bore, and that he also couldn't wait to go to his uncle Dan's at the weekend.

Adam told me all his news about the college and the apprenticeship and how cool Julie was. He said he was learning to drive, and that Tom was taking him out to practice and that, no, they'd not fallen out. I couldn't get over how much he'd changed.

The children also chatted with Michael. He told them about Australia. Max wanted to know if he knew any of the Neighbours cast. He was impressed to hear that the sister of one of the actors had once been a patient of Michael's. They asked about their cousins, and Michael asked them lots of questions about their lives. We had Chinese takeaway for dinner and, too soon, it was time for them to go. Michael was running them home. He went to fetch the car from the next street, leaving us to say our goodbyes. As the children were going out the door, I asked if their father would be at home when they got back.

"Oh yes, he should be back from Shee…" said Max.

"Shut up Max!" Jenny and Adam shouted together.

"Come on you!" Adam said to Max. "Bye Mum," he said to me and led his brother away to wait for Michael.

"Sorry, Mum," said Jenny. "I know the munchkin sort of let the cat out the bag about Dad and Sheena a few weeks back. Dad swore us to secrecy. He wants to tell you about it himself, of course. He's hoping you'll be pleased. It's good to see him so happy. He doesn't know that you know anything, so act surprised." With that she kissed me goodbye and went to join her brothers.

I closed the door and went and sat down on my bed in the darkness. So Tom was still seeing Sheena, and the children knew. They seemed very relaxed about it. Tom was happy with Sheena. I lay back on the bed and stared at the ceiling, numb, shut down with the shock, a sort of emotional concussion. I got up at some point and scribbled a note for Michael, saying that I was tired and had gone to bed. Then I crawled under the covers and, eventually, fell asleep.

The next morning I felt very low, but tried not to let it show. Michael said I looked tired and that he hoped I wasn't overdoing it. He insisted that he would come with me for the DNA test appointment, and I was glad of his support. It was all over very quickly. There was paperwork to complete and a few questions to answer and then, after the mouth swab, we were back out on the street. It was good to see Robbie. He'd told his school he had a dental appointment. He had to get back, so there wasn't much time to chat. He seemed very relaxed about the whole thing, a little shy with Rick perhaps, but that was all.

Karen Knox called me that afternoon. She'd made an appointment for me to go and see her in a couple of weeks and said that I was to have my scan on the same day. She said she'd spoken to her colleague in radiotherapy, and that I would start my course of treatment at the beginning of November. I asked her again if she thought I was going to beat the cancer. She said there was no reason to suppose that I wouldn't and that I was doing well up to now. Of course, this was all she could say, but it wasn't exactly what I wanted to hear. I wanted a definite answer. I wanted her to say I would certainly recover and live to be ninety. At least she didn't say I was doomed.

The rest of the week passed very slowly. I was looking forward to the wedding and, despite trying to be laid back about it, I was desperate to know the DNA results. I was desolate about what Jenny had said about Tom. But in spite of my desolation, I was still really excited about seeing him at the weekend. I fervently hoped that nothing would get in the way of us having our much needed talk after the wedding. I was more than ready now to hear Tom out. Hearing his story about Heather's last months, and about Robbie's birth, would be the end of an unfinished chapter in my life, but also the beginning of a new one.

And if Tom was moving onto a new chapter too, I told myself I would let him go with good grace. I would get over it. I would get over the cancer and I would get over Tom leaving me. That's what I told myself. Somehow, I got through the week.

Michael accompanied me again on the Thursday, when it was time to get the paternity test results. Kirsty was with Rick this time, and Sue and Bob came with Robbie. We met outside the test place. Everyone was nervous. There was no script for an occasion like this. As we were about to go in, my phone beeped. It was a text from Tom. It said he was thinking about me and to let him know how it went.

Rick was Robbie's father. The doctor and the counsellor spoke, first of all, to Robbie and Rick, and then to all of us. None of us was sure what to say at first. It was always going to be a shock whatever the outcome. The counsellor was brilliant, reassuringly professional and kind. She said we would all experience many different emotions, that we should all take time to come to terms with the news and how it affected each of us. She gave us her card, in case we wanted to talk anything over at a later date, and also some leaflets about other counselling services that we could access. And that was it.

# Chapter Forty Two

### *Tom*

I was incredibly nervous on the morning of the wedding. And it wasn't only because of my role in the ceremony. I was worried about whether the plan would work. Everyone in the wedding party was involved. Everyone that is , except Rosie.

I suppose Kirsty was the instigator. It was just after Rosie got out of hospital and I was recovering from the gastric bug. Kirsty phoned and told me about her and Rick and how they were going to get married. I was very touched when she asked me to give her away.

"Good, that's that sorted," Kirsty said. "Now we just need to get you and Rosie fixed." She hesitated for the shortest of moments. "You do know she thinks you're in a new relationship, don't you?"

I tried to keep my voice steady. "Michael asked me if I was seeing someone. I left him in no doubt. I'm not. I'm not interested in being with anyone else." My breath caught and reduced my voice to a whisper. "I just want Rosie."

"I thought so. I'm sorry, Tom. I didn't mean to upset you."

"It's all right. I know you're trying to help."

I considered asking her who Rosie supposed I was involved with, but it was way too painful a topic. I think Kirsty sensed how I felt, because she didn't seem inclined to get into any details.

"Somewhere along the line, wires got crossed and you're

going to have to untangle them. Have you two arranged a time to get together?" Kirsty sounded like a teacher questioning a seven year old.

"Yes, sort of, as soon as I'm in the clear from this virus, but we haven't got a firm arrangement yet."

I heard Kirsty sigh, could imagine her shaking her head.

"Right, you need a firm arrangement, one that can't be broken. My wedding will be the perfect opportunity. I'm going to ask Rosie to be a bridesmaid. You two will be in the same place at the same time. I know St Andrews didn't work out last month, but I have a good feeling about it this time. And I have a plan. You're going to surprise her, impress her, and sweep her off her feet!"

By the time it was fully formed, Kirsty's plan involved everyone and all were sworn to secrecy. The wedding itself had not required so much planning.

There was the home part of the plan. Dan knew that if things went well between me and Rosie, then Max would be staying with Ruby for the entire week after the wedding. Dan would drop Max off at Ruby's, if and when he got the call. Ma was similarly on standby for a week with Toby. Jenny and Adam were prepared for the possibility of me being away for longer than just the weekend. Even Sheena and Andy played a part in the plan, and both had done as much as they could to prepare me.

And then there was the away part of the plan. Lucy and Graham were instructed to make themselves scarce after the wedding ceremony as were Sam, Eilidh and Robbie. I also needed to leave immediately after the ceremony. Rick was primed to give me an excuse to do so. That way, when Rick needed a favour, only Rosie would be available.

The cottage, a crucial part of the plan, was booked by Rick. It was a holiday place, belonging to a mate of his, and was just outside St Andrews. As far as Rosie was concerned, the cottage was to be the venue for Rick and Kirsty's wedding night.

So, by the day of the wedding I was tense with anticipation. I was alone in the house on that morning. Even Toby was gone, picked up by Ma the day before. I packed the cool-boxes with the food shopping I'd done the previous evening, and put the last minute bits of packing into my holdall. I checked and rechecked that I'd put everything into the car. Then, at last, it was time to set off.

Before picking up Robbie, I went to the flat. There I collected the extra bag that Michael had secretly packed for Rosie. It contained clothes that Rosie didn't know she might need.

Once on the road, I just wanted to concentrate on getting to Fife, and on putting the plan into action. Robbie talked a bit about Rick and how he was getting his head round having found his real father. But he seemed to sense that I wasn't up to much in the way of conversation. He asked if I minded if he listened to his i-pod while we drove. I said I didn't mind at all.

We went to the cottage before making our way into St Andrews. I followed the directions Rick had given me. It was down a single track road and surrounded by fields. It was an old, traditional structure, with whitewashed walls. The key was where Rick said it would be, on a shelf in the shed behind the cottage. The shed also contained plenty of logs for the fire.

We let ourselves in. There was a welcome note to me and Rosie propped up on the kitchen table. I pocketed the note.

The kitchen seemed well equipped, which was a relief. I put the food I'd brought into the fridge and larder. I also put the pink champagne in to chill. I hoped it was still Rosie's favourite.

I'd also got flowers for Rosie. Robbie helped me carry them in. There were several armfuls, roses and freesias. The florist in Gullane was both bemused and delighted as I selected almost her entire stock of both types of flower. Suspecting, I'm sure, that flower arranging was not a skill-set that I possessed, she'd offered to arrange them and tie them into bunches, an offer I was pleased to accept. So all Robbie and I had to do was find some vases and get them in water.

"Only two vases, that's no use!" I said, after we'd scouted around.

Robbie laughed. "Nobody would be expecting this amount of flowers. Two vases are probably more than enough for normal people. You have gone a bit over the top."

"Yes, I probably have overdone it, haven't I?"

"Don't worry," Robbie said, smiling broadly. "Rosie will love it!"

"God, I hope so," I replied.

In the end we had to use two pails, a waste paper bin, a milk jug and a beer tankard as makeshift vases.

Robbie went back to the car to phone Eilidh and I was able to have a quick look round the cottage as I put flowers into every room.

The living-room had a huge, brown, leather sofa and three matching armchairs. A log fire was set in the grate, ready to light.

The master bedroom at the back looked out over open fields. I allowed myself only a quick glance at the large, white-covered bed.

As well as a shower room, there was a bathroom with an enormous free-standing bath at its centre, the sort that Rosie had often said she'd love to have at home.

The ceilings were low, and I had to watch not to bump my head on some of the doorways, but the overall effect was cosy and comfortable. The place had a good atmosphere. I started to hope.

Graham and Rick arrived at the hotel moments after Robbie and I got there. We all met up in the foyer. Graham called Lucy to say we'd arrived and she came to greet us. She said the girls were having lunch in Rosie and Sam's room. She told us who was to get ready in which room and that I was to be at Kirsty's room at five-to-three.

Before Lucy left us to go back upstairs, she gave me a kiss on the cheek and wished me luck. Rick protested that it was him who was getting married and did he not get a good luck kiss.

Graham said never mind that, he was Lucy's husband and he didn't even get a kiss. She just made a face, laughed and walked off.

Me and the other guys went to the bar for some lunch before going to get changed. And then it was time.

Kirsty opened the door to her room as soon as I knocked. She looked lovely in a long, cream dress, with a little jacket thing over the top of it. She was carrying a bunch of yellow roses.

"Wow," I said, "you scrub up nice."

She laughed. "Why thank you. You don't look so bad yourself. Rosie won't be able to resist."

I smiled weakly. "Ready?"

"Yes, very," she replied taking my arm. I don't know about Kirsty, but I was feeling quite sick with nerves.

As I approached the wedding room with Kirsty on my arm, I spotted Eilidh, Lucy and Rosie waiting just outside. When we got over to where they were standing, all three of them said how lovely Kirsty looked.

Rosie glanced at me at the same moment I looked at her. She smiled. She looked incredible, relaxed, happy and beautiful.

As a heart surgeon I should have known better, but it felt like my heart was going to explode out of my chest. I could hardly breathe.

Then we were being ushered inside the room and the processional music started. I took Kirsty's arm once more and walked her down to where Rick was standing with Graham. Lucy, Eilidh and Rosie followed us. Sam and Robbie stood up as we came in. They grinned at me. I think Sam actually winked. I couldn't have felt more nervous if it had been me getting married. My normally very steady hands were shaking and I thought my legs might give way. I was glad to be able to hang on to Kirsty. She seemed to be steadying me rather than the other way around, and she squeezed my arm as we walked. The music faded and the registrar smiled. I kissed Kirsty and passed her hand into Rick's outstretched one. Then I gratefully sat down beside Sam and Robbie.

As Rick and Kirsty exchanged their vows, I watched Rosie. She was standing beside Kirsty, looking intently from her to Rick. She looked gorgeous in a shade of blue that suited her perfectly. She wore a circle of yellow flowers in her newly-grown, short hair. I looked again. Yes, she definitely had hair.

Sam caught me gazing at her mother, squeezed my hand and smiled.

As I watched Rosie, she lifted her hand to her face and seemed to wipe away a tear. It was the bit in the ceremony where the rings were being exchanged.

I patted my pocket where I had Rosie's ring. She knew it had been given to me when she was in hospital, but neither of us had broached the subject of its return. If all went according to plan... I swallowed hard and tried not to think about it.

The ceremony was over and there was a flurry of handshakes, kisses and congratulations for the newly-weds. Sam nudged me in the back and reminded me it was time to go and speak to Rosie. I told her I wasn't sure if I could speak and, even if I could, that I would make any sense. But Sam wasn't having any of it. She just shoved me harder in Rosie's direction.

I took a deep breath and went over. She had her back to me and was speaking to Robbie. As I arrived, Sam swooped on Robbie and led him away.

"Hello, Rosie." My voice sounded hoarse.

She turned and smiled. "Hello, Tom, and well done. You did the giving away beautifully."

"Thanks. It was a lovely ceremony wasn't it? Kirsty looks lovely. So do you. Your outfit is lovely. Sorry, I seem to be experiencing adjective failure."

Rosie laughed. "Yes, it's all lovely." She laughed again. I prayed for rescue.

Rick called for silence. He was standing with his arm round Kirsty's shoulder. "Thanks, everyone, for coming. Mrs Montgomery and I..." He paused as we all laughed. "My wife..."

He paused again to kiss Kirsty. "My wife and I suggest that everybody goes and relaxes for a while. And we'll all meet in the bar for pre-dinner drinks at around six."

On that cue, Sam went over to Eilidh and Robbie. She spoke to them and the three of them left the room. They waved to me and Rosie. Then Lucy and Graham put down their glasses and they too gave us a wave and left.

Rick called over to me. "Tom, can I have a word, mate?"

"Sure," I called back to him. "Excuse me a moment," I said to Rosie.

The plan was now in action.

# Chapter Forty Three

### *Rosie*

On the morning of Kirsty's wedding, I awoke with a mixture of dread and anticipation. I was excited for Kirsty and Rick of course. But I was even more excited about seeing Tom and spending a day in his company.

I'd decided to make the most of it, to enjoy the present. I knew that in the coming week we'd meet to talk over our relationship, its past and its future. The dread I felt was that I'd pick up some signal from Tom that he no longer wanted to be with me. I knew I might soon have to face that possibility, but I wanted to remain ignorant for one more day, for this special day in particular.

Lucy, Kirsty and Eilidh joined Sam and me for a room-service lunch. But by then I was so nervous, I hardly ate any of the sandwiches that the others tucked into.

I looked at myself in the long, wall mirror before going downstairs to the wedding. It was ages since I'd worn makeup or anything remotely smart. I touched my hair. Even although it was still very short, it remained a lovely novelty to have any at all. I twisted right and left to see myself from various angles.

"You're looking great, Mum," Sam said, smiling. "You suit the short hair. It makes you look really young. Dad's going to be well impressed!"

"I hope so," I said, trying not to sound as scared as I felt.

Once we were downstairs we didn't have long to wait before

Tom and Kirsty appeared.

I couldn't look at Tom at first, but once I'd greeted Kirsty I allowed myself a glance. I took a breath and smiled at him. He smiled back. He looked really good in a new, navy-blue suit, pale blue shirt and patterned, grey, silk tie. My heart did several somersaults.

The ceremony was very simple and moving. I tried to focus only on what was happening now, in front of me. When I heard the bit about entering into a contract for life and watched the exchange of rings, I couldn't help crying a little. I remembered that Tom had not yet returned my wedding ring, but quickly suppressed the thought that perhaps this was significant.

After the ceremony, Tom came to speak to me. He seemed nervous. I was hoping to have him to myself for a little while, but then Rick called him away and the two of them left, deep in conversation.

I went and joined Kirsty, who also appeared to be on her own. She looked stunning. Her long, tight-fitting, cream silk gown was perfect for her figure and her colouring. Lucy had put Kirsty's hair up and woven little yellow rosebuds into it. They set off her auburn hair beautifully.

"So, Mrs Montgomery," I said, hugging her. "How are you feeling?"

"I'm feeling happy, very happy." Kirsty answered. "Come on, let's go and sit in the lounge."

Once we were sitting down, I asked Kirsty where everyone had disappeared to.

"Graham and Lucy are going to spend the rest of the afternoon with their boys. And Sam is taking Robbie and Eilidh round the university. I don't know what Rick's got Tom doing, probably planning some daft surprise for me." She laughed before adding, "Tom looked very handsome don't you think? Smart suit and that tie, very nice."

"Yes, they're new, I've not seen them before and yes, he was looking good."

Kirsty and I chatted some more, and then she said she thought she'd go up to her room and lie down for a little while, if I didn't mind. "I couldn't sleep last night. I was so excited. I think it's catching up with me now."

"I'll be fine," I said. "On you go. Get some rest."

I was wondering what to do with myself for the next hour or so when Rick came back and sat beside me. I told him he'd just missed Kirsty.

"It was you I wanted," he said. "I wonder if I could ask you a favour? Only, everyone else seems to have disappeared."

"Surely," I said.

"Could you go to the cottage and check the heating's on. My mate told me it would be, but if it's not, the place will be pretty cold. And could you check that the food shopping I ordered has been delivered and that the champagne is chilling. Just give the place the once over for me. I want everything to be perfect for Kirsty when we get there tonight. I mentioned to Tom that I was going to ask you and he said to take his car." He reached into his pocket and gave me Tom's car keys.

"Okay, you old romantic you," I said. "Where is Tom anyway?"

He tapped his finger to the side of his nose, " Oh, he's off preparing something else."

"Kirsty's a lucky woman," I laughed. "Maybe I should get changed first, though."

"No, no, you'll not have time, not if you want to be back and all dressed up and ready for six o'clock. Tom's got a jacket in the car. I remember seeing it earlier. Put that on if you're cold. Go, while it's still light. And here, I've written down directions for you. Head back out of town the way you came in. The keys are on the shelf in the shed." He seemed on edge, desperate to send me on my way. I put it down to the adrenalin of the day.

"Right then," I said, smiling. "I'd better go. See you later."

"Yes, see you," Rick said, seeming to give a huge sigh of relief as I walked away.

It was strange to be in Tom's car. It was months since I'd been in it. And sure enough, his old, winter jacket was lying on the back seat. I put it on. It smelt of him. I rubbed the sleeve against my face, and sat for a minute, enjoying how good it felt to be close to him, even in this small way.

I found the cottage easily. The gate was open and I turned the car into the driveway at the side. I retrieved the house keys and let myself in.

The heating was on. The cottage felt cosy as soon as I stepped in. I went into the kitchen and checked the fridge. It was full and the champagne was well chilled. It was pink champagne. I knew Kirsty would be impressed by Rick's choice of this most romantic drink. There was a fragrant bunch of yellow and lilac freesias in a little blue vase on the table. I breathed in their gorgeous scent.

Then I went through to the bedroom and I switched on the bedside lamp. It was a plain room, white-walled and with sheepskin rugs on the stripped wooden floor. I closed the heavy, dark blue velvet curtains. The bed was enormous and covered with a thick white quilt. On the dressing table there was a crystal vase full of the most beautiful red roses. "Kirsty, you're a lucky woman," I said to myself.

I peeped into the bathroom. I loved the bath with its silver claw feet. There were bottles of jewel-coloured bubble bath on the windowsill and thick, white towels on the rail. There were candles on the shelf above the bath and yet more beautiful flowers in a chipped, white enamel pail. This place was perfect for a wedding night.

I walked through to the living-room. I did think it odd that the lamps in there were already on and the fire was lit. The logs smelt wonderful. And, yes, there were flowers, this time in what appeared to be a wastepaper bin. Someone must have been into the cottage recently. Maybe Rick's friend, the cottage's owner, had decided to call in himself, to ensure a warm welcome for the newly-weds and would, presumably be coming back to keep an eye on the fire. I shrugged to myself. Whatever the explanation, everything was ready and I knew I should head back.

But I decided to sit down for a moment to enjoy the fire. I sat in the armchair nearest the hearth, facing the door. I slipped out of Tom's jacket and gazed into the flames. I held the jacket to my face. I missed him so much.

It was getting dark and I was just thinking I'd really better move when a voice said, "Hello, Rosie."

I jumped.

Tom was standing in the doorway.

# Chapter Forty Four

## *Tom*

The taxi was already waiting when Rick called me over. We dashed round to my car for the bags and I flung them into the taxi and jumped in.

"Good luck, mate." Rick said as he slammed the door shut.

As soon as I got to the cottage, I stowed the bags in the bedroom wardrobe and then set to work. I took off my jacket and tie but decided there was no time to get properly changed.

The fire was first and, I'm proud to say, it took first time and was burning away nicely within half an hour.

Next, I prepared the vegetables to accompany the main course of that night's meal. I had all my instructions from Andy and Sheena. Tonight's dish was beef in designer beer, one of Delia's finest recipes. I'd cooked it at home and it would just need to be reheated in the oven. I'd learned to cook this dish on one of my cookery lessons at Sheena's house. She'd suggested teaching me when I took her out for a thank you meal after the coq au vin recipe proved so successful. Andy had offered to help me too. So, in order not to offend either of them, I suggested they both taught me. I found that I really enjoyed cooking. Then I found that Andy and Sheena really enjoyed each other's company, and I began to feel like a bit of a gooseberry on lesson nights. But, fortunately for me, they didn't let their personal feelings get in the way of their teaching commitment.

I'd just finished doing the vegetables and hidden them away, when I saw the car approaching. I let myself out the back door and went and hid behind the shed. I heard rummaging from inside the shed and a little while later I saw the bedroom light go on. I crept up to the back door and listened. It was quiet.

I slipped back into the kitchen and, very quietly, switched on the oven and put the casserole dish into it. Then I crept down the hall to the living room door.

Rosie was sitting gazing into the fire. She was holding my old jacket. She looked breathtakingly beautiful. My heart was doing the hammering thing again.

"Hello, Rosie."

She jumped. "Tom!" she said, rubbing a hand across her face. "What are you doing here?"

"Long story. Are you crying?" I moved towards her.

She put my jacket down and stood up, shaking her head. "No, I'm fine." She put up a hand to hold me off.

"Please, Rosie, tell me what's wrong. Don't shut me out, please."

"Look, we better be getting back. How did you get here anyway? I've got your car."

We faced each other across the room.

"Sit down, Rosie, please, just sit down. I've got some explaining to do. I need to talk, even if you don't."

She looked at me, scared and sad. I so wanted to hold her, to comfort her. I took another step towards her. Again she gestured to keep me away. She really didn't want me to touch her. I couldn't bear it.

"Rosie, please."

"No," she spoke very quietly and shook her head. "Please, don't. Say what it is you have to say, and then we can get back to our friends' wedding."

"Right," I said, sitting on one of the sofas. "If that's the way you want it."

Rosie shrugged and returned to the fireside chair.

"But if we go back to the hotel now," I said, "our family and friends might never speak to us again."

"What? What do you mean?"

"Let's just say, you're not really here to check out the place for Rick. We – that is me and everyone who cares about us – we sort of planned it – for you and me to be here together – so we could talk."

Rosie frowned. "So this is all some kind of trick, to force me to be here with you, and everyone, except me, knew about it."

"Yes. I can see how you might feel tricked. But honestly, it was all done with the best of intentions. It was because everyone wanted to make sure we'd get time alone."

"But what about when Rick and Kirsty come?" she asked, sounding only slightly less wary.

"Ah, they're not coming. The cottage is for us. To quote Kirsty, she said, 'I'm not spending my wedding night in some old cottage. I'm having the bridal suite or there will be no wedding.' Or words to that effect."

Rosie gave a little smile. "Sounds like Kirsty."

"So you'll stay? And we'll talk?" I asked.

She shrugged, defeated. "Yes, if that's what you want. But surely we could have talked at the hotel, or back home like we arranged. It seems a bit extreme to rent a cottage for an evening."

I didn't want to tell her, yet, just how long I'd rented the cottage for, so I mumbled something about Rick's friend not minding and owing Rick a favour, and there being no time like the present.

She shrugged again and shook her head. Then she looked in the direction of the kitchen. "Is that food I can smell?"

"It's dinner, beef casserole. I put it in the oven before I came in here."

"*You* did?"

"Yes, I've been having cooking lessons with Andy and Sheena. They both volunteered to teach me, so we've been meeting at Sheena's place and they've turned me into a bit of a chef. At least,

I hope they have."

Rosie looked anxious, panicky almost. I desperately wanted her to relax so I kept talking.

"I kept the lessons secret because I wanted to surprise you. And here's another surprise. While I fell in love with cooking, it seems Andy and Sheena fell in love with each other! I think theirs will be the next wedding."

I hoped Rosie might laugh at this revelation, smile at least. But she just put her hands to her face and stood up. I assumed she hadn't been listening to me, had been wrapped up in her own thoughts. She turned her back and looked down into the fire. Her voice was so quiet I had to lean forward to hear her.

She muttered something about a secret.

"Sorry, what was that?"

She shook her head. "I thought I'd lost you." She gave a little sob.

I went to her. "Oh, Rosie…"

Tentatively, I put my hand on the back of her neck. I was still at arm's length. She didn't pull away. She was trembling. I stepped in closer behind her. I put my other hand on her shoulder and breathed in the smell of her. I could hear her breathing.

She turned to face me, but kept looking down at the floor. I put a finger under her chin and tipped her head up. Tears ran down her cheeks.

I held her face in my hands. "You've not lost me. I've been there all the time, waiting." I rubbed away her tears with my thumbs and looked into her eyes.

"Oh, Tom," she whispered. I put my arms round her. She turned her head and leant it on my chest. I pulled her close and held her tightly. She clung to me and cried with quiet sobs.

Eventually she moved back slightly and looked up at me. "I'm so sorry," she said.

I put my fingers to her lips and shook my head.

She moved closer again. Her breathing was fast and shallow. She put her hands up to my neck.

I kissed her, and she responded. It was the most tender kiss we'd ever exchanged.

Then she looked into my eyes again and said softly, "I want you, Tom."

"And I want you," I said.

The talking was going to have to wait.

I took her hand and led her through to the bedroom. I sat her down gently on the bed. She lay back on the pillows. We looked at each other for a long moment. I sat down on the edge of the bed, beside where she lay and I stroked her face.

I leant over her and we kissed again, more urgently this time. She unbuttoned my shirt and I took it off. Rosie watched me intently as I undressed. I lay back down on the bed and kissed her again. I ran my fingers down her neck. I unfastened her jacket and caressed her right breast. She caught my hand.

"Wait," she said. "Please, wait." She sat up. "I need to show you first. It's – I don't want you to be – it's…"

"Show me, Rosie," I said quietly, sitting up as she got off the bed. She slipped off her jacket and stepped out of her skirt. She stood there in her white, lacy underwear and stockings, incredibly sexy. I stared into her face and she held my gaze.

"You look amazing," I said.

She gave a small smile and glanced away momentarily. Then she undid her bra and removed it. "There," she said, resuming her stare, ready to gauge my reaction.

I lowered my gaze. There was a scar across her left chest. Her breast was gone. I felt such anguish for her, for what this loss must mean to her.

"Oh, my darling," I whispered.

Her hand went to the scar.

"Come here," I whispered, holding out my arms towards her. She came back to the bed and lay down beside me.

I lifted her hand away from the scar and traced along it with my finger.

She gave a little shudder.

I ran my lips along it and tasted my tears on her skin. "Your poor breast."

"I know," she said quietly. It was Rosie's turn to brush my tears away. "Tom?"

"Yes?"

"Would you make love to me, please?"

And so I made love to my darling Rosie. It was sublime to be able to touch her and to feel her hands on me. It was soft and incredibly tender. I wanted to linger over every look, every sensation, every touch. Rosie's eyes scarcely left mine. I don't think we'd ever been so – together. Then a little later, when Rosie kissed me and said 'more please', it became more urgent and utterly exhilarating.

Afterwards we lay exhausted, facing each other, looking, not speaking.

I traced the contours of her face and stroked her hair and then I just held her.

In the end it was Rosie who broke the silence. "I'm starving," she said. "When's dinner?"

I laughed. "Oh, right, dinner." I propped myself up on one elbow and glanced at the bedside clock. "The casserole's on at a low heat. It'll be fine for about another hour. So, why don't we have a soak in that lovely big bath before we eat?"

"Mmm, that sounds nice." She stretched and arched her back. It was an almost irresistible pose.

"Stop that," I said. "Or I'll never get out of this bed. Cover yourself up, woman."

She giggled. It was a wonderful, wonderful sound. I tore myself away and went to the wardrobe. I brought out two white towelling robes and put one on.

"Here," I said, holding the other one out for Rosie. "Make yourself decent."

Rosie laughed again. "If you insist," she said, getting out of bed and letting me slip the robe round her shoulders. "Mmm, that feels nice," she said, tying the belt.

She returned to the bed and, sitting back against the pillows, she watched as I unpacked. "You came prepared," she said, smiling.

"So did you." I reached into the wardrobe. I took out the bag Michael had packed, as well as the one she'd taken to the hotel. "Your luggage, ma'am. The cottage is ours for a week, if you want it, and you should have everything you need here."

"What? How?"

I explained more of the subterfuge and planning and that I'd paid a week's rental.

"My God!" she exclaimed. "You were determined, weren't you?"

"You don't know the half of it. Now, I'll get the bath started."

I left the bath to fill and went to the kitchen to get the champagne. Rosie was still lying, propped against the pillows when I returned.

"Drink?" I said, laying the glasses on the dressing table and starting to undo the cork.

Rosie sat up and beamed at me. "Oh, Tom, pink champagne, my favourite! What a lovely idea! Yes please."

The cork came out with a satisfying pop and I poured us both a glass. I handed one to Rosie. "To – the future?" I said, raising my glass.

Rosie smiled again and touched her glass to mine. "Yes, to the future."

# Chapter Forty Five

### *Rosie*

I experienced several emotions immediately after Tom's appearance in the cottage. There was the surprise of seeing him, and the shock as he revealed the plot to get me there. Then, of course, there was the mixture of shame and relief when I realised how wrong I'd been about Tom and Sheena. But my over-riding emotion was one of longing. It was a longing for him, to be held and be touched by him.

To find myself in bed with him was way more than I'd dared hope for. I'd been nervous, shy of showing him the effect of the mastectomy. But Tom's empathy and sympathy, when he saw my scar, was not only all the reassurance I needed, but it lessened my sense of loss.

And the lovemaking, oh, it was amazing.

The first time, it was tentative and tender. Our awareness of each other seemed incredibly heightened. We were careful, still vulnerable, searching for and finding deep reassurance and comfort. We were questioning and rediscovering.

The second time it was much more greedy and raw. There was a passionate assertiveness about it, an urgent reclaiming after the months of fear and mistrust.

But, as we lay back in the gorgeously scented bath, sipping champagne by the light of the scented candles, I wondered if the sex had been an ending or a beginning. On its own, wonderful though it had been, it wasn't enough to put everything right. Tom still cared about me, that was obvious, but how did he see our future? He'd changed over the last few months and so had I. I knew what I wanted; I wanted to be with Tom. But I realised, that if we were to be together, it would have to be in a new way.

Tom got out of the bath first and went to get dressed and see to our meal. I remained and luxuriated for a little while longer.

But when he shouted that the food would be ready in five minutes, I dragged myself out. I put on a pair of jeans and Tom's old, blue denim shirt. I'd deliberately not returned it. I'd found it comforting to wear and had deliberately packed it in my weekend bag.

When I went back to the living-room, the table was set, white cloth, candles and an open bottle of red wine. I stood at the fire. I could hear Tom at work in the kitchen. I tried to remain relaxed and enjoy the moment.

"Top up?" Tom was in the doorway, champagne bottle in hand. He smiled and nodded at his denim shirt, as he refilled my glass. "So, you've still got it."

I touched the collar. "I wasn't sure you'd want it back after what happened to it. And I've enjoyed wearing it. It's been a – a link to you." I now felt a bit shy with him, uncertain of my ground.

"Oh, right. That's nice." He raised his glass. "To us?"

I heard the question in his voice. I could only nod as I raised my glass in response. Tom put his hand in the pocket of his jeans and produced my wedding ring. He held it out to me. He ran his hand through his hair and cleared his throat. I could see he was as awkward and unsure as I was. "Will you – do you want this back?"

"Of course I do." I held out my hand and he replaced the ring on my finger. It was still slightly loose.

"You need fattening up, my girl." Tom raised my hand to his lips. "So drink up your champagne and come and sit at the table. I'll bring the food through. We'll eat first, talk later."

The dinner was delicious. The first course was a smoked salmon pâté with green salad and warm toast. Tom laid mine before me with a flourish, telling me proudly that he'd made the pâté himself and had even baked the bread. "I've got a bread making machine. Andy suggested I get one, and the pâté is a recipe of Sheena's. I made it all at home before I came up."

Mention of Sheena made me feel so embarrassed. I knew I'd have to confess what I'd suspected regarding Tom and her, but this wasn't the time. Luckily Tom didn't seem to notice my discomfort on that score. He was too busy watching and waiting while I took my first mouthfuls of the starter. The pâté was delicately flavoured, beautifully soft and luscious on my tongue, and the bread gorgeously fragrant and yeasty.

"Mmm," I said, between mouthfuls. "That is so good."

"I'm glad you like it," Tom said, in a decidedly seductive tone.

"Oh, I do." I smiled at him.

The main course was beef cooked in beer. It certainly lived up to the promise offered by the aroma of its cooking. The beef was meltingly tender, the sauce rich, dark and velvety. The fluffy potatoes and crisp, lightly cooked, sugar snaps and carrots complemented the meat perfectly, as did the intense red wine Tom had chosen to accompany it. Once again, Tom watched me closely as I ate, and once again I made approving noises as I savoured each mouthful.

"I'm amazed! That was absolutely gorgeous," I said, as I finished eating.

Tom's smile told me how delighted he was that I'd enjoyed it. "Do you want some more?"

"Oh, no, I couldn't take any more! I'm completely satisfied." I took a sip of wine.

"Not completely satisfied, I hope." Tom resumed the seductive tone. "I'm not finished yet. There's still dessert to come."

I spluttered on the wine. "Are we still talking about the meal?"

"Of course, what else?" Tom smiled and raised his eyebrows.

Dessert was a fluffily light, but gorgeously chocolatey, pudding with a melted fudgy sauce at its core and there was cream to pour over it. It was scrumptiously, spoon-lickingly, delectable. When I'd finished I leaned back in my chair and stretched.

"Well?" Tom asked.

I licked my lips. "Orgasmic." The combination of physical intimacy, alcohol and excellent food was a potent mix. It was wonderful to be this relaxed with each other. But, I think we both sensed it was temporary. We still had a lot of serious talking to do.

While Tom put more logs on the fire, I made us some coffee. We drank it sitting side by side on the sofa.

Tom beamed with pride when I pronounced the meal to be the best I'd ever had. "I know you've been making dinners for the kids, but I'd no idea you had this sort of talent."

"I had good teachers. Andy and Sheena were great and I love cooking. It's a wonderful way of unwinding. I'm just sorry I didn't learn sooner." He paused and took hold of my hand. "I'm sorry I didn't learn a lot of things sooner. These last few months, I've realised what I've been missing."

"Like what?"

"For one thing, I've got to know the children properly. They're great kids, Rosie."

"Yes, they are." I nodded.

"I still love my work, but I've found I love being at home too. The job share with Anna is working out really well and I'm going to take a sabbatical."

"You have changed!"

"I want to be more involved, be there for the children, if it's not too late that is. I..." His voice caught. He looked away. His earlier ease was gone.

I put my hand to his face and turned him back to look at me. "Of course it's not too late. You're a good father. Sam adores you. They all love you, Tom."

He took my hand. "And you, Rosie, do you love me?" His earlier look of uncertainty and apprehension had returned.

"Yes, Tom, I love you very much."

He clasped my hand more tightly and moved in closer. "And I love you, more than anything, more than ever. I never meant to hurt you. Please believe me, Rosie."

"I do. I do believe you. But–"

"But, what?"

"But things weren't right between us long before I knew about Robbie, or the cancer. I'd got lost. We'd got lost. There was no – no joy any more. It had all become a bit of a treadmill. I feared that once the kids were grown up and gone, we'd have nothing to keep us together."

Tom nodded and pulled me close. He placed his hand on the back of my neck and looked into my eyes. "I'm so sorry. I've been such a selfish bastard. I know things need to change. They will, they have."

I shook my head and moved away a little. "It's not all down to you, Tom. I shut you out. I was so wrapped up in the children and the domestic stuff, taking everything on myself. I could have told you how I felt, could have asked you to do more. I could even have left some of it undone."

"Yes, but–"

"No, Tom, I mean it. It's not only you to blame. I was a martyr. You said so, so did Sam." Tom looked as if he was going to protest. I put my hand up to stop him. "It's okay. You were both right. I must have been such a bore. Keeping busy, it was a way of coping, a way of making amends –to Mum, to Heather. It also gave me control. Even when I looked after Dad, it was a way of taking charge and of lessening the guilt."

Tom put his hands on my shoulders. "You're being too hard on yourself. Maybe, at some level, that's what you were doing. But you've been a loving, caring wife and mother in spite of your grief, not because of it. Your Mum died. Your sister died. There was nothing you could do."

"I could have made sure Mum got her treatment on time. I could have been there for Heather."

"No, Rosie, your mum was in charge of her illness. She made her own decisions, just like you have. I agree she was wrong to delay her treatment, in order to try to help Heather, but it was her decision and she had the right to make it. And Heather, she made her own decisions too."

"Yes, bad ones." I got up, walked over to the fire, stood looking into it.

"Not all bad, not all her decisions were bad." He spoke softly.

I turned to face him. "So, tell me, Tom. Tell me what happened to Heather, at the end. How exactly were you involved?" I sat down in the armchair by the fire.

And, at last, Tom told me it all. He told me how he'd kept an eye on Heather after she and I became estranged. He confirmed what Rick had already told me about her being off drugs by 1988. He told me about the church charity that supported her, about her little flat and about how pleased she was to be pregnant.

"I asked her who the father was, but she wouldn't say. All she'd say was, he was someone she was fond of, but he didn't need to know about the baby as he wasn't in a position to be its parent. It certainly didn't occur to me that it could be Rick." He paused for a moment. "And please believe me, Rosie, there was no possibility that I could be the baby's father, no possibility at all."

"I do believe you. I got that wrong. I'm so sorry I mistrusted you." I got up and went back to sit on the sofa. He put his arm round me as I nestled in at his side. I looked up into his face. "The crazy thing is that, in the end, I didn't actually care even if you were Robbie's father." Tom raised his eyebrows. "I mean, yes, I'd have been gutted, but I would still have wanted us to work, now and in the future. But I really am sorry, for doubting you."

He stroked my face and said, "I'd be lying if I said it didn't hurt, but I don't blame you. It's no wonder you had your suspicions." Then he kissed me.

A little while later I said, "It was a wonderful thing to do, to try and keep in touch with Heather when the rest of us couldn't.

But from what you've said, it sounded like she'd sorted herself out, that, for a time at least, she was optimistic about the future."

"Yes, she was optimistic. She'd started painting again. She'd really got herself together. I couldn't believe it at first, but the evidence was there before me. And the pregnancy seemed to have filled her with hope, with resolve for the future." He hesitated, cleared his throat. "She asked me to be with her for the birth."

"Oh?" I was both shocked and fascinated by this disclosure. "Did you go? Were you with her?"

"Yes, I was. She had no-one. She knew it was a lot to ask. If you'd been well, she'd have asked you."

"Would she?"

"Oh, yes. It was only because I'd told her you were ill after the twins that she thought she'd wait until after she'd had the baby before she got in touch. I agreed that was best. She was so looking forward to seeing you, Rosie, to showing you how she'd changed, to showing you her baby." He paused again. "Anyway, I justified being with her for the birth by telling myself that it's what you'd have wanted." He looked at me, waited for my reaction.

"Yes." I nodded slowly.

"The birth was straightforward. She was so happy. I took her home to her flat a couple of days later. The church group had got a load of baby stuff together for her and I bought her some bits and pieces. The social workers were hovering, but they seemed fairly relaxed about Heather's fitness as a mother. I arranged to drop in on her once a week, and for a few weeks it was fine."

"You were amazing, doing all that for her."

He shook his head. "You haven't heard it all yet, Rosie." He ran his hands through his hair, sat back, looked up at the ceiling and exhaled loudly.

I put my hand on his arm. "Tom, are you okay?"

He turned and looked at me, his face drawn and pale. "I'm all right. It's just – well this is difficult. It was cruel, Rosie, what happened to her. It was cruel." He sat forward, gazing into the fire as he spoke. "She found out she was HIV positive."

I put my hands to my mouth. I couldn't speak. A sob caught in my throat. I shook my head. "No, no…" The sob escaped.

Tom gathered me in his arms. "I'm sorry, I'm so sorry," he said. He stroked my hair. I don't know how long I stayed in his embrace, trying to take in what he'd said.

Eventually I said, "Poor Heather."

"Yes, poor Heather. She was terrified. HIV and AIDS were new and very frightening. Even the medics were panicking. She'd been offered the test as part of her post-addiction care plan as she was a former intravenous user. She'd agreed to it without any real understanding of what it could mean. And a positive diagnosis, it felt like a death sentence back then. It was a death sentence. In 1988 there was little anyone could do. She was desperate and she was afraid for Robbie. He was tested, not all babies born to HIV mothers were positive, and he was one of the lucky ones. But she was scared she could still infect him or that he might still develop it. As I said, nobody knew anything much about it then."

"It's awful, unimaginable how she must have felt. I'm so glad you were there for her, that you offered her support."

Tom shook his head. "I couldn't – didn't offer enough support. Oh, I tried. I found out what I could about the disease. But there was little to be found by way of reassurance. And then there was the stigma. She was so ashamed. It was portrayed as something very shameful. She didn't want you to know. She made me promise not to tell you. If I'd told you, she'd have had nothing more to do with me. She'd have been completely alone. So I agreed not to tell about the HIV or the baby." Tom got up from the sofa. He went over to the fire, poked at the embers, replaced the guard.

I watched him, could see what the telling of all this was costing him. "Do you want to stop,? Tell me the rest in the morning."

"No, no I need to tell you it all, now, tonight." He came back and sat beside me. "Anyway, I kept a close eye on her, dropped in on her as often as I could. I kept her up to date with every little development in treatment, went with her to doctor's appointments. I thought she was coping reasonably well, Rosie, honestly I did."

Tom looked scared. I knew he needed to see that I believed him. I nodded and squeezed his hand.

He sighed deeply before continuing. "The last time I saw her, she asked me to promise to see to it that Robbie was taken care of when she died. She didn't expect me to do the caring, but to arrange for good people to bring him up. I promised, but told her I didn't think I'd need to carry it out any time soon. But that's where I was wrong. I never suspected what she was planning. I swear I didn't. Anyway, a few days later…"

He got to his feet again, began pacing. "Christ, it was awful. I got a call from her. It was the evening. I was at home. She was crying. I tried to reassure her, but she said she'd phoned to say goodbye and to ask me to come and get Robbie. She said she'd fed and changed him and that he'd probably stay sleeping until I got there. I knew then. I knew it was too late, too fucking late." His voice cracked and he rubbed roughly at his eyes.

I let out a sob and put my face in my hands. He was over beside me instantly, holding me tight and rocking me in his arms.

When I could speak I said, "But you went to her?"

"Yes, I went. I decided to call Michael, get him to go with me. I told him the whole story as we drove to Heather's flat. Luckily I had keys, but, by the time we let ourselves in, she was gone, lying on the bed – dead. Christ, Rosie, I'm so glad it wasn't you who found…" It was Tom's turn to sob.

We held each other for a long time before Tom could go on.

"It was a drug overdose, heroin. She knew exactly how much to take to ensure there was no way back. She'd known it was only a matter of time before she caught a cold, or some other trivial bug, and that she'd be unable to fight it, be overwhelmed by it.

She knew enough to know it was a horrible way to die. There was no note. I think she knew I'd understand. She preferred that people thought heroin rather than AIDS was the cause of her death. I can't say I blamed her." Tom paused again.

I nodded, trying to take in what he was telling me. I couldn't speak.

Tom went on. He told me how social work had placed Robbie with the Sutherlands that night, as emergency foster carers, and how he and Michael agreed not to tell me the full story. He also explained how their shared secret ended their friendship. When he was finished he leant back and closed his eyes. He looked shattered.

I was dismayed by all Tom had told me. Not for myself so much as for him and for my sister. What a burden he'd taken on and continued to carry. He'd made a promise and he'd kept it. He'd been a true friend to Heather when she needed him. No wonder he'd been devastated when Robbie turned up.

And Heather, she'd turned her life around and been happy for a while at least. As for her death, it wasn't a pointless and futile act. It wasn't just another junkie overdose. It had been a positive and loving act as she saw it, sparing herself and those she loved further pain. I didn't think she was right to have killed herself, but at last I could understand why. As I sat, thinking, I became aware that Tom was staring at me, waiting for a reaction. I turned to him. He looked terribly sad and terribly scared.

"I'm sorry, so sorry. Can you forgive me? I understand if this changes things, but I'm so sorry."

"No, Tom," I put my fingers to his lips, "Stop it. It's me who should be sorry. I misjudged you, mistrusted you. You did an amazing thing and I love you even more because of it. You were right. I couldn't have looked after Robbie and I couldn't have coped with the truth at the time. Robbie's had a wonderful upbringing and now he's found us. Maybe you should have told me sooner, but you didn't. You acted in good faith. I know that now and that's what matters. There's nothing for me to forgive.

And you need to forgive yourself."

"But I took you for granted, Rosie, let you get exhausted and ill. I didn't mean to drive Adam or you away. I was scared for you both. I thought you needed protecting. I thought that Adam's future happiness depended on exam results. I was wrong."

"Yes, okay, you got some things wrong. Who doesn't? But you can't take the blame for me getting ill. Besides, Adam and I owe you. You pushed him into growing up, taking responsibility. And I love you all the more for letting me go, and for waiting for me to come back."

He didn't speak for a few moments. I could see he was having difficulty. He let out a long breath and then said, "I thought I'd turned into him, you know. I've always tried to be different from him. But in the end I was just as bad."

"As who? Who do you mean? Your father?"

"Yes, ironic or what?"

"No, Tom, whatever you've done, you've done out of kindness, out of love and wanting the best for me and the kids. I don't doubt that. I never have, not really, not deep down. You've been great these last few months. You've given me the space I asked for. You've kept everything and everyone going at home. I mean it, there's nothing to forgive."

At that Tom put his head in his hands and let out another long sigh. His whole body shuddered, and then he was sobbing and saying my name. All I could do was hold him, hold him very tightly. I rocked him like I'd rocked the children. I don't know how long we remained like that. He clung to me and I soothed and stroked him as he cried. I gazed into the glowing embers of the fire as he gradually became calm, and I felt so wanted, so full of love and gratitude.

At last he was able to pull back a little and speak. "I was so scared, Rosie. So scared I'd blown it. Lost you. No way back. I wouldn't have been able to bear it. I don't think I..."

"Shh, now," I said, standing up and taking his hand. "You're exhausted, let's go to bed."

# Chapter Forty Six

The next day we awoke side by side, in bed together for the first time in so long. Tom lay beside me with his hand on my hip, the way he always used to. When I opened my eyes he was already awake, watching me. He smiled and I moved into his arms.

Once we were up, we cleared up the debris from the previous night's meal. It felt good to be doing small, domestic things together.

"And we really have this place for the rest of the week?" I asked as we worked.

"If that's what you'd like. We can stay on, be together. Do you think you could stand it?"

"I don't know." Tom looked serious. I struggled to keep a straight face. "Oh, what do you think? Of course I want to stay."

He relaxed. "I almost believed you were uncertain. Don't do that to me." He reached for his phone. "I'll let the kids and Mum and Dan know we're staying on. And there are a few other people, including the honeymooners, who I'd better contact, people who are desperate to know all about how we got on."

"You won't tell them all about it, I hope, only the clean bits surely?"

"That'll keep the calls short," Tom said, grinning and pulling me to him.

"Actually, before I make the calls, let's make another bit of the story that'll have to be edited out on the grounds of decency."

I laughed, a laugh that Tom described as dirty, very dirty. Some time later Tom made his phone calls, while I had a long luxurious bath. When I eventually emerged from the bathroom, there were many text messages on my mobile, from the children and other co-conspirators. The briefest were from Adam saying 'Wicked', Kirsty saying 'Yes!' and Michael saying 'Good on ya, sis!'

Later that morning I called Michael. At last I could talk to him about our sister without him changing the subject. I was able to reassure him that I wasn't angry and that I understood what he and Tom had done.

After lunch we went for a long walk along the west sands in St Andrews. The east wind blew unimpeded straight off the North Sea. It was bitingly cold but it was a bright day and we were well wrapped up. We held hands as we walked, and I breathed in the sea air. Its tang made me think of home.

We talked more about Heather. Tom told me about her funeral, attended only by him, Michael and my father. "I was so scared you'd die too, Rosie. You were so depressed, so fragile. You really frightened me when you said you couldn't see any point in going on, and that we'd all be better off without you. I couldn't risk putting you under any more pressure. The effect on you of Heather's death was bad enough, without burdening you with the fact of Robbie and the HIV."

Tom was clearly still having difficulty believing I understood what he'd done. I stopped walking and pulled him round to face me. I put my arms around him and looked up into his face. "I meant what I said. I understand. I can't imagine what it must have been like for you coping with me and all the rest of it. I was in a bad way. You did the right thing." Then I pulled him closer and kissed him. He returned my embrace.

We resumed our walk and Tom told me about how he'd gone to meet Sue, when she first fostered Robbie, and how nobody wanted a baby from an HIV mother. Nobody, that is, except Sue and Bob. They fell in love with Robbie and applied to adopt him.

"He deserved a lucky break," I said. "And he certainly got that with the Sutherlands. You definitely did right by him."

As we walked back to the cottage in the fading afternoon light, Tom said, "There's still something I don't understand."

"What's that?"

"When I found you at the cottage, you wouldn't let me comfort you or even touch you. You kept pulling away. You said you thought you'd lost me. You said something about a secret?"

"Oh – that – yes." I could feel myself blushing. "It's embarrassing now, another misjudgement on my part." I told him about Max letting it slip about Sheena, and then what Jenny had said. "I thought you'd found someone else, Tom. I wanted you so much, it would've been unbearable to let you touch me, if I couldn't have you."

"Oh my God! So that's what Michael and Kirsty were on about," Tom said. He stopped walking, and turned me to face him with his hands on my shoulders. "*I* thought *I'd* lost you, that you'd moved on and didn't want me, that you couldn't bear to be touched by me! And all the time you thought that me and Sheena..." He hugged me to him and then he laughed. "Wait till I see Max. The Sutherlands might have another child to adopt!"

"We can't blame Max," I laughed too. "It was me who was the idiot. I'm sorry, Tom."

"Can we do a deal?"

"What?"

"Let's stop apologising now."

On our second evening at the cottage, Tom cooked another amazing dinner. Afterwards we sat on the sofa, drinking our coffee and gazing into the fire, me with my head on Tom's shoulder. It was Tom who broke the silence.

Still staring at the flames, he said, "I read his diaries, my father's diaries. I got them from Ma last week and I started to read them."

"You did?" I turned away from the fire to look at him. "You've always been so resistant to looking at them. Why now?"

"Like I said, lately I'd feared I'd turned into him, the way I was acting. Both Ma and Dan suggested, again, that I read what he'd written. The time seemed right."

"And did it help? What you read? Can you – do you understand him any better?"

"I've not read them all. Ma suggested I begin with the one he kept at the time of world war two." Tom paused for a moment, looked back at the fire, lost in thought. Then he turned back to me, put his arm round my shoulder and I leant against him as he began to speak again. "Yes, it did help. It helped a lot."

And as we sat there, watching the logs burn down, Tom told me what he'd read.

"My father was still a medical student when he joined the army medical corps in 1940, not much older than Adam. He was sent to Italy. Christ, he had a terrible time, tending to injured soldiers, appalling injuries. Then on top of that he was captured. He was a POW for almost a year, but then he escaped and had to find his way across enemy lines and home. He was very young and very scared." Tom shook his head and stopped.

I looked up at him, stroked his face. He put my hand to his lips, held it there for a moment.

"Did you not know any of that before?" I asked.

He shook his head. "No, he never spoke about it, any of it. I've not got to the worst bit yet. It was a fucking harrowing read."

"Do you want to go on?"

"Oh, yes. I want to, need to, share it with you." Tom got up as he spoke. He put another couple of logs on the fire.

"Okay, if you're sure," I said.

Tom remained by the fireplace, watching the newly added wood begin to burn, as he continued his father's story. "At the end of the war, he was one of the first medics sent into Belsen."

I gasped at this. "Oh – Tom – no."

"Yes," Tom looked grim. "I struggled to finish that section. There was little my father, or anyone else, could do for the few poor souls still alive there. The filth, the disease, the carnage, I can see why he found it to be, literally, unspeakable. He wrote of how he sat with a dying prisoner, a man called Heinrich.

Heinrich had been imprisoned in the camp because he was homosexual. He died in my father's arms."

"Oh, my God! How horrific. What he must have seen."

"Reading about it all, it's not hard to understand his bleakness, his black moments, his despair." Tom turned away, prodded the logs with the poker.

I got up and went to him, put my arms around him. If anything, he looked worse than he had the night before, when he told me about Heather. I took his hand. "Come and sit down," I said, leading him back to the sofa.

After a few moments Tom was able to go on. "No wonder he couldn't stand what he saw as signs of weakness in Dan and me. Weakness made us vulnerable to all sorts of unnamed suffering. No wonder he wanted Ma at home and not out at work. He needed her where he could see her and protect her. I don't think he was right, but I can understand. Yes, he was flawed. He was damaged. But I think he did love us. I understand his misguided attempts to keep his family safe, I understood that all too well."

For some time after Tom finished speaking, I just held him. Then I kissed him softly and said, "So forgive him, Tom. Forgive your father, and forgive yourself."

Tom nodded and held me very tightly.

Later that night, when we were lying in bed together, Tom ran his finger along the scar on my chest. He looked very thoughtful.

"What is it? What are you thinking?" I asked.

"Oh, just inspecting a fellow surgeon's work. Angus Campbell did a good job on that scar." He smiled, as I tried to look cross.

"Oh, very romantic. But praise indeed for your colleague!" I shook my head in mock despair.

Then Tom looked serious again. He took my hand and kissed it and then he moved nearer and put his arms around me. "I'm scared. I'm scared that, after all this, I'm still going to lose you."

"Oh, Tom, the outlook's good. Even Karen Knox is sounding optimistic. Let's just enjoy our lives together. We've been given a second chance." I paused to kiss him. "After all, nobody knows how long they've got."

Tom caressed my face, "You're very brave, much braver than me."

"I'm not brave. It wasn't like I had a choice. It's happened and I've had to face up to my mortality. But I don't buy all the talk of bravery. What does that make you if you don't get better? Don't get me wrong, I've fought back. I've given the witch-bitch a run for her money."

Tom looked at me, puzzled. "The witch-bitch?"

I explained how I visualised the cancer. "But bravery doesn't really come into it. I'm only doing what I have to do to stay alive. It's just normal. Before having cancer, I thought death was for other people, not for me. I was actually dreading getting old. Now, I say, bring it on. Getting older sure beats the alternative. I've no intention of dying just yet, but even if I died tomorrow, I'd die very happy."

Tom didn't seem able to speak. He buried his head in my shoulder.

I took his face in my hands. "And, Tom," I said, looking into his eyes, "I want you with me when I get the scan and the radiotherapy. I want you with me on what's left of this particular journey. And you can boss the medics around as much as you like."

He still couldn't say anything. He didn't have to. He just held me very tightly.

A little while later, as we lay side by side, I took his hand and interlaced my fingers with his. I told him how much I'd enjoyed our walk on the beach. "It made me think of home and how much I miss it. I've been in the city long enough."

Tom propped himself up on one elbow and looked into my eyes. He stroked my face. "So," he paused, cleared his throat. "So, you're coming home then, home to Gullane, to the kids, and me?"

"I'm coming home." It was indescribably wonderful to say those words.

Tom's smile showed just what this meant to him. He took me in his arms and kissed me. He managed to say, 'Oh, Rosie', and then he kissed me some more.

The rest of the week passed too quickly, in some respects. But, in other ways, I wanted it to be over so I could go home. We spent some time with Sam, of course. She was happy at uni and delighted with our news. She showed me her room in the hall of residence, and took us to all the places she went to in a normal week. I was so proud of her and told her so. On our last day in St Andrews we took her out to lunch and said our goodbyes.

After lunch we loaded up Tom's car. As we got in, Tom said softly, "You're sure? You're definitely coming home?"

"I'm sure," I said.

When we got home, Adam, Max and Jenny were waiting on the doorstep. Tom carried me over the threshold, and kissed me as he put me down in the hall. Max clapped, while Toby yelped ecstatically and ran in circles round me. Jenny and Adam rolled their eyes and muttered something along the lines of 'gross' and 'embarrassing parents.'

Feeling quite overwhelmed, I walked from room to room, reclaiming my territory. I left our bedroom till last. I went in and sat on the bed and looked out to sea. I thought about Heather, about our childhood bed, about her death bed, about labour ward beds, hospital beds, a bed in St Andrews, and this bed, Tom's and mine.

I lay back and fell asleep. I must have slept for a couple of hours. It was nearly six and dark outside when I woke up. Someone had put a blanket over me. It took a minute to remember where I was. I lay there, taking it all in again. I could hear movement downstairs, bits of voices and music in the background. I got up. The sounds were coming from the kitchen. I approached the doorway quietly and stood taking in the scene.

The radio was playing and Tom sang along while he prepared dinner. Jenny was helping him. Max sat at the end of the table, speaking on the phone about football.

Adam came up behind me, as I stood there watching. He hugged me, leaning against my back, and bent down to rest his head on the top of mine. "God, Mum, you're really quite little aren't you?" he said.

"No, it's you, you've got tall!" I laughed.

Tom turned round when he heard us. "So, you're awake. You looked so peaceful, I just covered you and left you to sleep." He came over and put his arm round me. "Come and sit down. Dinner's nearly ready."

"Hi, Mum, that was Uncle Dan on the phone. He said to say hello," Max said, getting up from where he was sitting. "Here, you can have your place."

"No, no stay where you are Maxy, you have it. I'll sit in your old seat, to be closer to your dad," I replied. Tom glanced at me and smiled.

"Okay, cool," said Max. "Does that mean I get to be one of the important people round here, sitting at the top of the table?

"In your dreams, munchkin," laughed Adam. "It just means it'll be easier to ignore you, stuck out on the end there."

Max frowned. "I hate being the youngest!"

"Aw, Maxy, I love you," said Jenny. She giggled and went up behind him. She put her arms round him, gave him a kiss and ruffled his hair.

"Get off!" Max waved his arms at his sister. "Yuck, Mum, help me!

I shook my head and laughed. Tom and I exchanged another look. It was good to be home.

# Epilogue

*Tom*

It's a whole year since that day, last May, when Robbie and Rosie met for the first time. I've spent most of today working in the garden, not doing anything creative, that's still Rosie's territory. I just clear the way for her. I've cut the grass and done some tree and hedge pruning.

Even now, I sometimes can't quite believe that Rosie's back. I hate to come home and find she's not in. My heart still lifts when I see her again, after any time apart. It's like I fell in love with her all over again and Rosie says she feels the same. But it's different from before. We both know we can't take anything, and especially each other, for granted.

The year has passed quickly. It seemed like no time from Michael going home until it was Christmas. It was a very special time for us all. I had Christmas Day off work and I cooked my first Christmas dinner. Ma and Dan joined us and stayed over. It was a happy day, all of us together, and everyone seemed to enjoy my efforts in the kitchen. On Boxing Day morning Ma and Rosie were sitting at the kitchen table, having breakfast and chatting to one another, as I emptied the dishwasher. Toby was snoozing in his basket and none of the children had surfaced yet. I remember watching those two women that I love so much, those two very brave, special women and feeling so grateful to have them both.

In January I started my six month sabbatical. I've enjoyed the chance it's given me to study, to research and to prepare and publish papers. But mostly I've enjoyed the time it's given me to spend with Rosie and the family. When the time comes though, I'll be happy to get back to my work at the hospital. It's still very important to me and I do miss it. I've negotiated a new work pattern, with more time off, and I'm determined to stick to it.

Rosie also began a twelve month career break last January and is using the time to think what she wants to do next, which may, or may not, be continuing to teach. We started our, temporarily, job free lives by going to Australia for six weeks, just after New Year.

Robbie is a frequent visitor to our home. He now knows the full story of Heather's death, and he continues to have long talks with Rosie about his birth mother. He's also been spending some time with Rick.

Then at the end of March, Rosie had a double celebration. She had her fiftieth birthday and she was told that she was in the clear. The cancer is completely gone, and other than regular check-ups, she's free to get on with living.

To mark both these wonderful events we had a ceilidh. All the people who are precious to us were there, including the Sutherlands. Ruby and her husband were also among Rosie's guests. Ruby has now retired from cleaning for us, but is still very much part of our lives. Dan brought his new partner, Simon, to the party and Sam's boyfriend, Calum, and Jenny's Stewart were also there. It was a magical evening. There was a ceilidh band and lots of reels were danced. The highlight was something I'd arranged as a surprise for Rosie. It was Eilidh singing 'My Love is like a Red, Red Rose,' accompanied by Jenny on her fiddle and Adam on his guitar. Jenny'd taught Adam to play it and, according to Kirsty, in whose house they'd practiced, he'd slogged at it to get it just right.

Robbie's fiftieth birthday present to Rosie was something unique and very special. He'd come to me with the idea not long after Christmas. He wanted to do a charcoal sketch of me to give to her. He was keen for it to be a surprise and asked me to sit for him in secret. I agreed in principle, after all it was a lovely idea, but something about it niggled me. It took me a couple of days to pin down exactly why I had reservations. I was visiting Ma when it dawned on me. I happened to glance at the photos on the mantelpiece in Ma's living-room and there was one of her and my stepfather. They were sitting on the garden bench, looking at each other and laughing. They just looked so together.

I wanted this picture of Robbie's to capture that same spirit. I wanted it to be of us, Rosie and me together. After everything that had happened I didn't want to be alone, not even in a portrait.

Robbie rose to the challenge. He captured Rosie's likeness perfectly from a photo I'd taken of her at Christmas time. The resulting sketch showed Rosie and me, head and shoulders in profile, smiling at each other. Robbie had it mounted in a plain silver frame. It was simple and utterly beautiful.

Robbie asked me to give the picture to Rosie. He said he felt that was the right way to do it.

So on the morning of her birthday, after I'd brought us breakfast in bed, eggs Florentine and smoked salmon, and after we'd finished eating, I gave her the drawing.

I was aware of holding my breath as Rosie unwrapped it. When she saw the picture, she gave a little gasp and put her fingertips to her lips.

"Oh, Tom," she said, passing the portrait to me. "Look at what Robbie's done. How on earth did he manage it, not from memory surely?" There were tears in her eyes as she took it back and gazed at it.

I explained how it had come about. When I finished she couldn't speak at first. Then she whispered, "I love it." In the end I had to prise it from her grasp so that I could show her just how much I loved her.

And now, as I tidy up the clippings and put away the gardening tools, I allow myself to look forward, and not only to getting back to work at the hospital. In July, we're going on holiday to Skye with Lucy, Graham, Kirsty and Rick. Yes, me and Rick in the same cottage for a week. Who'd have thought it? Kirsty has sold the family croft and she and Rick are having a house built close to where she grew up. They plan to move to Skye in October after Eilidh goes to university.

Walking back up the garden, towards the house, I admire the results of my labour. The garden looks good. It won't stay tidy of course. It'll keep growing and needing attention.

As I approach the house, I see Rosie sitting on the bench by the back door. Sam, home from uni now that first year is over, is lying back on my reclining, garden chair. She's reading and is plugged into her i-pod. She's working for most of the summer in a bookshop in Edinburgh and then, in September, she and Calum are going off round Europe by train. I'm trying to be cool about this plan, but it's not coming naturally.

Rosie bought me the recliner for my birthday earlier this year. It's to help me chill out, apparently, and I must admit I love it. I consider asking Sam to move so I can sit in it, but decide I can't be bothered with the negotiations this will inevitably involve.

Instead I sit down beside Rosie. Her face is turned up to the late afternoon sun and her eyes are closed. I kiss her on the cheek. I put my arm round her and she puts her head on my shoulder. We sit like this for a while, neither of us needing to speak.

It's me and Max on dinner duty this evening and Ma's coming to eat with us. I'm just thinking about moving, when Max and Jenny come out of the house.

"Here you are. We've been calling you," Jenny says.

"Hi you two, how was school today?" Rosie asks, as Max sits down at the end of the bench beside his mother.

"Okay," is all Max is prepared to say.

"It was just revision and practice classes for the music exam," says Jenny. "It was fine. I can't wait for next week, no more school ever! Budge up, Dad." She squeezes in beside me at the opposite end of the bench from her brother. Rosie and I push closer together. Rosie leans her head on my shoulder again. Jenny does the same on my other shoulder.

Then Adam arrives. "So this is where you all are," he says. He's now several months into his mechanic's apprenticeship and though he's still a man of few words, he seems to be enjoying it. He and Julie are still together. Rosie and I both hope their relationship will survive when Julie goes off to university, in the autumn, to begin her engineering course. But, whatever the future holds for my son I know he has the strength of character to cope. I'm still ashamed that I ever doubted him and I'm still so proud of him. However, he did tell me recently that I was to stop telling him so. He said it was cool that I was proud, but not cool to keep saying it over and over again.

He plucks his brother from the bench and plonks him down on the grass. He then sits down beside his mother. "Hey, Ma," he says and puts his head on her shoulder. He stretches out his legs, grinning at his brother and gives an exaggeratedly happy sigh for Max's benefit.

"Adam, that's my place! That's not fair!" Max's protests are drowned out by the rest of us laughing. I wonder why I didn't think of doing that with Sam, but realise my back wouldn't be up to it.

"It's not funny," Max complains. "Why's it always me that's picked on? Some things never change round here!"

Rosie and I glance at each other and smile, each knowing what the other is thinking.

Anne lives in Scotland, UK

Anne writes contemporary fiction for people who enjoy a good story which informs, entertains and satisfies. There's usually a good dash of romance thrown in.

For more about Anne Stormont and her writing
visit http://putitinwriting.me

Anne can be contacted at annestormont@putitinwriting.me

# Also by
# Anne Stormont

# *Displacement*

*A novel about the search for settlement after the upheaval of loss.
A journey of insight, forgiveness and love.*

Divorce, the death of her soldier son and estrangement from
her daughter, leave Hebridean crofter, Rachel Campbell grief-
stricken, lonely and lost.

Forced retirement leaves former Edinburgh policeman Jack
Baxter looking for a new direction in life.

When Rachel meets Jack in dramatic circumstances on a wild
winter's night on the island of Skye, a friendship develops, despite
very different personalities. Gradually their feelings for each
other go beyond friendship
- something neither of them
feels able to admit. And it
seems unlikely they'll get the
chance to because Rachel is
due to leave for Israel, where
she hopes to re-root and
reroute her life.

Set against the stunning
backdrops of the Scottish
island of Skye and the
contested country of Israel-
Palestine, *Displacement*
is a story of life-affirming
courage and a love-story
where romance and realism
meet head-on.

Printed in Great Britain
by Amazon.co.uk, Ltd.,
Marston Gate.